# The Promise

# The Promise

Benita Brown

**headline**

First published in 2008
by HEADLINE PUBLISHING GROUP

1

Cataloguing in Publication Data is available from the British Library

ISBN 978 0 7553 3475 9

Typeset in Sabon by Avon DataSet Ltd,
Bidford-on-Avon, Warwickshire

Printed and bound in Great Britain by
Clays Ltd, St Ives plc

Headline's policy is to use papers that are natural, renewable and recyclable
products and made from wood grown in sustainable forests. The logging and
manufacturing processes are expected to conform to the environmental
regulations of the country of origin.

HEADLINE PUBLISHING GROUP
An Hachette Livre UK Company
338 Euston Road
London NW1 3BH

www.headline.co.uk
www.hachettelivre.co.uk

To Norman,
for his enthusiasm, patience and support

# Part One

# Chapter One

Newcastle, September 1885

Marion Brookfield lit the lamps, then went to the window to draw the curtains. She paused with one hand on the rich red velvet and with the other moved the lace curtain aside. She stared out into the street. It was only just past seven o'clock, but it had been one of those days when the sun had barely penetrated the sooty pall that hung over the city. Coal fires burning in every hearth sent never-ending plumes of smoke up into the sky. And today there had been no wind to blow the gloom away.

She peered through the murk and realised that part of the problem was a gathering fog that might soon make walking in the streets both difficult and dangerous. She ought to send Betty home. Before closing the curtains, she paused to watch the familiar figure of the lamplighter emerge from the mist, raise his long pole to light the lamp nearest to the house, then go on to the next one; the fog swallowing him up as he went. Once lit, disembodied lights surrounded by a hazy nimbus seemed to float mysteriously above the menacing shadows. She shivered. She hoped her father would stay at home tonight.

Marion caught sight of her reflection. Tall and slim, her chestnut-brown hair pinned back from her finely drawn face, she knew she had come to resemble the portrait of her mother that her father kept in his study, especially as now, when she wore forest green, her mother's favourite colour. Beyond her own reflection, as if there were another room out in the street, she could see the mirror image of the hearth where her sister sat with her slippered feet resting on the padded footstool.

Annette, at sixteen two years younger than Marion, and not as tall, had hair of the same rich hue, but the lines of her face were less well defined and her young figure was childlike in her school grey flannel skirt and high-necked white blouse. Marion's anxious expression softened into a smile as she observed Annette flicking impatiently through the pages of the book she was supposed to be studying for homework. She was chewing on the end of a pencil, but her notepad had fallen to the floor.

Marion let the lace drop into place and drew the curtains. She turned her back on the nebulous and vaguely threatening world that lay beyond the window and stood still for a moment, absorbing the warmth, the comfort and the security of their home. How lucky we are, she thought, and how right our father is to do what he does.

The clock on the chimneypiece chimed the quarter-hour and Marion roused herself from her reverie. It was time to see if Betty had prepared the sandwiches for her father and Daniel. She decided not to ring the bell but rather to go along in person. She saw no need to summon the girl to the sitting room when she herself was perfectly capable of going to the kitchen.

As Marion walked to the door, Annette leaned over to retrieve her fallen notebook. But instead of beginning to write, she frowned and shook her head. She gave an exaggerated sigh. Marion knew the sigh to be a cry for attention.

'What is it?' she asked.

'This stupid essay!' Annette looked up at Marion, her light brown eyes wide with despair. 'I don't know where to begin! We're supposed to choose one of the comic scenes in the play and write about it, but I don't think the play's funny at all!'

'You don't think *A Midsummer Night's Dream* is funny?'

'No.' Annette scowled. 'Do you?'

'Yes, I do.'

'Tell me why.'

'Well, for a start there are the young lovers being led a merry dance by Puck, and then what about Bottom being transformed into an ass?'

Annette's eyes widened. 'And you think those things amusing?'

'I do.'

'Well I don't. Squeezing juice in people's eyes and making them get lost in the forest then fall in love with the wrong people. And as for poor old Bottom, well that's just unkind to give him a donkey's

4

head and then make anyone as beautiful as Titania fall in love with him!'

Annette's voice and face expressed indignation. Then suddenly her eyes widened and she smiled. 'It's a trick question, isn't it?' she asked. 'Miss Thomas wants to catch us out.'

Marion hated to disillusion her sister. 'No, Annette, it's not a trick question. The problem is that you have simply missed the humour of the situation.'

Annette frowned. 'Are you saying I'm stupid?'

'No, of course not. And it's a credit to you that you feel so sorry for poor old Bottom.' Marion smiled. 'But now I must go and see Betty, and if you start going through the play again – for instance look at the scene where the amateur actors are rehearsing their play – then I'll help you as soon as I can.'

Annette's smile was luminous. 'Thank you, Marion. You're too good to me, really you are!'

She turned back to her book, her long hair falling forward to obscure her face. Marion watched her for a moment and smiled wryly. She supposed she should have told her sister to persevere and get on with her homework by herself, but rather than risk tears, she had taken the line of least resistance. Marion acknowledged this was not good for Annette's character, but it was also important to make sure that the household ran smoothly. She did not want their father to be distracted from his important work.

Marion hurried along the passage to the kitchen. The kitchen was empty and the cold draught that slammed the door behind her informed her that the back door that opened into the yard from the scullery was open. A moment later she heard the door close and Betty, the Brookfields' maid of all work, hurried through from the scullery carrying a large scuttle full of coal. She saw Marion and smiled.

'Miss Brookfield,' she said, and shivered. 'By, it's real damp out there. Not quite raining, but not dry either.' She smiled at Marion. 'But you've come about the sandwiches, hevn't you?'

Marion nodded.

'Don't worry, I hevn't forgotten them but I thought I'd better see to the bedroom fires first. It's getting quite chilly, isn't it?'

'Yes,' Marion agreed. 'I think the year has turned. But let me do the fires.'

5

'You?' Betty's smile widened into an outright grin.

'I'm getting better at it,' Marion insisted.

'Aye, you are, and I'll larn you yet. But I've let them burn low and I'm afeard if you start raking them out you'll put them out altogether. No, Miss Brookfield, pet, I'll see to the fires; it won't take long, and then I'll make the sandwiches and take them in to your da and Mr Brady.'

'All right, Betty, have it your own way, but I'll make the sandwiches.'

'Divven't fret. I'll wash me hands before I start.'

'I know you will. But it's not that. The fog's getting worse and I think you should go home.'

'Home? But I hevn't put me hours in.'

'Don't worry about that. My father would never dock your pay.'

'No, he wouldn't, would he? He's a good man and you've grown into a kind mistress, young as you are, and I'm lucky to be working here.' Betty paused and then, as if realising that Marion was embarrassed, she added with a grin, 'Even if Miss Annette isn't as easy to get on with as you are. Sometimes I think she lives in a different world to the rest of us.'

'I know what you mean. Her drawing and her painting mean so much to her that sometimes she can appear to be a little selfish. But she's not really.'

'I'll take your word for it!'

By now the two young women were smiling at each other like old friends, as indeed they were. Betty was only four years older than Marion and she had been working for the Brookfields ever since their previous maid of all work had retired six years before. The widowed Mr Brookfield was a kind master and a devoted father, but his work as a newspaper reporter often made him late home, and in the early days, Betty, not much more than a child herself, became responsible for looking after the growing girls.

To Betty's way of thinking, Marion had always been thoughtful; her only fault being that she took life too seriously and often forgot to enjoy herself. Annette, on the other hand, was less easy to deal with. To be fair, it wasn't entirely her own fault. She had been such a little thing, just a toddler, when her mother had died of consumption that even sensible Mr Brookfield had tended to indulge her. Not that he didn't love the older girl any the less, but Marion's nature was such that nothing could spoil her.

Pretty Annette, though, usually got her own way, and if she didn't, she sulked. Most of all Betty hated it when Annette took advantage of Marion's kind nature.

'All right, then,' Betty said. 'You can make the sandwiches. There's some boiled ham ready cut in the larder and a dish of pease pudding. There's enough of both to make a bit supper for you and Miss Annette as well. Now mind you divven't cut yourself slicing the bread.'

'Of course I won't cut myself,' Marion began indignantly before she noticed Betty's smile. 'You're teasing.'

'Aye. Now, I'll be off upstairs before I break me back carrying this scuttle.'

'I'm sorry, Betty, I should have thought . . .' Marion began to say, but the maid had gone and a moment later Marion heard her hurrying up the stairs.

While Betty was upstairs, Marion made the sandwiches and set the tray. She took a bottle of beer from the cold floor of the pantry, opened the spring top, and put the bottle on the tray along with two glasses. Then she left the tray on the scrubbed table and went along to the room that ought to have been the dining room but that had become her father's study.

As soon as she knocked, her father called, 'Come in, Betty.'

'It's not Betty,' she said as she opened the door and entered. 'If you agree, I would like to send her home now.'

'Would you?' her father asked. 'Is there some trouble there?'

Henry Brookfield looked concerned. He rose from behind his desk. Daniel Brady, who had been sitting opposite him, also rose and turned to face Marion, regarding her gravely, his eyes level with her own.

'No, there's no trouble,' she said. 'At least I don't know of any. It's because I don't want her walking home in the fog.'

'Fog?' Her father turned to look out of the window behind him. He had not drawn the curtains and the top half of the window, above the nets, was an opaque grey. 'Oh yes, it is bad,' he said. 'I should have noticed and thought of that myself. You're right. She must go immediately.'

'Thank you. Now, shall I bring the tray along?'

'I'll carry it for you,' Daniel Brady said. 'That is, if I may?' He turned to look questioningly at Henry Brookfield.

'By all means,' Marion's father said. 'You go along with Marion; I'll build up the fire.'

Daniel followed Marion along the passage. He didn't speak, but she was overwhelmingly aware of his presence. Once in the kitchen, she stood aside and with one hand indicated the tray on the table. When he walked over to collect it, she had time to let her glance linger on his broad shoulders and the way the light from the overhead gas mantle shone on his black hair.

He picked up the tray and Marion's glance fell on his hands. They were large and work roughened, but his fingernails were clean, as were his clothes. She knew that he must go to great pains to look presentable whenever he came to their house for his lessons with her father.

Still without speaking, he was about to walk past her when she stopped him. 'Mr Brady,' she said. 'Why do you never talk to me?'

He looked dismayed. 'Hev – I mean, have I been rude?'

'No, of course not. It's just that your silence is disconcerting.'

'I'm sorry.'

'No, no, don't apologise.' Marion was aghast. She had upset and worried him and probably made the situation worse. 'No, you haven't offended me. I – I imagine it is simply that your mind is so taken up with the work you are doing with my father that you cannot – I mean you just don't notice me.' As the words left her mouth she knew how they sounded. 'But then,' she hurried on before he could answer her, 'why should you?'

Daniel Brady didn't answer but he regarded her thoughtfully, his eyes as grey and as cool as a stream in winter.

She turned away. 'Well, if you can manage the tray I'll just . . . I'll just stay here.'

In the ensuing silence she heard the tick of the clock on the mantelpiece. She gazed at the burning coals in the hearth and felt another sort of heat burn up inside her.

'Miss Brookfield.'

She turned, startled. Daniel Brady was still standing there. 'Yes?' she said.

'If you don't mind, I would like you to come and open the study door for me.'

'Oh yes, of course.'

'And another thing . . .' He paused, and his smile reached his eyes. 'I could never not notice you.'

8

Now it was Marion who could find nothing to say. She hurried along before him and preceded him into the study. Her father had attempted to clear a space on the desk for the tray.

'Just put it there,' he told Daniel, 'on top of those papers, but before we start on the sandwiches, would you mind going along to Osborne Road and fetching a cab? I've decided that will be the safest way to send Betty home tonight.'

Daniel set off to the cab stand and Marion returned to the front parlour, where Annette was still sitting by the fire. Her head was bent over her notebook and her pencil was moving across the paper. She was concentrating so hard, she did not hear Marion enter the room.

She must have decided to start without me, Marion thought, and this pleased her. She moved quietly across the room, not wishing to break her sister's concentration, but when her shadow fell across the page, the younger girl looked up quickly and closed the notebook so that Marion could not see what she had been writing.

'You startled me!' she accused. 'Creeping up on me like that!'

'I'm sorry. But I'm glad you've made a start. May I see what you've done?'

'Oh, not very much. I've been waiting for you to help me.'

'But you *have* made a start?'

'Mmm.'

'Then show it to me.'

Annette was obviously most unwilling to show Marion her work, but after a moment she smiled and said, 'Oh, all right then. You might as well see it. But don't be angry with me.'

She opened the notebook, resting it on her lap, and Marion sat on the arm of the chair and looked down at it. She drew in her breath. Annette had made no attempt to begin her essay, but far from being angry, Marion was amazed at what she saw.

Instead of writing anything, Annette had drawn two of the characters from the play. The fairy queen, Titania, beautiful and graceful, was sitting on a flower-starred bank with Bottom's ass's head resting on her lap. He lay at her feet looking up at her with delighted bewilderment as she laid a graceful hand on his muzzle.

'But Annette, this is wonderful!'

'Do you think so?'

'Yes, I do.'

'And you're not angry because I haven't started on my essay?'

Marion shook her head. 'I know I should be, but . . . but you have quite taken my breath away.'

'Marion – you will talk to Father again, won't you?' Suddenly Annette's eyes were filled with real concern.

'About?'

'Don't tease! It's not kind. You know what I want you to talk to him about. I want to leave the silly old Girls' High School and go to art school.'

Marion sighed. Annette had been pleading with their father to let her leave school since she was fifteen, and he had been just as adamant that she should complete her education. Marion had found herself attempting to keep the peace between them.

'You know, Annette,' she said, 'you are lucky to have a father who thinks that education is important for girls.'

'Of course I know that. You keep reminding me! But going to art school would still be an education, wouldn't it? Furthermore, it would be more useful to me than learning about stuffy old Shakespeare!' Annette's eyes filled with tears.

'Don't cry,' Marion said. 'As a matter of fact, I've already spoken to Father and persuaded him that your talent should be encouraged.'

'Have you? And what did he say?'

'He said, and I agree with him, that you must stay at school until the end of this term, and then, depending on your report, he will allow you to go to art school.'

'My report?' Annette looked horrified.

'I'm afraid so.'

'I suppose that means he expects me to work hard and come top of the class like you did.'

'No, you're wrong. Father simply wants you to do your best, and if you do, you shall go to art school next January.'

'Really?' Annette's eyes were shining. 'Do you promise me that's true?'

'I promise. So how about making a good start and getting on with your homework?'

'Oh, I will. And you know, Marion, I can just about see why that scene when Quince and Flute and Bottom and the others are rehearsing their play is funny, but I don't think it's kind to mock them, is it? I mean, they were only doing their best to please the Duke, weren't they?'

Marion looked down into her sister's earnest eyes and realised that Annette was quite sincere. 'Yes, dear, they were,' she said. 'And now, seeing that you've promised to do your best, I'm going to leave you to write the essay all on your own.'

Betty sat well back in the hansom and tried not to breathe deeply. The soot-laden air was bad enough, but the nearer they got to the east end of the city, the worse the smells from the stagnant waters of the Ouseburn, the Dead House and the bone yard.

Her family was respectable. Her father and her two grown brothers worked in the shipyards and brought home good money; enough to ensure that her mother did not have to seek employment outside the home. Her days were busy enough, cooking and cleaning and looking after the youngest members of the Sutton household, the eight-year-old twins, Dinah and Daisy.

The hansom turned into Raby Street, and to Betty's mind the horse's hoofs seemed to make an unearthly clatter on the cobbles. She saw curtains at lighted windows twitching and imagined that her coming home in style would be a subject for gossip for many a day after this one. Not that Mr Brookfield hadn't sent her home in a cab before.

There was the time the heavens had opened and the rainwater ran down the streets like a river, and then the time she had fallen down in the yard and twisted her ankle. She hadn't been able to hobble back to work for nearly a week, and when she'd returned to the Brookfields' house in Jesmond she'd discovered that Miss Marion had taken time off school to look after her father and her sister. Bless her. She'd managed very well, although she'd never quite got the hang of laying and lighting the fires. Thank goodness Mr Brookfield had stirred himself to do that.

Betty thought about Mr Brookfield and how he compared with her own father, who never lifted a finger to help in the house. That was women's work, he said. But he did clean the boots and shoes every night until they shone so you could see your face in them. He was a good man, her da, and so was Mr Brookfield in his own way, although Betty often reflected that he cared for his work so much that he might just be neglecting the welfare of his own daughters. It was a good job Miss Marion was so capable.

By the time the cab pulled up at her door, the twins had already pulled it open and were out on the pavement, hopping up and down with excitement.

'Here comes our Betty, just like a princess!' they called in unison.

'Whisht!' Betty said, and the cab-driver laughed.

Mr Brookfield had already paid Betty's fare, so after wishing her good night, the driver pulled away. Betty stood for a moment holding her sisters' hands and watched as the cab, its coach lamps sending hazy rays of light through the mist, turned expertly and headed up the hill again.

'Come in and shut the door, for heaven's sake,' their mother called from the house, and as they turned towards the door, Betty noticed the old besom who lived opposite dropping her curtain.

No doubt she's had a good look and she'll hev something to say about me getting above meself, Betty thought. Well, that can't be helped. Then, as the night and the fog enclosed them, she gripped her sisters' hands all the tighter. 'Hawway inside, me bairns,' she said. 'The streets at night are no place for little 'uns like you.'

Daniel Brady put his books into a small satchel and prepared to take his leave of Henry Brookfield. He rose from his chair, put his hand in his pocket and took out a shilling. He stood awkwardly for a moment, not knowing, as ever, exactly what to do, then he put it down on the only part of the desk that was not covered with books and papers.

'Your – erm – fee,' he said.

Henry Brookfield was attempting to tidy the pile of papers on the desk in front of him. He looked up distractedly and smiled his thanks. But he did not reach for the shilling.

Daniel wondered if his tutor ever picked up the coins or whether, if the books and papers were moved aside, a small fortune would be found scattered across the desk. For Daniel, every penny counted, and he found it hard to understand Mr Brookfield's seemingly casual manner; for surely he wouldn't take on this extra work if he didn't need the money.

Over the weeks Daniel had been coming for lessons, he had realised that clever man though he was, brilliant even, Henry Brookfield was not wealthy. His work as a journalist earned him only a modest living. He seemed to have enough to pay the rent on this comfortable but not too large house in a respectable terrace just off

Osborne Road, to bring up his daughters without hardship, and to keep one general maid.

But even if, as Daniel suspected, Mr Brookfield found it a struggle, there was a world of difference between the Brookfield household and the house in Byker where the Brady family lived. Daniel had enjoyed school and had been considered scholarship material. But when he was twelve his father was killed in an accident in the shipyards, and Daniel had had to leave school and find a job in order to support his mother and his younger sister, who was only seven years old.

With no training, and unable to afford an apprenticeship, he had found work clearing stones away from the digging of the tracks for the new tramlines. Although he was not tall he was already sturdy, and the hard labour filling and wheeling the barrows away soon made him as strong as many a grown man.

From that job he had progressed to general labouring. He worked long hours and made good money, but it was hard being the main wage-earner. As soon as she had pulled herself together, his mother found the odd cleaning job, but she had never been robust and often her health let her down.

Daniel accepted what had happened but he had never forgotten his yearning for education and his love of books. When any of his fellow workers had finished with their daily newspaper, he would ask for it and read just about every word in it.

One day he had found a notice in the evening newspaper advertising Henry Brookfield's services as a tutor to working men. Immediately, without even knowing exactly what he wanted for his future, he had seized the chance and gone to the house in Jesmond and asked Mr Brookfield to take him on.

Henry Brookfield had agreed, and from that moment Daniel's life had changed. It wasn't just the learning; it was the whole ambience of this house that he loved. One day, he decided, he would have a home like this. Modest but comfortable, and most importantly, as many books on the shelves as he could afford. His daydreaming always stopped short of imagining who would share this imaginary home with him.

But sometimes, without being bidden, the figure of a young woman materialised at the other side of the dining table, and she bore a striking resemblance to Marion Brookfield. Daniel would dismiss this image quickly and shake himself back into the real world; for he knew in his heart that someone like Henry Brookfield's daughter would never share her life with a working man like Daniel Brady.

Daniel arranged to come the following week at the same time, and was about to take his leave. Henry Brookfield was as pleasant as ever, but his air of distraction had increased. Daniel guessed it would be something to do with the investigation he was undertaking. He had been collecting evidence for months now, but all he had revealed to Daniel was that the report he was writing was something to do with slum landlords.

'Wait a moment, Daniel.' Henry Brookfield looked up just as Daniel was about to leave the room.

'Yes?'

'Would you like to borrow another book or two?'

Daniel smiled. He had returned the books he had been reading and was desperate for something new. 'Yes please,' he said.

'Let me see.' Mr Brookfield looked at the books that Daniel had left on the edge of the desk next to the tray. 'Pope's translation of *The Iliad* and John Milton's *History of Britain*. Hmm . . . I think I know what you should read next.'

He went to the bookshelves set into one of the alcoves next to the fireplace. He reached up, took two books, and, turning, handed them to Daniel, who looked at them and then frowned.

'What's the matter?' Mr Brookfield asked.

'These books . . . they're . . . well, they're fiction.'

'Yes, novels. Don't you ever read novels, Daniel?'

'I do, I borrow them from the library, but I thought . . . I mean . . .'

'You thought that while you are coming here for lessons you should only read serious stuff?'

'I suppose so.'

Mr Brookfield smiled. 'Time for a little relaxation, Daniel. Even my daughter Marion enjoys reading for fun now and then. Have you read either of these two?'

Daniel looked at the books. 'No.'

'Well, that one . . .' Henry Brookfield pointed to the book on top, 'Anstey's *Vice Versa*, is amusing. Thanks to a magic stone, a father and son change places so that the father has to go off to a grim boarding school and the son gets a chance to run his father's business in the city. It's great fun, but in case you think you shouldn't be enjoying yourself, there is a more serious point to it: they both learn from the experience and are left with a better understanding of each other.'

'And this one?' Daniel held out the second book and read the title aloud. '*The Leavenworth Case*?'

'It's a detective story.'

'But it's written by a woman.'

Henry laughed softly. 'Yes, indeed, Anna Katherine Green. And why shouldn't a woman write detective stories?'

'Well . . . no reason, I suppose.' Daniel felt as though he had blundered.

'No reason at all. And lest you think that reading such books is entirely frivolous, Miss Green is very good at warning the reader not to take anything for granted – not to trust circumstantial evidence, and to look beyond the obvious. Now, you'd better go home before the fog gets any worse.'

'Yes – well – thank you. I'll see you next week as usual.'

Henry Brookfield's attention had already strayed back to the papers on his desk, but as Daniel put the two books he had loaned him in his satchel, his tutor looked up again. 'I did set you a written exercise, didn't I?'

'Yes.'

'Good. Now, as I've already sent Betty home, you'll have to see yourself out.'

'Of course.'

On his way home Daniel had much to think about. He knew he was doing well because Mr Brookfield had told him so. And he had also told him that he ought to start thinking about his future; that he should find some employment where he would have to rely on his brain rather than his brawn.

But that would be difficult. He didn't want a clerical job in some stuffy office that would bring home hardly enough pay to support his family. But a job in any of the professions would require training, and that training would have to be paid for. And that was the point where Daniel's speculations about his future life ground to a halt.

'You could always apply for a job on a newspaper,' Mr Brookfield had said one day.

Daniel had thought he was joking. When he realised that was not the case he had asked, 'Would they take me on?'

'You'd have to prove you were capable,' Henry Brookfield replied.

'And how could I do that?'

'Write an article or two – choose something newsworthy – and send them in to the editor. You never know, he may even buy them outright. Or on the other hand he might ask you in for an interview.'

'And that would be the end of it,' Daniel said.

'Why so?'

'The way I speak.'

'You speak like the honest man you are, Daniel,' Henry Brookfield had said. 'It is the way you write that will be more important – and I think you are just about ready to prove it.'

As he made his way home, Daniel thought it was a night to drive all decent people indoors. The fog had enveloped houses and whole streets. The sounds of the city were muffled and his footsteps struck eerily on the pavements and the cobbled roads. It was as if he was the only person left in the world. But Daniel's sense of direction took him safely through the sedate suburbs and on towards Byker and the steep rows of old houses that tumbled downhill towards the river.

As ever, in his head, he carried home with him everything he had learned that night, and with it came a sense of intense pleasure. If only his mother could share his enthusiasm, he thought. But Daniel's mother, Hannah Brady, thought he was wasting hard-earned money on something that would never profit him. And Dora Gibb, the young woman whom everyone assumed he was going to marry, thought the same.

Marion helped her father into his overcoat and wound a long muffler around his neck. She pulled it up a little to partly obscure the bottom half of his face. Then she handed him the cap he wore when he ventured out at night. It was a working man's cap, for anything more fashionable would draw attention to him in the part of Newcastle that was his destination.

'Has Annette finished her homework?' Henry Brookfield asked.

Marion smiled. 'Don't worry, I'll see everything is done properly before she goes to bed.'

'Then you should go too.'

'I'd rather wait up for you.'

'I know, and I wish you wouldn't.'

'I'll sleep better when I know you're safely home, and besides, you know I look forward to talking to you by the fire with our cups of cocoa.'

'I must admit it's a comfort for me to come home and be pampered. But sometimes I think I ask too much of you, Marion. You're not much older than Annette and yet you have taken on all the cares and worries of looking after her and also of running the household.' He paused, and then said quietly, 'Your mother would have been so proud of you.'

For a moment father and daughter looked into each other's eyes, then Marion smiled reassuringly. 'I wouldn't be happy doing anything else,' she said.

'Wouldn't you? You have a good brain – you should be furthering your education – maybe going to college.'

'Perhaps I will when Annette is a little older.'

'You know, I worry about Annette sometimes,' her father said. 'She is so single minded about her art that she can think of nothing else. It's fortunate that you seem to be able to guide her as I never could. She's lucky to have a sister like you.'

'I am lucky to have a sister like her, and we are both lucky to have a father like you.'

Henry Brookfield laughed. 'It seems we are a very fortunate family.'

'We are. Now go, although I wish you wouldn't, not on a night like this.'

Henry Brookfield had already opened the door, but at Marion's words, he hesitated, and doubt filled his face. Before he could speak, Marion said, 'I know how important your work is. Don't worry about Annette and me. I promise you I can look after things until you come home.'

No matter how important he thought his work, Henry Brookfield was only human, and he regretted having to leave his comfortable home on a night like this. For many months, after his normal working day was over, he had been investigating the scandal of slum housing. Newcastle, with its manufactories, mines, shipyards and railway yards, was one of the richest cities in Europe, and yet the wealth and luxury this brought the city did not extend to its poorest inhabitants. There were many wrongs that needed righting, but

Henry had chosen to investigate and report on the appalling conditions in which some people lived.

Henry believed slum landlords should be exposed, but in most cases they hid behind impersonal companies and their names were not known. Since beginning his investigations, he had followed a labyrinthine trail, and now he was close to discovering the identity of one of the worst of these men. And in this case there might be something more to discover, for Henry suspected that this man, whoever he was, was also growing rich from prostitution of the most evil kind.

Young girls, little more than children, vanished from the streets and were lured, or in some cases forced, into a short life of vice, disease and despair. Henry had been told that at least two of the brothels where child prostitutes were available belonged to the very same landlord who owned some of the worst, most insanitary and rat-infested housing.

Henry wondered if the man he was going to meet would venture out on such a night. Perhaps he should turn round now and go home to his warm house and the company of his daughters. He stopped and considered this thought for a moment, but the tempting image of the fireplace and his comfortable chair only made him more keenly aware of those who did not have such a chair, or even coal to burn on a night like tonight.

Now and then, as he made his way down a steep cobbled street towards the river, he thought he heard footsteps other than his own. But when he stopped and glanced behind him, the other footsteps stopped too. He decided it must be some kind of echo. Eventually he reached the meeting place behind a ramshackle deserted boathouse near the place where the Ouseburn emptied its black and sullen waters into the River Tyne.

He peered around him but he could not make out whether anyone was there. Drunken shouts and laughter echoed across the sludgy water from the Mushroom Inn near the old Glasshouse Bridge. He hasn't come, Henry thought, and I can't blame him.

Then he heard the footsteps again, and as he himself was standing still, there was no denying that someone was coming up behind him. He turned to see the figure of a man emerge from the mist and walk purposefully towards him. Henry was puzzled. Surely this man was not as tall as the man he had arranged to meet? Or perhaps the swirls of mist were playing tricks with his vision.

'Brookfield?' a voice hissed.

Was that the same voice he had heard before?

'Yes. Is that you?' he asked, and felt foolish because he had never discovered the man's name.

The man did not reply. He stopped and held out a hand. Henry knew what he wanted. He took a leather pouch from his pocket and heard the coins jingle as he handed it over. To his puzzlement, the man did not check the contents to see if it was enough. He merely slipped it in his pocket and then, without warning, drew one arm backwards and lunged straight at Henry, knocking the breath out of him. Henry gasped with pain. Why had he punched him? He looked into the man's face and frowned. He staggered forward helplessly, but his assailant struck him again.

Henry clutched his stomach, trying to hold in the pain, and realised that his hands were wet. He raised them towards his face and saw that they were covered with some dark liquid. Blood. He was bleeding. He hadn't been punched, he had been stabbed.

He felt himself keeling over, and his senses began to slip away. As he fell, he struck his head on a stone, and despite the pain he smiled. Now he understood what it meant when they said a blow to the head made you see stars. Except that there weren't any stars. Not real ones. He couldn't even see the night sky. All he could see was someone bending over him, looking at him keenly.

And in that moment he had the answer to many of his questions, but the agony of it was that he would never be able to publish those answers. For he knew he was dying, and he wept that his life should end like this, lying in the fetid mud, far away from his home and the daughters he loved.

His daughters . . . Terror took hold of his remaining senses. What would happen to his daughters? Marion so sensible and kind; Annette so talented and yet so immature. In his last moments Henry Brookfield offered up a prayer to the Almighty. 'God take them to your heart,' he whispered, 'protect them from danger, keep them safe from anyone who would do them harm.'

Just before the darkness claimed him, there was one last moment of light. Marion, he thought. She will look after Annette . . . she promised . . .

# Chapter Two

Early the next morning the fog had thinned and an unwilling sun shone through the mist and gleamed on the damp cobbles. On most mornings Betty enjoyed the walk to the Brookfields' home. At this time of day the streets were lively with delivery carts taking bread, milk, meat, ice and all kinds of provisions to the shops and houses long before the toffs were out of bed.

Just as she was about to turn the corner of her street, she saw two policemen running down the hill towards the river. They were running so fast their boots struck sparks off the cobbles. Betty thought she recognised the lanky form of one of them, and she stopped and watched them, curious as to why they should be in such a hurry. But whatever it was, she knew that word got round fast and that her mother would no doubt have found out what the commotion was by the time she got home.

A moment later Betty popped into Brown's Bakery on Shields Road to buy a loaf, as she did on most days. She wrapped it in the clean tea towel she had brought and put it in her basket, savouring the delicious smell of new-baked bread all the way to Jesmond.

When she arrived, she opened the back door with her own key, and before taking off her coat and hat in the scullery, went through to the kitchen to place the bread on the table.

Something was wrong.

Betty paused with the handle of the basket still over her arm and looked at the tray, which should not have been there. On it were two willow-pattern beakers with spoonfuls of cocoa and sugar in each one. Marion hadn't made her father his usual bedtime drink. Betty turned and looked at the glowing remains of the fire. A pan of milk still sat on the top of the range, ready to be pushed on to the hob. A skin had formed over the top.

Now Betty knew for sure that there was something wrong. If Mr Brookfield had not felt like a cup of cocoa, Marion, probably very tired, might just have left the beakers on the table. But she would never have left the milk uncovered until the next morning.

Betty wasn't sure what to do. She took the loaf out of her basket and set it down on the breadboard on the table, then went back into the scullery, put the basket on the floor of the pantry, removed her hat and coat, and hung them up on the hooks on the back door. Then, because it was what she always did, she built up the fire in the range, filled the larger of the two kettles at the kitchen sink, and put it on to boil. As soon as it began to steam slightly, she left the kitchen and walked along the passage.

The house was quiet. It was too soon for Annette to be stirring, but Marion usually came downstairs early so that she could have breakfast with her father before he went to work at the newspaper offices in the city. Betty looked into the room that Mr Brookfield had appropriated for his study. It was empty.

Next she tried the front parlour, and at first she thought nobody was there either. The heavy curtains shut out the morning light; the room was dark. As Betty's eyes became accustomed to the dimness, she saw first the dull glow from the remains of the fire, then that there was someone sitting in the armchair, the one with its back to her. She could see a graceful arm lying on the armrest and a pair of slippered feet resting on the little footstool.

As the furniture gradually emerged from the shadows and swam into focus, Betty hurried over to the window and opened the curtains as quietly as she could. She turned towards the fireplace and saw that as she had guessed, it was Miss Marion sitting in the chair. She was sleeping with her head dropping awkwardly sideways. Betty took in the fact that she was fully dressed. Either she had got up and come downstairs in the early hours, or she had never been to bed at all. And remembering the unused cups and the pan of milk in the kitchen, Betty thought the latter explanation the more likely.

Had someone been taken ill? Annette or Mr Brookfield? Had Marion been up all night nursing them? Or was it Miss Marion who was ill? Whatever the truth of it, Betty couldn't leave the poor girl sitting so uncomfortably like that or she would have the most awful crick in her neck.

21

Betty crossed over to the fireplace quietly and placed a gentle hand on Marion's shoulder; she didn't want to frighten the lass. Marion opened her eyes straight away, and in the morning light, Betty could see how pale her complexion was and that there were dark circles under her eyes.

'Father?' Marion said uncertainly.

'No, it's me,' Betty said. 'What's the matter? Has your da taken poorly?'

'Poorly?' Marion sounded as if she was trying to remember something. Whatever it was, the knowledge must have come flooding back for she sprang from the chair and said, 'My father . . . my . . .' She swayed and looked as though she was going to fall.

'Here, let me!' Betty caught her and lowered her gently back into the chair. 'You got up too quickly,' she said. 'Now, what were you saying? Does Mr Brookfield need the doctor?'

'No, he isn't unwell — or at least he might be, I don't know.' Marion looked anxious — no, more than anxious; she was obviously worried sick.

'You're not making sense,' Betty said. 'Try again.'

Marion looked up at her, and Betty noticed that strands of hair had escaped from their pins and were framing her face, giving her a dishevelled look that was most unlike her. 'He didn't come home last night,' Marion said. 'At least I don't think he did. Perhaps he came home after I fell asleep in the chair here. Perhaps he went straight up to bed thinking I hadn't waited for him.'

'You've been sitting here all night?'

'Yes.'

'No wonder you look so washed out.'

'Thank you.' Marion managed a weak smile.

'Come along to the kitchen. It's warmer in there and you need a cup of tea.'

'Thank you, but first I'll go upstairs and see if my father is there.'

Betty went through to the kitchen, but before she had even got her pinny on, Marion appeared in the doorway. Her face was pale as parchment.

'He's not there,' she said. 'My father did not come home.'

Betty was stumped. She had no idea what to say. She knew Mr Brookfield went out on some kind of business most nights; she thought it was to do with something he was writing for his paper about poor people's houses. She had gathered that much from over-hearing the odd remark he made to his elder daughter.

'Do you know where he went?' she asked Marion.

'Not exactly.'

'Hev you got a rough idea?'

'I suppose so.'

'Well, first of all we'll get Annette up, give her her breakfast and send her off to school, then you and me will go looking for him.'

'Annette . . .' Marion looked stricken.

'Divven't fret, Miss Marion, pet. There's no need to worry her. I'll make porridge and toast and a nice big pot of tea and you'll hev breakfast together as usual.'

'No . . . I couldn't . . .'

'Yes you could. You'll eat every last morsel that I sets afore you. You don't want your sister to guess that there's something wrong, do you?'

'But she'll wonder where Father is – why he's not having breakfast with us.'

'Tell her that your da has had to go to the office early today. He does that sometimes, doesn't he?'

'Yes . . . but . . .'

'Lissen, if you can't bring yourself to tell a fib, then I'll tell one for you. Now go upstairs and hev a wash. I'll bring jugs of hot water up for both of you.'

Annette, sleepy and a little grumpy as she usually was in the morning, accepted Betty's explanation as to why her father was not joining them for breakfast. There was a small dining table in the front parlour, but the family had got into the habit of having breakfast in the kitchen because it was warmer there first thing in the morning. Before Betty went home each day, she made sure that the range fire was set to last all night.

Annette didn't seem to sense that anything was wrong. She ate her breakfast as enthusiastically as usual, and Marion, mindful of Betty's watchful eye, ate everything she was given. After breakfast, when Annette was ready to leave the house, Marion asked her, 'Did you put your homework in your satchel?'

'Oops! It's still on the table where I left it last night.' Annette hurried into the parlour to get her notebook. 'Honestly, sister dear,' she said when she came out again. 'I don't know what I'd do without you!'

She hugged Marion and set off happily enough for school.

As soon as Annette had gone, Marion put her coat on and started to button it up.

'Wait a minute,' Betty told her. 'You sit down and have another cup of tea while I wash the dishes.'

'But—'

'Lissen, if your da comes home while we're out, I don't want him to find the place abandoned like the *Mary Celeste* – dishes on the table, the teapot still warm. He'll think something awful has happened.'

'Do you think he might?'

'Think something bad has happened? Bound to. I mean, why else would his daughter be missing and his housemaid have left everything in a mess? He'd probably think one of us had been taken off to the hospital.'

'No, I didn't mean that. I meant do you think he might come home while we're out?'

Betty felt the stirrings of unease, but she forced herself to smile and said, 'It's a possibility, isn't it?' She poured Marion another cup of tea. 'Drink that, and while you're sitting there, scribble a quick note to leave for your da – say we've gone to the shops together. We sometimes do, don't we?'

Marion did as Betty suggested, although she found it strange to be writing a note to stop her father from worrying when she was the one who was nearly out of her mind.

A short while later, Marion and Betty closed the door behind them and walked to Osborne Road. Marion knew approximately which part of town her father had been visiting, and she had decided they would take a cab as far as the top of Byker Bank and then continue on foot. They were silent as they travelled; neither knew what to say, and Betty began to feel more and more uneasy. When they reached the end of Heaton Road and turned into Shields Road, she said to Marion, 'Let's stop the cab now and get out here.'

Marion looked puzzled. 'Why here?'

'Because I've decided that it just won't do. You and me going alone to those streets down near the Ouseburn. It might not be safe.'

'But that's where my father is likely to be.'

When Marion didn't ask the cab-driver to stop, Betty did so herself and persuaded Marion to get out.

'Now what are we going to do?' Marion looked bewildered.

Betty took her arm and guided her across Shields Road. 'We're going to the police station in Headlam Street.'

Marion blanched. 'You think something's happened to him, don't you? Something bad?'

'Maybe. Maybe he's had a fall or something. Maybe they've taken him off to the infirmary, and if that's the case they'll know about it at the police station.'

'And if they don't know anything?'

'Then we'll look for him just as you suggested. But we'll ask one of the constables to come with us. All right?'

'Yes.' Marion realised that this made sense, and she made no further objection as they walked to Headlam Street.

Betty kept glancing at her uneasily. The lass was behaving so unlike herself. Marion was usually so decisive and practical. It must be shock, Betty thought. That would be it. Betty admitted to herself that she had a bad feeling about this, and she only hoped that Marion would be strong enough to face whatever lay ahead of her.

Once inside the police station, Betty was pleased to recognise the young constable sitting on a high stool at a desk in the reception area. It was the lanky lad she had glimpsed earlier, running down the bank with another policeman. They had been in the same class at school. He was writing in a large ledger, and when he looked up, his eyes opened wide in surprise. Then he smiled his recognition.

'Betty! Betty Sutton, isn't it? Do you remember me?'

'Aye, I do. You're Arthur Robinson. I was at school with Arthur,' she explained to Marion.

'Well, what can I do for you?' he asked.

Marion stood back a little and allowed Betty to tell Constable Robinson what the problem was.

The young police constable looked grave. 'So this lady's father is missing?'

'That's right,' Betty said.

'But what makes you think he could be in this part of town? I mean, excuse me saying so, but Miss Brookfield looks – I mean . . .'

'It's all right, Arthur,' Betty said. 'You're right. Miss Brookfield lives in Jesmond. I work for the family,' she added.

'So, as I said, why would Miss Brookfield's father be here?'

Marion stepped forward. 'My father is a newspaper reporter,' she said. 'He was doing some investigations for something he is writing. This necessitates him going out at night. And as Betty told you, he didn't come home. He's never stayed out all night before. He wouldn't do that – he knows I would worry.'

Betty saw that Marion was close to breaking point. She also saw that Arthur had begun to look uneasy.

'Could you describe your father?' he asked Marion.

'He's tall – quite thin. He has dark hair and a beard.'

'What was he wearing when you last saw him?'

'An old overcoat over his suit, a long muffler, a cap.'

'Excuse me, miss,' Arthur said, 'but why an old coat and why a cap?'

'He doesn't like to stand out. He doesn't want to arouse suspicion.'

Arthur looked more uneasy. He closed the book in which he had been writing and rose from his stool. He towered above them.

'If you don't mind, Miss Brookfield,' he said, 'I'm just going to have a word with Sergeant Wilson. Would you like to sit down?' He waved his long arm in the direction of a wooden bench placed against a tiled wall.

'He knows something, doesn't he?' Marion asked, when he had gone.

Before Betty could think of an answer, Arthur returned with an older, more solidly built man. The senior officer surveyed each of them and then addressed Marion. 'Miss Brookfield?'

Marion looked as though she was holding her breath; her eyes were unnaturally bright. 'Yes,' she said.

'Arthur here has told me that you are enquiring about your father. A tall, dark, bearded man, you say?'

'Yes.'

'And dressed – shall we say disguised? – in working men's clothes.'

'That's right.'

Betty saw Marion begin to sway and she stepped closer.

'Then I'm sorry to say that we think we may have found him.' He paused, his eyes filled with compassion. His voice was gentle as he continued, 'And we'd like you to come with Arthur and me to – to identify him.'

Betty took hold of Marion's elbow.

'Identify him?' Marion said. 'Are we going to the infirmary?'

'No, Miss Brookfield, not the infirmary. We will be escorting you to the morgue.'

It was Betty who fainted.

Henry Brookfield had been taken to the city mortuary. Known locally as the Dead House, it overlooked the River Tyne at the boat landing near Spiller's flour mill. Somehow the old building did not look imposing enough to act as a resting place for the dead before their final journey. Marion wasn't sure what she had been expecting – a dignified church-like edifice in grey stone, perhaps, but not this ancient jumble of whitewashed old brick dwellings.

On the pavement near the entrance to the mortuary there were some grappling hooks and coils of chain. Marion overheard Arthur Robinson telling Betty quietly that they were for pulling dead bodies from the river. Dead bodies, Marion thought, and found herself wondering if any of the poor souls fished out of the river turned out to be alive after all.

Far above, a seagull swooped over the water and screeched with what sounded like mirth. Marion suppressed a shocking desire to join in the laughter; she worried that she might be approaching a state of hysteria.

Sergeant Wilson led the way through a wide doorway. The door, old and needing a coat of paint, had been propped open. Marion walked behind him. She began to tremble. Their footsteps echoed on the bare stone floor and the white-tiled walls seemed to be closing in on her. Fear surged through her body and she suddenly felt as though she might choke. Clenching her fists, she prepared herself for the ordeal that lay ahead.

Betty followed, still looking pale. Constable Robinson brought up the rear and kept a watchful eye on Betty as if he was worried that she might keel over again, as she had at the police station. In fact he had caught her before she hit the floor, lifted her up as though she were a child and carried her through to a room where there was a table and a few chairs. It was the room where the police officers took a break and brewed themselves a cup of tea, the sergeant explained.

While Arthur lowered Betty into an armchair near the fireplace, the sergeant himself went off to the kitchen and reappeared with a tray and two cups of tea. He insisted that Marion sit down and drink one of them. It was very sweet, but he said that sugar was good for the shock she must be feeling. Betty had come round by now and had accepted her cup gratefully. As soon as they had finished, they had set off for the mortuary.

It hadn't taken long to walk down from Headlam Street, and now Marion stood and waited while Sergeant Wilson went to seek the attendant in charge. She was aware of Betty standing behind her and keeping close to her old schoolfriend Arthur Robinson.

Despite their physical proximity, Marion felt as though a gulf was opening up between them. Betty and Arthur would remain anchored in this familiar, everyday place, whereas she was about to enter a new, terrifying world; a world without her father.

The sergeant returned with a portly, self-important-looking man wearing a white coat unbuttoned over a dark blue suit. His greying hair was parted in the middle and he had half-moon spectacles perched on his nose.

'I suppose it's all right,' he was saying to Sergeant Wilson. 'I mean, if you say so.'

'I do say so,' the sergeant replied.

'Well I hope you've explained to the – ah' – he glanced at Marion – 'to the young lady that we have only recently received this – ah – the deceased, and that we have not yet had the opportunity to – ah – tidy him up.'

Marion blanched. She sensed that Betty had moved up behind her, but she had no intention of fainting and she shook her head slightly, meaning that she did not need supporting.

'You have at least covered him decently,' Sergeant Wilson said quietly.

'Of course.'

'Then let us not waste any more time. Will you lead the way?' He turned to Marion, 'Do you wish your maid to come with you?'

Marion, mindful of the way Betty had reacted earlier, said, 'No, that's all right. I would rather be alone.'

'We cannot allow you to be quite alone,' Sergeant Wilson replied. 'I must come with you – and of course Mr Potts here.'

The mortuary attendant led them through a door, and their footsteps echoed almost deafeningly along a dismal corridor where the smell of some sort of chemical, carbolic perhaps, grew stronger as they reached a set of double doors at the end. Marion was not prepared for the fact that there would be more than one body in the room. Her eyes widened with barely controlled horror as she took in the neat rows of tables. On most of them lay forms covered in white cloths. On the floor under one of them a pool was forming as water dripped steadily from whatever it was that lay beneath the cloth.

Mr Potts saw the direction of her glance and explained, 'The poor soul was taken from the river this morning. But please, follow me.' At the far end of the room he stopped at one of the tables. 'Are you ready?' he asked, and his voice was reverential.

'Yes,' Marion whispered.

She was aware of Sergeant Wilson standing close. He didn't speak, but he placed a hand under her elbow. Mr Potts drew the cloth back a little and Marion saw what she had been praying she would not see. His eyes were closed, but in the harsh overhead light she saw no peace, no acceptance of death in the fine lines of her father's face. She noticed the scattering of grey hair in his dark beard and at his temples. But he wasn't old. He was surely in the prime of his life. He should not be lying here so still on this uncomfortable wooden table. She suppressed a sob that was prompted as much by rage as sorrow.

'Miss Brookfield . . .?' Sergeant Wilson murmured.

'Yes,' she whispered, 'that is my father. But how . . .?'

'Mr Potts, may we use your office?' Sergeant Wilson asked.

'Of course.'

In the mortuary attendant's office, which was little more than a cubicle, Marion sat on a leather armchair near the fire. She had the strangest sensation that she could actually see herself sitting there. She was two people. One, the surface Marion, was practical and matter-of-fact as she dealt with everything that had to be done. The other Marion had been pushed deep inside her being. And this inner Marion was seething with emotion; her grief welling up and aching to burst forth.

The sensible Marion asked Sergeant Wilson how it had happened. He told her as much as he knew.

'There is no question but that he was murdered,' the sergeant said, and Marion gripped the arms of the chair.

'How?' she asked.

'The police surgeon has still to examine your father, but when my men found him this morning, there was – forgive me – there was a pool of blood. It looks as though he had been knifed.'

'Who would do such a thing?'

'A thief.'

'But when my father went out at nights he did not carry anything very valuable with him.'

'No money at all?'

'Well, yes, he did carry money in a black leather pouch. Not sovereigns, small coins.'

'Very much?' the sergeant asked.

Marion frowned uneasily. 'Sometimes. You see, he liked to be able to give those with nowhere to sleep sufficient to pay for a bed for the night in a common lodging house.'

'So the sum could have been considerable – at least it would be to the type of person he would encounter on the streets. And would there be anything else? A watch, for example?'

'Yes, he had a watch.'

'Was it valuable?'

'It was to my father. My mother gave it to him just a few months before she died. She had his name engraved on the case.'

'Gold?'

'Silver, the fob also.'

The sergeant looked grave. 'When we found him, there was no watch; there was nothing in your father's pockets. Nothing at all.'

Marion stared bleakly into the fire. It looked bright enough, but it seemed to give off no heat. 'Where did you find him?' she asked.

'Near one of the coal wharves. Poor folk go there with baskets and bags and they stand in the water and salvage any coal that falls overboard from the keels. Some bairns who had been sent there by their mother found the body – your father – lying on the shore.'

'How dreadful for them.'

'Why do you say that?'

'They must have been shocked – frightened.'

'Ah, you're imagining they would be like the children in your part of the city; children who have been nicely brought up – who have been cared for, not to say cosseted. I'm afraid to say that these bairns are not so lucky and that they've probably seen much worse. Likely this isn't the first time they've seen a dead body lying in the streets, and it won't be the last.'

Marion felt as though she had been reprimanded. 'Of course,' she said. 'I should have remembered.'

'Remembered?' Sergeant Wilson looked puzzled.

'Remembered why my father was working here.'

'And why exactly was that? A charity worker?'

'As I told the constable, my father was a journalist. He has been investigating the conditions that so many of our fellow citizens have to live in. The housing, the lack of sanitation, the disease.'

'Ah, your father thought he could change things, did he?'

Marion sensed a certain cynicism in the police sergeant's manner and she flushed. 'Of course he did. He thought that by writing about such matters, by exposing people who needed to be exposed, he could begin to stir consciences.'

'It seems that he has paid for his good intentions by being murdered by one of the very people he was trying to help. He was killed and robbed for the little he had in his pockets. But please be assured, Miss Brookfield, we will do our utmost to apprehend the wretch who did this. And now . . .' Marion realised that the interview was coming to an end, 'you had better contact an undertaker. Tell him that we will release the body as soon as possible.'

'Thank you.' Marion rose to her feet. 'I should go home now.'

'Will you be alone there?'

'I have a sister – a younger sister.'

The sergeant looked aghast. 'And you must break the news to her.' It wasn't a question.

'Yes.'

'Have you no relatives? An older lady, perhaps?'

'No, we are alone.'

'Then, Miss Brookfield, my thoughts will be with you.'

'Thank you.'

'At least you have your maid. She seems to be a good soul. A canny lass, as they say.'

'She is.'

'Now, if you would excuse me, I must have a word with Mr Potts.'

When they left the office, the sergeant hurried away along the corridor and Marion went the other way to the entrance hall. There was no one there, but she could hear the low murmur of voices coming from outside. The sun had broken free from the clouds, and for a moment, Marion stood in the doorway and let her eyes become accustomed to the world outside. Betty and Arthur Robinson were sitting on a low wall overlooking the river. While Betty talked to him, he was writing something in his notebook. Marion supposed he was doing his duty and asking Betty to tell him everything she knew.

As soon as Betty saw Marion, she rose and came towards her. 'Can we go home now?' she asked.

'Yes.'

'Arthur is going to walk up to Shields Road with us and get us a cab.'

'Very well.'

'Then he's going to my house to tell my mother what has happened. I've given him a list and he's going to bring everything along when he's finished work.'

Marion frowned. 'I don't understand. A list?'

'Aye, pet, a list of the things I'll need for the next few days. Arthur will tell me ma that I'll be staying with you for a while.' She raised her hand when she saw that Marion was about to object. 'Divven't fret. Me ma won't object. In fact she would probably hev suggested this herself.'

'But where . . .?'

'Will I sleep? On the sofa; it'll do me fine.'

Marion was bemused, but she was happy to let the older girl take charge, for her practical self was beginning to weaken and the other self, the self that was howling with rage and grief, was close to the surface. But she knew she must not give way to this other Marion yet. She must keep her under control until the lonely hours after she had gone to bed. For now she must remain as strong and as calm as she could. She had to tell Annette that their father had been murdered.

When her sister came home from school, Betty left them alone in the front parlour and Marion told Annette as gently as she could that their father was not coming home, and why. After a long, uncomprehending silence Annette said, 'Father has had an accident?'

'No, dear, not an accident. I told you, he was attacked by a thief. There must have been some sort of struggle and – and Father was mortally wounded.' Marion had decided at the outset that Annette must be told the truth; at sixteen she should not be treated like a child.

'Mortally wounded?' Annette's eyes filled with tears.

'Yes.' Despite her resolve, Marion's own tears began to flow.

'We will never see him again?' Annette sobbed.

'No. I'm so sorry, Annette.' Tears ran down Marion's cheeks unchecked until she saw her sister's grief give way to anxiety.

'But who will look after us?' Annette asked.

Marion suppressed her own grief in order to comfort her sister. 'I will.'

'Will we be able to stay here? In this house? Our home?'

'Of course,' Marion said, although she suspected there was no 'of course' about it.

'How will we pay the rent?'

'Father had some savings. No doubt we will inherit them. That will keep us going for some time. And I . . .' She paused; she had not really thought this through, 'I will find some sort of employment.'

'Will you?' Annette looked at her doubtfully. 'But what will you do?'

'I don't know. Work in an office – a shop – something like that.'

'And will you earn enough for us to live on?'

'Yes.' Marion had no idea if that were true, but she could see that her sister was getting more and more anxious and she wanted to reassure her. 'You mustn't worry. Whatever happens, I will look after you.'

Annette was frowning; she looked far from reassured, but at that moment Betty knocked on the door and came in.

'Your tea is ready,' Betty said. 'I've made Welsh rarebit and some treacle drop scones. We'll eat in the kitchen. I've built up the fire so's it's nice and cosy.'

When Marion and Annette had been younger, Henry Brookfield had asked Betty to sit and eat with them whenever they took their meals in the kitchen. 'More like a family,' he had said. As they grew older, the custom continued. As Marion had once remarked, 'The kitchen is your domain, Betty. Of course you should sit with us.'

Betty had gone ahead, and Annette was just about to follow her when she turned to Marion and said, 'And will I still be able to go to art school?'

# Chapter Three

The fire in her bedroom burned low and shadows flickered on the ceiling. Usually Marion found this reassuring, but tonight there was no solace in the warm glow nor in the comfort of her feather bed. Outside a dog barked, the sound echoing intermittently along the back lane. A wind had risen, whistling round the chimneypots and loosening the roof tiles.

Towards morning the wind died and the rain began, drumming against the window panes. Marion, her head aching, was sleepless when the early-morning rattling of the delivery carts began to wake the respectable streets from their slumbers.

There was a knock on the door and Betty entered balancing a tray. 'I thought you'd be awake,' she said. 'Here, drink this tea, and I've brought meself a cup as well, if that's all right with you. We've got a lot to do today and I thought we'd better discuss things before Annette gets up.'

Marion pulled a shawl around her shoulders and Betty built up the fire before perching on the end of the bed. They knew they would have to tell Henry Brookfield's employers what had happened, and decided that Marion should write a letter to the editor of the paper and Betty would take it to the newspaper office. They must also think about the funeral. They kept their voices down because they did not wish to disturb or upset Annette.

When Annette came down to the kitchen for breakfast, she was subdued. 'What shall I do today?' she asked Marion.

'You should go to school,' Marion said. 'I've thought about it and I don't think it would be good for you to sit at home with nothing to do.'

Annette ate her breakfast without making any further comment. By the time she was ready to leave for school, the rain was heavier. A steady downpour slapped the leaves of the laurels in the front gardens, bounced off the pavements and turned the gutters into narrow swift-flowing streams. Marion saw that Annette put her mackintosh on over her coat and also slipped her galoshes over her shoes. But her sister refused to wear a waterproof hat.

'Those hats are so ugly,' she said.

'Here you are, then.' Marion handed her an umbrella. 'Luckily school isn't too far away. Wait a minute, I want you to give this letter to your form teacher.'

'What's in it?' Annette asked. 'You're not going to tell Miss Thomas that I said school was boring and Shakespeare was stuffy, are you?'

Despite her grief, this made Marion smile. 'No, dear, I would never let you down like that. This letter explains about Father – what has happened – and that I believe you would be better occupied at school rather than being at home.'

Marion stood on the doorstep and watched her sister set off through the rain. When Annette had turned the corner, she closed the door and turned to find Betty looking at her quizzically. 'What is it?' Marion asked.

'You fret too much about your sister,' Betty said.

'She's just lost her father.'

'So hev you.'

'But she's only a child.'

Betty sighed. 'That's how you see her, I know, but it won't do the lass any good if you go on wrapping her up in cotton wool.'

'Betty . . . stop this . . . don't let's quarrel. Not today of all days,' Marion said.

Betty looked mortified. 'Is that what we're doing? Quarrelling? Eeh, pet, I'm sorry. It's just that I think Annette expects too much of you sometimes.'

'If she does, I don't mind.'

'I know you don't, and I'll try to keep me mouth shut in future. Now, hawway, we've got jobs to do.'

They smiled at each other, but Marion was troubled. She didn't like anyone else to say so, but she knew that at times Annette's behaviour left much to be desired. She might be sixteen years old, but she was not very mature. She didn't even look her age. And now that their father had been taken from them, Marion foresaw some troubled times ahead.

As the day wore on, the rain grew heavier. The streets where the new tramlines were being laid were awash with mud. By mid-afternoon Daniel was not surprised when the foreman came round and told them that work was finished for the day. Despite the fact that they were soaked through, many of the men groaned with disappointment. No work meant no pay for the casual labourers, and only 'wet money' for the regulars.

Daniel had been with the same gang since he had left school at twelve, so he would be entitled to half-pay as long as the rain prevented them from working. He hoped it wouldn't be for too long. He was responsible for his mother and his sister and he needed every penny he earned, but today he was almost pleased to have a rest from the backbreaking work. He would go to the library and sit in the reading room. He would find the peace there he was denied at home.

His canvas bait bag was stored in the workmen's hut; he collected it and pushed it down inside his jacket. He didn't want the bag to get wet, for as well as his sandwich tin, it contained one of the books Mr Brookfield had lent him.

There was a new library assistant behind the desk whom Daniel had never seen before, and there was no mistaking the look of disdain the young man gave him. 'Yes?' he said. 'Can I help you?'

Daniel was aware of what he must look like in his rough working clothes. 'I want to use the reading room,' he said.

'The *reading* room?' The library assistant emphasised the word as if he doubted that Daniel could read.

'Yes, I often go there.'

'It's all right, Mr Chalk,' a female voice called, and Miss Bennett came bustling out of her office. 'I know Mr Brady. It's perfectly all right for him to use the reading room.'

Mr Chalk could hardly argue with his superior, but he had one last try. 'But Mr Brady is soaking wet – and what's more, he should wash his hands.'

The elderly librarian smiled at Daniel as if asking him not to take offence. Then she turned to her young assistant. 'You're right, Mr Chalk. I think Mr Brady should be allowed to use the rest room to wash his hands and to dry himself as much as he can, and then you can put the kettle on for a cup of tea.'

Mr Chalk was taken aback, but he wilted under Miss Bennett's determined gaze and contented himself with saying, 'Food and drink are not allowed in the reading room.'

'I'm perfectly aware of that,' Miss Bennett said. 'Mr Brady can have a cup of tea and a biscuit in my office.'

From the look the young man shot him, Daniel knew he had made an enemy of Mr Chalk – and he knew why. He was a labouring man, and there were those who thought that people like him shouldn't get above themselves. The irony was that by dint of hard, backbreaking work for as many hours as possible, Daniel was probably taking home more pay than young Mr Chalk in his cut-price suit and shirt with sleeves too short to cover his bony wrists.

Now Miss Bennett was a real lady, Daniel thought. She might not be from a wealthy family – otherwise why would she have to seek employment – but she spoke in well-modulated tones and had perfect manners. The kind of manners that taught you to treat every-one with respect no matter which part of town you came from.

She had never asked Daniel too many questions – that would have been considered rude – but she had watched with interest the sort of books he was borrowing, and sometimes, when he was doing his 'homework' in the reading room, she had entered quietly and left a selection of books that she thought might be helpful on the table.

Once he had cleaned himself up, she made him sit by the fire in her office. He became acutely aware of the steam rising from his clothes. He knew that the odour was unpleasantly musty and he scalded his mouth in an attempt to drink the tea quickly. Miss Bennett had left the door open and was coming and going with various files. At one point when she was out of the room, Daniel made his escape and went to the reading room.

He was the only person there. He guessed that sensible folk would not be prepared to brave the weather on such a day. When he sat down and took the book from his bag, he sighed with satisfaction. He was not going to do any written work today. He was going to do as Henry Brookfield had suggested and read for relaxation.

He opened *The Leavenworth Case* and was soon immersed in a world thousands of miles away, in a solicitor's office in New York. He hadn't been reading for very long when he decided that he liked detective fiction.

The time passed all too quickly, and he looked up in surprise when Miss Bennett came in and told him that it was time to close the library. She looked down at the book as he was about to put it back into his bait bag. She smiled.

'It's good to see you reading for entertainment for once, Mr Brady. You work so hard usually.'

Daniel sensed a question in her voice. He guessed that she must have been curious as to why he had been studying so earnestly. She would probably want to know what the purpose of all his efforts was, and the truth was he couldn't tell her – not exactly.

'I . . . I want to better myself,' he said, and he was aware how awkward he sounded.

'Very worthy.' Miss Bennett smiled. 'May I ask why exactly? I mean, what are your hopes?'

'My hopes?' Daniel was momentarily distracted by a vision of a modest but comfortable house; a house full of books where he would sit reading at one side of the hearth, and glance up to see a tall, graceful, dark-haired young woman completely absorbed in her own book. She would sense his glance . . . look up and smile . . .

He thrust the image away from him and repeated, 'My hopes? I can't tell you exactly.' Then he smiled as her remembered what Henry Brookfield had said to him. 'I suppose I want to make myself fit for some sort of employment that will exercise my brain rather than my brawn.'

'I'm glad to hear that, Mr Brady, and if ever there is anything I can do to help you, don't hesitate to ask me.'

Miss Bennett, Mr Chalk and Daniel left the library at the same time. Miss Bennett locked up and said good night to Mr Chalk, who opened his umbrella and scuttled away through the rain. Miss Bennett also had an umbrella, and after smiling and nodding to Daniel, she too hurried away.

Daniel watched her slight figure merge into the crowds and he wondered what sort of life she might lead away from the library. She was unmarried, but did she have sisters, brothers, elderly parents? Despite her unfailingly cheerful manner, he could not shake off the impression that the kindly Miss Bennett was lonely.

Feeling the rain beginning to soak through his jacket, Daniel turned for home. He stopped on the corner to buy an evening paper from a ragged paper boy sheltering in a shop doorway. He folded it quickly and pushed it into his bag. Poor lad, he thought, out in all weathers selling papers for very little money. Money that no doubt his family couldn't manage without.

Passing carriages threw up sprays of filthy water, and as Daniel hurried through the streets, a variety of odours assailed his nostrils. Horse droppings, the sudden foulness of a blocked drain, the smell of frying bacon from a small café, and the rich aroma of roasting coffee from an Italian grocer's shop.

And then, as he approached the narrow cobbled streets where he had always lived, the ever-present stink from the bone yard, mingled with the more appetising smell of hundreds of meals being cooked for the men returning from work.

Many of these meals would be some sort of soup or stew; cheap cuts of meat cooked slowly on the range in an attempt to make them tender. His mother always had such a meal ready for him. Her cooking was unimaginative but she saw to it that his plate was piled high. He was the man of the family, the worker, and he must be fed as well as they could afford.

Tonight was no exception. Mutton broth by the smell of it, probably made from a sheep's head. His mother would buy the head from the butcher for as little as a penny, soak it in salt water overnight to clean it, and then wash it and put it in a large pan of water with chopped carrots, turnip, onions, celery and a good helping of barley.

Hannah Brady was stirring the pot when Daniel came in, and she spoke without turning. 'You're late.'

Daniel glanced at the clock on the mantelshelf. 'No later than usual,' he said.

'Didn't they send you home early today? Surely you couldn't do much in this weather?'

'You're right. I've been to the library.'

Daniel could not lie to his mother, but he wished she had not asked. He did not know why, but she seemed to resent the time he spent with his books. Often when he was working at home with his papers spread out across the table, she would interrupt him, telling him what she had been doing that day, gossiping about the neighbours and expecting him to reply.

If he didn't, she would complain to his younger sister, Susan, that he was being grumpy and the pair of them would keep up a constant flow of chatter that drove him to distraction. But how could he complain? After all, this was their home too, and he couldn't

really expect them to curtail their usual pleasures just to accommo-
date him.

'Go and wash in the scullery,' his mother told him. 'This broth is
good and ready. You and me will eat now and I'll warm it up for
Susan when she gets home.'

'Where is Susan?' Daniel asked.

His sister was seventeen and very attractive, with a creamy
complexion, glossy black hair and blue-grey eyes. She loved clothes
and always made the most of herself, even though she was paid very
little for her job behind the counter in a tobacconist's in the
Haymarket.

Daniel worried about Susan. She had a loving nature and an air of
innocence, but he couldn't deny that she was immature and somewhat flighty. She seemed to have room for nothing in her head
except the latest fashions.

'She's working late,' his mother said.

'I wish she wouldn't.'

'Why ever not? She gets paid extra, and you know she's saving up
for that little fur muff she saw in Bainbridge's.'

'I don't like her being in town when the pubs start filling up.'

'Divven't worry, Daniel. She'll go straight to the tram stop; she
won't wander about the streets. She's got more sense than that.'

'I hope so,' Daniel said, but he remained uneasy. If the fancy took
her, his sister was perfectly capable of going off to do some window-
shopping – especially now that the autumn fashions were on display.

'You fret too much,' his mother told him as she placed a bowl of
broth on the kitchen table in front of him. 'You may not realise it, but
you're turning out just like your da.'

Hannah Brady had served up a small bowl of broth for herself, and
she sat down opposite Daniel. Daniel cut them each a generous slice
of bread and she smiled her thanks.

'Do you remember much about your father?' she asked after she
had taken a mouthful or two.

'Of course.'

'He was a fine-looking man – you take after him. In fact I think
you may be even better looking.'

Daniel smiled. 'You see me through a mother's eyes.'

'Aye, I do, but it's true all the same. And you're like him in other
ways.'

'And what are those?'

'You work hard. You're a good provider. Whoever you wed will be a very lucky lass.'

'And whoever I wed will have to put up with you, won't she?'

'You could always pack me off to the workhouse,' his mother said. They smiled at each other. This was an old joke.

'I might just do that. Especially if I have to endure all this blather every time I sit down at the table.'

Hannah Brady laughed, but as she watched her son finish his bowl of broth she suddenly looked serious. 'Divven't leave it too long, will you, Daniel?'

'Leave what too long, Ma?' he asked, but he knew what was coming.

'Your da was wed to me and we had two bonny bairns by the time he was your age.'

Daniel's humour died. 'So you keep telling me.'

'It's not fair to the lass to keep her hanging on like this. Her bottom drawer must be overflowing by now.'

Daniel suddenly felt trapped. He knew perfectly well which lass his mother was referring to: Dora Gibb. The Gibb family lived next door, and Dora and he had known each other since they were children. Dora was one year older than Daniel and she was pretty in a rounded, comfortable sort of way. But her pleasant face was rather vapid, Daniel thought, and her conversation dull.

He felt guilty for thinking of her in this way; Dora was what people called 'a canny lass', meaning kind and good natured. She had always got on well with his mother and she provided the female company and gossip that Hannah enjoyed. Dora helped her mother with the younger bairns, but she worked some days in the corner shop. Hannah would give her a list, and Dora would bring her shopping home for her.

Daniel couldn't remember when their childhood friendship had changed into something more. Perhaps he had simply got used to Dora always being around, but at some point it had seemed natural for them to go out together – for walks in Heaton Park, or even on a train ride to the coast to enjoy the fresh sea air and the beautiful golden beaches.

It was on one of these trips to the seaside that something had occurred that would change everything – and it was something that

Daniel wished with all his heart had never happened. Yet he only had himself to blame.

They had been walking on the beach in Cullercoats Bay when it had begun to rain. Just a few drops at first, and then suddenly a downpour. They had turned and run for the nearest cave, but by the time they arrived, laughing and breathless, the feathers on Dora's hat were a sorry sight. They were drooping limply down over the brim, one of them hanging directly over her nose and making her go cross-eyed.

Most young women, including Daniel's sister Susan, would have been upset about the ruined hat, but Dora laughed, then stuck out her lower lip and tried to blow the feathers up off her face. She didn't succeed, and still laughing, she removed the hatpin, took the hat off and shook it vigorously. Then she looked at it in mock despair.

'Is it ruined?' Daniel asked.

'Only the feathers,' she replied, and smiled ruefully.

'I'll buy you some more,' Daniel said. 'Feathers, flowers, ribbons – anything you like!'

'Will you, Daniel?' Dora asked, and she moved closer and looked up into his eyes.

The dim warmth of the cave enclosed them. The sound of the waves beating on the shore and then drawing back across the shingle seemed to fade. The smell of rain in her hair mingling with her perfume – a light rose – engulfed his senses. Daniel took Dora in his arms and kissed her.

She returned the kiss with passion, pressing her body against his in a way that aroused him. Then the harsh cry of a gull, the flapping of powerful wings and the shadow of its flight moving across the wall of the cave shocked them to their senses.

'I'm sorry,' Daniel said, letting her go and stepping back. 'Please forgive me. I shouldn't hev done that.'

Dora was flushed but far from upset. 'No need to apologise,' she said.

Her hat had fallen to the floor. She picked it up, tore off the ruined feathers and flung them to the ground, before putting it on again. They left the cave and the beach, hardly talking on their way back to the station. But Dora slipped her hand through the crook of Daniel's arm. It would have felt brutish to remove it.

He didn't know how much of it she had confided to his mother, but she must have told Hannah something of what had happened, for since that day, there had been an understanding. They were walking out. Dora had taken it for granted that they would be married and she had started putting things in her bottom drawer. She might have wondered why he had never kissed her again, but she probably took it as a mark of respect.

Why on earth had he done it? He didn't love her. But their closeness in the cave, their senses already roused by the run up the beach and the shared laughter, had brought them together. There was no doubt Daniel had enjoyed the moment, but he knew such a thing must never happen again.

His mother took his empty bowl away and placed a plate before him containing apple pie and custard. 'There you are, hinny, your favourite.'

'That's right, Ma,' he said to please her, although in truth his mother wasn't a very good pastry cook.

But when he started eating, he looked up in astonishment. His mother laughed. 'That surprised you, didn't it? Dora made it. She's a better cook than I am.'

Daniel didn't respond. What could he say? After a while he looked up and asked, 'Shouldn't Susan be home by now?'

His mother glanced at the clock and frowned. 'I'm not sure. She didn't say exactly.' At that moment they heard the back door open and smiled at each other in relief. 'That'll be her,' his mother said.

But when the door that led from the scullery opened, it was Dora who walked in. She must have sensed their concern, because her ready smile faded.

'What is it?' she asked. 'Is something wrong?'

'No, pet, we were expecting Susan, that's all. She hasn't come home from work yet.'

'But she said she was working late tonight, didn't she? Until eight o'clock, if I remember right.'

'Aye, she did. But Daniel gets worried when she's in town after normal hours, and it rubs off on me.' Hannah paused and added, 'Well, in truth I suppose he's right to worry. There's some bad folk of late.'

'You mean the Toff,' Dora said.

'Aye, I do. Preying on young lasses, indeed, some little more than bairns, the newspapers say.'

They were referring to a shadowy figure who had been glimpsed talking to various young women who had subsequently disappeared. Either he was a murderer – except that no bodies had ever been found – or he was procuring girls for prostitution. No witnesses could swear they had actually seen him up close, but somehow a rumour had started that he wore an opera cloak and a top hat. This had prompted a reporter with a fertile imagination to dub him 'the Toff'.

'Don't worry, Mrs Brady,' Dora said. 'Susan would have more sense than to speak to someone like that.'

'I suppose so,' agreed Hannah. But Daniel could see the doubt in her eyes.

He rose from the table. 'I think I'll go and meet her,' he said.

'Do you want me to come with you?' Dora asked him.

'No.'

Dora looked stricken, and Daniel realised that his answer had been too abrupt. He smiled at her and added, 'I'd like you to stay with my mother, keep her company. We don't want to leave her on her own, she'll only worry.'

'Oh . . . of course.'

Daniel had washed before sitting down for his meal, but rather than go into town in his work clothes, he went upstairs and changed into a decent shirt and his best suit. In fact it was his only suit. Every other jacket or pair of trousers he owned had been worn for working on the roads.

It didn't take him long, but by the time he went down again, his mother was sitting by the fire with a cup of tea and Dora was in the scullery washing the dishes in the sink. She gave him an encouraging smile as he left.

Daniel walked up to Shields Road and caught a tram that went over Byker Bridge into town. He got off at the end of Newbridge Street and walked up Northumberland Street to the Haymarket. On Tuesdays, the Haymarket was taken over by countrymen with strings of horses and fragrant high-piled carts of hay and straw. But in latter years the old Tudor houses that had provided the background had gradually been replaced by tall, impressive buildings more in keeping with a great industrial city.

Now, in this area of the city, there were proper theatres instead of sideshows, and one or two fine restaurants in place of ale and pie stalls. And in the evening, when the shops and offices were closing, a different atmosphere suffused the sober, busy streets. The pavements became crowded with people determined to enjoy themselves.

Daniel knew that many of these folk would be perfectly respectable. Couples out for a meal or a visit to the theatre, young men who only wanted to sit with their friends for an hour or so and sup a pint or two of ale. But for some of them a pint or two would not be sufficient, and as the beer took hold of them, they would become rowdy and stagger out on to the street and become a nuisance and perhaps even dangerous.

After dark, others, less law abiding, would emerge from the shadows: thieves, women driven to prostitution, and other desperate souls who would prey on the unsuspecting. But Susan had always come home long before the streets grew dangerous – until recently, when she had started working extra hours. Maybe as the man of the family he should put his foot down, Daniel thought. Tell her that there was to be no more working late. He smiled as he imagined her reaction. He admitted to himself that it was partly his own fault. Along with his mother, he had indulged and spoiled the enchanting little girl who had grown into such a beautiful young woman. A young woman who liked getting her own way.

Before Daniel reached the shop, he spied Susan emerging from the doorway. She was dressed in emerald green, and a ridiculous concoction of flowers and ribbons masquerading as a hat was perched on her magnificent upswept black hair. The hat was what Daniel imagined would be called sophisticated, and was not the sort of thing a girl of Susan's age should be wearing.

An older, well-dressed man followed her out and they stood chatting animatedly. Daniel could hear them laughing. Very soon the gentleman tipped his hat politely, gave one last smile, then turned and walked away. Susan stood gazing after him, and when she turned to face Daniel she was still smiling. But when she saw him her smile turned into a scowl.

'What are you doing here?' she demanded.

'That's not a very pleasant greeting,' Daniel replied.

'I didn't intend it to be.'

'I thought I would come and meet you,' Daniel said, answering her question. 'See you home safely.'

'I'm grown up enough to see myself home.'

Without warning, she suddenly started to walk towards the top of Northumberland Street.

'Where are you off to?' Daniel asked as he hurried after her.

'Home, of course. Isn't that what I'm supposed to do?'

'But why the sudden hurry?'

'I don't want anyone to see us.'

'Why ever not?'

'It would be embarrassing.'

'Why? Isn't it perfectly natural for your brother to meet you from work?'

'Yes, but . . . I mean . . . it's not that. It's just that . . .' She stopped walking so abruptly that they collided. She looked up into his face, then glanced away evasively.

'You're ashamed of me!'

'No, of course not.' But she couldn't meet his eyes.

'Yes you are. You don't want to be seen with me because I'm not smartly dressed. Even in my best suit it's obvious that I'm an ordinary working man. That's it, isn't it?'

Susan didn't answer him. Dashing tears from her eyes with a slender gloved hand, she turned and hurried ahead once more. She's ashamed to be seen with me, that's the truth of it, Daniel thought. She dresses as well as she can afford and she is adopting the speech and manners of a lady.

'Wait for me!' he said loudly, and several passers-by turned their heads. She didn't stop, so he hurried after her and took hold of her arm. 'Didn't you hear me? I said wait!'

A young man came towards them. 'Are you all right, miss? Is this ruffian bothering you?'

Daniel glanced at him and suppressed a smile. The young fellow was small and painfully thin, and yet such was Susan's beauty, he was prepared to take his chances with an obviously stronger man – someone he had deemed a 'ruffian'.

Susan glanced at her would-be rescuer, and for a moment Daniel thought she was going to say that yes, this ruffian was indeed bothering her. He would have hated himself if he'd had to manhandle the gallant young man, so he sighed with relief when his sister said, 'It's all right, thank you. This man is . . . is my brother.'

Daniel thought she almost choked over the words. The young

46

man looked at Daniel and his eyes widened briefly, then he bowed his head and walked away.

'Thank you for that,' Daniel said.

'For what?' Susan frowned.

'For saving young Sir Galahad from a pasting.'

'Sir Galahad? Pasting? I don't know what on earth you're talking about.' She shook his hand off her arm and hurried on towards the tram stop.

Once on the tram, Susan would not look at Daniel; she stared resolutely ahead. He felt both exasperated by her and sorry for her. Like many young women, she resented being told how to conduct herself – and she did not realise that the restrictions on her would have been much more severe if their father had been alive. Daniel had always tried to be fair.

He had no wish to quell her independent spirit, but he had to protect her from her own naivety. She was seventeen and she thought herself grown-up, but she was still an innocent in the ways of the world. He hated playing the tyrant, but he loved Susan and would do anything necessary to keep her safe.

Lost in his thoughts, he was hardly aware of the journey home, but as they alighted from the tram on Shields Road, a laughing group of young dandies, taking up most of the pavement, pushed past them. They were probably on their way to the Grand Theatre. Daniel was vexed by their seeming unconcern for other pedestrians, but as he watched their swaggering progress and noted how well dressed they were, another image sprang to mind.

'Who was that you were talking to?' he asked Susan.

'I beg your pardon?'

'Outside the shop. You were talking to a gentleman.'

She gave him a sulky look. 'I wondered how long it would take you to bring that up.'

'Well? I'm waiting for an answer.'

Suddenly she laughed. 'Oh Daniel, if only you could see yourself and hear the way you're talking to me. You are behaving like a grouchy old killjoy.'

The smile she gave him was so genuine that he couldn't help responding. 'I know,' he said, 'but it's only because I care about you.'

'You do, don't you?' She slipped her hand into the crook of his arm. 'You are a good brother and I'm lucky to have you to take care of me. Ma often says she doesn't know what we would do without you.'

Daniel wondered how genuinely artless she was. He was reluctant to spoil her good mood, but she hadn't answered his question. 'So who was that gentleman?' he asked.

To his relief, she smiled. 'Oh, just a customer. He comes in regularly to buy a cigar. He's very pleasant.'

They had reached their door, and Susan swept in ahead of him and straightaway began talking to their mother and Dora. Daniel realised that for the moment he would have to be satisfied with her answer, but he couldn't help remembering how animated she had been when he saw her chatting outside the shop. He wondered if she was aware how her vivacious manner might easily be taken for flirtation. The best he could do would be to ask their mother to talk to her.

Daniel was pleased that he had spent a few hours at the library, for there was no chance to do any reading that night. The three women kept up a flow of conversation that would have made it impossible to concentrate even on a novel. And even though they didn't expect him to join in, his mother would have considered it rude of him to bury his nose in a book while Dora was there.

When at last Susan admitted that she was tired and needed her beauty sleep, Dora said that she'd better go. She said it as though she expected them to tell her there was no need, but thankfully Hannah was tired too and also wanted to retire.

'Daniel will see you home,' she added.

'But Dora only lives next door,' Susan said.

'I know that fine well.' Hannah looked scornful. 'But the streets aren't safe for respectable women at the moment. Daniel will see her home, won't you, lad?'

'Of course.'

He knew very well what his mother was up to. Of late she had taken every opportunity to throw him together with Dora. He wondered fleetingly if Dora was in on this too when he saw the two women exchange what he considered to be a significant look.

'Well, I'm off to bed,' Susan said.

Hannah gave an exaggerated yawn. 'Me too. Daniel, divven't be too long, will you,' she said knowingly. 'And when you get back, will you see to the fire?'

Daniel did his best to conceal his irritation. 'Yes, Ma, I'll see to things.'

'Good night, then.'

Hannah and Susan left the room and went upstairs.

When they were alone, Dora smiled at Daniel. 'I don't have to go just yet. I mean, if you'd like me to stay a little while longer . . .'

Daniel faked a yawn and hated himself for it. 'That would be nice, but I'm tired too. I've an early start, you know.'

'Very well.'

Dora's lips thinned and her smile turned into a moue of displeasure, and Daniel had a glimpse of an entirely different side of her, an aspect of her personality that was at odds with her seeming good nature.

They left by the back door, through the yard and out into the lane. Just a few steps took them to the door that led into Dora's back yard.

'This will do,' she said, 'I think I can make my own way across the yard without coming to grief.'

She opened the door, went in and shut it behind her; all without another word. Daniel sighed. Should he tell her that he didn't want to marry her? But he had never told her that he did. There had never been any tender words between them. It was what had happened in the cave that had given Dora the idea that they might be courting.

And Daniel admitted that she was probably entitled to think so. What should he do? He couldn't let things go on like this. Sometimes he even found himself thinking that perhaps they should get married. Dora would make a good wife for any man.

But not for me, he thought. Not when my dreams are haunted by another woman. A tall, slim girl with chestnut hair and with the same passion for books as I have.

A dog barked and a cat yowled as it leapt down from the brick wall and fled up the lane. The wind coming up from the river was cold, and Daniel was glad to get back into the warmth of the kitchen. He saw to the fire, banking it down so it would last the night, and remembering his bait tin, took it out of his bag and put it on the bench in the scullery. His mother would make him some sandwiches or cut a slice of pie first thing in the morning. Then he took the newspaper he had bought out of the bag. He decided that now that the house was quiet, he would sit by the fire for a while with the paper he had not had time to read.

49

The first page was taken up with the usual five columns of advertisements in tiny print. There were advertisements for auctions and livestock markets, for sales of bankrupt stock and for all kinds of household necessities: Fry's Cocoa; Carter's Little Liver Pills; Carbolic Smoke Balls, to cure colds in the head, colds on the chest, sore throats, sore eyes and even influenza. Then there was Pond's Extract, a toilet cream and lip salve that was unequalled for the alleviation of frostbite, wounds, cuts, chilblains, sores and piles. Daniel was always amused by the claims that were made for these products and thought the people who wrote them very clever.

It amused him to spend time reading this page, and it was here that he had found amongst the singing and piano teachers and the teachers of elocution Henry Brookfield's announcement that for a modest sum he was prepared to take on pupils who wished to improve their reading and writing.

After a brief glance at some of the more outrageous claims, Daniel opened the paper and was struck at once by a lurid headline:

HORRIBLE MURDER! BODY FOUND!

The body of Henry Brookfield, a well-respected journalist, was found stabbed to death on the banks of the Ouseburn. It is a mystery why he was there, but Mr Brookfield, who was employed by this very newspaper, was in all likelihood working on an important assignment. Police are investigating this matter. It must be hoped that they will apprehend the perpetrator of this heinous crime and bring him to justice as soon as possible.

Daniel stared at the page in horror. This couldn't be true. The man he respected beyond all others taken away so cruelly from his friends and his family. Marion, Daniel thought, what will become of Marion?

# Chapter Four

'May I assure you, Miss Brookfield, your father will get a decent burial with all the respect that is due to him.' Mr Portley's smile combined sympathy and encouragement.

'Thank you,' Marion said.

Betty had shown the funeral director into Henry Brookfield's study. Annette was doing her homework in the front parlour and Marion did not want her younger sister to be distressed by over-hearing details of the plans for their father's funeral. Mr Portley looked at Marion expectantly.

'Please do sit down,' she said.

Betty was hovering by the door. For a moment it seemed that no one knew what to do. Marion realised that the funeral director and Betty were both looking at her expectantly.

'Betty, would you—'

'Shall I stay here with you, Miss Marion?'

The two young women had spoken in unison.

Marion's smile expressed her relief. 'I was just about to ask if you would. I'd be glad of any advice you can give.'

Betty closed the door. 'Divven't fret, Miss Marion, hinny. I'll help keep you right.'

So with Mr Portley, the undertaker, sitting at one side of the hearth and the two young women at the other, the discussion began.

'If you are content to leave things to me, we shall – erm – collect the deceased from the police surgeon,' Mr Portley began, 'and take him to the funeral parlour, where we will do everything necessary. Then he will remain with us until the day of the funeral.' He paused. 'That is, if you wish it.'

'I don't understand,' Marion said.

'I mean, do you want us to bring him home after we have laid him

51

out and placed him in his coffin so that friends and family may pay their respects?'

The room began to spin and Marion gripped the arms of the chair. Her father's death had caused her secure and comfortable world to come tumbling down. The man sitting opposite her, although subdued and respectful, was leading her towards decisions that she had not faced yet – that she did not want to face. She breathed in deeply in order to control her sense of panicky unreality.

'We do not have any other family,' she said. 'There is only my sister and myself. My father's work colleagues and friends will call at the funeral parlour if they wish to.'

Betty had already warned Marion that she would have to make this decision, and they had both thought that for Annette's sake it would be better not to bring Henry Brookfield home, even though Marion felt that this was somehow betraying him.

'Very well,' Mr Portley said. 'That's quite in order. And – erm – you and your younger sister will also be calling at the funeral parlour in order to say goodbye before we close the coffin.'

It was a statement rather than a question. Marion began to feel sick.

'Yes.' Her voice was barely more than a whisper.

Mr Portley nodded and then continued, 'On the day of the funeral, the cortège will call here before setting off for the cemetery. That is the custom, you know.'

'Of course – whatever is proper.'

'And now,' Mr Portley continued, 'if you would glance at this little booklet, we must make some further decisions.'

Marion was glad that Betty was sitting beside her. They looked at the pages of the catalogue with the illustrations Mr Portley had described as 'tasteful' but that Marion thought somewhat mawkish. They saw almost immediately that there was really no choice at all. Marion handed the open book back to the funeral director and pointed wordlessly to the page she had chosen. He looked at it and made an effort to hide his disappointment.

'Ah, let me see.' Mr Portley produced a pencil and began to tick the items off. 'A stout elm coffin with three sets of handles, a mattress, a pillow and a pair of side sheets, a hearse with one horse, a mourning coach with one horse, and silk hatbands and gloves for the coachmen and attendants. That will come to five pounds. Is that what you want?'

Marion nodded.

Mr Portley looked at her quizzically. 'Please do not take offence at what I am going to say, Miss Brookfield, because I mean it kindly.'

'I won't.'

'This is the least expensive funeral we provide. Do I take it that the cost is – erm – the deciding factor?'

'Yes, sadly it is.'

Mr Portley's rather portentous air melted and his smile became truly compassionate. 'I understand. Your father has left his two young daughters to fend for themselves, and as the elder of the two you will bear the heaviest responsibility. But I must advise that there be a wreath.'

'Yes, I should have thought of that, but—'

He held up his hand to stop her from saying more. 'I hope you will allow me to provide the flowers at my own expense,' he said. 'Lilies, I think, a wreath of beautiful white lilies to place atop the coffin. Would you object to that?'

Marion felt the grief rise in her throat. Overwhelmed by the compassion of this stranger, for the moment she could not speak. She shook her head and then managed to say, 'You are very kind.'

Mr Portley gathered his papers together and stood up. 'Leave everything to me,' he said. 'And God bless you, my dear.'

Daniel was pleased that the rain had stopped the road gang from working again. While the others were grumbling, he hurried home. The house was empty and he boiled a kettle to wash in the sink in the scullery.

When his mother came in through the back door, he had already changed into his suit and was standing by the fire in the kitchen looking up into the mirror over the mantel shelf while he combed his hair. He turned to look though the open door into the scullery.

Hannah Brady shut the back door quickly to keep out the rain. She was carrying her shopping basket over her arm. She put the basket down on the scullery bench and taking off her shawl shook it over the sink. She glanced at him over her shoulder. 'Is that you, Daniel?' she said.

'Who else would it be? Unless you've taken a lodger and haven't bothered to tell me.'

She laughed. 'Divven't tease, bonny lad. But it's a pity that foreman didn't wait a while before sending you home; the rain's easing off a bit now.' She hung her shawl up on a hook on the back door, then came through into the kitchen. She stopped in her tracks and looked him up and down.

'Where are you off to all dressed up in your best like that?' she asked.

'To pay respects. Mr Brookfield – my tutor – has died.'

His mother drew in her breath and her eyes rounded. 'Brookfield – I thought the name rang a bell. They were talking about it in the corner shop. They say he was murdered. Dreadful business. I suppose that will mean the end of your lessons?'

'I suppose so.'

Daniel couldn't be sure, but he thought he saw a fleeting look of satisfaction cross his mother's face. It was overtaken by a look of avid curiosity. 'What do you think a man like that was doing down by the Ouseburn – and at that time of night?'

Something in his mother's tone, something in the prurient look in her eyes, raised his hackles. 'I've told you before, Mr Brookfield was a reporter. He must have been investigating something,' he said. 'Something that needed putting in the newspaper.'

He could well imagine what the talk had been like in the corner shop. His mother was a good woman, a kindly soul, and yet, just like the other women around here, she enjoyed a gossip. Many a poor neighbour had had his or her character blackened by malicious speculation. This was something Daniel hated.

'Eeh, divven't look at me like that, son. It's natural to wonder what folk are up to.'

Daniel realised that he and his mother were on the verge of quarrelling, and he didn't want to do that because he loved her. 'Of course it is,' he said. Then he softened his words with a smile. 'But if only folk wouldn't always think the worst of people.'

Hannah looked at him for a moment and then said, 'You're right, son. And you do right to go to the Brookfields' house. It's the proper thing to do. Mrs Brookfield will appreciate it.'

'There is no Mrs Brookfield; she died some time ago. There are only two daughters.'

'Poor bairns. I wonder what will become of them?'

'Miss Marion is very capable – and strong.'

'Miss Marion?'

'The elder girl. She's eighteen, and her sister, Annette, is sixteen.'

His mother gave him an odd look. 'So you're going to call on Miss Marion?'

'I told you, I'm going to pay my respects, and you agreed it was the right thing to do.'

'That was before I knew that the head of the household is only a slip of a girl. I'm not sure that it's proper.'

'Mr Brookfield's daughter will not be there alone.' Daniel flushed. He was angry that he felt he had to defend himself. 'They . . . they have a companion,' he said, and he wondered what Betty would think if she knew of her elevation. 'That is, a woman who has been looking after them since their mother died.'

'Nice comfortable soul, is she?'

'Yes.' Betty was indeed both nice and comfortable, but he had deliberately not told his mother that she was also young.

'And she will be in charge of things?'

Daniel nodded.

'Well, that's a relief,' his mother said, but she frowned all the same. Then he saw that with an effort she dismissed the matter from her mind. She looked at Daniel critically. 'Here, let your mother tidy that hair of yours. Bend down so's I can reach.'

She took the comb and Daniel suffered her to adjust his parting. When she had finished, she stood back and looked at him and smiled. 'Fine head of hair you've got – just like your da.'

Daniel said, 'Will I do?'

'Aye, you'll do, but I think you'd better wear the black necktie. More respectful, like.'

Every house had a black tie, kept for funerals. Hannah opened the cupboard set in the wall next to the range and took out the tie that had belonged to Daniel's father.

Daniel took it from her, then put one arm around her shoulders and gave her a hug. 'You're right, Ma. What would I do without you?'

The rain had stopped altogether by the time Daniel reached Jesmond. There was a carriage in the street outside the Brookfields' house and he hesitated. He did not want to intrude if Marion had visitors. He looked up into the impassive face of the coachman as if for guidance, but the man stared straight ahead. Daniel opened the gate and walked up the short path.

Black crêpe was tied with a white ribbon to the bell knob. This was a sign that he must either wait until the occupants had some cause to open the door or somehow attract their attention without actually ringing the bell. As he stood there wondering what to do, the door opened and a tall, top-hatted gentleman dressed in black stepped out. He nodded civilly to Daniel and walked towards the coach.

'Mr Brady?' a voice said, and Daniel realised that the Brookfields' maid, Betty, was standing in the doorway watching him.

'Yes . . . I, erm . . .' Daniel didn't know what to say.

'Have you come for a lesson?' she asked, 'because if you have, I have some very sad news for you.' She looked distressed.

'I know,' Daniel said. 'I read about it in the newspaper.'

'Then why are you here?'

'To pay my respects.'

The maid frowned, and for a moment Daniel thought she was going to send him away, but then she said, 'Wait here a moment.'

In Henry Brookfield's study, Marion was standing at her father's desk looking down perplexedly at the untidily scattered papers. She heard Betty's gentle knock and called for her to enter without turning round.

'What am I to do with all this?' she asked.

'I'll help you sort them if I can,' Betty said, 'but right now you have a visitor.'

Marion turned to look at Betty in surprise. 'Visitor? Is it something to do with . . . I mean, is it Sergeant Wilson? Constable Robinson?'

'No, it's Mr Brady.'

'Has he come for a lesson? This isn't his usual evening, is it? But Father might have changed his appointment, I suppose. Well, anyway, you must tell Mr Brady what has happened.'

'He knows. He read it in the newspaper.'

'Then why has he come here?'

'He wants to pay his respects and I think you should see him. He was very fond of your father – anyone could see that.'

Marion's anxious expression softened a little. 'Yes, he was, wasn't he? And my father was fond of him. You had better show him in.'

'I will. And I'll make a pot of tea as well.'

★

Daniel Brady felt awkward. 'Miss Brookfield,' he said, 'may I offer my condolences?'

How marvellous she looks in black, he thought, so tall, so slender, so serious, and yet so vulnerable. He felt himself flushing, knowing that his thoughts were inappropriate. She didn't speak, and suddenly he realised that she was as much at a loss as he was.

'I want to say much more than that,' he said, 'but I don't know the proper words – the right form, if you like. So all I can do is tell you from my heart that I am sorry. Your father was a good man, he taught me much, and I shall miss him, not just as a teacher but I like to hope as a friend. A good friend.'

Marion still did not speak.

'Have I gone too far?' he asked. 'Have I presumed too much?'

'No, of course not.' Her voice was husky. 'I know that my father was fond of you and had great hopes for you.'

'Did he?'

'He often told me that you had a natural style of writing, and that you should seriously consider changing your occupation. Perhaps become a journalist, like him.'

'Yes, he was kind enough to tell me so, but I cannot think of that now.'

'Why not?'

'I have so much more to learn.'

They fell silent. The only sounds in the room were the crackling of the fire and the ticking of the clock on the mantel shelf. Then Marion sighed and smiled sadly. 'Please sit down,' she said. 'Betty is making a pot of tea.'

They had hardly taken their seats when the door opened and Betty entered, balancing a tray. She had brought slices of fruit cake as well as tea. 'Me mother made it,' she said. 'And I want you to eat a great big slice, Miss Marion. Do you realise you've hardly had owt to eat since your . . . for days. Now, Mr Brady, if you could pull that footstool forward, I'll put the tray on it and go and see if Miss Annette wants owt.'

The footstool, though wide enough for the tray to balance on, was low, and Marion found it easier to kneel on the hearthrug while she poured the tea. The lamps were not yet lit, but the skies were grey and the room was becoming shadowy. The glow from the fire reflected on Marion's glossy hair and seemed to warm her skin. The picture of her kneeling there performing a simple domestic task was uncomfortably like the images that haunted Daniel's daydreams.

She looked up to hand him his cup of tea and her eyes widened as if she had read his thoughts. She looked away quickly and got up on to her chair.

'Please help yourself to a slice of cake,' she said.

'Only if you have some too.' He smiled at her surprised expression. 'Betty said you must.'

With those light-hearted words the tension seemed to ease between them. They ate their cake and drank their tea and Daniel wondered how much he should say about the seemingly senseless murder of a good man. He was saved embarrassment when Marion brought up the subject herself.

'Betty told me that you read about my father's murder in the newspaper.'

'Yes, I did. Have the police any idea why it happened?'

'Robbery. They think it was a thief.'

'Was anything stolen from him?'

'A small amount of money, and the watch my mother gave him.' For a moment her voice wavered, but she quickly regained control. 'It seems so little to die for.'

'It may seem so to you, but maybe it would be a fortune to the desperate soul who took it.'

Her eyes flashed. 'Do you expect me to feel sorry for him? For the evil scoundrel who took my father's life?'

'No, of course not. I simply want you to understand the act. No one could condone it.'

Marion stared at him speechlessly and then turned her head and looked into the fire. 'I do understand,' she said. 'My father told me what life is like for some of the citizens of this great city. But he was trying to help them – to improve things by his writing.'

'I'm sure whoever murdered him didn't know that,' Daniel said, and he could have added that the unfortunate wretch probably didn't even care, but he knew that would break Marion's heart anew.

She turned her head to look at him again. 'Do you think the police will apprehend him?' she asked.

Daniel thought it unlikely, but he said, 'It will be difficult, but I'm sure they will do their best.'

'Well, thank you for coming.'

Daniel's heart sank when he realised that he was being dismissed. He leaned forward and put his cup and saucer on the tray, then rose to go.

'May I come to the funeral?'

'Of course.'

'When . . .?'

'It may be the day after tomorrow but I don't know for sure. The police surgeon hasn't . . . hasn't . . .'

'I understand,' Daniel said quickly.

Now Marion rose and stood facing him. 'I will put an announcement in the newspaper.'

'Goodbye, then. I'll see myself out.'

Daniel had started to walk to the door when Marion called, 'Wait.'

He turned to see her staring at her father's desk. 'My father always prepared his lessons in advance. Those he intended for you must be here. Would you like them?'

'I would indeed.'

Marion began to sort through the papers. She looked up and smiled. 'He wasn't very orderly, was he?'

Daniel, pleased to see her mood had lifted a little, returned her smile. 'Your father once told me that Betty could clean the windows and beat the carpets to her heart's content, but she had strict instructions not to tidy his desk or he would never find anything. He said he knew exactly where everything was.'

They both laughed.

'I'm not too sure about that,' Marion said. 'I can remember times when he couldn't find the article he'd been writing just the night before and everything would end up on the floor while he rummaged about. When he found what he was looking for, he would put it in his briefcase and then pick all the papers up from the floor and dump them on the desk again.' Her smile faded and she said, 'Betty has promised that she will help me to tidy this up somehow.'

'You'll want to keep his papers?'

'Yes, I would never part with them.' She paused. 'Except those I will give to you.' She picked up a pile of papers and examined the top page. 'I think these are the lessons he prepared for you – look, he has pencilled your name at the top.'

'Thank you – there are quite a lot.'

'I'll get Betty to make a parcel for you. No, wait, better than that
. . .' Marion went behind the desk and bent down to pull something
out from the kneehole. She put it on top of the papers. 'I would like
you to have this dispatch case.'

Daniel gazed down at the black leather-covered box. 'No . . . it's
too good.'

'My father would want you to have something – some memento
– and I'm sure he would wish you to fulfil his hopes for you and
become a writer of some sort. And a writer ought to have his own
dispatch case.'

She opened the catch and lifted the lid to reveal the red watered-
silk lining. 'Look, there are pockets on the inside of the lid for your
pencils and your notebooks and any other bits and pieces, and the
main compartment will hold your papers. Please say you'll take it.'

'I'd love to, but . . .'

'I insist.'

Marion began to put the papers she had identified as Daniel's
work programme into the dispatch case, and as she did so she dis-
lodged some other papers and they cascaded on to the floor. She
stared at them in dismay, then laughed weakly, but Daniel could see
there were tears in her eyes.

He kneeled down swiftly and began to gather the papers up. As he
did so, a coin or two fell out, and then more, until there was a
considerable sum of money scattered over the rug.

Marion shook her head and, clutching the briefcase, sank down
into her father's chair. Daniel continued to pick up papers and coins
and put them on the desk, arranging them as neatly as he could.
When he had finished, he glanced at Marion, who stared back,
bewildered.

'It's the money I paid him for my lessons,' Daniel explained, 'I
suspected he just left it there. But looking at the amount, I'm sure he
has been doing this for years, long before I became his pupil.'

'Poor Father. He would never have become rich, would he?'

'I'm sure he would be pleased that you have the money now.'

'Yes, he would.'

'Well . . . I suppose I'd better go.'

'Yes.'

Suddenly they did not know what to say to each other. Then
Daniel remembered something.

'I have two of your father's books,' he said. 'He loaned them to me for light reading. *Vice Versa* and *The Leavenworth Case*.'

'*The Leavenworth Case*? Oh, I love detective stories!' Marion said.

Daniel remembered how Henry Brookfield had told him that even Marion, an outwardly serious young woman, enjoyed reading for fun.

'I should have brought them back today. I just didn't think.'

'Have you finished reading them?'

'No, not even the first one.'

'Well keep them until you have, and then – well, perhaps you would like to borrow some more.' Marion half turned and indicated the tall bookcases set in the alcoves at each side of the chimneypiece.

'Could I?'

'Of course. You must treat my father's bookshelves as your own personal library. Apart from me, there will be nobody else to take advantage of his collection.' She became more animated. 'And as we work our way from shelf to shelf, perhaps we could have discussions about the books.'

Her smile was warm. Daniel, starved of intelligent conversation in his everyday life, did not trust himself to say how much such meetings would mean to him. As well as discussing books with her, he wondered if he might persuade her to take on the role of his tutor, but he sensed this was not the time to ask. So he said nothing.

'Would you like to be my reading companion?' Marion asked.

'There's nothing I'd like better.'

'Good. Then we will arrange things after . . . after . . .'

'The funeral.'

'Yes, I'll write to you.'

After Daniel had gone, Marion deliberately put away all thoughts of future meetings with him and stared down at the pile of coins they had found under the papers. She realised there was enough there to tide her and Annette over until their father's affairs were settled and anything owing to them was released.

Meanwhile she would pay for the funeral with her own money; she had a small legacy left to her by her mother. Annette's school fees were paid until the end of term, when she would be leaving anyway, and hopefully their father had left enough money to cover the fees at the art school.

But Marion suspected they would not inherit enough for this state of affairs to last indefinitely. She thought once more about the possibility of finding employment.

'You'd better come and talk to Annette.'

She turned to find that Betty had entered the room. She had been too preoccupied to hear her knock.

'What's the matter?'

'It's her homework. She's getting herself into a right state about it. I think you'd better help her.'

'Of course.'

Betty pursed her lips.

'What's the matter?' Marion asked.

'I telt her not to bother you.'

'Oh, it's no bother. I enjoy helping her with her lessons; it's just that I feel she ought to do more for herself.'

Later, when Annette was working more happily, Marion sat in the kitchen with Betty. The maid was blackleading the kitchen range but was happy to chat as she worked.

'Hev you ever thought you ought to be a teacher?' Betty asked.

'I have thought about teaching, but I've left it too late.'

'Too late for what, exactly?'

'I would have to train, and I don't think we could afford that right now.'

'Well why not teach at home, then?'

'At home?'

'Yes, like your da.' Betty smiled when she saw Marion's startled expression. 'Oh, I don't mean great hulking working men. I mean small children who are hevin' troubles with spelling and their tables – or older girls like your own sister who just need a little guidance. You could do that easily, couldn't you?'

'Yes . . . I suppose I could.'

'Well, there you are then.'

Betty looked pleased with herself, but Marion suddenly had a bleak vision of her possible future. Once Annette had flown the nest, she would be left here, a lonely spinster eking out her existence by teaching a succession of cross and unwilling pupils. I know what I would rather do, she thought, but I would be foolish to hope for it. She sighed. How could I ever have a future with Daniel Brady?

★

'Look, he's waiting outside again,' Maisie said. The shop assistant was looking out of the window at the customer who had just left. He was bending his head to light his cigar, but Maisie thought this was just an excuse to stay there.

'Is he?' Susan's tone was studiedly careless. She did not look round but went on tidying the section of the shelves where the tins of pipe tobacco were kept. 'We haven't any Evening Glow left,' she said. 'You'd better tell Mr Jacobs when he gets back from the wholesaler's.'

'Why me?' Maisie asked.

'Because I'm going home now.'

Maisie lifted up her pendant watch so that she could see the face and said, 'But you still have another hour to work.'

'Not today.' Susan turned her attention to the racks of pipes, straightening them unnecessarily, Maisie thought, rather than turn to look at her.

'Why not today?' Maisie's tone betrayed her exasperation. She hated it when Susan acted all mysterious like this.

'I'm going home early.'

'You've just said that. My question was why?'

She glared at Susan, who had turned to examine the tall glass-fronted cupboard that held the boxes of cigars. She was pretending to be checking stock when Maisie knew very well that she was admiring her own reflection.

Susan raised one hand to capture a stray lock of hair and sweep it up. Then, with the other, she adjusted her comb until the wayward strand was secured. She turned to smile sadly at Maisie.

'I told Mr Jacobs how ill my mother is. Of course he said I must go home early and make a nourishing meal for her and my brother.'

'Your ma is ill?' For a moment Maisie was taken in, but when she saw Susan struggling to keep her mouth straight she exclaimed, 'I don't believe you! You're . . . you're going to flirt with that man.'

'What man?'

'You know very well what man. The one who's waiting for you outside there.'

Susan made a play of looking out of the window, turning her head from side to side. 'I don't see anyone waiting, do you?'

Annoyingly, she was right. The man had gone, but in Maisie's mind he would not have gone far.

Susan didn't give Maisie the chance to respond. 'You're imagining things,' she said. 'And you do so because you're jealous that such a prosperous gentleman should pay me any attention. But in any case,' she shrugged, 'believe what you like. I'm going, now.'

'But that's not fair! This is the busiest time, when men begin to leave their offices and others arrive early in town for a night's entertainment. You shouldn't leave me to cope by myself.'

'Mr Jacobs will be here any minute. He said he'd get back as quickly as possible.'

Maisie sensed she was losing the battle, but nevertheless she said, 'Well, why don't you stay until he arrives?'

Before Susan could answer, the bell on the shop door tinkled and a stooped, elderly man in a shiny-elbowed business suit walked in. He was a regular customer, and Maisie half turned to take a packet of ten Plain Cut Virginia cigarettes from the well-stocked shelves behind her. She put them on the glass-topped counter, where the old gentleman had already placed five pence.

'There you are, Mr Parker,' she said.

'Thank you, Miss Collins.' Mr Parker nodded and smiled and looked as though he would have liked to stay for a chat, but he succumbed to a coughing fit and left the shop.

In the short time this exchange had taken, Susan had disappeared into the back shop and now came out again wearing her hat and gloves and ready to go. Maisie stared stonily at the cash register as she heard Susan lift the flap in the counter then lower it when she had reached the other side. She pursed her lips while she deposited the five pence in the drawer and didn't reply when Susan said, 'I'm off. I'll see you tomorrow.'

Annoyingly, Susan didn't close the door properly behind her, and a whiff of horse manure blew in from the busy street to mingle with the ever-present aroma of fine tobacco. Maisie went to close the door and couldn't resist glancing outside to see if Susan turned towards the tram shop or walked in the other direction, where the customer who called most evenings for an expensive cigar was still standing.

Frustrated – she could hardly pop out on to the pavement to see what was happening – she stood there for a moment and then had to dodge back smartly when Susan walked past the shop. She was not only accompanied by the man, who had obviously been waiting for her, but she had linked her arm through his.

Maisie felt a surge of bitter rage. She was angry with Susan, who had lied about going home to a sick mother, and angry with herself because, although she would never admit it, Susan's remark had hit home.

She *was* jealous. Maisie knew she was a good-looking woman, with bright blonde hair and a voluptuous figure, and in her day the customers had paid her much flirtatious attention. But ever since Susan, with her lustrous black hair and her smoky grey eyes, had come to work at the tobacconist's shop, Maisie's flirtatious followers had deserted her, preferring to pay court to the much younger girl.

Two young men, office workers judging from their cheap suits and ink-stained fingers, pushed past her none too politely and entered the shop. Usually she would have scolded them, but today she simply gave them their cigarettes, took their money and dropped it in the cash drawer all without a word or a smile.

Soon the shop got busy and she had little time to think about Susan until Mr Jacobs got back and joined her behind the counter. Her employer was a short but hefty man whose expensive tailored clothes pronounced him to be a successful businessman. Maisie glanced at him as he opened the cigar cabinet and took out a box of coronas. He served the customer with a smile and they exchanged gossip about the stock market.

Maisie wondered what would happen if she told him that Susan had lied about needing to go home to her sick mother. Maybe I will, she thought, or maybe I should get some sort of proof first. And if I do, I'll decide how I'm going to deal with that hoity-toity little madam. She hugged the idea to herself, and in a thoroughly good mood again greeted her next customer with a radiant smile.

'So it was Daniel's teacher who was murdered, was it?' Dora asked.

'Aye, that's right, pet,' Hannah replied. 'Now sit yourself down and we'll have a nice cup of tea and a bit chinwag.'

Dora sat at the oilcloth-covered table and watched as Hannah spooned tea into the old brown teapot. The kettle was gently steaming on the hotplate of the range and the glow from the fire made the room look cosy. It was not yet time to light the lamps, but the sky was dark and the shadows deepening.

Hannah kept everything clean, tidy, and respectable and it was a pleasure for Dora to be sitting here doing nothing but gossiping rather than in her own overcrowded and higgledy-piggledy house where her mother would expect her to help with the younger children.

Hannah set the cups on the table and poured the tea. 'Help yourself to sugar, hinny,' she said and pushed the sugar bowl towards her.

A moment or two later, when both women had enjoyed their first sips of hot sweet tea, Dora put her cup down on its saucer and said, 'So I expect Daniel won't be going to his lessons any more?'

Hannah Brady gave a smile of satisfaction. 'No, thank the Lord.'

'Why are you pleased?'

'Because that man was putting a lot of silly ideas into the lad's head. Making him think he could have a different sort of life to what he's been brought up to.' She shook her head. 'I mean, there's no shame in being a labouring man. Daniel works hard and earns good money and one day he could even be the foreman of a gang, and if he is he'll earn much more than if he was an inky-fingered clerk in some dusty office.'

'Is that what he wants to do?' Dora said. 'To work in an office? It doesn't seem the right sort of work for a proper man, does it?'

'I agree with you there. That's not a real man's job. In truth he hasn't actually said that's what he wants, but what else could he do with his book learning?'

Dora looked perplexed. 'I don't know, I'm sure.'

The two women stared at each other for a moment, each trying to imagine exactly what sort of job Daniel could do, and then Hannah shrugged and said, 'Here, pet, let me fill up your cup.'

They were still sitting there when Daniel came home. His mother rose hurriedly and reached up to pull the chain that lowered the overhead gas lamp. She lit the mantle and raised the lamp again. By the time she had done this, Dora had opened the drawer set into the table and taken out knives and forks for three.

Hannah glanced at what she was doing and said, 'Lay a place for yourself, Dora pet, there's mince and dumplings enough for four.' Then she frowned.

'What is it?' Dora asked.

'Where's our Susan?'

Daniel looked at his mother sharply. 'Isn't she home yet?'

'No.' Hannah looked at him helplessly. 'But divven't fret. There must be some explanation.'

Daniel had been just about to take off his jacket, but now he shrugged it on again and headed for the door. 'I'm going to look for her,' he said.

But before he got any further, they heard the back door open, and a moment later Susan walked into the room. She looked happy, but when she sensed the atmosphere her smile faded and she looked at her brother nervously.

'Where have you been?' Daniel asked.

'Nowhere – I mean, the trams were full. I had to walk as far as Byker Bridge before I could get on one.'

'Really?' Daniel asked.

'Yes, really!' Susan's spirit returned and she glared at her brother. 'Surely you don't think I would lie to you!'

Daniel looked at her long and hard. 'I don't know what to believe,' he said.

Suddenly Susan burst into tears and her mother hurried over to her.

'Now then, hinny,' Hannah said. 'Don't take on.' She turned her head to glare at Daniel. 'Look what you've done,' she said. 'Upsetting the poor bairn like this. She's been working hard all day and then had to walk halfway home. It's unkind of you, Daniel, it really is.'

Hannah produced a handkerchief from the pocket in her pinafore and Susan sobbed into it. Daniel stood and watched awkwardly. He was pretty sure the tears Susan was shedding were crocodile tears, but he did not want to upset his mother. He became aware that Dora was watching him. Until now he had not really registered her presence. He sensed that she was trying to attract his attention and looked at her. He was surprised to find that she was smiling slightly as she shook her head and looked first at Susan and his mother and then at him.

Dora thinks so too, he thought. She is as little fooled by Susan's tears as I am. He inclined his head in Dora's direction, grateful for her silent support. Eventually Susan stopped sobbing and Hannah told her to go and wash her face. Without being asked, Dora calmly went about serving up the meal, and soon peace was restored.

When they had done eating, Hannah eased her bones down on to the chair near the fire and declared herself exhausted. Susan took the cracket and placed it by her mother. She glanced reproachfully at Daniel before reaching for the hairbrush that was kept on the mantel.

She sat down on the small wooden stool and looked up into her mother's kindly face.

'Will you brush my hair, Ma?' she asked. She started taking out the pins, putting them on the broad sweep of the pinafore on her mother's lap. 'You do it so gently, it fair relaxes me.'

Hannah took the brush and began to brush her daughter's hair as if she were a child again. In many ways she *is* a child, Daniel thought. A beautiful child who is on the verge of becoming a woman. But her emotions and her intellect were still immature. Again he sensed that Dora was watching him. He looked at her and thought he saw understanding there – and also agreement. Then she cast her eyes down as if embarrassed to have ventured into territory so personal. She rose from the table and began to clear the dishes. Daniel rose too and helped her take the dirty plates into the kitchen.

Dora raised her eyebrows and looked at him with mock astonishment. 'Go and sit down,' she said. 'This is no place for a man. I can manage in here.'

Her easy smile prompted all the familiar feelings of guilt. He put the dishes he was carrying on the scrubbed wooden bench and fled from the scullery.

# Chapter Five

Marion watched a leaf detach itself from a branch of one of the sheltering trees. Twirling as it fell, it landed on her father's coffin just as the gravediggers began to lower it into the open grave.

A sudden eddy of warm wind shuddered through the trees, sending more leaves whirling above the heads of the mourners. The leaves were stained red and yellow with the colours of autumn, but paradoxically, today was more like a summer's day. She was reminded of 'A Song for September', one of her father's favourite poems.

> *Sorrow and scarlet leaf,*
> *Sad thoughts and sunny weather,*
> *Ah me, this glory and this grief*
> *Agree not well together.*

The day of a funeral is not supposed to be like this, Marion thought: the old gravestones warmed by the mellow sun; blue skies and soft clouds, and the gentle breeze bringing a fragrant remembrance of summer flowers. In novels she had read, the rain would be driving across the funeral party huddled under large black umbrellas; the leaves would hang with all life drained from them, forlornly dripping, and the sky would be overcast, the clouds heavy with gloom.

Marion glanced at the assembled mourners. She had been surprised by how many people had turned up at the church. She had expected one or two neighbours, and indeed they had come, but so had almost all the staff of the newspaper her father had worked for. She realised with pride how well liked he had been.

The traditional words from the prayer book echoed through the sweet air, and when she was handed the silver shovel in order to throw the first sod into the grave, she heard her sister gasp with shock. Betty put her arm round Annette and drew her back from the graveside.

The sound of the earth thudding on to the lid of the coffin was shocking. Suddenly the air was tinged with the sharp smell of the exposed soil. Marion felt herself sway, but before she could fall, someone standing behind her gripped her arms and kept her upright.

'Thank you,' she murmured, and turned her head to find herself staring into the face of Daniel Brady. She saw that his eyes were glittering with unshed tears, and the look that passed between them spoke of their mutual heartache

Daniel did not presume to walk with her, but fell in behind along with the other mourners as the party walked away from the grave. As they came out of the cemetery through the imposing stone archway to where the carriages were waiting, a large bear of a man approached Marion. She recognised Charles Earnshaw, the editor of the newspaper.

'The others should go back to the office now,' he said. 'We must get the paper out. I hope you don't mind.'

'Of course not, it's what my father would have expected.'

The big man smiled at her. 'He was one of my best reporters. I shall miss him.'

There was nothing Marion could say, but she looked at him gratefully.

'Perhaps I shouldn't mention this today, but . . .' Mr Earnshaw looked irresolute but then seemed to make up his mind. 'There was something he was working on – some project.'

'That's all right,' Marion said. 'I don't mind talking about it.'

'Well, if you would find a moment for me when we get back to your house . . .'

'I will.' Marion was aware of Daniel still standing beside her and she said, 'Mr Earnshaw, I'd like you to meet Mr Brady, a – a friend of my father's.'

Marion saw that Daniel was self-conscious, but nevertheless, he shook the editor's hand firmly.

Then Marion heard her sister call, 'I want to go home.'

Annette looked distressed and Marion worried that the day's events had been too much for the younger girl. Betty hovered beside her along with a tall young man in a suit the sleeves of which did not reach far enough to cover his bony wrists. It was Arthur Robinson.

So far the day had gone by in a haze of anxiety and grief, and Marion had not realised that the police constable had been in the church. How kind of him to come, she thought. She invited him to join the party that was going back to the house.

Once home, she was glad that Betty had suggested that her mother should come to help. Mrs Sutton was a plump, comfortable-looking woman who didn't say much. She had set the dining table with plates of cold roast beef sandwiches and slices of ham and egg pie, and she moved quietly about the room making sure that everyone had a cup of tea. She told Betty to tell Marion that it was up to her to serve sherry. Mr Earnshaw, seeing Marion's hesitation, offered to do that for her.

Even though the funeral party was small, the front parlour was crowded. Their neighbours were there: Miss Cudlip from one side and Mr and Mrs Thomson from the other. Then there was Mr Earnshaw, Arthur Robinson, Daniel Brady and a small, elegant lady Marion could not remember ever having met before. She had slipped into the church unobtrusively and kept in the background throughout. She had not travelled back in the coach provided by the funeral director, nor had she taken a hansom cab as Mr Earnshaw had done, nor had she walked back like Marion's neighbours. She had her own carriage.

The mystery guest took a glass of sherry from the tray Mr Earnshaw offered, and from the way she thanked him, Marion got the impression that they knew each other. A moment later her supposition was confirmed when the editor brought the woman over and introduced her.

'This is Lady Cressington,' he said. 'She was a friend of your father's.'

Lady Cressington clasped Marion's hand and looked up at her with compassion shining in her extraordinarily beautiful blue eyes. 'I'm so very sorry, my dear,' she said. 'Your father was a good man. He did not deserve to die like that at the hands of one of the very people he was trying to help.'

Marion was puzzled. She had never met Lady Cressington – hadn't even heard her mentioned. 'I'm sorry,' she said, 'but I don't . . .'

'You don't know who on earth I am!' Lady Cressington said, and she smiled. 'I admired the work your father was doing, and some time ago I wrote to him and offered to help in any way I could.'

'You helped him with his writing?'

'Oh no, he didn't need help with that. No, one of his pieces in the newspaper was about the children who have nowhere to live but the streets. Apart from giving them clothes and food, it is difficult to help them because they are suspicious of strangers and don't want to leave their friends. But I told your father that if there were any children he could persuade to leave their wretched lives on the streets, I would find homes for them.'

'And that is exactly what Lady Cressington has been doing,' Charles Earnshaw said. 'She has worked indefatigably.'

'So now we must hope there will be someone to take up your father's work,' Lady Cressington said. 'Someone with as much dedication.' She sighed. 'But that is not your worry, my dear.'

'No, that will be my task,' the newspaper editor said, 'although it will be hard to find someone who can write as well as your father did – with so much passion, so much fire.' He paused. 'And that is what I must talk to you about, my dear Miss Brookfield. Your father's papers.'

'His papers?' For a moment her father's untidy desk sprang to mind, and Marion smiled faintly.

'Yes. He must have left notes – half-written articles, lists of names.'

'Names? I don't understand.'

'Names of people who had been helpful to him during his investigations.'

'Oh, I see. I suppose he will have done.'

'Then I wonder if you would mind handing them over to me? When you have had a chance to sort everything out.'

'Why do you want them?'

'As I explained, I would like someone else to continue his work. It would be a crime if all his efforts had been wasted.'

Marion nodded solemnly. 'Of course. If I find any such papers, I'll bring them to you personally.'

'Thank you. And now, if you will forgive me, I must go. I have a newspaper to get out.'

Lady Cressington had been listening. 'I must take my leave too,' she said. 'But I want you to know that should you ever need help or advice, you must come to me. Here is my card.' She turned to Charles Earnshaw. 'May I take you back to the office, Charles? My carriage is at your disposal. It will save you finding a cab.'

The titled lady and the newspaper editor said goodbye and Betty saw them out. After they had gone, Marion's more homely guests seemed to relax a little. They spoke with less restraint about times past and what a good neighbour Henry Brookfield had been and how well he had brought up his motherless daughters.

Miss Cudlip, a wrinkled spinster of indeterminate age, told everyone how Marion, right from being a small child, had always been willing to run errands for her. And Mr Thomson, a thin, sandy-haired middle-aged man, spoke of how Henry Brookfield had always been ready to give advice and how he had helped him write a letter to their mutual landlord that time the tiles had blown off the roof during a storm.

'Of course I didn't expect any trouble,' Mr Thomson added. 'Mr Bateman is a good landlord. We're lucky to have him. It's just that your father could write a much better letter explaining things than I could.'

'That reminds me,' his wife said, 'does Mr Bateman know what has happened?'

'I'm not sure,' Marion said. 'I mean, I haven't told him. Why do you ask?'

'Well,' her neighbour said, 'I mean, will he . . . oh dear . . . will he be all right about your staying here?'

'Whisht, Muriel,' Mr Thomson said. He looked sternly at his wife. 'Fancy worrying the lass today of all days.'

His wife, a plump, fresh-faced but untidy woman, looked uncomfortable. 'I didn't mean to worry her. I just thought—'

'That's the trouble,' her husband told her. 'You don't think before you speak. Now come along home.' He softened his peremptory tone with a smile, and putting a hand under his wife's elbow, he led her away.

'What was that about?' Marion asked Betty when everyone had gone.

'Mebbe Mrs Thomson was wondering whether you would be able to afford to stay here but didn't like to come right out with it.'

'Oh, I see.' Marion supposed it was natural for people to wonder how the Brookfield girls were going to manage. 'Well, if she had asked outright, I would have told her.'

'Humph,' Betty said. 'It's none of her business, the nosy parker.'

'Don't think the worse of her,' Marion said. 'I believe she was genuinely concerned about us.'

Betty looked at Marion for a moment, then said, 'Perhaps you're right. There's no harm in Muriel Thomson. Now, why don't you sit by the fire and I'll get you a plate of sandwiches. You've had nowt to eat all day. Go on, while you've the chance to be alone – put your feet up on the little velvet stool.'

'Alone?' Marion looked around the room. 'So I am. But where . . . ?'

Betty smiled. 'Your sister got bored with the occasion long ago and is sitting at the kitchen table with her drawing book.'

'And . . . and Mr Brady? Has he gone? I wanted to thank him for coming.'

'Divven't fret. When me mam began to clear the plates, he offered to help her. I think he was a little overwhelmed by some of the guests.'

'So where is he?'

'In the kitchen, like I said. Me mam promised him a cup of tea. Now, are you going to sit down like a good lass?'

'No – I mean, yes, but not in here. I'll come through to the kitchen and have my tea with everyone else.'

When Marion entered the kitchen, she found that Betty had neglected to tell her that Arthur Robinson was there as well. The young police constable and Daniel Brady were in the scullery. They had removed their jackets and each, self-consciously, wore one of Betty's pinafores as they saw to the dishes; Arthur washing and Daniel drying. Even though they had just met, they were chatting to each other as comfortably as old friends. Marion stared at the scene in amazement.

'I never did hold with the idea that a man should be a stranger to the kitchen,' Betty's mother said, 'and these two offered to help so I set them to work.'

'I see,' Marion said. But the day seemed to be taking on a surreal atmosphere.

Annette was sitting at the table concentrating on her sketchbook. Marion glanced over her sister's shoulder and caught her breath. Annette had drawn the scene in the front parlour just a short time ago: the assembled guests chatting awkwardly as they balanced their plates and Betty pouring tea at the table while Charles Earnshaw graciously offered a glass of sherry to Lady Cressington.

She had caught the scene so well, the guests both humble and grand. Marion imagined she could almost see them moving and hear them talking. In that moment she realised that her sister was more than gifted; she was a truly exceptional artist, and somehow, no matter what the circumstances, Marion must fulfil her promise to see that Annette went to art school.

'Sit down,' Betty said. 'Me mam's brewed a pot of tea and we'll eat up the sandwiches and these scones I put by just for us.'

'Our Betty made the scones, she's a dab hand at baking,' her mother said as she put the plate on the table, and Marion fancied the remark was directed at Arthur Robinson, who had just emerged from the scullery and was taking off his apron.

Daniel followed him, looking rather self-conscious, but soon they were all sitting at the kitchen table quietly discussing the day as they ate the sandwiches and scones obediently and drank several cups of hot sweet tea.

Despite the occasion, it was a comfortable gathering with everybody at ease with one another. Marion was almost moved to tears as she realised that these good people were the nearest thing to a family that she and Annette now had.

After everyone had gone, another visitor called and Betty showed him into the front parlour. Marion joined him there and asked him to sit down. Mr Percival was a small, neat, silver-haired gentleman and he was carrying a briefcase.

Marion sat in the armchair facing him. 'I got your letter,' she said. 'It's very kind of you to come to the house.'

Mr Percival smiled kindly. 'Solicitor's offices can be intimidating places,' he said, 'and you are so young to have such a burden placed on your shoulders.'

Marion shook her head. 'To look after my sister is no burden,' she said.

'Of course not. I'm sorry if I offended you.'

'Please . . . it's all right.'

The solicitor looked at her searchingly for a moment and then he opened the briefcase that he had placed on his knee. He took out some papers. 'Your father's Will,' he said. 'Shall I go through it with you?'

'Yes.'

Mr Percival sighed. 'I wish I had better news for you but there's not much to explain, I'm afraid. You father was not a rich man.'

'I know that.'

'Your inheritance is modest to say the least.'

Marion smiled faintly. 'I didn't expect it to be a fortune.'

The solicitor looked at her anxiously. 'But I believe your mother left you and your sister each a little money.'

'She did.' Marion did not want to worry him further by telling him how little that was.

'Well, then,' Mr Percival glanced down at the papers, 'this won't take very long.'

After the solicitor had gone, Marion sat alone in the front parlour a little longer. Then, hiding her fears for the future for Annette's sake, she rose and went to join her sister and Betty in the kitchen.

The next day the weather was just as fine. It seemed that the summer sunshine was reluctant to give way to the uncertain weather of autumn. Marion woke early, dressed and crept downstairs. She opened the door of the front parlour softly and peeped inside to reassure herself that Betty was still asleep. The older girl lay on the sofa. An eiderdown covered her sleeping form and only her head embellished with rag curlers could be seen on the pillow.

Marion closed the door gently and went along to the kitchen, where she wrote a note and left it on the table. Then, taking her coat from the stand in the hall, she left the house. Fifteen minutes later she was walking across the large area of common land known as the Town Moor. She marvelled at the wonderfully green open space so close to the great industrial town. It's like a lung, she thought, providing great breaths of fresh air. Looking back towards the suburbs, she could see wisps of smoke rising from the chimneypots as people began to light their morning fires.

She turned her back on the wakening streets and set off across the tussocky grass. In the distance she could see the cattle that the free-men of the city were allowed to graze on the moor. A wind sprang up, and although it was playful, tugging at her hat gently rather than lifting it from her head and sending it flying, it was keen enough to bring tears to her eyes.

Maybe it was the wind that first provoked the tears, but she allowed them to flow freely. Here, alone on the sweet-smelling moor, she gave in to the grief that she had held at bay for days. At home and at the funeral she had had to be strong for Annette's sake. But now, with no one to see her, she could cry not just for her father but for herself and the life the three of them had lived together: happy and secure and full of the sort of gaiety their father had provided with his quick and unusual mind and his admittedly advanced notions about how girls should be brought up to think for themselves. Now, with their beloved father gone, long before his time, it was up to Marion to provide the love and security Annette deserved. And she vowed to herself that she would.

When she reached the top of a rise in the ground not quite big enough to be called a hill, she turned and looked back the way she had come. The tree-lined road that led into the city from the north seemed far away and the numerous horse-drawn trams and carriages looked like mechanical toys.

She wondered how long she had been walking and looked at her wristwatch. She was shocked to discover that she had left home more than an hour before. She realised that by now Annette would have come down for breakfast. Hurriedly she set off for home.

There was a carriage outside the door. Marion had never seen it before and she wondered who could be calling at this hour of the morning. She supposed whoever owned the carriage could be visiting one of her neighbours, although she couldn't imagine any of them having such a grand acquaintance, but as soon as she opened the door she saw the gentleman's hat on the hallstand and knew that whoever it was had indeed come to see her.

Betty must have been listening for her return, for she hurried down the passage to greet her almost before Marion had finished unbuttoning her coat.

'Here, let me help you,' she said and slipped Marion's coat from her shoulders the way she used to when Marion was a child and needed help with dressing.

'Who is it?' Marion asked as her glance lingered on the hat.

Betty hung up the coat and reached for Marion's hatpin. She removed the hat deftly and turned Marion to face the mirror set into the coat stand. 'Tidy your hair,' she said. 'You look as though you've been dragged through a hedge backwards.'

Impatiently Marion caught at stray wisps of hair and pushed them back, while Betty took out a few pins and secured them. 'But who is it?' she asked. 'And why do you look so worried?'

Betty stood back and examined Marion critically. 'You'll do,' she said. 'Now take a deep breath and calm yourself.'

'I'm perfectly calm,' Marion retorted. 'At least I was until you started behaving so oddly. Now tell me who this hat belongs to!'

Betty picked up a calling card that had all the time been resting on the shelf of the hat stand and handed it wordlessly to Marion

Marion looked down at the neatly engraved writing. 'Mr Victor Bateman,' she said. 'But that's the landlord.'

'Aye, it is,' Betty said, and there was no disguising how worried she was.

'Why should he call?' Marion asked, but she had a horrible feeling that she knew the answer.

'I don't know,' Betty said, 'but you'd better go in and find out.'

Marion had never met their landlord, but she knew that her father had always got on well with him – at least he had never had cause for complaint. The houses Mr Bateman owned were well maintained, and any repairs that needed doing were always seen to as soon as they were reported. The rents were fair and Marion had never heard of any evictions.

She gripped the handle of the parlour door and paused to breathe deeply as Betty had instructed her. Then, adopting a calm and what she hoped was an adult and businesslike expression, she opened the door and entered the room. As soon as she did so she was thrown off balance. Betty had not told her that Annette was in there.

Her sister was sitting at the dining table, her sketchbook laid out before her, and was turning the pages while Mr Bateman looked down appreciatively. Neither Mr Bateman nor Annette seemed to be aware of Marion's presence. Annette was smiling as Mr Bateman praised her work, each new page seemingly impressing him further.

Neither of them seemed to have noticed her, and Marion had time to observe Mr Bateman keenly. He was younger than she expected. She knew him to be wealthy, so she supposed she must have been expecting a sober older gentleman in a business suit. Instead she saw a good-looking, even handsome man who must be about forty years old and who was wearing discreetly fashionable clothes as portrayed in the Harrods and Gamages mail-order catalogues that she and Annette loved to look at. Mr Bateman had light brown hair with a slight wave in it, and when he looked up at last, she saw that he had intensely blue eyes.

She glanced down quickly, hoping that he had not noticed that she had been staring at him.

'Miss Brookfield,' he said, 'may I offer my deepest sympathy.' His voice was cultured and well modulated. 'Your father was a good man and he is a great loss to his newspaper – and to all of us.'

'Thank you.'

Is this why he has come? Marion wondered. Simply to offer condolences? Or is he going to ask whether we can afford to go on paying the rent and perhaps advise us to start looking for somewhere else to live?

'May I sit down?' he asked.

'Oh, of course.' Flustered and feeling gauche, Marion indicated the fireside chairs.

Victor Bateman walked over to one of them and stood there looking at her expectantly. Marion realised he was waiting for her to take a seat, and she did so quickly.

'I didn't just come to offer condolences,' he said once they were both seated. 'I came to make sure that you and your sister were – this is awkward – that your father has provided for you.'

'Do you mean to ask if we can go on paying the rent?'

Mr Bateman raised his eyebrows and said with a slight smile, 'Well, I wouldn't have put it quite so bluntly, but yes, I would like to know the answer to that question.'

'We can,' Marion said. She stared down at her hands, which were clenched in her lap.

Their landlord waited, as if expecting her to say more, but when it was obvious that she was not going to, he said, 'That's good. But I want you to know that if life becomes difficult for you, I have no intention of acting the part of a wicked landlord in a melodrama.'

She looked up in surprise. Mr Bateman was smiling.

'Something tells me that was what you were expecting when you walked into the room just now,' he said.

'Oh no! I mean . . .'

'Please don't distress yourself, Miss Brookfield. One of the reasons I wanted to see you today was to tell you that if there is anything I can do to help you, I will.'

'But why should you?' Marion asked. 'You've never met Annette and me before.'

'I am motivated by respect for your father.' He paused. 'But I'm sure he's left you well provided for?'

Marion remembered that she hadn't answered his question. 'Yes, he has.'

'Well, I shall take my leave. But you have my card and you must not hesitate to come to me for help or advice if you should need it.'

'Thank you.'

They both rose, and Marion reached towards the bell pull. 'Betty will see you out.'

While they waited for the maid to appear, Mr Bateman asked, 'Do you know if your father's newspaper means to carry on with his work?'

'I believe so. Mr Earnshaw has asked me to sort out my father's papers.'

'I'm pleased to hear it. The men he was investigating are the sort who give all landlords a bad name.'

Betty had barely closed the front door behind Mr Bateman when Annette hurried to the window. She pushed the lace curtain aside and peered out.

'What are you doing?' Marion asked.

'Looking at his carriage. Isn't it grand? Do come and see.'

'I saw it when I came in, and you really shouldn't do that.'

'Do what?'

'Lift the curtain and look out like that. It's bad manners.'

Annette ignored her and went on looking.

'Annette – please come away from the window. What do you suppose Mr Bateman will think if he sees you staring like that?'

'He already has seen me, and don't worry, he smiled and waved.' In her own good time Annette let the curtain fall and returned to her seat at the table. 'Mr Bateman thinks I'm very talented. He said he had never seen such delightful drawings.'

Marion was perplexed. Annette was behaving badly, but perhaps that was understandable. What had happened had been a great shock. Poor Annette, her whole world changed in an instant. And now, with no father to love and indulge her, she had responded hungrily to Mr Bateman's attention. I must be patient with her, Marion thought, as I know Father would have wanted me to be.

Victor Bateman had been amused when he saw the younger Brookfield girl peeping out of the window. She was a pretty little thing and very talented. He wondered if he should encourage her. It would be a pleasure to foster such a talent, and, he suspected, such an act on his part would surely win favour with the elder girl.

Marion. What was he to make of her? So grave, so serious and yet so attractive. He had been struck by her beauty one evening a week or two ago when he had observed Henry Brookfield and his elder daughter coming down the steps of the Literary and Philosophical Society along with other serious folk who had been attending a lecture. He had been tempted to stop and ask Henry to introduce his daughter, but he was on his way to the theatre and it would soon be curtain up.

Today Victor had seen that even in unrelieved black, Marion Brookfield could rouse the senses, and she obviously had no idea of the effect she had on men. He settled back in his carriage and narrowed his eyes as he thought, as he often did, how sad it was that all that youthful appeal would one day fade. But meanwhile he must concentrate on the challenge that lay ahead. For he sensed that Marion Brookfield's air of reserve masked a keen intelligence. It was not going to be as easy as he had imagined.

Marion started to walk to and from school with Annette. They didn't talk much but were simply glad of each other's company. One day, when they returned for tea, Betty met them in the hall.

'There's a parcel for you,' she said.

'For who?' Annette asked.

'Both of you,' Betty replied. 'At least both your names are on the label.'

'But who is it from?'

'How should I know?' Betty smiled teasingly. 'Why divven't you open it and find out? I've put it on the table in the front parlour.'

Marion stood back and allowed Annette to open the parcel. Inside the sturdy cardboard box there were two packages: one rather solid-looking affair and another, much smaller. Annette saw with delight that a label bearing her name was attached to the larger of the two parcels.

'Presents!' she said. 'For us! Look, this one is for you. Who can have sent them?'

'The landlord,' Betty said, and both girls turned to look at her in surprise.

'Mr Bateman?' Marion asked.

'Aye, that's the one. At least that's what the chap who delivered the parcel said, and I hev no cause to doubt him.'

Annette was already opening her present, tugging at the string and almost tearing the brown paper off. Betty hurried over to the table. 'Carefully does it,' she said. 'That string and paper can be used again.'

Betty undid the knots and wound the string around her fingers before putting it in the pocket of her pinafore, then eased the brown paper away and folded it. For a moment Annette didn't utter a word. She stared at the oblong cherrywood box, finally turning shining eyes towards her sister.

'It's a sketch box,' she said. 'And look, the lid props open to become an easel – a tabletop easel.' She lifted the lid to demonstrate, and then exclaimed with delight. 'Just look!' she said.

The inside was divided into several compartments, and each contained something that would delight an artist. Brushes, pastels, crayons, calligraphy pens and nibs, and in one long compartment there was an artist's lay figure: a jointed wooden manikin about six inches long.

'This must have cost him a fortune!' Annette exclaimed.

'Aye, I dare say,' Betty said. She looked impressed.

'I don't know if we can accept it,' Marion said.

Annette uttered a sound somewhere between a shriek and a howl. 'Not accept it! Why ever not?'

'Because, as you've guessed, it's a very expensive gift and we had never met Mr Bateman before the day of the funeral.'

'Oh no, Marion, please don't say I have to send it back!' Annette's face was flushed and her eyes were brimming with tears. 'He said I was very good – no, more than that: he said I was exceptional and that I must be encouraged. How ungrateful and rude he would think us if we refused his gift!'

'The lass is right,' Betty said unexpectedly. 'And besides, you divven't want to upset your landlord, do you?'

'I suppose not,' Marion said, but she was troubled.

Annette, taking this to mean that her sister had changed her mind, smiled and said, 'Well go on, then, open your parcel and see what Mr Bateman has sent you.'

Marion's present was a book. The title was picked out in gold lettering: *Poems to Comfort You in Your Bereavement*. She opened it. Each page had a black border and the poems were interspersed with illustrations of angels, funeral wreaths and angelic children kneeling in prayer.

'Isn't that beautiful?' Betty said as she peered over Marion's shoulder.

'Mmm,' was Marion's noncommittal reply.

'I must say, Mr Bateman must have put his mind to it. He knew that artist's paraphernalia would please your sister and that you were a more bookish sort. Now, if you divven't mind, just give us about ten minutes and then come along to the kitchen for your tea.'

Annette started taking everything out of the sketch box. She counted the pencils, the brushes and the pastels and arranged them on the table in front of her before putting them back neatly. Marion sat by the fire and looked at her book. As she turned the pages, she stared with growing dismay at verses about silent lips, smooth sinless brows, snow-white hands, wreaths of lilies and lone vigils beside marble tombs. She did not find the poems comforting. In fact, she was irritated, even angered by their mawkishness, especially as she knew her father would have hated such manufactured sentimentality.

She found herself imagining his reaction as they read the poems together, and she realised that with his dry sense of humour, he would have found them both dreadful and amusing. She could picture the astonished expression on his face and hear his laughter. She startled herself by laughing out loud, and Annette glanced up in surprise.

'What is it?' she asked. 'Have the poems cheered you a little?'

'In a way they have.'

'Then you must write to Mr Bateman and tell him so.'

'I will,' Marion agreed, although she knew she would have to word her letter very tactfully. 'And you must write too, and thank him for his wonderful gift.'

Annette smiled. 'We'll write our thank-you letters together.'

At that moment Betty came in to tell them their meal was ready.

Annette left her present on the table reluctantly, and Marion put her book down on one of the shelves in the alcove at the side of the fireplace. She doubted if she would ever open it again.

Betty joined them at the tea table as had become her habit, but she was much quieter than usual. 'I don't know how to put this,' she said eventually, 'but I think it's time I took me things and went home.'

Marion looked at her in alarm.'

'Divven't fret,' Betty said. 'I don't mean that I'm leaving you – you just try getting rid of me – but it's time I slept at home again. Me mam misses me company at nights when me da's on night shift at the railway yards.'

'Of course. I've been selfish keeping you here,' Marion said.

'You didn't keep me here, pet, I stayed of me own accord. I've been with you two since you were young lasses. Your da trusted me to look after you and I'm sure that's what he would hev wanted me to do – stay here and see you through the worst of it.'

'And I'm truly grateful,' Marion said.

She knew what Betty meant by 'the worst of it'. She meant the terrible days after her father had been murdered, but she wasn't sure if the worst of it was over, would ever be over, at least for her. She glanced at Annette, who was looking dreamy and preoccupied as she ate a piece of raisin cake.

She's thinking about Mr Bateman's gift, Marion guessed, and what she will draw next. And I'm glad she has that to distract her. Despite her great talent, or maybe even because of it, she is not yet ready to cope with the world. I must do my best to protect her.

After Betty had cleared the table and washed the dishes, she put on her coat and hat. Marion noticed that she had made a brown paper parcel of the clothes she had brought with her. It was large and unwieldy.

'Can you manage that? Should I get you a cab?'

'Bless you, no. Arthur will carry it for me.'

'Arthur? You mean Constable Robinson?'

'Aye, that's the fellow. He said he'd help me take my bit stuff home. That's him now,' she said when there was a knock on the back door. 'I hope you divven't mind him calling?'

'No, of course not,' Marion said.

She noticed that Arthur seemed quite at home. They mean more to each other than old school friends, she realised. What if Betty decides to leave and get married? What will we do without her? Nevertheless, Marion managed a welcoming smile.

Arthur didn't return the smile, and Marion noticed that he looked nervous. 'Miss Brookfield,' he said. 'I have some news.'

Betty looked at him keenly. 'Wait a minute, Arthur,' she said. She moved her head to indicate Annette.

'Oh, yes.'

Marion took the hint. 'Annette,' she said, 'do you want to go to the parlour and have a look at your present? I'll see Betty out and then I'll come and join you.'

Annette needed no second bidding. Smiling briefly at Arthur without really focusing, she hurried back to the front parlour and her new sketch box.

'Sit down, Arthur,' Betty said.

The police constable glanced at Marion to see if this was all right, and she nodded wordlessly.

'It's about your father,' he began. He paused and looked hesitant.

'What is it?' Marion asked.

'They've found the culprit.'

'Culprit?'

'The black-hearted villain who murdered him.'

Marion stared at him. 'Found him? Where? How do you know that he is the man?'

'He was lying in the gutter outside the Crow's Nest – that's a drinking den down by the river. It's not the kind of place respectable working men go to. But even so, the landlord wanted him moved. He found him lying there one morning when he opened up. The wretch was so drunk that he couldn't stir himself when he was asked to move on. There was an empty gin bottle lying beside him.

'The landlord wondered how the man could hev afforded a whole bottle, so he sent a lad up to the police station. When the police constable examined him, he found nothing in his pockets but a black leather pouch. It was empty. Whatever money it might have held had been spent.'

He paused and looked concerned as he heard Marion gasp.

Then he continued in a grave voice. 'And there was a watch. The watch had a name engraved on the case.' He looked at Marion anxiously.

'Henry Brookfield,' she breathed.

85

'Aye, I'm afraid so,' Arthur said.

'I wonder why he hadn't sold it,' Marion said.

'No doubt he would hev if we hadn't found him first.' Arthur paused. 'And then we would never have discovered who had killed your father.'

No one spoke. In the silence, Marion could hear the ticking of the clock on the mantel shelf and the comforting sound of coals settling in the hearth. She stared down at the tablecloth and noticed a few crumbs and a raisin where Annette's plate had been.

Eventually Betty said, 'Arthur, I'd be obliged if you would call and tell my mother that I'm not coming home tonight.'

Marion looked up. 'Oh no,' she said. 'Your mother is expecting you, and I'm all right, really I am.'

Betty shook her head. 'All right, are you? I divven't think so. Why, lass, your bonny face is whiter than that tablecloth. I'm staying here tonight, whatever you say.'

# Chapter Six

After the rainy spell in early September, the fine weather held and work on the new tramlines progressed without too many problems. But as soon as the darker evenings set in at the beginning of October, the working day was shorter and the men grumbled about the reduced pay.

Once Daniel would have been just as unhappy as the rest of them, but now he welcomed the chance to get home early, wash, eat, and then spread his papers out on the table. He missed the money, but there was a growing need within him to earn his living another way. His first task was to sort out the muddle of papers that Marion had given him and try to work out what Henry Brookfield's plan for him had been.

Most of the time he was able to lose himself in his work and ignore his mother's occasional tut of disapproval. She had made it plain that she thought he was wrong to attempt to get above himself. To Hannah Brady, the class structure was ordained from above, and no one should attempt to rise higher than their proper station in life.

Daniel made sure that he gave his mother the same amount of money as he had during the good days of summer, even though this left him with less to spend on himself. But as he didn't smoke and didn't frequent the public houses, that was no great hardship. Not that he didn't like a glass of ale now and then, but he would take a jug up to the Raby and bring home enough to share with his mother beside the comfort of their own fire.

He carried on with the assignments Henry had planned for him. He could only hope the results of his efforts would have pleased his patient tutor. He also continued to buy a newspaper and would read it before he started his studies.

A week or two ago he had read of the arrest of a vagrant suspected of murdering Henry Brookfield, and he had wondered if he should visit Marion and see if she was all right. But even though she had invited him to the funeral, he worried that she might think him presumptuous, so he stayed away. He had every intention of taking up her offer of becoming her reading companion, but thought that he should wait until she invited him. She had told him that she would write to him when she was ready.

Then one day the newspaper carried notice of the trial. Daniel was overcome with the urge to see for himself what kind of wretch had murdered the man he had thought of as a friend. Even though it meant taking a full day off work, he decided that he would go.

'Aren't you going to do any book learning tonight?' his mother asked.

Daniel looked up in surprise. 'Why do you ask that?'

'Because you've been staring at the same page of the newspaper for a good half an hour, just staring at it, and I can see you're not really reading it. If you ask me, you've exhausted yourself. You should give all this sort of thing a rest before you give yourself brain fever. Put those books away, son, and let me make you a cup of tea – or would you like cocoa?'

Daniel folded the newspaper and put his exercise books and papers away in the dispatch case that Marion had given him. 'All right, Ma. I'd like some cocoa, on condition that you have a cup too.'

His mother smiled. 'Go on, sit by the fire, bonny lad. I'll make the drinks, and mebbes we should hev a slice of toast. Would you like that?'

'Aye. You slice the bread and I'll toast it.' Daniel rose from the table and crossed to the fireplace. He took the toasting fork down from its hook. He would allow his mother to have her way tonight, and would do his best to chat to her about nothing in particular.

Daniel put a slice of bread on the prongs of the toasting fork and held it towards the bars where the fire glowed hottest. When one side was done he drew the fork back and turned the slice over as quickly as he could so as not to burn his fingers. His mother had cut three slices of bread from the loaf, and when they were all toasted satisfactorily, she carried the plate to the table and began to spread them thickly with butter. She handed Daniel a mug of cocoa and two of the slices of toast.

'Two for you and one for me,' she said.

Daniel munched his toast and sipped his cocoa, and for a while they sat in companionable silence; but then he noticed that his mother kept glancing at the clock on the mantel shelf.

'What is it?' he asked.

'Nothing,' Hannah replied.

'Then why do you look so anxious?'

'Well . . . I was just wondering when our Susan would get home.'

'I thought she was going to her friend Maisie's house, and that Maisie's father had promised to walk her home.'

'Yes, that's right. Well . . . not exactly.'

Daniel felt a stirring of unease. 'What do you mean, not exactly?'

'Well Maisie – that's the lass she works with . . .'

'I know that. Get on with it.'

'Well, it seems that Mr Jacobs gets complimentary tickets for the theatre . . .' Hannah paused and looked anxiously at the clock again.'

'What has Mr Jacobs got to do with this?'

'He said he didn't want to use the tickets this week, so he gave them to Maisie and Susan.'

'And who exactly is going to see Susan home?'

'Eeh, divven't look at me like that, Daniel. You look just like your father did when he was vexed with me. And divven't fret, I gave her the money to come home in a cab.'

Daniel fought to control his irritation. 'Ma, I'm not vexed. I'm worried about Susan. I don't like the idea of her coming home alone late at night.'

'I wouldn't hev let her go if she was going to come home late.'

Daniel stared at his mother. 'You're not talking sense.'

Hannah Brady recovered a little of her confidence. 'Yes I am,' she said. 'Mr Jacobs promised to let them off work early so's they could go to the first house. That starts at six o'clock and gets out at eight. And that's not too late, is it? I mean, every now and then she works in the shop as late as that.'

'And if she does, I meet her and bring her home,' Daniel said. He looked up at the clock. 'It's quarter to nine. Even if she had to queue for a cab, she ought to have been home by now.'

Susan had never sat in a box before. Previously, when she had been to the theatre with her mother and Dora, they had queued for seats in 'the gods', as the upper circle was known, which was so dizzyingly

89

high and so steeply tiered that Susan would cling to her seat in terror until the show began. Once the curtain rose, she was able to put to the back of her mind the notion that if she stood up too quickly she would pitch over and fall down on to the heads of the more fortunate people sitting in the stalls.

But this evening she was sitting in a box – like Lady Muck, as their next-door neighbour Dora might have said. Just like Susan's mother, Dora didn't like anyone to get above themselves and adopt airs and graces.

Well, what a surprise Dora would have if she knew what Susan's gentleman friend, Mr Mason, thought of that kind of attitude. He had told Susan that no matter that she lived in Byker, she was as good as any lady he knew and that he would be proud to take her anywhere – starting with this visit to the theatre.

She loved the way the important-looking gentleman – she thought he must be the manager because he was dressed in evening clothes – showed them to their box. He seemed to know her escort, for he bowed and smiled a lot and said he was very pleased to see him and he'd be glad to take their order. It was then that Susan realised that the important-looking chap was in fact a waiter of some sort, because her gentleman asked him to bring coffee and cakes to the box in the interval.

'Would you like that, my dear?' he asked, turning to Susan with an indulgent smile.

'Oh yes,' she had said. 'Very much, but . . .' She faltered.

'What is it?' Gilbert Mason looked perplexed.

'Perhaps the young lady would like ice cream rather than cakes?' the waiter said.

'Oh, of course!' Her gentleman friend smiled. 'Bring ice cream for the young lady and brandy for me. It's such a crush at the bar.'

'Of course, sir,' the waiter said and withdrew discreetly.

Susan noticed that Gilbert sat well back in the box, in the shadows almost, but he made no objection when she leaned forward and gazed out. She was entranced by the view of the auditorium. She watched the seats in the stalls below and in the dress circle fill up with respectably dressed folk, then her eye was drawn to the upper circle, where some sort of disturbance had broken out.

Two women sitting in the front row were arguing about something, and their raised voices echoed around the theatre before

90

two hefty commissionaires in uniform jackets embellished with rows of brass buttons edged along the row, seized them and hauled them away, still screeching.

People in the stalls were turning and craning to look upwards. Some smiled but others shook their heads disapprovingly. Susan heard her companion laugh softly and turned to see him smiling. 'Riff-raff,' he said. 'The inhabitants of the gods can always be relied on to provide a lively and amusing diversion before the real entertainment begins.'

Susan was glad that the light inside the box was dim and he could not see her mortified expression. I hope he never finds out that that is where my ma and I sit, she worried. But when the house lights dimmed, the conductor tapped his baton on his music stand and the orchestra began to play, she soon put aside all qualms and prepared to enjoy herself.

Carried along on the light-hearted tunes, her eyes were already shining like those of a child by the time the curtain was raised on a world of magic. So absorbed was she by what was happening on the stage that she had no idea that her gentleman friend, rather than watching the stage, was watching her.

He was entranced. She is so young, he thought; so unaware of the ways of the world. I don't believe that I will be able to resist her for much longer.

After the final curtain fell, Mr Mason remained sitting.

'Let them all get out first,' he said. 'We don't want to be caught up in the crush.'

The theatre gradually emptied. The audience were smiling and laughing and discussing the entertainment that had lifted them out of their mundane lives for a while. Susan began to fret about getting home. She was relieved when Gilbert, as she was beginning to think of him, eventually deemed it the right time to go. But once they had reached the street, he asked if she would like to come with him for an early supper at Alvini's.

'I could secure one of the private dining rooms. There would be no one to interrupt us or spoil our fun.'

'Alvini's! Oh, I'd love to!' she said, wondering how she could ever let that priggish Dora know that she had dined at the most fashionable restaurant in town.

But then she remembered that she had promised her mother that she would go straight home after the theatre, so reluctantly she told him that she couldn't have supper with him.

Suddenly his blue eyes looked quite cold, but he smiled when he said, 'Your mother must be quite a dragon.'

'Oh no, not Ma. It's my brother, Daniel. He thinks he has the right to tell me what to do.'

'Well, if your father is dead then I suppose he has,' Gilbert said. 'Tell me, how did you persuade him to let you come to the theatre with me tonight?'

'I didn't. He thinks I'm at Maisie's house. Maisie from the shop. As if I would go anywhere with that miserable old bat! But I told my mother that I was going to the theatre with her.'

Gilbert laughed. 'Two different stories? What a wicked child you are. Won't you get in a muddle?'

Susan looked flustered. 'Well, no, my mother knows where I am really − or where I'm supposed to be. Oh dear!' She began to laugh too. 'Anyway, I told Ma to be the judge of what to tell Daniel, but if I'm late home I wouldn't put it past him to come looking for me.'

'Well then, I had better send you home forthwith. Come, let me see you into a cab.'

They walked across to the cab stand together and he helped her in. 'Here you are,' he said as he handed her a small leather pouched purse.

'What is it?' she asked.

'Your cab fare.'

'Oh, but my mother . . .'

'Take it, I insist. Now, tell the cabby where to take you. Perhaps we will dine out another time.'

Susan managed a smile as the cab drew away, but inwardly, she was seething with regret. She would have loved to have gone to Alvini's and she had sensed Gilbert's exasperation when she had told him that she couldn't go. She settled back miserably and thought about his last words to her.

*Perhaps we will dine out another time.*

What did he mean by 'perhaps'? Was it a way of telling her that he was no longer interested in her? It was unsettling enough that she never knew exactly when he would be waiting for her. This visit to the theatre had been the only meeting that had been planned.

When the cab reached Shields Road, the cabby turned round and asked her if he could drop her at the top of her street rather than going down Byker Bank, a steep road that was difficult for the horses.

'Oh, of course,' Susan said distractedly.

He told her what the fare was and she opened the purse her gentleman had given her to extract the money. When she saw what was inside, she nearly cried out in astonishment. As well as some small change, which added up to more than enough for the cab fare, there was a golden sovereign. She paid her fare, and as the cab drew away, she stood on the corner and stared at the golden coin glinting in the light from the streetlamp.

It must be a mistake, she thought. He must have pulled a handful of loose change from his pocket not realising that there was a sovereign amongst it. But then she saw that there was also a folded piece of paper in the purse. She took it out carefully so as not to displace the sovereign, and opened it.

*Buy yourself another hat or some such*, the note read.

A hat? Susan thought. I will be able to buy a hat, gloves and maybe a pretty little scarf as well, and still have change left over. She had already imagined her shopping trip before it crossed her mind that her mother and her brother would certainly not approve of her accepting such a gift.

She remembered the old saying warning young women not to accept gifts of clothes from men: *whatever a man puts on you, he wants to take off again*. She considered for only the briefest of moments handing back the money next time she saw him, and then she smiled and refolded the note. Well, even if he does want to take it off, it's only a hat, she thought. What harm can there be in that? She put the note back into the purse with the sovereign and drew up the leather strings, then tucked the purse deep into the pocket in her skirt.

My mother and Daniel need never know, she thought. And if they ask where the new hat came from, I shall say that Maisie bought it for herself, decided she didn't like it and gave it to me. She smiled, pleased at how clever she was to think of such a plan.

She hurried down the bank towards her home and cut through the back lane. She was still smiling when she walked into the kitchen. 'What a lovely time I've had,' she exclaimed to her mother and her brother. She was just about to describe the show she'd seen when she remembered that Daniel had been told she'd gone to Maisie's.

Then he disconcerted her by asking her if she had enjoyed the theatre. So her mother had told him.

She flushed but did not allow Daniel's severe look to deflate her spirits. 'The show was marvellous,' she said. 'And Maisie is such good company. We've decided that we shall go to the theatre together again as soon as Mr Jacobs has some more spare tickets.'

'That's nice, pet,' her mother said, but Daniel, seeing Susan's flushed cheeks and the way she could not meet his eyes, was troubled.

On the day of the trial, Daniel woke to hear wind howling up the cobbled streets from the river and rain lashing against the window. The weather was so foul that he was pretty sure there would be no work that day. Nevertheless, the men were expected to turn up even if it was to be told to go straight home again. He looked at his work clothes and his best suit and debated with himself about what he should do.

His mother and sister were still asleep, so he put on his working clothes and crept downstairs quietly to fetch his tool bag from under the bench in the scullery. Then he looked in the fireside cupboard for some brown paper and string. Back in his room, he folded his good clothes as neatly as he could and, after wrapping them in the paper in order to keep them clean, put them in his tool bag.

He was in the living room making a pot of tea when his mother came down, yawning and crumpled in her flannel dressing gown.

'Eeh, Daniel lad, you're up sharp the day. I've overslept and so has Susan. But you sit by the fire and I'll get the breakfast on the table.'

Breakfast that morning, like most weekday mornings, consisted of thick slices of bread and dripping and hot sweet tea. When Susan appeared, she was dressed for work but she hadn't done her hair and it hung down, partly obscuring her pretty face. She sat and waited quietly at the table, and Daniel thought she looked troubled. No, troubled was not the word, but she was definitely bothered about something.

He watched as she reached for the bowl of dripping and, taking her knife, dug deep to find the layer of rich, dark jelly. But she seemed to shrug off whatever unsettling thoughts she had had and appeared to enjoy her breakfast as much as she always did. Whatever was bothering her had not put her off her food.

After breakfast, Daniel had time for another mug of tea. He watched as his mother put Susan's hair up. Seeing Hannah's expression as she worked, he realised how proud she was of her beautiful daughter. With a pang, he realised that his mother must have been just as beautiful once. Under the faded skin, her cheekbones were finely drawn and her eyes were the same blue-grey as Susan's. But the years had not been kind to Hannah Brady. No matter what her hopes might have been as a young bride, early widowhood and the resulting life of hard work and near poverty had taken their toll.

By the time she was ready to leave, Susan was grumbling that no matter how big the umbrella, she was sure to get soaking wet, and that the trams would be full of fusty-smelling people with dripping clothes. Daniel could see that Hannah was upset, and instinctively he put his arm around her shoulder and gave her a hug.

'Don't worry about it, Ma,' he said. 'Susan is young and healthy; she'll survive.'

His mother managed a careworn smile. 'And what about you?' she asked. 'Will they expect you to work in this downpour?'

'Probably not,' Daniel said. 'But there are always odd jobs to be done for the foreman. Most likely I'll be sitting in his warm hut checking off lists of supplies.'

'They trust you with that kind of thing, don't they? They must think well of you. Eeh, Danny boy, they'll make you the foreman one day, I'm sure of it.'

'Perhaps. Now, I must be off.'

He felt guilty because he had deceived his mother; nevertheless, when the foreman told the men that there would be no work today, he headed for the library and asked Miss Bennett if he could change his clothes in the gentlemen's cloakroom. She agreed without asking why, so when he was ready to go, he felt that he should offer her an explanation.

'I thought I would go to the trial,' he said.

Miss Bennett knew which trial he meant. 'Mr Brookfield was your tutor, wasn't he?'

'Yes.'

'And I suppose you want to make sense of it,' she said. 'I mean, you want to discover why such a good man should be murdered by one of the people he was trying to help.'

Daniel nodded.

Then she surprised him by asking, 'Have you got a notebook in that bag?'

'A notebook? No. Why?'

'I thought you might take notes.'

'Why should I do that?'

'Write it up afterwards – as if it were a report for the newspaper.' Before he could reply, she hurried on, 'I'm sure you'd make a good job of it, and that has been the whole point of all your studying, hasn't it? To find employment more suitable for your intellectual capabilities?'

Daniel flushed. 'I suppose so,' he admitted reluctantly.

'Well, there you are then. Here.' She handed him one of her own notebooks. 'See what you can do, and remember, Mr Brady,' she smiled, 'that's how Mr Dickens started, you know.'

'Started?'

'As a reporter; although in his case he was a parliamentary reporter. But just look what he went on to achieve.'

'You think I should write novels?' Daniel grinned.

'Why not? One day. But as for today's task, I would be very pleased to look over it for you – if you would like me to.'

'Thank you. I would.'

Miss Bennett pushed a pencil across the counter and Daniel slipped it into his tool bag along with the notebook.

'And you'd better take this umbrella,' Miss Bennett said.

'Oh, but I couldn't. I mean, you—'

'Don't worry, it isn't mine. It's lost property. I keep it behind the counter along with the scarves and the gloves and even the odd pair of galoshes. Someone left it here about a year ago, and whoever it was, they haven't been back for it. You must return it, of course, in case the owner suddenly remembers about it.'

Daniel smiled and thanked her, then, acutely aware that Mr Chalk had observed the entire exchange and was sniffing disapprovingly, left the library and hurried through the rain down to the quayside and the Moot Hall.

The courtroom was crowded; it usually was for murder trials. Daniel, seeing the avid expressions on the faces of the spectators lining the gallery, realised that for them this was some form of entertainment. He sat down and, sliding his umbrella under the bench, took out his notebook.

'Not here.' He looked up to find a court official standing over him.

'I beg your pardon?'

'You don't sit here. Look, down there.' The man pointed to a sort of wooden pen near the front of the courtroom. 'You must go downstairs and sit there with the rest of the reporters.'

'Oh, but—'

'Now be a good man and do as you're told,' the official said. 'Gentlemen from the press must sit together where the judge can keep an eye on them.'

'Why?'

'Probably because you're like a cartload of monkeys and his honour wants to see that you behave yourselves. Now come along, don't waste my time or I'll have you out of here altogether and on to the street.'

Bemusedly Daniel groped for his umbrella, picked up his tool bag and did as he was told.

Nobody questioned him when he took his place among the reporters, and although he felt like a fraud, he decided that he might as well learn from this experience and watch closely how real journalists went about the job of reporting a trial.

He was barely settled when a sort of groan went up from the crowd. He looked up to see that the accused had been brought into court. The man who stood in the dock between two hefty jailers was not at all what Daniel had been expecting. This was no hardy criminal, no tough bully boy, but a frail, timid-looking wretch who stood there blinking and looking utterly confused.

Daniel was puzzled, but he supposed that if a man were desperate enough, he would be able to summon up superhuman strength. And then he realised that in any case it would not take much vigour to slide a knife between someone's ribs – especially if your victim trusted you and had been taken by surprise.

He soon became caught up in the drama of the trial and could hardly keep up with his note-taking. At one stage, when hurrying to turn the page, he dropped both notebook and pencil. The pencil began to roll forward and Daniel got down quickly to retrieve it. While he did so his neighbour, an elderly gentleman with untidy hair and half-moon spectacles, had picked up the notebook. Daniel flushed when he saw that the man was looking at it critically.

'Shorthand, dear boy,' he said when he handed it back. 'You must learn shorthand.'

The trial did not last long. It seemed to Daniel that this was no case of the suspect being presumed innocent until proven guilty. Everybody, judge, jury and most of the people in the courtroom, had already made up their minds. Apparently the evidence of the empty purse and the watch was strong enough, and although the accused man claimed repeatedly that he had no idea how they had got into his pockets, no one believed him.

When the judge placed the black cap on his head, everyone in the courtroom held their breath, and at the words 'hanged by the neck until you are dead', they let it out again in a long, satisfied sigh. Justice had been done.

And then Daniel was almost knocked over in the rush as the journalists scrambled to get out of the courtroom and back to their newspapers in order to write up their reports.

'New to the game, are you?' the elderly reporter asked, but didn't wait for Daniel's reply before hurrying off after the rest of them.

Daniel decided not to join in the rush and let the others go ahead. As he did so, he glimpsed two men talking earnestly as they walked towards the door. With their backs to him all he could see was the sharp-nosed profile of the taller man as he lowered his head to listen to what the other one was saying; his attitude and his expression were respectful. Daniel wondered who they were.

He forgot about them as soon as he glimpsed the slim, black-veiled woman just rising from her seat at the far end of a row near the back of the room. His heart skipped a beat, that was the only way to describe it, and he smiled ruefully at his own reaction, for he knew immediately who it was. And she knew him. She made her way along the row of seats towards the centre aisle. There she stood and waited for him.

'Mr Brady,' she said softly.

'Daniel, please.'

She lifted her veil, arranging it across the brim of her hat. 'And you must call me Marion.'

They looked at each other solemnly.

'It doesn't make sense, does it?' she asked. 'I mean, a man like that. So inadequate, so ineffective – not at all the evil scoundrel I had imagined him to be.'

'Me neither,' Daniel replied. 'But maybe he was so drunk that he didn't know what he was doing.'

'Maybe.' She looked towards the dock where the prisoner had stood shaking with fear, and frowned. 'He insisted that he didn't know how my father's wallet and watch came to be in his pockets.'

'Well he would, wouldn't he? And if we accept that he was inebriated, then perhaps he really doesn't remember what he did – how he came by them.'

'But he had no qualms about spending the money, did he?'

She looked into his eyes searchingly, as if she would find an explanation there. Daniel ached to be able to help her but he was confused himself. Throughout the trial he had been overwhelmed by the strangeness of the occasion, but he had attempted to write down everything he thought significant. When he went over his notes he might be able to make more sense of it all.

'We must accept that the wretch was beyond hope,' he said.

Marion gazed into the mid-distance and nodded thoughtfully. 'I suppose so.' She paused and dragged her gaze back from whatever dark image she was imagining, and said, 'I should go now.'

'Must you hurry?'

'No. As long as I am home before my sister gets back from school, my time is my own.'

'Then would you – I mean, we could walk along to Olsen's and have coffee and cakes. That is, if you would like to?'

Daniel saw her eyes widen with surprise and shrank within himself, waiting for the rebuff that would come.

'Thank you,' she said. 'I would like that.'

Olsen's was a café on the quayside that specialised in Norwegian food. Not only was it popular with the Norwegian and Danish sailors, but it had also become somewhere where Scandinavian immigrants heading for the New World via the Tyne could have a last taste of home. It was popular with local people too, and Daniel had been there before on such occasions as his mother's or Susan's birthday. It was his treat to them.

'Have you been there before?' he asked Marion.

'Yes. With my father. He liked the potato dumplings. It would surprise you how many he could eat! Annette and I would have the cardamom cake or the almond bars.'

They walked out on to the steps and halted in the doorway when they saw that it was still raining. Marion began to unfurl her umbrella. Daniel remembered that his umbrella was still under the seat where he had been sitting. 'Wait a moment,' he said, and, feeling foolish, hurried back to collect it.

When he returned, Marion was talking to someone; a well-dressed man. The same man Daniel had glimpsed earlier. His companion had disappeared. The man turned to look when he heard Daniel approaching, then glanced at Marion questioningly. 'This is Daniel Brady,' Marion said. 'Daniel, this is Victor Bateman, my landlord.'

Bateman didn't offer to shake hands, but his smile was pleasant enough when he asked, 'And your interest in the trial, Mr Brady?'

'I was a pupil of Mr Brookfield's,' Daniel said. 'I admired and respected him.'

'A pupil? A trainee reporter?'

Bateman's surprise was obvious. Daniel fought the temptation to hide his large work-roughened hands behind his back.

'No – I mean, I haven't made up my mind what I want to do. I simply wanted to be better educated.'

'Very worthy. I admire your dedication.'

'Dedication?'

'Yes. I imagine that you are a working man and that you must labour long and hard. So to give up your free time – time when many other working men might snatch an hour or two's enjoyment in a public house – is admirable.'

Daniel understood that Victor Bateman was complimenting him, and yet he felt patronised. Throughout this exchange Marion had been silent, and now the three of them stood awkwardly, each wondering what was expected of them. Victor Bateman took the initiative.

'My carriage will be here soon,' he said. 'May I offer to take you home?'

He was looking directly at Marion, and Daniel knew that he was not included in the invitation.

'That's kind of you,' she said, 'but Daniel – Mr Brady and I are going to Olsen's.'

'Along the quayside?' Victor Bateman asked.

'Yes,' she replied.

'But it's pouring,' he said. 'You will be soaked through by the time you get there.'

'We have our umbrellas,' Marion said. 'One each since Mr Brady remembered that he had one too.' She smiled faintly at Daniel, who returned the smile, and for a moment Bateman was excluded.

But then he said, 'Well then, I suppose I should take my leave.'

Daniel sensed the disapproval that the landlord was too polite to give voice to.

At that moment the sun struggled weakly through the clouds, the rain eased off and Victor Bateman's horse-drawn carriage arrived with a clatter of hoofs on the wet cobblestones.

'Remember, Miss Brookfield, if you should need help or advice, I am yours to command.' Stiffly, he took his leave, and Daniel and Marion watched him hurry to his carriage. At a command from the coachman, the gently steaming horses set off again, and as soon as the coach began the steep ascent up Dene Street, Daniel felt the mood lighten.

'Perhaps you should have taken advantage of his offer,' he said, although he knew he would have been devastated if she had.

'He asked me why I had come to the trial,' she said. 'I think he imagined that I would be too – oh, I don't know – too frail to do so.'

'Frail?'

'That's not quite the right word. He thought I would not be strong enough to hear the bald facts about my father's murder. He did not realise that I had to hear them – that terrible though they were, it would have been even worse to go on imagining and not really knowing. Do you understand my feelings?'

'Of course.'

As one, they opened up their umbrellas and began to descend the steps. Then the umbrellas collided and threw them off balance. Daniel took hold of Marion's arm to steady her. When equilibrium was restored, Marion raised her umbrella and said, 'Why don't we share this one? It's large enough to shelter both of us; it was my father's.'

# Chapter Seven

Daniel managed to get to the library before it closed. He returned the umbrella to Miss Bennett and then changed back into his work clothes. Miss Bennett asked how he had got on at the trial. Daniel told her he had taken notes but that it had been an effort to keep up with the proceedings.

'You'll have to learn shorthand,' she said.

Daniel remembered what the elderly reporter had said when he'd looked at Daniel's notebook. *Shorthand, dear boy. You must learn shorthand.* He'd been too embarrassed to tell the man that he didn't know what shorthand was. But now he was able to ask Miss Bennett.

'It's a quick way of taking notes,' she told him. 'A fast method of writing using symbols to represent letters words or phrases. You can go to classes to learn how to do it, but Mr Dickens bought a book and taught himself.'

'Do you think shorthand is essential?' Daniel asked.

'If you want to be a reporter.'

'But I'm not sure about that. You see, I don't think I would be very well paid.'

'Not at first, that's true.'

'I can make more from labouring.'

'Forgive me for asking, and heaven forfend that this sounds arrogant, but is the money so important?'

'If I only had myself to worry about, I would be happy just to make enough to keep body and soul together. But there's my mother and sister; I'm responsible for them. It's true Susan is working now, but she doesn't earn very much.'

'I see.' Miss Bennett looked thoughtful. 'Well, it's something to think about. Meanwhile, are you going to let me see the results of your work today?'

'As soon as I've sorted out the notes and written them up,' Daniel told her.

When Daniel arrived home, his mother greeted him anxiously. 'Such weather,' she said. 'It was raining cats and dogs earlier. I hope they didn't hev you outside getting soaked through.' She looked at him keenly, and her worried expression eased. 'Your clothes are only a little damp – so the foreman found you work to do inside?'

Daniel nodded. 'I wasn't out in the rain.' He felt guilty even though his crime was evasion rather than an outright lie. I'm just like Susan, he startled himself by thinking. I have secrets from my mother. Then he wondered why he was so sure that Susan had a secret. Why he was convinced that something was going on that she did not want her family to know about.

His mother had already placed a bowl of ham and pea soup before Daniel and was cutting generous slices of homemade bread when Susan arrived home. She put her arm around her mother's shoulder when she apologised for being late. Her eyes were shining.

'How lovely to come home to hot soup,' she said. 'Mmm, it smells good!'

But Daniel thought it was more than the soup that had brought the smile to her face. There was a certain heightened exuberance in her manner, and he noticed that she did not look directly into anyone's eyes.

After the meal, Dora came to visit. She sat by the fire with his mother and Susan while he put the notebook Miss Bennett had given him on the table and opened one of his own exercise books. The women kept up a flow of chatter and Daniel had the impression that they were deliberately talking more loudly than usual in order to disturb him. He felt a surge of guilt when he looked up at one stage to see Dora looking at him wistfully, but he lowered his head and concentrated on his notes once more.

To his surprise, he found that once he had started, the flow of words came easily. He wrote up the report in the manner he imagined Henry Brookfield would have adopted, but all the while tried to make sure that he was not simply copying his tutor's style. Henry had told him some time ago that he had a distinct style of his own.

While he was working, Susan yawned, said good night, and went up to bed. Dora stayed.

'Right, lad,' his mother said when the clock on the mantel shelf struck eleven. 'If you're going to get up and do a good day's work tomorrow, it's time you went to bed.'

'I'm not a little bairn, Ma,' he said, but his tone was light hearted.

'You're not so big that you divven't hev to do as your ma tells you.' Hannah was smiling too. 'And just see Dora home, will you? Right to her own back door, mind.'

Daniel put his papers in his dispatch case and closed the lid. He rose from the table and smiled at Dora with as good grace as possible.

'Don't be too long!' his mother said suggestively.

Daniel concealed his irritation. It was natural for his mother to want him to marry and provide her with grandchildren.

As soon as they stepped out into the yard, Dora said, 'You don't have to see me home, you know. It's only a couple of steps away.' She seemed subdued.

Daniel, who had resented this chore being thrust upon him, nevertheless replied, 'Of course I'll see you home. The lane is dark.'

Dora didn't reply, and as soon as they got to the door that led into her yard, she opened it and turned to face him. 'Good night then. No matter what your ma says, you needn't see me to the house.'

She closed the door so quickly that Daniel stepped back in alarm. He could hear her quick footsteps hurrying across the yard.

When he returned, his mother was washing the cups in the sink in the scullery. She looked up in surprise.

'You're back quick,' she said.

'Dora was tired,' he lied. He didn't want to get into any discussion with his mother tonight. 'And so am I. I'm going up. Good night.'

Vexed with himself because he knew he had left his mother surprised and hurt at his curt tone, he went to bed. And then, at last, he was able to give himself up to memories of the day. Not the trial – his weary brain had had enough of that – but thoughts of Marion. He relived the time they had spent together in the café and began to savour the memory.

Olsen's had been full, and they had been lucky to find a table for two at the back of the room near the stove. The stove with its tall iron flue gave off so much heat that they very soon realised why that table had not been taken. Marion slipped off her coat but Daniel could hardly take off his jacket, so he contented himself with surreptitiously opening the buttons of his waistcoat.

The waiters were busy, carrying the trays high over their heads, balanced on one hand. Marion and Daniel had time to look around. The floor was of pale wood, which was scrubbed twice a day. The tablecloths were of snowy white linen. Various aromas mingled in the warm air. Pickled herring in barrels of brine, cardamom cake and strong, rich coffee.

Suddenly Daniel noticed that Marion's face was very pale. She closed her eyes and swayed slightly. He reached across the table and grabbed her upper arms. Startled, she opened her eyes and stared at him.

'Are you all right?' he asked.

'Yes. What happened?'

'You looked as though you were going to pass out.'

She seemed startled. 'Did I?'

Then she became aware of his hands on her arms; she looked down and glanced from side to side. She appeared steady enough, and a little colour had returned to her face, so he withdrew his hands slowly.

'Look,' she said. 'You've knocked over the sugar bowl.'

Daniel stared in dismay at the bowl tipped over on its side and the little mountain of sugar on the tablecloth.

'I can't remember whether that's good luck or bad, spilling sugar,' Marion said. 'I know there's trouble ahead if you spill salt.'

'Well, I don't believe in such things,' Daniel replied, 'except right now there'll be trouble ahead when the waiter sees this mess I've made.'

'Don't worry, he won't see it.' Marion's whole manner had lightened and Daniel looked at her smiling face in surprise.

She righted the bowl, pushed the pile of sugar towards the back of the table and concealed it behind the cruet. They grinned at each other like mischievous children, and suddenly the cares and worries of the day seemed to fade a little.

Then Daniel remembered what had caused him to spill the sugar in the first place. 'Are you ill?' he asked.

'No. I think it's just because I haven't been sleeping well.'

'That's natural in the circumstances. And it looks as though . . .' He trailed off, not wishing to say anything too personal.

'What? Tell me? I shall just worry until you do.'

'You look as though you've lost weight. Have you been eating properly?'

Marion sighed, and she seemed exasperated when she said, 'You sound just like Betty. She's been nagging me to clean my plate.'

'She's quite right, too.' Daniel grinned and was pleased when Marion responded with a smile. 'But now we'd better order something,' he said, 'because that waiter keeps sending looks our way.'

Ignoring Marion's protests, Daniel ordered the potato dumplings she had told him that her father loved, to be followed by her favourite cardamom cake and a large pot of piping hot coffee. He was pleased to see that she cleaned her plate as Betty would have wished, and over the coffee and cake they began to talk about the books they both loved to read.

'Have you finished the novels my father lent you?' she asked.

'I have.'

'Then you must bring them back and choose two more. I know, why don't you come on Sunday? Come after your midday meal and stay for tea. Would you like that?'

'Mmm,' Daniel mumbled. He had just taken a bite of cake, and as his mouth was full he nodded.

'Good,' Marion said. 'I'll look forward to that. But now I really must go. I couldn't bear Annette to come home to an empty house.'

Daniel frowned. 'Betty will be there, won't she?'

'Yes, of course. But I'm Annette's sister. She needs me.'

And you probably need Annette, Daniel thought. Caring for your younger sister has given you a purpose in a life that has suddenly turned topsy-turvy.

'Why are you looking at me like that?' Marion asked.

'Like what?'

'So solemnly.'

'I didn't mean to look solemn. I'm sorry.'

And with that exchange, some of the gaiety of the last hour seemed to fade and drift away. Daniel insisted on taking care of the bill, although Marion wanted to pay her share.

'I won't hear of it,' he said. 'It was my suggestion that we come here.'

The rain had held off and a pale sun glinted on the choppy waters of the river, seeming to break it up into scattered fragments of silver. The quayside was as busy as ever with a mixture of sail and steam vessels lying at anchor. When they reached the cab rank at the bottom of Dene Street, Marion asked Daniel if he wished to share her cab.

'No thank you. I don't have to go up into the city. I can walk along the quayside and then up Byker Bank.'

'Very well. You'll come on Sunday, then?'

Daniel thought she looked nervous. Perhaps she regretted having asked him.

'Yes – if you want me to.' He prepared himself for disappointment.

'Of course I do.'

They looked at each other for a moment, and then she pulled her half-veil down once more and he helped her into a cab. The brief touch of her gloved hands in his set his pulses racing. As he watched the cab go, he experienced a burgeoning sense of exhilaration. She thinks of me as a friend, he thought, she enjoys being in my company.

Daniel had turned and made his way through the busy throng, forcing himself to suppress hopes of anything more than friendship. But despite his determination, he had found himself overwhelmed by the now familiar mix of joy and despair induced by thoughts of Marion Brookfield.

Annette was sitting at the kitchen table when Marion arrived home. She was enjoying tea and a plate of buttered drop scones but she looked up with a pained expression.

'Where were you?' she said.

Marion looked at Betty, who pursed her lips and shook her head. She hadn't told her.

'I've been into town,' Marion said. She didn't want her sister to know that she'd been to the trial of the man who had killed their father. She was worried that it would upset her. 'I – I needed to get out for a while. I'm sorry.'

Annette resumed eating the drop scones. Betty placed some more on the table and poured another cup of tea.

'Take your coat and hat off and sit down,' she told Marion. 'Try to eat a scone or two. It will keep you going until I hev the tea ready.'

Marion did as she was told. 'Isn't this our tea?' she asked Betty.

'No. Like I said, that's just to keep you going. I'm making macaroni cheese, and there's a rice cake I baked this morning.'

Marion felt she couldn't tell Betty about the potato dumplings she had eaten at Olsen's, not when their maid had gone to so much trouble, so she tackled the scones valiantly and managed, to her surprise, to eat two.

'My, that's better,' Betty said. 'Just lately you've hardly eaten enough to keep a sparrow alive. I hope this means your appetite's coming back. Now, if Miss Annette has finished, she can go to the parlour and start her homework while you hev another cup of tea.'

Annette went obediently enough, then Betty poured herself a cup of tea and sat down opposite Marion while they discussed what had happened at the trial.

'So they found him guilty?' Betty said.

'Yes.'

'That's that, then.'

'I suppose so.'

'Never mind suppose so, they found the cold-hearted scoundrel guilty and now they'll hang him. That's justice, isn't it?'

Marion licked one finger and dabbed at the crumbs on her plate absent-mindedly. 'I'm not sure.'

Betty looked outraged. 'I beg your pardon, Miss Marion, but what do you mean, you're not sure? The man murdered your father.'

'That's what I'm not sure about. He didn't look much like a cold-hearted scoundrel; he looked like a pathetic lost soul.'

Betty's features softened into a fond smile. 'Eeh, Miss Marion hinny, you're too tender hearted for your own good. You mustn't be deceived by what folk like that look like. Murderers don't go round with a label pinned to their clothes. Most of them look like ordinary people. Or so Arthur tells me.'

'Oh yes,' Marion smiled, 'your friend Constable Robinson. I saw him at the trial. He looks very smart in his uniform.'

'He does, doesn't he? Although he needs someone to let his cuffs down a bit. He's got such long arms, you know.'

Betty rose from the table and gathered the cups and plates together. 'Now put your mind at rest, pet, and go and sit with your sister until I call you for your tea. Oh, wait a moment, a letter came for you after you'd left. Delivered by hand. Here it is.' She took an envelope from the shelf on the dresser. 'Posh paper, isn't it? I wonder who it's from. The landlord, d'you think?'

'Don't worry, Betty, I'll let you know.'

The two young women smiled at each other and Marion took the letter with her to the front parlour. On the way she collected her father's silver paper knife from his study and glanced briefly at the piles of papers she had only just made a start on sorting out. Not today, she thought, and went to join Annette in the parlour.

The letter was from Lady Cressington inviting her for lunch the next day. She must have taken Marion's acceptance for granted, because she said she would send a carriage at eleven o'clock. Marion remembered how surprised she had been on the day of her father's funeral to discover that he and Lady Cressington had known each other.

But when she thought about it, it wasn't so surprising. Henry Brookfield had been the sort of man who had been equally at home with titled ladies and labouring men. He had been the most unpretentious person Marion had ever known. No, what had surprised her was the fact that apparently Lady Cressington had been assisting him in his work with the homeless.

The following day was Saturday, and when Marion awoke she realised that she could not go to Lady Cressington's for lunch. There was no school on Saturday so Annette would be home, and Marion did not want to leave her on her own.

'What do you mean, on her own?' Betty asked. 'I'm here, aren't I?' Betty was washing up the breakfast dishes and Annette had already gone along to the parlour to set out her drawing materials on the table.

'Of course you are,' Marion said, 'but you know what I mean.'

'No, I don't.' Betty sounded vexed. 'Your sister's not a bairn. She doesn't need you fussing over her the whole time.'

'I don't fuss over her.'

'Yes you do. Oh, I know you feel responsible for her and all that, but you've got to hev a life of your own, you know. Go to Lady Cressington's for lunch and then you can come back and tell us how the other half live.'

At that moment the kitchen door opened and Annette came in. She was round eyed with surprise. 'I heard raised voices,' she said. 'Have you two been quarrelling?'

Neither Betty nor Marion answered her. They just stared at each other and laughed.

Then Betty said, 'No, not quarrelling. I've just been telling your big sister what she ought to do today.'

'Oh, I hope it doesn't involve me,' Annette said.

'Why not?' Marion asked her.

'Because I've asked Miss Cudlip to come and visit after luncheon.'

Both Marion and Betty stared at Annette in surprise. Marion was puzzled. Why would her sister want to spend time with the old lady who lived next door, nice as she was?

It was left to Betty to ask, 'Why hev you done that?'

'I want her to pose for me.'

Marion was dumbfounded, and again it was left to Betty to say, 'You want Miss Cudlip to pose for you? But she's as wrinkled as a prune.'

'It's *because* she's wrinkled that I want her to pose for me,' Annette said. 'It will be a challenge. I want – oh, I don't know how to say this – I want to draw her with all her wrinkles without making a caricature of her. I want to be able to show the living, breathing person that she is. Do you know what I mean?'

Marion was astounded. Her sister, so immature in many ways, was like a different person when the artist in her took over. 'Yes, I know what you mean, Annette. And to answer your question, no, my plans for today don't involve you.'

Annette was already losing interest, but she asked, out of politeness it seemed to Marion, 'So, what are you going to do?'

'Lady Cressington has invited me for luncheon.'

'Has she?' Annette's expression became animated once more. 'Now there's another interesting face. She must be quite old – oh, at least forty – and yet she is still beautiful. There's something about her – something that draws you in. I would love to try and capture what it is that makes her so attractive.'

Marion considered Annette's appraisal of Lady Cressington and realised that her sister was quite right. Lady Cressington was conventionally beautiful, but she also had a seductive charm that she seemed to exercise quite naturally; there was no artifice there.

The Cressington house was just a little way north of Gosforth and stood in large, beautifully kept grounds. When Marion arrived, the young maidservant who answered the door bobbed a curtsy and said, 'You're to come to the drawing room, Miss Brookfield.'

No one had ever curtsied to Marion before, and she was still feeling bemused when the girl opened the door and stood back to allow her to precede her into the most lavishly appointed room Marion had ever seen. The maid shut the door and left her there.

Marion walked a little further into the room and then stopped and gazed round in wonder.

The ceiling was high and the mouldings were elaborately carved and painted in a lighter shade of green than the wallpaper, which was covered in vines and exotic birds. The dark green brocade curtains were held back with tasselled gold-coloured ropes, and scalloped valances adorned the tops. The green and gold carpet had an oriental design and the room was filled with cretonne-covered sofas, chairs and footstools, but Marion could not imagine finding anywhere to sit where she would feel truly at ease.

She wandered over to the fireplace, where a comforting fire burned in the hearth. The only sounds were the ticking of a large ormolu mantel clock and the crackling of the coals. Marion stared down into the flames, seeking pictures in the fire as she had done as a child, but no images presented themselves to her. Lost in contemplation, she did not hear the door open, so when Lady Cressington spoke her name, she almost jumped in fright.

'I'm so sorry, my dear, did I startle you?'

'Just a little.'

'You seemed so far away – in a brown study, as my dear late husband would have said. I think that means lost in thought, doesn't it?'

Marion smiled and nodded. It was only then that she realised that Lady Cressington spoke English with the faintest of foreign accents.

'But come,' her hostess continued. 'Shall we go to my little morning room? It is much more intimate – more cosy, I think you would say. No – there's no need to go back into the hall. See, there is a door over here.'

Marion followed Lady Cressington through a door she had not noticed in the corner of the room. A door curtain with an oriental design hung there but the door itself was open, and Marion realised that Lady Cressington had entered the drawing room this way.

The decor of the morning room was in complete contrast to the room they had just left. The ceiling was just as high but the mouldings were cool white and the pattern on the cream wallpaper consisted of a subtle tracery of small pale pink flowers. The same flowers – were they hedge roses? – formed the pattern on a rich cream carpet, and the furniture was light and feminine; it looked how Marion imagined French furniture would look.

Lady Cressington indicated that Marion should sit in one of the fireside chairs, then she sat down opposite her. 'That's better,' she said. 'It is more friendly in here.'

Marion wondered why she had not been shown into this room in the first place. Her puzzlement must have shown.

Lady Cressington said, 'I told the maid to show you into the drawing room because my previous visitor was still here. She is one of the poor unfortunates whom I'm trying to help. She's gone now,' she added unnecessarily. 'I sent her to the kitchen to be given a good meal.'

With a delicate hand she indicated another door, which Marion thought must open into the hall.

'In a moment we will go to the dining room,' Lady Cressington said, 'but I thought we should have a little talk before we do.'

'Talk?' Marion said.

'Please don't look so anxious, my dear. I only wish to know how you are coping. It is quite a responsibility for you, at your age, to have to look after your sister and sort out your father's affairs.'

'I'm happy to look after Annette,' Marion said, 'but I'm not sure what you mean by my father's affairs.'

'Oh – mundane things like going through his papers, deciding what to do with them. I could come along and help you, if you wish.'

Marion tried to hide her surprise. 'Oh no, I couldn't trouble you to do that. And I've made a start.' She thought guiltily of the mass of papers on her father's desk and how she had only just started trying to separate them into relevant piles. Despite the sad memories she smiled. 'My father was very untidy, you know.'

'But he had a tidy mind, didn't he? I mean, he couldn't have written the way he did if he had not planned his work carefully. And no doubt he made notes for all his projects. Or did he hold everything in his memory?'

'He had an excellent memory,' Marion told her, 'but I'm sure he would make notes as well. Despite appearances, he was methodical.'

'But you haven't found anything important yet?'

'No – well, I mean, to my father all his work was important.'

'Yes, of course.'

'But I haven't found anything to do with his work on the homeless and the slum-dwellers. Is that what you mean?'

'Yes. That is a project dear to my heart.'

112

Lady Cressington looked at her searchingly and Marion felt disconcerted. Then her hostess smiled. 'But that is enough talk of serious matters. Now we will go through for luncheon.'

On the way home in the carriage, Marion tried to make up her mind about Lady Cressington. She had been warm and welcoming and had assured Marion of her friendship. But despite her apparently open manner, there was something about her. Something secretive. Marion smiled to herself as she recalled one of her favourite books, *Lady Audley's Secret*. Did Lady Cressington also have a past life that she did not want to reveal?

Marion remembered the way Lady Cressington had turned the conversation to more cheerful matters, matters as varied as her favourite hot-house plants and her trips to London in order to go to the theatre – on her last visit she had seen *The Mikado*, an opera by Gilbert and Sullivan.

'My dear, I think it is their best collaboration yet!' she had exclaimed.

After a luncheon of mutton cutlets followed by cherry pudding, they had retired to the morning room again to take coffee and ratafia biscuits.

'So much nicer than amoretti, don't you think?'

Marion rather liked the Italian biscuits but she didn't want to disagree with her hostess, so she had simply smiled and nodded.

Then, hardly pausing in her conversation, Lady Cressington had risen and gone over to the fireplace, where she had pulled the bell cord to summon a servant.

'I mustn't keep you from your sister any longer,' she had said. And although she had continued to smile graciously, Marion could not help feeling that she had been dismissed.

When the carriage drew up outside her door, the coachman dismounted and helped her down. He was very smart with his shiny boots, gold buttons and top hat, and Marion could see more than one curtain twitching as, with a crack of the whip, the carriage drove away again.

She was glad to be home. Once enfolded in dear familiar surroundings she began to relax. For pleasant as her luncheon with Lady Cressington had been, she had somehow felt as though she ought to be on her guard. She had no idea why. She removed her coat and hat and Betty placed them on the hallstand. Marion was about to enter the front parlour when Betty smiled and said, 'Miss Cudlip is still here. She complained that sitting still has made her weary, so I'm going to make her a cup of tea.'

The scene in the parlour was peaceful. Annette was concentrating on the drawing on her table easel and her model was dozing by the fire. Annette looked up and smiled, then placed a finger to her lips.

'Hush,' she whispered. 'Miss Cudlip is taking a nap. It seems holding a pose is very tiring.'

Marion walked quietly over to the table and gazed with admiration at her sister's work. Annette had caught the spirit of the old lady perfectly and had even managed to find traces of the beautiful girl she must have once been.

'It's marvellous!' Marion said, forgetting to whisper.

'She won't let me see it.'

Marion and Annette looked up, startled, to see Miss Cudlip glaring at them.

Annette suppressed a giggle and said, 'You can see it when it's finished, Miss Cudlip. I don't want you to be disappointed.'

'Am I likely to be?'

'Definitely not,' Marion assured her.

'Do I have to pose any longer?'

'No, that's all right. I just want to – well, tidy it up a little,' Annette said.

'And then can I see it?'

'Not today. I'll come to your house and show you when I'm satisfied with it. I promise you.'

'Humph,' Miss Cudlip said. 'Where's Betty with that cup of tea I was promised?'

'Here I am,' Betty said as she entered the room carrying a tray. 'Now, where shall I put this?'

Marion helped Annette make room on the table for the tray and asked Betty to bring through a cup and saucer for herself.

'Now tell us all about your visit to the grand lady,' Miss Cudlip said when they were all settled with tea and biscuits.

After describing the house and the furnishings, Marion tried to describe the lady herself. 'It's hard to say how old she is,' she began. 'Maybe in her forties. But she's elegant and still beautiful. She has light brown hair and the most amazingly expressive eyes. She is charming, good company and I think very clever.'

'She's clever all right,' Miss Cudlip said, and they all looked at her in surprise.

'Do you know her?' Marion asked.

'I know of her.' Miss Cudlip nodded but didn't say any more.

'What do you know about her?' Annette asked.

The old lady's eyes sparkled. 'Your new friend was the talk of the town once upon a time. Everyone wanted to know what on earth the old man was thinking of.'

'Which old man?'

Miss Cudlip pursed her lips and nodded wisely again.

'Oh, don't be so mysterious!' Annette said, and Marion sent her a warning look. It was obvious that the old lady was enjoying herself and would take her time drawing the story out.

Miss Cudlip sipped her tea, asked Betty to refill her cup and then continued. 'Well, maybe she set a trap for him, the clever little minx. But she made him a good wife. She took care of him and proved them all wrong, give her her due.'

'You mean Lord Cressington?' Marion said.

'Of course I do. He was old enough to be her father – her grandfather. He'd been a hero in his time. Led some charge or other at the Battle of Waterloo.'

'Waterloo!' Annette exclaimed. 'But that was centuries ago!'

Miss Cudlip looked at Annette over the rim of the cup. 'It may seem so to you, miss, but it was the year I was born and I'm only seventy, if I remember aright.'

'I'm sorry,' Annette said, and Marion could see that her sister was dangerously close to laughing.

'Well, anyway,' Miss Cudlip said, only slightly mollified, 'old John Cressington was a hero. After Waterloo he had a distinguished career in the army – that's how they put it in the newspaper when he died. But he'd never married. After leaving the army he travelled a lot. And that's when he found her.'

'Found Lady Cressington?' Marion prompted.

'Yes, that's who I mean. There was he, an old man in his seventies, and there was she, a slip of a girl in her twenties. Her father was some sort of diplomat – that's what it said in the newspaper. But her folks had died and she was all alone in the world, so Lord Cressington married her and brought her back to England. Everyone said he'd regret it. But they were wrong. He didn't last long after that, but from all accounts the lass made him very happy, and as far as I know, she's been faithful to his memory.'

'What do you mean?' Betty asked.

'Well, she's never married again, has she? And there's never been a breath of scandal about her. At least not in the newspapers that I read. In fact, you hardly see anything about her these days. Not like when she first arrived here and there were reports of how she was refurbishing the old man's house from top to bottom and buying the best of everything. It's said he gave her complete control of his bank account.'

Miss Cudlip handed Betty her cup and saucer and rose shakily to her feet. 'Now, miss,' she said to Annette, 'I've obliged you by posing for you this afternoon, so now you can oblige me by giving me your arm and seeing me safely home.'

After Annette and Miss Cudlip had left the room, Betty surprised Marion by asking her to follow her to the kitchen.

'Look at this,' she said, and her expression was grave as she handed Marion the newspaper. 'I kept it from your sister, although she never bothers to read the paper anyway.'

'What is it?' Marion asked. 'What do you want me to look at?'

'You'd better sit down, pet. That's right. Now open it up – another page – that's right. Now read it.'

Marion did so. The words seemed to blur. She closed her eyes and handed the newspaper back to Betty. 'Burn it,' she said. 'I don't want to think about this ever again.'

She had just learned that the man who had murdered her father had gone to the gallows that morning.

# Chapter Eight

Hannah was surprised when a young man she didn't know called that night and asked Daniel to come 'for a gill'. But she could hardly object to her son, a grown man, going for a drink with a pal just like any other man. She asked the caller in to wait by the fire while Daniel finished his meal.

Daniel looked up and smiled, then caught sight of his mother's questioning look. 'This is Arthur, Ma,' he said.

'Good evening, Mrs Brady,' the young fellow said, and he shook hands with her just like a gentleman.

She asked him to sit down by the range and then took the chair opposite him. She frowned as she contemplated his big feet planted firmly on the new hooky mat that she'd only just taken out of the frame and laid before the hearth.

'Don't I know you from somewhere?' she asked.

'You'll hev seen me about,' he said.

Daniel finished his meal and carried the plate through to the scullery, where he proceeded to have a wash at the sink.

Hannah stared a little longer at the visitor's long legs and his large hands holding his cap on his bony knees, and then she smiled.

'Oh aye. I didn't recognise you out of uniform. You're that lofty young copper from the police station in Headlam Street, aren't you?'

'That's me.'

Hannah waited until Daniel went upstairs to change into a clean shirt and his good trousers and jacket before she asked: 'And hev you known my son for long?'

'Well, we went to the same school but we never really got to know each other until recently.'

'But now you're pals.'

'Aye, I suppose we are.'

117

Hannah was eaten with curiosity, but it was obvious that Arthur was not going to say any more, so she gave in with good grace. That didn't mean that she wouldn't be quizzing Daniel about his new pal later.

She sighed. Susan had told her she would be going to Maisie's house after work again – it seemed those two were getting really pally – so if Daniel was going to go out she would have to sit here on her own. Maybe Dora would drop in, she thought, but Dora had been a little bit moody lately and Hannah didn't blame her. The lass had her pride.

Daniel came down looking as smart as a new pin. Arthur got up, ready to go. Daniel looked down at his mother and asked, 'How is Susan getting home tonight?'

'Divven't fret,' Hannah said. 'Maisie's brother is going to see her to the door.'

'Brother? She's never mentioned a brother before.'

'Well, why should she?'

Daniel frowned. 'We don't know much about Maisie's family, do we? We don't even know where she lives.'

'No, I don't suppose we do.' His mother looked uneasy, then brightened a little. 'But we know where she works, divven't we? If you want to see what the girl's like, you could always pop in the shop for a chat, couldn't you?'

'Yes, Ma, I could, and maybe I will.'

Hannah looked anxious again. 'Susan won't like that,' she said.

'Probably not. But if she's going to make a habit of this, that's what I'm going to do.' He leaned down and gave his mother a hug. 'I won't be too long. We'll have a bite of supper together.'

Hannah dragged up a smile. 'Off you go. You work hard and it's nice to see you going out for a drink like a proper man instead of sitting over those dratted books.'

The wind was blowing up from the river and Daniel and Arthur hurried to the Raby on the corner of Shields Road. When they had been served at the bar, they found a small table by the fire and sat there with their beer. Arthur had insisted on paying for it because it had been his idea that they should go out for a drink.

Daniel took a sip from his glass before asking, 'So what is it? Why did you come for me?'

Arthur grinned. 'I fancied a drink, like I said.'

Daniel studied the policeman's face and thought the smile strained. 'It's more than that, isn't it?'

Arthur's smile faded. 'I had to talk to you.'

'So what couldn't you talk about in front of my mother?'

'You've read today's paper?'

Daniel knew what Arthur was referring to. 'I have. They hanged him this morning.'

'Aye.' The young policeman swallowed a mouthful of beer, replaced his tankard on the table and shook his head.

'Were you there? Is that it?'

'Aye, God help me. I've never been to a hanging and Sergeant Wilson thought I should go.'

'I'm sorry. Sorry for you, I mean. It's not something I should like to witness.'

'I hope you never have to.'

'Was it bad?'

'Very bad.' Arthur paused. 'The man was crying.'

Daniel remained silent. There was nothing he could say.

'He kept asking why nobody would believe him. He swore he had never harmed another human being in his life. When it got through to his muddled brain that his end had come, he began to shake with terror. He . . .' Arthur paused and looked down at his beer. 'The poor wretch wet himself.'

No matter that they were sitting by the fire, Daniel felt chilled to the bone. He could imagine all too vividly the scene Arthur was describing. Arthur remained silent for so long that Daniel looked at him keenly. He saw the anguish in the policeman's face and could only guess at the torment he was suffering.

Arthur sensed that he was being observed, and he seemed to make an effort to pull himself back from the brink of some dark abyss. 'I'm sorry,' he said. 'I'm sorry to tell you all this, but I had to talk to someone.'

'Of course.'

'He struggled and fought for his poor wretched life until the end. His last words before they put the hood over his head were, "I'm innocent."' Arthur paused again and stared into the fire without seeing it. Then he looked at Daniel with a mixture of terror and anguish. 'That's why I had to tell you,' he said. 'You see, I believe we've hanged the wrong man.'

★

'I can stay a bit longer, if you'd like me too.'

Betty had just finished scrubbing the kitchen table and was drying her hands on the roller towel that hung on the back of the scullery door.

'No, that's all right. Sunday is your half-day. You must go home and spend time with your mother.'

Betty came and sat with Marion. It was just the two of them. Annette had retired to the front parlour to get on with her drawing. The room was still filled with the lingering aroma of roast beef. The fire glowed in the hearth, sending dancing shadows on to the ceiling. The clock on the mantel shelf ticked the hours away, and although it was only one o'clock, the sky outside was darkening.

'You should get home before it starts to rain,' Marion said.

Betty glanced out of the window. 'Do you think those are rain clouds?'

'Mmm.' Marion nodded.

'Well, I'm not so sure. I think mebbe it's just one of those days when the sun never manages to shine. And even if it does rain, I've got me brolly and me galoshes.'

'No, really, you should go.'

'But . . .' Betty hesitated. She looked embarrassed.

'What is it?'

'Well I don't know if it's proper.'

'Proper? What do you mean?'

'To leave you in the house on your own with Mr Brady calling.'

'I won't be on my own. Annette will be here.'

'But she's just a little lass.'

'She's only two years younger than I am, as you keep reminding me!'

Betty had the grace to look abashed. 'You know what I mean. Just two young lasses in the house. You'll get a reputation.'

Marion stared at Betty helplessly. She was right, she supposed. Here I am, she thought, in charge of this little household, and yet I'm not considered old enough to have a gentleman friend for tea unless there is an older woman in the house.

'Tell me,' she said to Betty, 'would your mother leave you alone in the house with Arthur?'

'Not on your life!' Betty grinned. 'Not until the date is set at the very least.'

'Has it come to that, Betty? Already?'

Betty looked down into her cup, and even though it was hard to tell in the firelight, Marion could have sworn that she was blushing.

'Perhaps it has.' She looked up and laughed. 'Although he hasn't exactly said anything yet.'

'Then how do you know that he will?'

'I just do. I can tell he's interested in me just like I can tell Mr Brady is interested in you.'

Marion stared at her.

'There now,' Betty said. 'That's shut you up, hasn't it? And by the look on your face, I'm pretty sure the same thing has occurred to you, and that's why I'm going to stay here today.'


If only Betty hadn't said that, Marion thought later. For now, instead of enjoying the talk about books that she had been so looking forward to, she sat uneasily at one side of the hearth in the study and Daniel at the other, desperately trying to think of something sensible to say.

He was looking at her questioningly, obviously waiting for her to start the discussion.

'Erm . . . which of the books did you like best?' she asked at last and mentally cursed herself for the inanity.

Fortunately Daniel didn't seem to consider the question too asinine, because he smiled and said, 'Is that a trap?'

'A trap? What do you mean?'

'Well, although the books are both fiction, they are quite different. One is a comic fantasy with a moral and the other is a detective story – a lesson in logic. You can't really compare them – unless you are simply asking me which type of book I like best and then I would have to say I haven't found a type I don't like. At least not yet.'

Daniel was leaning forward in his chair. His eyes were shining. It was as if he had been waiting all his life to be able to talk like this to someone, and Marion was touched. She began to relax.

They talked for a while about books they had read and books they would like to read, and they hardly noticed the time ticking away until there was a knock at the door. It opened before Marion had time to call out, and Betty entered the room.

'Would you like a bite to eat before Mr Brady goes home?' she asked. 'I've made some sandwiches.'

'Oh . . .' Marion pulled her attention back to everyday matters with an effort. 'Oh, yes please, Betty. Would you bring a tray?'

'It's nice and warm in the kitchen.'

'It's just as warm in here,' Marion replied, and she fixed Betty with a determined stare.

'Right-oh,' Betty said, accepting defeat, and left the room, leaving the door open behind her.

Daniel had risen to his feet. He looked flustered. 'Have I outstayed my welcome?' he asked.

'No, of course not. Please sit down again.'

'But your maid . . .'

Marion laughed. 'Betty – well, she likes to look after me.'

'And she obviously thinks I've stayed too long.'

'Whatever Betty thinks, I can assure you that you haven't. I've enjoyed this talk of ours immensely and I'm sorry we were interrupted.'

As she spoke, Betty returned with a small table and placed it on the hearthrug between them. 'There you are,' she said. 'That's better than balancing everything on your knee.' She left the room again and returned very quickly with the tray. Then she hovered for a moment and said, 'Do you want me to pour the tea?'

'No thank you,' Marion said. 'I can manage.'

'Well, I suppose I'd better go and keep Miss Annette company,' Betty said. 'We don't want her sitting all alone, do we?'

'That's thoughtful of you,' Marion said, and struggled to conceal her amused irritation.

When they were alone, Daniel asked, 'What was all that about?'

'About?'

'It's obvious that Betty doesn't like me and wants me to go.'

'Oh no, it's not because she doesn't like you. Please don't think that. It's just that she probably thinks we have been alone together for too long.' Marion felt herself flushing. 'You see, she . . . erm . . .' Embarrassment nearly overcame her but she stumbled on. 'She has appointed herself my chaperone.'

'Chaperone?' Daniel looked astounded. 'Do you mean she doesn't think we should be left alone together?'

'It seems that way.'

'What does she think I would do?'

Marion stared at him in consternation. She could feel her cheeks burning. She leaned forward and concentrated on pouring the tea. Neither of them spoke. The easy atmosphere that existed between them when they were discussing books had vanished. Conversation after that was stilted, and when Daniel had eaten the sandwiches pressed on him by Marion and, at her insistence, finished a second cup of tea, he told her that he had better go home.

'Of course,' she said tersely. She was furious with Betty for introducing this awkwardness between Daniel and herself. 'But don't you want to choose another book or two?'

'Yes, if that's all right with you.'

'I wouldn't ask if it wasn't,' she said and immediately regretted her snappy tone.

Daniel's grey eyes widened with hurt. The bookcases were set in the alcoves at each side of the fireplace. He walked over to one of them. Marion watched as he scanned the books, running his fingers lovingly over the spines. His hands were large, the hands of a man who laboured for his living, but his touch was gentle. Marion shivered and wondered why she felt so disturbed.

'I thought so,' he said as he pulled out a book. 'I thought I saw this here when your father asked me to choose a book.'

'What is it?'

'Another novel, I'm afraid.'

'You don't have to apologise for wanting to read a novel.'

'It's by Thackeray – your father said it was a satire, using wit and humour to criticise society.'

'*Vanity Fair*,' Marion said.

'That's right.'

'You'll enjoy it. And when you've finished reading it, you'll have to tell me what you think of Becky Sharp?'

'Becky Sharp?'

'She's a character in the book. The most interesting in my opinion.'

Marion was moved by Daniel's eagerness to read and learn. The mood had lightened once more and she smiled at him. 'You may need more than a week to read *Vanity Fair*. Would you like to come again in two weeks' time?'

'Yes. And thank you.'

'Why do you thank me?'

'For this.' Daniel looked around the room as if he was savouring every detail of it. 'For allowing me to spend time here.' He paused and looked at her intently. 'And with you.'

Marion returned his gaze for a moment and then looked at a point over his shoulder. 'I'm glad you came,' she said. 'But now . . .'

'I know. I must go.'

Marion did not ring for Betty. She saw Daniel to the door herself. The day had faded to dusk. The air was cold and frost sparkled on the pavement. They said goodbye awkwardly and Daniel turned to walk away. Marion stood in the doorway and watched until his wide-shouldered figure merged into the darkness at the end of the street.

After she had closed the door, another figure emerged from the shadows on the other side of the street. It was Dora Gibb. Daniel had told his mother that he was going to return some books that Mr Brookfield had loaned him and that Miss Marion Brookfield, the elder of the two girls, had kindly asked him to have tea with them.

'What on earth for?' Hannah asked him, and he told her that Miss Brookfield had offered to lend him any of her father's books that he would like and that they were going to talk about them.

As Mr Brookfield had been teaching Daniel, Dora supposed that could be true. But all the same she decided to find out what she could about Marion Brookfield. And the first thing she needed to know was where she lived. Straight after she had helped her mother clear up and wash the dishes from the midday meal, she put on her hat and coat and waited by the front parlour window until she saw Daniel go past, dressed in his Sunday best. Then she slipped out of the house and, keeping as much distance as she could, she followed him.

When they reached the smarter suburbs, there were fewer people about and reluctantly she had to let the distance between them lengthen. When she saw him stop and push open a gate, she backed away. From the corner of the street she saw him walk up the garden path, knock on the door of the house and a moment later enter.

She knew where the Brookfields lived now, but she wasn't sure what she was going to do with that knowledge. Neither did she know what she should do next. Seething with resentment that Daniel should choose to spend his Sunday afternoon this way, and in a haze of indecision, she waited on the corner, attracting curious glances from one or two passers-by, and growing colder and colder.

When the shadows stretched across the pavement, she nerved herself to move closer. She looked at the house enviously. No wonder Daniel liked to come here. The Brookfields' house was part of a neat terrace with small, tidy gardens, and although it wasn't as big as some of the nearby villas, it was obviously well kept. It was a clean, comfortable haven for people who lived what she imagined must be worry-free lives. They weren't the sort of folk who should be inviting a working man like Daniel Brady to visit them.

She was standing in the shadow of the tall hedge of the house opposite when the lamplighter came up the street and folk inside the houses began to light their own lamps and draw their curtains. A lamp was lit inside the house she was watching and a woman came to the window. The lace hanging there made it difficult for her to make out anything more than that the woman was wearing a black dress and a white cap and pinafore. So she must be a servant. Daniel had told his mother that there was an older woman looking after the Brookfield girls. Dora wondered what this woman thought about Daniel coming to call.

Once the curtains were drawn, she knew she ought to go. There was nothing more to see. But she found she couldn't tear herself away. She had to know how long Daniel would stay with Miss Marion Brookfield, and all the time she waited, her emotions were seething with a mixture of longing and jealousy, for she could not believe that any proper man would visit an eighteen-year-old girl simply to talk about books.

At last her vigil was rewarded. The door opened, Daniel emerged and the figure of a woman stood in the lighted doorway. She wore a black dress, but this was not the woman Dora had seen at the window. She was taller and more slender. There was no cap on her shining chestnut hair and her voice, when she said good night to Daniel, was not the voice of a servant.

Miss Brookfield seemed as reluctant to close the door as Daniel was to leave her. Dora thought that he dragged himself away unwillingly, and Marion Brookfield stood in the lighted doorway watching him walk down the darkened street until surely she could see him no more. Choking with rage and jealousy, Dora remained where she was until the door closed.

She had no clear idea what she was going to do. Daniel would be appalled and angry if he learned that he had been followed – been spied on, for that was how he would view it. And Dora didn't know if she could even tell Hannah about this, for she still had some pride and she did not want anyone to know how desperate she had become.

With these thoughts tormenting her, she set off to follow Daniel. But very soon, to her dismay, she realised that she had lost track of him. She looked around her at the unfamiliar streets and experienced a moment of panic. Then she began to run. As she turned corners and crossed roads, she had no idea whether she was going in the right direction, and when she saw the stone columns and lintel of the lighted porch of a grand house that she was sure she had passed before, she began to cry.

She was shaking as she stopped to wipe her eyes, and then, to her relief, she heard the rattle of a tram and realised that she must be near Osborne Road. She followed the sound of the horses' hoofs and the rattle of the wheels, and cold and miserable she continued on her way. By the time she reached home, a passionate hatred for Marion Brookfield had entered her soul.

Daniel had no idea that he had been followed. As he walked home, he had much to think about. In his mind he went over and over the events of the afternoon. He had enjoyed being with Marion in the friendly yet scholarly atmosphere of her father's study. Henry Brookfield had been a remarkable man, and Daniel would always remember and revere him for the way he had encouraged him and given him confidence.

He had been elated when Marion had invited him to become her reading companion, and he thought she had been looking forward to his visit as much as he had. But now he was not so sure. There had been an awkwardness between them. There were moments when she had appeared to be regretting the invitation, and then the next minute she gave the impression that she was thoroughly enjoying their discussion. Daniel had never known anyone to blow hot and cold like that, and he searched his mind for what he might have done to cause such behaviour.

But by the time he got home he knew that no matter what happened next time he called, he would persevere, and not just because of his love of learning. All the books in the world were not as precious as time spent with Marion Brookfield.

A few days later Betty answered the door to find Mr Bateman standing there. Her stomach lurched. In the world she lived in, a landlord calling was not usually a good thing. But his tone of voice was friendly when he asked, 'Is Miss Brookfield at home?'

'Aye, I mean yes, sir.'

'Well, may I see her?' His smile was amused but charming.

'Oh – of course – sorry. Do come in.'

Betty felt awkward. She had kept the man standing at the door a little longer than was polite. She stood back to let him enter the hall, closed the door after him and then said, 'Miss Brookfield is working in her father's study. If you'd like to step into the front parlour I'll go and tell her you're here.'

'Why don't you just show me to the study?'

'Well, I would, but it's an awful mess.'

Victor Bateman raised his eyebrows and Betty realised that he might think she was a slovenly housemaid, so she added quickly, 'With all the papers, you see. Miss Brookfield is trying to tidy up and make sense of her father's papers.'

'I understand, and I don't mind one little bit.'

'But—'

Before Betty could protest further, Victor Bateman walked past her and halted outside the study door.

'I presume this will be the study?'

Without waiting for an answer, he knocked and entered. Marion was kneeling on the floor surrounded by sheets of foolscap covered with small, neat writing. It looked as though she had been attempting to classify them. She looked up and her eyes widened in surprise.

'Mr Bateman. Betty shouldn't have shown you in here.'

She rose gracefully, still clutching a sheet of paper that looked different from the rest. To Victor's practised eye it appeared to be an invoice.

'Don't blame your maid,' he said. 'She quite properly wanted me to wait in the front parlour. I think I have upset her sense of the order of things.'

He smiled like someone who knew they had transgressed but sought forgiveness.

'But why did you?' Marion asked. 'I mean, why did you come to the study?'

'I didn't want to disturb you.'

'But you have.'

Taken aback by her forthright manner, Victor glanced at her sharply to see if this was a reproof, but decided Marion was simply being logical – and artless. 'I'm sorry,' he said contritely. 'I didn't mean to interrupt your work, but I have been concerned about you.'

'That's kind of you, but there is no need to be.'

'I think there is. I wanted to talk to you after the trial but you were intent on hurrying off somewhere with Mr Brady.'

'Yes,' and he thought that her voice had softened. 'We went to Olsen's.'

'You are friends?'

'I suppose so.' She looked as though she was considering the matter.

'Miss Brookfield,' he said, 'may we sit down?'

'I'm so sorry. I should have asked you. What on earth was I thinking of ?'

Marion looked round the paper-strewn room and then indicated one of the fireside chairs. It too was covered with papers, and she hurried forward to gather them up. As she did so, the piece of paper she had been holding slipped unnoticed on to the hearthrug.

Victor waited until she had placed the papers on the floor, carefully keeping them apart from the other piles, then cleared the chair at the other side of the fireplace, again placing the papers in a separate pile, and sat down herself before he took his seat. Marion looked flustered and his expression was full of concern.

'Is the job proving too difficult?' he asked.

'No, it's just time consuming. If my father had a filing system, I've yet to break the code.'

She looked around the room at the avalanche of paper and smiled. Victor caught his breath. Usually Marion Brookfield placed a barrier of reserve between herself and the world at large. He had sensed it was a defensive measure. But at moments like this, when she let her guard down, she was ravishingly beautiful. No wonder that good-looking young labourer was so obviously besotted with her. But she deserved a much better man than that.

'So have you devised a system for all – for all this?' he asked, and he gestured with a wide sweep of his arm.

'Yes.' She looked round eagerly. 'There are copies of articles and reports that have already been in the newspaper; I've decided to file them not just by their date but also by subject. Then there are articles that he had written but was not quite satisfied with; I'll file them the same way. There are letters, mostly business, and the notes and lesson plans he made for his pupils . . .'

'Ah yes,' Victor said. 'Pupils such as Mr Brady.'

'That's right.' Suddenly she couldn't meet his eye.

'And what other papers?' Victor prompted.

'Other papers?'

'Well . . . you know . . . his research. I'm assuming that he did extensive research before he embarked on his more serious projects.'

'Yes, he did,' Marion said. 'And that's a puzzle. The work must be here somewhere. Probably in there.' She nodded towards a rolltop desk against the wall. 'I haven't looked in there yet.'

'Why not?'

'Because I can't find the key.'

'You don't know where he kept it?'

'I don't. Although I suppose it could have been in the fob pocket of the jacket he was wearing. It was quite small. It could have been missed. And if it was . . .' Her expression was bleak.

'If it was?'

'It has been buried with him.' Marion fell silent as she stared into the fire.

After a decent pause Victor said, 'Let's hope not. But if you can't find it, you must allow me to recommend a reliable locksmith.'

'That's kind of you,' she said, 'but I'm not quite sure why you want to help me like this.'

'Because I admired your father. He had become what some call a crusading journalist. He exposed the wrongs in our society and he hoped that by telling the truth he could put things right. If you can find anything to do with his most recent investigations into the living conditions of the poor, then maybe someone else could continue this important work.'

Marion looked thoughtful. She remembered that on the day of her father's funeral Mr Earnshaw, the editor of the newspaper, had told her that if she could find any papers to do with her father's investigations – notes, half-written articles, lists of names – then he would try to find someone to take over where he had left off.

'That's what Mr Earnshaw wishes,' she said.

'Ah, yes, the editor. And do you trust him?'

'Trust him?' Marion looked at Victor Bateman in surprise. 'Why should I not trust him?

'I mean, will he find anyone good enough to assume your father's mantle?'

'I don't know.' She looked perplexed.

'Well, think about it. I have many contacts. I could get in touch with first-rate men. Men who work in London on the national newspapers. I could find someone worthy of the task. If you wish it, that is.'

Marion frowned, She had begun to looked tired and strained, and Victor realised that he had pushed her too far.

'But I shouldn't be wearying you with such matters now,' he said. 'I came to offer help, and I fear that I have just added to your burden.'

'No . . . it's all right. I'm pleased that you think so highly of my father's work.'

'Speaking of which, you dropped this paper before.'

He leaned down and retrieved the paper that had fallen and settled under the chair he was sitting on. He handed it to Marion, but not before he had taken a good look at it.

'It seems to be a bill of some kind.'

'Yes.' Marion took it from him. 'It's just one of those my father dealt with regularly, in this case for the coal. He never kept anyone waiting,' she said defensively. 'It's just that now I must find where on earth he put them.'

Her expression softened into a rueful smile.

'Miss Brookfield, I admire you, I can't say how much,' Victor said as he rose from his chair. 'And I have taken up enough of your time. I should go.'

'Oh, no!' she said.

'What's the matter? Is there something wrong?'

'I should have offered you tea,' Marion said. 'My manners are appalling.'

'Please don't worry. If we're talking about manners, then I should not have called uninvited.'

Marion rang for Betty to show her visitor out and then sank down on to the hearthrug and knelt among the papers she had scattered there.

'What did he want?' Betty reappeared in the doorway.

'I'm not sure.'

'Didn't he tell you?'

'Not in so many words . . . I mean, he said he came out of concern.'

'Kind of him.'

'He said he admired my father.'

'Many people did.'

'And he asked if I had discovered any papers – important papers to do with my father's work.'

'Yes, well I suppose that's as good an excuse as any.'

'What on earth do you mean?'

'Miss Marion, sometimes I despair of you. You really shouldn't be let out on your own. Mr Bateman is interested in you, just like Daniel Brady is interested in you. Anyone with eyes in their head can see that.'

Marion stared up at Betty in alarm. 'Do you think so?'

'Aye, I'm glad to say, I do.'

'Glad?'

'A fine gentleman like that? He's not just good looking; he's got a lovely way with him, and as if that wasn't enough, he must be one of the richest men in Newcastle. What a catch!'

Marion's temper flared. 'Don't talk like that. I'm not out to catch anyone!'

Betty put a hand to her mouth. 'Eeh, I'm sorry, pet. Of course you're not. You're too much of a lady – a proper lady – to behave that way. But now I want you to forget about those blessed papers for a moment and come along to the kitchen. You and me will hev a nice cup of tea and a fresh-baked slice of currant loaf before Miss Annette gets home from school.'

They sat in companionable silence over their tea and currant loaf. Then Annette arrived home, full of the latest horrors inflicted on her by the teachers and expressing more than once how glad she was that she wouldn't have to go back to that horrid school next term.

'I can't tell you how thankful I am that I'll be going to art school in January,' she said. Then she added dramatically, 'I shall leave the humdrum world behind and my life will take an entirely different course!'

Marion didn't have time to reflect on Betty's opinion of Mr Bateman until she was in bed and the house was quiet. Uneasily she considered the possibility that Betty was right. Victor Bateman did seem to be unusually concerned about her. Perhaps he was attracted to her. That would explain the way he had seemed to be displeased when he questioned her about Daniel. But why would a man from such a different world be interested in her? She turned restlessly and tried to get to sleep but it was nearly dawn before she succeeded.

Victor Bateman also lay awake until the early hours. He had a decision to make. When he had returned to his grand villa in Gosforth he had found his elder sister Charlotte entertaining friends. This in itself did not displease him. His sister had doted on him since he was a small boy, and when their parents had died, she had given up all hopes of marriage in order to look after him, taking over the running of the household and making sure things went smoothly for him. And for this he would always be grateful. He supposed he had imagined this happy state of affairs would go on for ever, but of late, Charlotte had started to worry about the fact that he remained unmarried.

'A man like you,' she would say, 'handsome, clever, a successful businessman of faultless reputation, could take a wife from any one of the best families.'

At first he would answer teasingly, saying such things as, 'But if I marry, what will become of you? A young wife might not be willing to share this house with my sister.'

And then Charlotte would smile. 'Nonsense. I trust you not to marry anyone who would be so disagreeable. Someone of whom I did not approve. Victor, my dear, like any sister would, I want to see you settled. A wife, children, people to care for when I am gone.'

'Gone? You are contemplating leaving me?'

At this Charlotte would lose patience. 'You know very well what I mean.'

Sometimes she would cry at this point, and Victor would feel guilty. 'Very well,' he would say. 'I will think about it.'

But he had dragged his feet and Charlotte had grown impatient. She had started arranging small dinner parties to which girls she deemed suitable would be invited. To give her her due, most of the girls were not bad looking, if a little serious minded like Charlotte herself. They would sit at Victor's table and, with their eager mothers, try desperately to impress him with their conversation. And it was this desperation that irritated Victor beyond measure.

132

The latest sacrificial lamb had been served up this evening. Daisy Walters was small and prettily plump; the daughter of a tea importer whose commercial empire spanned the globe. She was more animated than some of the poor girls whom Charlotte had summoned to his table, but her high-pitched voice and simpering tone would very quickly drive a man crazy, Victor thought. As he did his best to join in the conversation, he had a sudden vision of himself putting both his hands around Daisy's milky-white neck and throttling the life out of her.

This cannot go on, he acknowledged. Charlotte can be as single-minded as I am and she will not let the matter drop. I must marry. But it will be someone of my own choice. He smiled as he remembered where he had been that day. And I think that fate may have chosen for me.

# Chapter Nine

A few days later, Marion and Betty tackled something they had been dreading. Henry Brookfield's clothes were still hanging in his wardrobe or lying folded neatly in the tall old chest of drawers. Marion opened the wardrobe door, releasing a faint smell of mothballs. She paused, staring at the familiar garments hanging there, and clenched her fists before sighing and reaching in to take them down. She and Betty worked without speaking, the silence of the house enfolding them.

At Marion's request, Betty had arranged for someone in the Salvation Army to come to collect the clothes. Marion knew that her father would have wished them to go to those in need, and she kept this in mind as they got on with their forlorn task.

When everything was neatly parcelled, Marion's attention was drawn to the washstand. She looked at her father's shaving mug, brush and razor and she knew that she could never part with them. She remembered how as a small child she had been allowed to watch, fascinated, as her father lathered his face with the brush and then took up the razor and began to shave, stopping now and then to wipe the blade on the clean towel he had draped over one shoulder.

She picked up the badger-hair brush and stared at it. It would never be used again. Then she caught sight of herself in the washstand mirror. She looked at her reflection for a moment, and tried to imagine that it was her father's dear face reflected there.

'I'll go down and put the kettle on,' she heard Betty say. 'We'll have a cup of tea in the kitchen. We're done for now and it's cold in here.'

Marion turned to see Betty cross her arms across her body and hug herself tightly. The fire in this room had not been lit since Henry Brookfield had died. The grate was clean and the coal scuttle empty.

'All right,' Marion said, and she turned back to replace the shaving brush. The only other item on the dresser top was a small leather cufflink and stud box. She picked it up. Thinking that she might take it to her own room and maybe keep her earrings in it, she unfastened the small clasp and looked inside. The interior was partitioned into six small compartments. Three of them were empty. In one of the other compartments there was a spare pair of cufflinks; another held some shirt studs; and in the third there was a key.

'Why have you brought me here?' Susan asked her gentleman friend.

She had been expecting him to take her to the theatre again, or at least for an early meal at Alvini's, but instead he had hailed a cab to take them to the station, where they had caught a train to the coast.

Susan had left work early, not long after her lunch break, feigning a headache and drooping dispiritedly until Mr Jacobs had decided she was putting the customers off and told her to go home and go to bed. Maisie had sniffed audibly and Susan had not been able to resist slanting her eyes up and flashing a brief but triumphant smile as she walked towards the door.

Now here they were walking along the promenade in a brisk sea breeze that tugged at her hat and brought tears to her eyes. Susan was sure her nose had turned red.

'Be patient,' Gilbert told her. 'We're almost there.'

'Almost where?' Susan said plaintively.

'It's a surprise. Now be a good girl and stop complaining or I shall send you home.'

His tone was teasing but there was an edge to it that made Susan glance sideways surreptitiously. Had she annoyed him? Would he really send her home? To her relief she saw that he was smiling. As soon as they had left the railway station he had pulled her arm through his – he never did that in town – and now he gave her hand a squeeze.

'Here we are,' he said when they had walked a little further and turned in to a little row of terraced houses.

He let go of her hand and she watched in surprise as he walked up the short path of one of the houses and, taking a key from his pocket, unlocked the front door. He pushed it open, stood back and made a theatrical gesture, inviting her to lead the way.

'Here we are, madam,' he said as if he were a manservant. 'Please enter.'

Susan had a moment of misgiving. Why had he brought her to this house? Why was he being so mysterious? For one panic-stricken moment the melodramatic romances she loved to read in the penny story papers sprang to mind. Was Gilbert, outwardly so kind and charming, in reality a sort of Bluebeard? If she entered this admittedly ordinary and pleasant-looking house, would she ever emerge again?

She heard him laugh. 'Do you intend to stay out here in the cold, allowing your delightful little nose to grow redder and redder?' he asked. 'It's already glowing like a beacon.'

'Oh!' Susan was mortified. How could he talk like that about her poor nose?

'Oh, do go in,' he said. 'Jane will have the tea ready.'

'Jane?' she asked. So the house wasn't empty.

'Yes, Jane. And here she is to greet you.'

To Susan's surprise, a young woman appeared at the door. She was dressed as a servant in a dark green rayon dress with a frilled pinafore, cap, collar and cuffs in starched white muslin. She had a friendly manner and her face was fresh complexioned like a country woman. She was what Susan's mother Hannah would have called bonny rather than beautiful. She further surprised Susan by dropping a curtsy.

'Please come in, Miss Brady,' she said. 'Let me take your coat.'

Once in the hallway, which was decorated with green and white striped wallpaper Susan thought very tasteful, she took off her coat and handed it to the maid. Then she hesitated; she was not sure what she was supposed to do with her hat and gloves. She'd learned from fashion magazines that ladies did not remove their hats.

The friendly maidservant solved the problem. 'I'll take your gloves, shall I, miss?' she said. 'They might get spoiled when you have the sugar fancies. The icing can be quite sticky, you know.' She turned to Mr Mason and said, 'I've set up a little table in the front parlour as you ordered, sir. The table and chairs for the dining room have not been delivered yet.'

Susan remained perplexed. She'd had no idea that she was coming here today, and yet the maidservant had obviously been expecting her. Furthermore, she had curtsied and treated Susan as if she was a lady rather than a shop girl.

The front parlour also looked as though it had recently been decorated, only this time the wallpaper was red and gold. An oriental rug of deep jewel colours covered the floor and the gilded chairs were upholstered in crimson velvet to match the curtains. There was a large gilt-framed mirror over the fireplace and several gilt-framed pictures on the walls.

Susan had never seen a room like it and she gazed round in wonder. It was very grand, but for some reason a little strange. She wondered what sort of people lived here.

She took her place in one of the fireside chairs, glad of the cosy warmth after the biting winds on the promenade. She leaned towards the fire and rubbed her hands together, then looked up to see Gilbert looking down at her. He had removed his hat and coat and left them in the hall. He was smiling.

'You look as though you belong there,' he said.

'What do you mean?'

'So dainty – so appealing in the rosy glow of the fire. It would be good to come home after a busy day and find you sitting waiting for me.'

She caught her breath. What was he suggesting? Was he going to propose marriage? But before he could say anything more, the maid-servant knocked and entered pushing a wheeled trolley. Susan gazed in delight at the contents of the trolley, the dainty rose-patterned china cups and saucers, the matching teapot, sugar bowl and milk jug, the three-tiered cake stand laden with the most delicious cakes.

If only she could tell her mother about this! But of course Hannah must never know. Never discover that Susan had taken time off work to come alone with a gentleman to this delightful little house in Whitley-by-the-Sea.

Jane stayed long enough to pour the tea and then she left them alone. Susan wondered whether her gentleman friend would resume the interesting conversation that had begun just before the maid entered, but instead he pulled up a chair and urged her to help herself to whichever cake she fancied – and then take another, and another if she so wished.

She hesitated before taking a third cake. Would he think her greedy? But no, she decided, they were only little cakes, hardly more than a mouth-watering bite. She took another one, hardly noticing that he ate sparingly.

'There's a crumb on your chin,' he said at one point. He leaned towards her and picked up the napkin from her knee. 'Let me . . .' he said and he brushed her cheek gently.

Susan caught her breath. He had never been so close to her before. She could smell his hair dressing – a lovely lemony smell with a touch of something more exotic, something spicy.

'There,' he said when he had done, and he replaced the napkin on her knee. He laughed. 'What a child you are. A delightful child.'

Susan could not meet his eye. Trembling, she poured another cup of tea. Then she remembered her manners. 'Would you like another cup?' she asked.

'No. If you don't mind, I shall have a cigar.'

'Mind? Why should I mind?'

'It is usual to ask a lady, you know.'

'Oh.' Suddenly Susan felt out of her depth, but seeing his expectant expression she said, 'Please go ahead. I – erm – I don't mind at all.'

She watched fascinated as he walked to the table by the window, opened a cigar cabinet and chose a cigar. Then, using a silver cutter, he cut off the end and lit the cigar carefully with a cedarwood matchstick. He always chose the very best cigars Mr Jacobs had to offer, but it was only now that Susan began to wonder exactly how wealthy he was.

He sat opposite her for a while, enjoying his cigar, his legs stretched out, gazing at her through the wreaths of smoke. She did not know what was expected of her and she began to feel uncomfortable. Her gaze strayed to the pictures on the walls. Each one portrayed a man and a woman. The women were young and beautiful and wore low-cut gowns that revealed their shoulders and the rise of their breasts. Their skin was creamy, their hair fell loosely about their shoulders and the looks on their faces were coyly flirtatious.

The men, on the other hand, were more ordinary, although very well dressed. Each couple was captured in what Susan decided was a romantic pose. One pair sat on a love seat and merely gazed at each other; in another picture the gentleman was kneeling before the young woman and reaching towards her; a third picture made Susan feel more uneasy.

In this one the gentleman stood behind the girl and she leaned back into his arms. His hands were on her shoulders, and Susan realised to her dismay that the girl's gown had slipped until one of her breasts was completely revealed. She averted her gaze quickly but saw that her gentleman had been watching her, his eyes narrowed, an amused expression on his face. He laughed softly.

'Do you like the pictures?' he asked.

'I think so.'

He paused and then said, 'And this house? Do you like it?'

'I do.'

'Would you like to live here?'

Susan's eyes widened and she drew in her breath so quickly that it made a small choking sound at the back of her throat. 'Live here? Me?'

'Yes, you.'

She stared at him. Had the moment come again? Was he going to propose to her? But he remained silent, and at that moment the ornate clock on the mantel shelf chimed the hour. It was five o'clock.

'I must take you home,' he said. 'We don't want that brother of yours investigating what you get up to, do we?'

Susan had told him that Daniel was becoming more and more suspicious and that her mother had said that he might even come to the shop to talk to Maisie.

'I suppose not,' she said and pouted sulkily.

'What a delightful child you are,' he said again when he saw her expression. 'I would keep you here longer if I could, but we must allay your brother's suspicions until the moment is ripe.'

Susan, too embarrassed to admit that she had no idea what he was talking about, watched as he rang the bell to summon Jane, and then allowed the maidservant to help her into her coat.

To her chagrin, Gilbert bought an evening newspaper at the kiosk in the railway station and read it all the way home on the train. There was so much she wanted to ask him, but she didn't know how. While he buried his head in the paper, she stared out of the window, not really seeing the passing countryside or the small pit villages with their smoking chimneys.

Unable to sate her curiosity or vent her frustration, she kept her temper under control until she reached home, where she scowled her way through the evening meal, was short with her mother, and went to bed early.

However, Susan's moods were mercurial, and the next day, when Daniel got home from work, he was greeted by the cheerful sight of his mother and his sister sitting by the fire. Susan had come straight home from work and she seemed to be quite happy to sit and chat with her mother. Daniel was pleased, but all the same, he sensed a restless streak in his sister and he wondered how long this exemplary behaviour could continue.

By the time he had washed and changed, the plates of mince and dumplings were on the table, and as they enjoyed it together, his mother and Susan left him in peace while they talked in hushed tones.

At last, feeling guilty that he had been ignoring them, Daniel began to listen to their conversation with a view to joining in. Their talk had returned as it did every so often to the worrying matter of the children who just seemed to vanish from the streets.

Hannah was of the opinion that most of the folk they knew minded their bairns well. But it had to be said, there were those who lived further down the bank who simply let their children wander the streets at all times. Sometimes both parents were working long hours and left the bairns in the charge of some old woman or another child of ten years or more, and you had to feel sorry for them.

'What else can the poor folks do?' Daniel's mother said. 'They hev to put bread on the table.'

But others left their children unminded while they went out to drown their sorrows at the public house, and in Hannah's opinion, folk like that didn't deserve bairns; in fact, they ought to be locked up.

Hannah saw that Daniel was paying attention and she said, 'There's another one gone. Such a pretty little lass, you know, only ten years old. Last night she went out to take a message to her grandma only three streets away and she never got there. There's some that say her ma should never have sent her out after dark, but what could she do? Her man was on the night shift, the little ones were tucked up in bed and the poor woman had gone into labour.'

'Have the police been informed?' Daniel asked.

'Whey aye,' his mother said. 'But what can the polis do?'

'Search the streets,' Daniel replied. 'Look in empty buildings.'

'They've done all that and so has the little lass's father along with his pals, and most of the men in the street, but they're not going to find her. It's my opinion that the Toff's got her.'

'Do you believe this Toff, as they call him, is a real person and not something made up by the newspapers?' Daniel asked.

'He's real all right. He's been seen in his dark cloak and his top hat and he's a right nasty piece of work. Hevn't you noticed it's always the bonny little lasses that disappear?'

Daniel regarded his mother gravely. 'Yes, I have, and you're probably right. As a matter of fact, Mr Brookfield discussed the matter with me. In fact, I believe he was trying to discover the truth of the matter. Maybe that's what got him murdered.'

His mother shook her head. 'No, Daniel lad, your friend was murdered by a witless drunkard who simply wanted his money. The man was found guilty by twelve good men and true, wasn't he?'

'Yes.' Daniel said no more. He remembered Arthur Robinson's distress and his growing concern that they might have hanged the wrong man. But there was no point in sharing this with his mother.

When the table had been cleared and the pots washed, Daniel got his books out as usual. Susan, who had returned to sit by the fire and had been idly staring into the flames, got up and came to look over his shoulder.

'What do you want?' he asked.

'Nothing. Just to see what it is that keeps you so occupied. My goodness, what's that?' She reached down and picked up the textbook he had been studying. 'What are all these little squiggles?'

'It's shorthand,' he said. He took the book from her and put it back on the table.

'And what's shorthand when it's at home?' Susan sat down beside him and pulled his notepad towards her. 'You've been copying it – just like we had to copy the alphabet at school.'

Daniel concealed his irritation at the interruption because he sensed that Susan was genuinely interested rather than just being annoying.

'It's a way to write speedily,' he said. 'These little squiggles, as you call them, represent letters of the alphabet, or whole words or even phrases.'

Susan frowned.

'A phrase is a group of words that are used together, like—'

'Like "the cat sat on the mat",' Susan exclaimed.

Daniel smiled. 'Yes, something like that.'

His sister pored over the pages of symbols for a while and then said, 'Well, it's very interesting, but why on earth would you write like this when we've already got a perfectly good alphabet?'

'Because it's quicker.'

'Why would you want to write quickly?'

'Well . . .' Daniel was reluctant to mention that reporters used shorthand – that would only start his mother off – so he said, 'Sometimes you need to write quickly as people speak. Clerical workers use shorthand. Imagine if you worked in an office and your employer asked you to take down his words as he spoke to you and then to write them up neatly as a letter or a report.'

'Yes – or typewrite them! I've heard women typewriters are paid well – better than shop assistants.'

'Yes, I think they are.' Daniel gazed at his sister. Her expression was animated; her eyes were shining. 'Would you like to work in an office, Susan?'

Susan sighed and the light in her eyes faded. 'I'm not clever enough.'

'I think you are.'

'Those girls have to take tests and exams.'

'So?'

'I'm out of the habit of schoolwork.'

'You could go to evening classes. I would pay for them.'

'Would you?' She looked eager for a moment, then frowned. 'But evening classes are in the evening.'

Daniel laughed. 'Of course they are.'

'Then I couldn't go.'

'Why not.'

'Well, I have things to do. I mean, I might want to go out or something.'

Daniel was baffled. A moment ago the bright child that Susan had once been had returned, but then she suddenly seemed to remember something, something she didn't want to talk about. He knew it was no good pursuing the matter right now, but he might try again another time.

Susan rose from the table saying that she was going to wash her hair, and Hannah went with her into the scullery to help her. Soon mother and daughter were sitting peaceably by the fire, Susan leaning forward as Hannah brushed her shining dark hair until it was dry. Daniel was quickly immersed in his work, but every now and then he allowed himself to think with pleasure of the next time he would see Marion Brookfield.

★

Marion decided to go to Annette's school and have a word with the headmistress. When shown into the severely practical room that was Miss Clarkson's office, she was greeted with a warm smile.

'I'm pleased to see you, my dear,' the headmistress said. 'I should not say this, but you were always a favourite pupil of mine.'

Encouraged, Marion asked if it would be possible for the school to employ her as a teaching assistant.

'I would love to employ you as such,' Miss Clarkson said, 'but you do realise that the position would be unpaid, don't you? That is, until you are qualified.'

'Oh, I see.' Marion knew how crestfallen she sounded.

After a small pause the headmistress said, 'Are you finding life, shall we say, difficult since your father died?'

Marion decided to be frank. 'No, not exactly difficult. But as you know, my father agreed that Annette would start at art school after Christmas, and I promised her that I would make sure that she does.'

'And you must find the fees?'

'Yes.'

'I think I can help you in a small way.'

'How?'

'You know, my dear, you were a very bright pupil when you attended this school. I had great hopes for you, but your father needed you to run his household.'

Marion responded to the implied criticism of her father swiftly. 'I didn't mind. That's what I wanted to do.'

'Of course. Please don't get upset. As I said, I have a great respect for your intelligence and I would be happy to recommend you to any of our parents who wish to pay for extra tuition for their daughters.'

Marion cheered up a little. 'I've already thought of that, but I didn't know how to go about finding pupils. I wasn't sure if it was correct for me to advertise in the newspaper.'

Miss Clarkson smiled. 'Your problem is solved, my dear. In fact I would be very grateful to you if you would work with me to help these unfortunate and recalcitrant girls.'

'Recalcitrant?' Marion was alarmed.

'Don't worry, I wouldn't send you anyone impossibly unruly. Just those who seem to have a reluctance to learn. I'm sure your nature is such that you could coax them to find their schoolwork interesting.'

'Thank you, that would be wonderful,' Marion said.

Miss Clarkson told her that she would be hearing from her very soon and they said goodbye. Marion was not so sure that the head-mistress's confidence in her was justified, but she began to feel more optimistic.

That night, when Betty had gone home and Annette was asleep, she sat by the fire in her father's study and read into the early hours. When the fire had died to all but a few glowing embers, she put up the cinder guard and went to bed. A hesitant feeling of warmth and happiness welled up inside her. She was going to be able to earn some money, and she had Daniel's next visit to look forward to.

The day of their next meeting was bitterly cold, a hint of the winter to come perhaps, and Daniel arrived at the Brookfields' house to find the fire in the small hearth blazing and the lamps lit. Marion's eyes were shining; he could see she was trying hard to conceal some kind of excitement.

'What is it?' he asked. 'Has something happened?'

'The key to my father's rolltop desk was missing,' Marion told him, 'But now I've found it and I think his most important papers are in there.'

Daniel looked at her in surprise. 'You only *think* so? Why haven't you opened the desk yet to make sure?'

Marion smiled. 'It's been difficult.' She could barely contain her excitement. 'But I wanted you to be here.'

Daniel was speechless. He was both astounded and pleased that she should think his presence important.

'Shall we open it now?' Marion asked.

Still overcome, Daniel responded by nodding.

'Hold this for me,' Marion said. She took a small oil lamp from the occasional table and gave it carefully to Daniel. 'Bring it over here.'

The rolltop desk was in the semi-darkness at the back of the room. Daniel followed Marion and their shadows moved across the ceiling behind them. At first Marion fumbled. Daniel saw that her hand was shaking as she tried to insert the key. He would have offered to unlock the desk for her, but he knew how important this moment must be for her.

At last she fitted the key in the lock, turned it and then pushed the slatted cover up to reveal the contents. A pile of papers tumbled to the floor.

Marion stared at them. 'He was so untidy,' she whispered.

Although she was smiling, Daniel saw that there were tears in her eyes. They glittered in the lamplight. He put the lamp back on the little table, kneeled down and began to pick up the papers. Marion joined him. After a while her mood lifted and she began to laugh.

'We are like children crawling around the nursery floor,' she said.

She sat back on her heels, clutching an armful of papers; the exertion had brought a gentle flush to her face and strands of her magnificent hair had escaped their pins. Daniel had to restrain a powerful urge to drop the papers he was holding, reach out for her and pull her into his arms.

'What's going on here?' A shocked voice rang out from the doorway.

They looked up, startled, to see Betty standing there.

'We . . . I opened my father's desk,' Marion said, and then added unnecessarily, 'These papers fell out.'

'I see,' Betty said, but she pursed her lips in disapproval. 'You should hev rung for me. If you just get yourself up, Miss Marion, I'll do that.'

Marion scrambled to her feet, and clutching the papers she had gathered, she walked over to the large writing desk and deposited them as carefully as she could. Betty and Daniel between them brought the others over, and then Betty, her mobcap askew and her cheeks flushed, told them that there were sandwiches and cakes waiting for them on the table in the front parlour.

'You can start sorting that lot when you've had a bite to eat,' she said.

Marion and Daniel joined Annette in the parlour. Annette was frowning.

'What is the matter?' Marion asked.

'Betty made me take all my drawing things off the table,' Annette said. 'I asked her why we couldn't have tea in the kitchen like we usually do and she said that she wanted Mr Brady to know that we do things properly in this house.'

Daniel wondered if this was Betty's way of making clear to him the gap between his and Marion's position in society, but the meal was jolly enough, with Annette soon cheering up and telling him how pleased she was that she didn't have to go back to school after Christmas.

145

'I'm going to go to art school,' she said, and her eyes were shining. 'Marion promised that I could.'

Marion said nothing, and when Daniel glanced at her he thought he saw a fleeting look of worry. At that moment it occurred to him that Henry Brookfield might not have left his daughters adequately provided for, but he knew he would not be able to question Marion about this. He sensed that her pride would forbid her to confide in him.

After they had finished the meal, he and Marion hurried back to the study. Marion picked up a few sheets of her father's notes and glanced at them eagerly. Then he saw her expression change. She frowned.

'I can't make head nor tail of this,' she said.

'Why not?'

'It's the writing – it's just scribbles.' She held one sheet of paper towards him. 'Look,' she said, 'what do you make of it?'

'I believe it's shorthand.'

Marion's frown cleared. 'Of course. My father explained that when he was interviewing people he used a quick way of taking down what they said.' She turned back to the writing desk and hastily looked through all the papers. 'Apart from a few pages they're all the same. I suppose I'd better give them to Mr Earnshaw as he requested, but I would have liked to know what my father was working on. He thought it so important.'

'You don't have to give them to Mr Earnshaw,' Daniel said. 'At least not yet. I can transcribe them for you.'

'You?'

He was sure that Marion's surprise was not meant to be insulting, but nevertheless, Daniel felt himself flushing. 'Yes,' he said. 'I'm teaching myself shorthand. I've only just started, but if you would be patient I'll do my very best.'

'But that's wonderful. And of course I will be patient. Keep them for as long as you need.'

'Keep them?'

'Yes, I'll bundle them up and you can take them home with you.'

Daniel was disappointed. For a moment he had imagined that he would come here as often as he could and work in Henry Brookfield's study. But of course that would be impossible. Marion would not want him to become too familiar.

Perhaps she guessed the way his thoughts had been going, for she smiled and said, 'I would ask you to come here to work on the papers, but the headmistress of my sister's school is going to send me some pupils, little girls who need extra coaching, so I will need the study myself.'

It was just as well, Daniel thought. His mother would have been upset if he had gone out every night.

Marion took her father's papers to the kitchen to ask Betty to parcel them up with brown paper and string. When she returned to the study she smiled and said, 'So – the time has flown, but I would still like to talk about *Vanity Fair* with you. Have you finished it?'

'I have.'

'Good. Before you go, you must choose another book to read for when you come again – shall we say in two week's time?'

On his way home, Daniel carried his precious parcel carefully. He felt privileged to have been trusted with Henry Brookfield's papers. He had respected the man above all others and he would do his very best to help his daughter.

Violet Kilmartin and Florence Mortimer, both nine years old, sat opposite each other at Marion's large writing desk, copying letters, words and sentences from the school's approved copybook. Miss Clarkson had wasted no time sending Marion some pupils, and these two had come with the instruction that before anything else was done, they must learn to write with a fair hand.

Marion stood nearby and watched as Violet, small and spiky looking, jabbed her pencil crossly on the paper. She had already broken the point twice and Marion imagined that her writing looked as cross as the child herself. Florence, softer and more rounded, had not smiled at all since her mother had deposited her there after school. Her movements were lethargic, and as she wrote she bent her head over her work until her nose was almost touching the paper.

Every now and then Florence seemed to flinch, and at the same time Violet would grin. Eventually Marion realised that Violet was swinging her legs under the desk and kicking Florence, who was obviously too intimidated to complain.

'Stop that, Violet!' Marion said more sharply than she had intended, but she could not abide bullying behavior.

'Stop what, Miss Brookfield?' Violet asked, looking up with an assumed innocence written all over her freckled face and shining from her pale blue eyes.

'Swinging your legs like that,' Marion said.

'Why?'

Marion was taken aback by the impertinent tone but she was also aware that Florence was looking at her warily. The poor child thinks that if she complains, Violet will only be nastier to her, Marion thought.

'Because it's affecting your writing,' she improvised. 'See how erratic – how jerky – it looks.'

Violet scowled and bent over her work again. She stopped swinging her legs but she gripped her pencil even more fiercely and actually made holes in the paper when she crossed each t and dotted each i.

She just hates being here, Marion thought, and poor Florence is obviously unhappy about it too. I shall have to think of a way of making this tedious work more interesting. I must make the lessons a pleasurable experience rather than something merely to be endured.

When their mothers called to collect them at the end of an hour, Marion marvelled at how different the women were from their daughters. Or rather how, if she had not known, she would have matched the wrong mother to the wrong daughter. Prickly little Violet's mother was plumply pleasant and, it seemed, too in awe of her bossy child to properly discipline her. Whereas Florence's mother, who was in fact her stepmother, was thin and sharp featured with what appeared to be a permanent look of dissatisfaction with the world. Marion was disturbed to see that Florence seemed to be frightened of her.

After they had gone, Betty brought her a cup of tea. 'Well? How did it go?'

'Quite well,' Marion said, and she supposed it had. The girls had done what was expected of them, even though it had been with little enthusiasm. Marion knew from experience that her old school insisted that every girl should learn to write with a fair hand and that those who didn't faced hours of boring exercises.

She didn't think it would be too hard to devise some way of making the lessons more interesting. Perhaps she could find some amusing poems to copy out instead of rows of letters. She felt guilty that she had rushed into this without being fully prepared. The children deserved better and she resolved to try harder, but she could not help feeling daunted. Was this all her life was going to be about? Coaching reluctant children to reach the standard expected of them by the school and their parents? Resignedly she supposed that it was. Somehow she had to make enough money to spin out their inheritance and send Annette to art school.

Unfortunately she was still feeling disheartened when, only just after she had finished her cup of tea, Betty announced that Mr Bateman had called to see her.

'You'd better show him in,' Marion said, wondering why he had returned to visit her so soon.

When he entered, Victor Bateman glanced at the writing desk, and instead of the piles of papers that had been there previously, he saw school books. Marion told him without being asked, 'I have decided to take private pupils.'

'I see.'

Victor was at a loss. He guessed that this meant the Brookfield sisters needed the money, but he could hardly say as much. Instead he asked, 'Will you enjoy that?'

Marion smiled, a little wearily it seemed to Victor, and said, 'Needs must.'

He was taken aback by her frankness, but of course, she had too straightforward a nature to allow her to dissemble. 'I'm sorry,' he said.

'There's no need to be. But may I asked why you've called?'

'I've come because I am concerned about you . . . and your sister. I wish there was something I could do for you.'

'No – please – there's no need.'

At that moment the maid knocked and entered. 'Shall I bring tea for your visitor, Miss Marion?'

'Oh – yes, of course. Would you like to sit down, Mr Bateman?'

'Thank you.' After the maid had left the room, Victor said, 'You are lucky to have such a devoted servant.'

'I know.' Marion's smile was warm.

'Forgive me for mentioning it,' Victor said, 'and please don't answer if you find it painful, but your mother died when you and Annette were very young, didn't she?'

'Yes.'

149

'How did your father manage with two small daughters to care for?'

'The maid we had at the time, Agnes, was very kind, but she was old and eventually she had to retire. That's when Betty came into our lives. She has looked after us ever since.'

'And even though you are not much older than your sister, I believe you have cared for Annette as a mother would. Why is that, I wonder?'

Marion looked solemn. 'There may be only two years between us,' she said, 'but I was so much luckier than Annette.'

'Why do you say that?'

'Because I was just old enough to have wonderful memories of our mother. Of her humour, and her warmth and her love for us. Annette doesn't have the same memories . . .' Marion faltered.

'So you feel you owe her something?'

'I suppose so. But here is Betty with the tea.'

Victor sensed that Marion was glad of the interruption, but he had already learned much about the Brookfield sisters and he was content to let the matter drop.

When they had drunk their tea, Victor judged the time right to mention something that had been uppermost in his mind. He rose from his chair and walked over to the rolltop desk. 'Did you manage to open it?'

'Yes, we found the key.'

'And?'

'Oh, it was full of my father's papers.'

'Were they – were they of interest?'

Marion laughed. 'I don't know,' she said. 'They were all in shorthand.'

'And you don't know shorthand?'

She shook her head.

'If you like, I could find someone to transcribe them for you.'

'No – that's all right. I've already done so.'

'Someone at the newspaper office?'

'No. Daniel. Daniel Brady.'

'But how can he help? Forgive me, Miss Brookfield, but surely Mr Brady is simply a labouring man.'

'Yes, he is. And there's no shame in that.'

'No, of course not,' he soothed. 'I simply meant that, as such, he will not have learnt shorthand.' Then he remembered that Daniel Brady had been one of Henry Brookfield's pupils. 'Unless you father had been instructing him in the art.'

'No, he hadn't. Mr Brady has decided to teach himself.'

There was no denying the pleasure that gave Marion, and Victor realised with a shock what a threat Daniel Brady might be.

'And has he started work on the papers yet?'

'Only just. I'm sure he'll tell me if he has begun to make sense of them when he comes to tea again.'

Victor concealed the dismay he felt at the fondly familiar manner Marion had come to adopt when she talked of Daniel Brady. Had she and Daniel grown close? Would Marion consider forming an alliance with someone so far beneath her?

He decided that even though the Brookfield sisters were in mourning, he must make his intentions clear. He had made his decision after his sister Charlotte's last little dinner party, and although he would have preferred a more leisurely courtship, he could not allow the likes of Daniel Brady to steal Marion away from him.

When the time came for him to leave, Victor only hesitated for a moment before he took Marion's hand, holding on to it longer than was strictly proper. Then he raised it to his lips and kissed it.

Still bending over her hand, he glanced up and saw her startled expression. 'My dear Miss Brookfield,' he said, 'surely you have guessed that I have become more than fond of you.'

'No . . . I mean, why should I?'

Victor concealed a smile. There had been something – a flicker of awareness in her eyes – that made him suspect that, like all women surely would, she had considered the possibility that he had come courting.

'Well, it's true, my dear. I know you are in mourning and I am defying convention, but I can't hold back any longer. You see, I would like it very much if you would consider marrying me.'

He had held on to her hand throughout this speech and now she withdrew it quickly.

'I have shocked you,' he said. 'Forgive me. But let me assure you that society would not condemn you. You have been left fatherless, you and your sister; you need someone to look after you.'

'I am perfectly capable of looking after myself, and Annette too.' She had recovered from her shock and sounded affronted.

'Of course you are. I didn't mean to insult you. It's just that I could make your life so much easier. You would not have to take private pupils in order to make ends meet, and neither would you have to worry about paying your sister's fees at art school. I would be happy to send her there myself. I have already seen how talented she is.'

'But . . .'

He laughed softly and captured both her hands. 'Oh, Marion, I have just realised that I have neglected to say the words that every young woman deserves to hear. I have fallen in love with you and you would make me the happiest man in the world if you would consent to be my wife.'

Marion stared at him. He could see that she was on the verge of an outright rejection but perhaps didn't know how to phrase it politely.

He released her hands and held up one of his own. 'No, don't answer me now. But promise to think about it. I have to go away for a while. I have promised to take my sister to London to do her Christmas shopping before the shops get too frantic. I shall come to see you as soon as I get back. Give me your answer then.'

Not long afterwards, Victor Bateman took his leave. Marion decided that she would not tell Betty what had transpired. She suspected that her maidservant, who was also a dear friend, would urge her to accept the proposal. And how could she? How could she marry another man, no matter how suitable the world would deem him to be, when she had already given her heart to Daniel Brady?

# *Chapter Ten*

Marion was in the front parlour helping Annette with her homework when Betty appeared at the door. 'Mr Brady is here,' she said. 'I've already told him this is a bit late in the day to make a visit. It's nearly supper time.' She sounded vexed.

'Today? But I'm not expecting him until a week on Sunday.'

'I know you're not. Shall I tell him you're too busy to see him?'

Marion laughed. 'That would be a fib – and you brought us up not to tell fibs, didn't you?'

Betty sniffed, but she couldn't help herself and she grinned. 'All right, shall I show him in?'

'Yes – I mean, no, not in here. I'll see him in the study.'

'But you *are* busy,' Annette said. 'You're helping me learn my French vocabulary.'

'I know, and I'm sorry. But I can't actually memorise the words for you. Only you can do that. If you go over that page again, I'll test you when Mr Brady has gone.'

'Honestly,' Annette said, 'what with Mr Brady and those two little monsters, you hardly ever have time for me these days and I'm your own sister.'

Marion refrained from telling Annette that she had to devote time to the 'two little monsters' in order to save up money to pay for her to go to art school. Dispirited as she was, she did not want to quarrel with Annette. She smiled determinedly and dropped a kiss on top of her sister's head before leaving the room.

Daniel was waiting in the study. He was clutching a bundle of her father's papers and he looked excited. 'I hope you don't mind my coming,' he said, 'and so late, but I had to wait until I got home from work.'

'No, of course I don't mind. But surely you can't have transcribed them already?'

'Not completely. In fact hardly at all, but enough to be able to tell you what they are.'

'And what are they? Is it the investigation my father was working on when he was . . . when he died?'

'I'm sorry, I don't think so.' Daniel turned round and spread the papers out on the writing desk. 'They are reports of trials,' he said.

Marion joined him at the desk. 'How do you know that?'

Daniel looked eager. 'Well, I haven't read them word for word but I soon worked out that some of the symbols were occurring on nearly every page, so I concentrated on them and realised that they meant "judge" and "court" and "police constable" and "prison", things like that. So far I haven't come across a single document that doesn't fit the pattern.'

'I see.'

Daniel's enthusiastic smile faded. 'You look disappointed.'

'Oh no – I'm very grateful, really I am. It's just that it's not what we were looking for, is it?'

'No.' He looked perplexed. 'You father must have kept some kind of record of his recent investigations. Can you not think of anywhere he would have put it?'

Marion shook her head. 'No, I've emptied the wardrobe and the chest in his bedroom. There's nowhere else in the house I can think of.'

Totally baffled, they looked at each other in silence, then Daniel said, 'I suppose I should go.'

'Yes.' Marion sensed how unwilling he was to leave but she could not encourage him to stay any longer. Annette was waiting for her.

His next words surprised her. 'May I keep these papers for a while?'

'Of course you can. But why?'

'I . . .I'd like to study them.' He spoke self-consciously.

Marion sensed that there was something he would like to tell her and she smiled encouragingly, but he remained silent. 'Very well.'

'Thank you. I'll take great care of them, I promise you.'

'I know you will.'

They looked at each other awkwardly and then Daniel bundled up the papers, wrapping them once more in brown paper and tying the parcel with string. Marion did not ring for Betty; she saw him to the door herself. After they had said goodbye, she lingered in the doorway and watched him walk away into the night.

Daniel was disappointed that he had not discovered evidence of Henry Brookfield's investigation into the slum conditions in which some people lived, or the disturbing reports of children vanishing from the streets.

He knew that the work had been very important and he had hardly dared hope that he might be able to continue with it himself. That was why he wanted to keep the trial reports. He hoped that by studying them he would learn more and more about the correct way of doing things, because the conviction had been growing within him that he might become a reporter himself.

He remembered that day at the trial when the court official had mistaken him for a member of the press and the other journalists had not questioned him when he took his seat alongside them. Once he had mastered the art of shorthand – Miss Bennett at the library had told him the last time he called that it had taken Mr Dickens, the novelist, a year to teach himself – maybe he would start going to other trials.

Daniel knew that his mother would not be pleased with him if she learned of his intentions. She needed every penny he could give her to keep their little household going. Susan hardly made enough at her job at the tobacconist's to buy her own clothes, so in reality, Daniel was responsible for keeping all three of them.

If he was lucky enough to get taken on by a newspaper, he knew he would earn very little at first, so he had decided that he would have to work as many hours as possible in his labouring job and start saving money. He needed to have something put by to make it easier for him to change his way of life.

He was so caught up in his hopes and dreams and plans for the future that he had not noticed the shadowy figure who had been leaning against a garden wall at the bottom of the street. When Daniel had walked by, the figure straightened up and began to follow him. Like a wily hunter, at first Daniel's pursuer kept his distance, walking as quietly as possible, but when they reached the busier streets he became bolder and closed the distance between them, his footfalls drowned out by the rattle of passing carriages and cabs.

Then, once they crossed Shields Road and turned into the terraced streets where respectable working people lived, the hunter began to run. At last, when he was within yards of his own front door, Daniel heard the feet pounding the pavement behind him. He stopped and listened as they drew closer and closer. He felt the hairs rising on the back of his neck and, with a prickle of alarm, turned to see who it was. But all he had time to glimpse was the raised arm holding some kind of club before the weapon came crashing down on his head.

He dropped to the ground, twisting one leg as he fell. Still conscious but with blurred vision, he saw the tall figure of a man stoop and pick up the parcel of papers from where it had fallen on the pavement in front of him. He tried to protest but the only sound he uttered was a groan. And then even that was silenced as his assailant aimed a vicious kick at his ribs. Winded and in agony, he heard the footsteps receding into the distance.

Daniel tried to lift himself up, but the pain made him catch his breath. He lay still until it passed, feeling the cold seeping up through his body from the pavement. His head was aching and his vision was still blurred. He sensed that he might be slipping into unconsciousness. He tried to keep his eyes open, but his eyelids grew heavier and heavier until they closed and all he could see was a red mist.

He wondered why anyone would do this. Why steal a brown paper parcel whose contents the thief could not have guessed at? Perhaps the man thought it was something valuable, like a new shirt, which he could sell at Paddy's market? Well, in that case he was going to be disappointed.

As he lay there, helpless with pain, Daniel was overcome by distress. He was angry with himself not simply because he had lost Henry Brookfield's trial reports but because he had promised Marion that he would take care of them, and she had trusted him. The upset these thoughts caused him was almost harder to bear than the physical pain.

His state of consciousness ebbed and flowed. He had no idea how long he had lain there, but he was aware that rain had begun to fall and that a chill wind was blowing up from the river. The cold rain falling on his face brought him round a little and he tried to move again, but his limbs were heavy and would not obey him. He felt his heart thumping against his ribcage and could hear the pounding in his head.

Then the darkness around him seemed to lighten. An oblong of light fell across the pavement not far from his face. There was a shrieking sound. Was it the screeching of gulls circling high above the river?

No . . . it was a woman screaming . . . then shouting . . . and then another woman joined in. He was dimly aware of two people kneeling down on the pavement beside him. They began to sob and call out.

Footsteps . . . other voices . . .some words made sense . . .

'Someone run and get the polis.'

'He needs a doctor, more like.'

A woman's voice he recognised: 'Daniel – oh, Daniel . . .'

And another woman, older, stronger. 'For God's sake stop blethering, everyone, and help me get him into the house!'

'Ma . . .' Daniel said, and then the blackness closed around him.


'There's nothing broken. Your son is young and strong. He's going to be sore and bruised, and he may limp for a while, but he'll survive.'

Dr Cameron looked up to find Hannah openly weeping – as was the young woman, Daniel's sweetheart he supposed, who had insisted on staying with Mrs Brady while he examined her son.

'Thank God, for that,' Hannah Brady said, and then added, 'What's the matter? Why are you frowning?'

Dr Cameron sighed. He knew that Daniel was the main wage-earner in this household, and what he had to say was bad news. 'As I said, Daniel will survive the beating, but I fear that lying on the pavement in the rain has not done him much good. Do you know how long he was there?'

Hannah shook her head. 'Dora here found him, and thank the Lord she decided to open the front door instead of slipping out the back way.'

'I beg your pardon?' Dr Cameron said.

'Well, you see, she was keeping me company. Susan had gone to bed early – she's always going on about her beauty sleep, but I believe she just doesn't want to sit and talk to her own mother . . .'

'Mrs Brady.' The doctor held up a hand to interrupt the flow. He guessed that the poor woman was in a state of shock, but he had not the time to listen to her ramblings. 'You were telling me that this young woman opened the front door and . . .?'

'Aye, well, it was getting late and we were worried that Daniel had not come home. He's not a lad to go drinking and stay out late like some men. He prefers to sit by the fire with his books and papers.'

'Mrs Brady.' Dr Cameron looked at her impatiently.

'Eeh, I'm sorry. Well, anyways, Dora just opened the door to look out and see if he was coming before she had to go home, and she saw . . . saw him . . .'

Hannah buried her head in her hands. She could not go on. The young woman took up the tale.

'I saw something lying on the pavement. It was in the dark – in between the street lamps. I was frightened at first – there's been some terrible goings-on round here of late – but suddenly I knew, I just knew who it was. And I thought he was dead. I screamed, then I shouted for Daniel's mother and the neighbours must have heard us . . .'

The young woman began to weep again and the doctor said gently, 'Please don't distress yourself further. He wasn't dead and you got him into the house. But now, if you could both remain silent for a moment.'

Hannah and Dora watched him as he took his watch from his pocket and held it in one hand as he took hold of Daniel's wrist with the other. After a while he laid Daniel's hand down on the bed and replaced his watch.

'It's as I thought,' he said. 'He's running a fever. At this stage I have no idea how this will develop, but I will call again in the morning.'

'Can't you give him something?' Hannah asked.

Dr Cameron shook his head. He reflected for a moment that if the Bradys had been better off, he might have been tempted to sell them one of his own mixes of cream and tartar, lemon, orange and sugar. It wasn't a cure, simply a pleasant and cooling drink, but wealthier patients were reassured by having a bottle from the doctor, so he didn't feel too badly about it. The same result could be achieved by simply giving the patient water to drink – so long as it had been boiled to purify it and then allowed to cool.

He told Hannah this now and then added, 'And don't smother him with blankets. Make the bed coverings light and keep him cool. If he gets hotter during the night you must sponge him down with tepid water for at least ten minutes. Or you could wring out a sheet in cool water and wrap him up in it. And keep this window open.'

Hannah looked shocked. 'The window open? But what about the night air?'

Dr Cameron smiled faintly. He knew that many folk had a dread of night air, which they believed to be foul. 'There's nothing wrong with the night air, Mrs Brady,' he said. 'You must take my word for it that your son will be all the better for your keeping the window open.'

The doctor took hold of Daniel's wrist again and tried to conceal from the two women that he was worried to find his patient's pulse rate speeding, indicating that his temperature was still rising.

'I'll call before morning surgery,' he said as he took his leave. Then he climbed gratefully into his waiting carriage and instructed his coachman to take him home.

Later, as he lay beside his wife in his comfortable bed, he could not help thinking of the anxious night that lay before Hannah Brady.

The next morning, weary and haggard from lack of sleep, Hannah was sitting at the table downstairs drinking the hot sweet tea that Dora had placed before her. She put the cup down, pushed her greying hair back from her face and smiled at Dora gratefully.

'I can't thank you enough, lass,' she said. 'I don't know how I would hev managed if you hadn't stayed the night to help me.'

Dora stirred a spoonful of sugar into her own cup and shook her head. 'You don't hev to thank me,' she said. 'I couldn't hev gone and left you alone.'

It crossed Hannah's mind that had Dora not stayed, she would not have been alone, for she had Susan. But the night before, although Susan had expressed surprise that her brother was not yet home, she had gone to bed as usual.

'I have to be fresh and bright for work,' she'd said. 'Mr Jacobs expects us to look our best.'

When Daniel had been discovered lying in the street, Hannah had been too distracted with grief to even think about waking Susan, and in any case, Dora had been there. Ever-loyal Dora.

'What did your ma say about your staying here?' Hannah asked Dora.

'Divven't fret. When I popped in to tell her what had happened, she said that good neighbours must help each other.'

Hannah looked at Dora thoughtfully. The girl was pasty faced through lack of sleep, and her light-brown hair, not much to boast about at the best of times, looked thin and straggly. Poor lass, Hannah thought, she's tired out and now she'll have to go to work. Hannah reflected gratefully that nothing had ever been too much trouble for Dora, and over the years she had proved to be a good friend. Furthermore, when she married Daniel, there would be no friction between mother-in-law and daughter-in-law. Not like some families, where the new wife took over the running of the household and the old woman was pushed into the rocking chair.

And there was no doubt that Dora loved Daniel. She had loved him ever since they were bairns and she had toddled around after him when he'd been playing with his pals in the back lane. Daniel hadn't seemed to mind, and Hannah had taken this as a sign that he was equally fond. But of late she'd begun to have doubts. Maybe the lad was just too good natured for his own good, and not wishing to hurt Dora, he had let her go on believing that he loved her too.

All through the night that had just passed, Dora had proved her worth. She had helped Hannah to sponge Daniel down and had dried him as tenderly as she would have dried a bairn. Uneasily Hannah realised that the lass, still unmarried as she was, might hev seen just too much of Daniel for it to be quite proper.

She pushed these thoughts out of her mind. The main thing was that together they had pulled Daniel through. They had fought off the fever, and when Dr Cameron had called first thing this morning, just after Susan had left for work, he had said that the crisis was over.

'Your son will be in a weakened state for a while,' he'd told Hannah. 'He'll probably sleep a lot and he won't be able to stir from the house or even dream of going back to work.' Then the good doctor had added, 'Will you be all right?'

Hannah knew what he meant. He was wondering if she had enough money to tide them over.

'Aye, Dr Cameron,' she'd said. 'We'll manage.'

'I suppose Susan will help you – financially, I mean?'

Hannah laughed. 'Susan help me? The lass never has two ha'pennies to rub together. But it's not her fault,' she had added when the doctor raised his eyebrows. 'She doesn't earn that much in the tobacconist's, and what she does get she has to spend on clothes. She has to look presentable to work behind the counter, you know.'

Dr Cameron smiled. 'You're too easy on her,' he'd said. 'A daughter ought to help her mother, but as you had Daniel's sweetheart here, I suppose it doesn't matter.'

The doctor refused Hannah's offer of a cup of tea and told her that he might call again the day after next. But he asked if she could settle her bill for the two visits he had made so far. She'd taken the old cocoa tin from the cupboard next to the fireplace and counted out three shillings.

After Dr Cameron had gone, Hannah stared worriedly at the remaining coins in the tin. She was sure there had been more than that the last time she had taken money out. She shook her head. Mebbes she was wrong. After all, she wasn't getting any younger. She put the lid back on and returned the tin to the cupboard. She just hoped that she would have enough to see her through until Daniel was on his feet and back at work again.

Hannah finished her cup of tea and refused Dora's offer of another one. 'I'd best stir meself and get some broth going,' she said. 'Daniel might be able to sup a little.'

'Let me do that.' Dora said. 'I've got time. You must be exhausted. Why don't you sit by the fire and put your feet up on the cracket.'

Hannah sank gratefully into the fireside chair. 'You're a good lass,' she said, and she pushed her worrisome doubts about Daniel's intentious towards Dora to the back of her mind.

'Will you please sit down, Miss Marion,' Betty said. 'You're giving me the jitters.'

'I'm sorry.'

'Go on then, sit down by the fire and let me draw the curtains. You won't make him come any quicker by staring out the window like that.'

Marion moved away from the window reluctantly and sat in one of the fireside chairs. The other chair was occupied by Annette, who had her head bent over her sketchbook.

'And you should stop that now, Miss Annette,' Betty said. She had closed the curtains and turned to face the room. 'You'll ruin your eyes if you go on drawing in this poor light.'

Annette sighed exaggeratedly and closed her sketchbook. 'I would have stopped long ago if only you'd had the tea ready.'

'It's ready and waiting but your sister wants us to wait until Mr Brady arrives.'

Annette glanced up at the clock on the mantel shelf. 'I don't think he is coming this Sunday,' she said. 'It's too late now.'

'Well, I'm glad you agree with me for once,' Betty said. 'Now why don't we all go along to the kitchen and have our tea – although it's more like supper time now, and seeing as I usually go home earlier on a Sunday, my mother will wonder where I've got to.'

Marion rose from her chair looking distressed. 'I'm sorry, Betty. I didn't think.'

'No, you didn't, did you? Your head's so full of Mr Brady you have no room for anything else.'

'I'm truly sorry, really I am, and I can't bear it if you're going to be cross with me.'

Betty's features softened into a fond smile. 'Eeh, lass, I'm not cross with you. It's that fine black-haired gentleman that's going to get the sharp edge of my tongue when he shows up here again, whenever that will be.'

'Then you don't think he's coming today?'

'No, pet, I don't. Now come along the both of you and have your tea.'

Reluctantly Marion followed Betty and Annette to the kitchen. She tried to convince herself that she was disappointed because she would not be discussing books with Daniel, but in her heart she knew that it was simply being with him that she had been looking forward to.

Betty, seeing how downcast Marion was, found herself vexed with Mr Daniel Brady. She hadn't put him down as plain bad mannered. Arthur might know what was going on, but he'd been on night duty and she hadn't seen him for over a week. She supposed she could ask him if he knew anything the next time she saw him, but she suspected Marion would be vexed with her if she did. After all, it was clear to see, the lass had her pride.

Well, maybe it was just as well, Betty thought. The less Marion saw of Daniel Brady, the more she might favour Mr Bateman.


Daniel's temperature seemed to have settled, but Hannah was worried that he didn't seem able to stay awake for very long. At the end of a day when he had barely opened his eyes, she sent Dora for the doctor.

'It's because of his head injury,' Dr Cameron said. Alarm flared in Hannah's eyes. 'No, don't worry about it,' he continued. 'He's a big strong lad and nothing is broken. I don't believe there will be any permanent damage, but he's having dizzy spells. Let him rest and make sure that he doesn't attempt too much too soon.'

Hannah paid the doctor another one shilling and sixpence and saw him to the door. She returned to the cosy living room to find

Dora frowning – well, to call it a frown would be kind; it was more like a scowl. The lass obviously had something on her mind and it was bothering her.

'Is owt the matter?' Hannah asked.

'No, there's nothing wrong. It's just that I've been thinking. Daniel won't be able to go to Miss Brookfield's house with his books, will he? At least not for a while.'

'You're right, he won't, but there's nowt we can do about that.'

'But don't you think we should tell her why? I mean, she might be wondering why he doesn't call. It would only be polite, wouldn't it?'

'I suppose it would.' Hannah looked at Dora and saw that the lass couldn't meet her eyes. She was up to something. 'What do you suggest?'

'I could go and tell her. And I could take her story book back to her in case she's worrying about it.'

Hannah frowned. Although she didn't approve of Daniel's visits to the Brookfield house, she wasn't sure if they ought to go behind his back like this.

'I mean,' Dora continued, 'she might think Daniel is never coming back and has stolen her book.'

Hannah was outraged. 'Our Daniel steal something? Never on your life!'

'Of course not. We know that, but Miss Brookfield might not.'

Hannah sighed. 'I suppose you're right.' She used both hands to push herself up. 'I'll gan upstairs and get the book. It's on the little table by his bed. He keeps everything else in the bottom of his wardrobe.'

'That's all right, I'll go.'

And before Hannah could say anything else, Dora had left the room and was hurrying upstairs.'

Dora stood just inside the door and watched Daniel turn restlessly in his sleep. He had thrown back the bed coverings and his nightshirt was open at the neck, revealing his strong throat and the beginnings of the dark hair that covered his chest.

She had seen that for the first time when she had helped Hannah sponge him with cool water. Hannah had made her turn her back when she had stripped her son. When Dora turned round again, Daniel's lower body was draped in a towel. But even now she flushed at the memory of his muscular bare limbs and his strapping torso.

Dora remembered how they had worked desperately that first night, both of them near to tears, terrified that Daniel would develop an inflammation of the lungs. But the next morning Dr Cameron had seemed satisfied that the worst danger was past, although Daniel was by no means better. And goodness knows how long he would be bedridden.

Dora picked up the book from the bedside table. She opened it and looked at the title page.

*The Mayor of Casterbridge*
*By Thomas Hardy*
*The story of a man who sells his wife and child*

How disgusting, she thought as she closed the book forcefully. So this is the sort of thing Miss Marion Brookfield encourages him to read. She slipped the book into the large pocket of her pinafore, then walked over to the wardrobe and opened it. The door creaked loudly on its hinges. She held it steady with one hand and turned to see if the noise had disturbed Daniel, but he lay still, his dark hair tousled, a lock of it falling across his brow. She resisted the urge to go over to the bed and smooth it back.

She bent down to look on the floor of the wardrobe. She had expected to see a lot of papers lying there. She had seen Daniel working at the table downstairs and she had a rough idea of what she should find. But there was nothing to be seen except Daniel's best shoes and a fancy-looking leather case.

She took it out, and feeling only the merest twinge of guilt, knelt on the floor and opened it. After all, this wasn't really prying, was it? She was doing this from the best of intentions: to return to Miss Brookfield anything that might rightfully belong to her.

But wherever the bundles of papers were, they were not in here. Well, there were a few pages, all covered with those funny scribbles Daniel had been poring over, and there was another book. Dora opened it and found more of the funny scribbles instead of proper writing. She also found a library ticket, so this book, at least, didn't belong to Marion Brookfield. She put the library book back and was about to close the lid when she paused and looked properly at the case.

With its fine black leather covering and its red silk lining, it looked as if it had cost quite a bit of money. When she and Daniel got married and maybe needed a bit of cash, they would be able to sell this for a tidy sum. She put the case back where she had found it.

Dora stood up and was about to close the wardrobe when she caught sight of Daniel's reflection in the mirror set on the inside of the door. She caught her breath. His eyes were open and he was looking straight at her. What should she say to him? How could she explain what she had been doing. She closed the door firmly and gave herself time to think before she turned to face him.

'I was just tidying . . .' she began when she realised that his eyes were closed again.

She walked over to his bed. He was breathing evenly but his brow was creased into a frown. Dora leaned over and held her breath as she tried to soothe the frown away with her fingers. Daniel moaned softly and turned his head away. Then, with his eyes still closed, he whispered hoarsely, 'I'm sorry.'

Dora's heart melted. 'There's no need to apologise, Daniel,' she said. 'I'd do anything for you, you must know that.'

Daniel groaned and turned his face into the pillow. His words were muffled, but Dora understood them well enough.

'No,' he said. 'I lost them . . . her father's papers. You must go and tell Marion that I'm sorry.'

Dora could taste the bile rising in her throat. She clenched her fists so tightly that her knuckles whitened. Then she turned and stumbled from the room. Almost hating Daniel as much as she loved him, propelled by cold rage, she hurried down the stairs. She would go to see Marion Brookfield all right, and she knew exactly what she was going to say.

Hannah was in the back scullery filling the poss tub with hot water when Dora hurried past her like a fury and went out, banging the door behind her. She hadn't even said goodbye, never mind given Hannah the chance to ask her something that had been puzzling her. Dora had offered to take the books back to Marion Brookfield, but how did she know where the Brookfields lived?

Hannah's doubts about Daniel's intentions suddenly took on a new dimension. There was more to Dora than she had imagined. She began to wonder – and felt guilty for doing so – whether Dora was the right wife for Daniel after all.

My Dear Marion,

Forgive me for writing to you so soon after we last met, but I cannot help myself. I am missing you already and may I dare to hope that you are missing me just a little bit? We get on together so well, don't we?

My sister Charlotte is enjoying herself thoroughly visiting all the department stores in Kensington and choosing assorted fabrics and patterns for new gowns. I must say she has excellent taste when it comes to quality and colour, but once the garments are made up by her dressmaker they never seem to do her justice. I am very glad that she has not succumbed to the second coming of the bustle, but I fear her tastes are a little old fashioned and I wish she had a younger woman – you, perhaps? – to advise her.

And then poor Charlotte gets so bored when I have to leave her in the hotel while I conduct my business affairs. I am buying some property here in London and it was necessary that I come to inspect it and talk to the architect I have engaged to draw up plans for necessary alterations. If you were here, and your sister too, of course, you, Annette and Charlotte could visit the great museums and the art galleries. Oh, how Annette would love the galleries!

Marion, I hope you are giving thought to my proposal. I could offer you so much. A comfortable way of life, security for both you and your sister and, of course, my love.

Yours sincerely,
Victor Bateman

Marion sat at the desk in her father's study, took the letter from its envelope and read it again. It had arrived by the morning post and she had read it hastily after Annette had gone to school and while Betty was upstairs making the beds. She had been surprised and startled by its contents. The letter read as though they were on much more intimate terms than they actually were. Did they really 'get on together so well'? She thought back over the few times they had met, but could not remember any conversation that would lead him to believe such a thing.

166

And they were from such different worlds. She had lived a quiet life here with her father and her sister, whereas Victor moved in a different level of society. How could he think she would be a suitable wife for such a man as he, unless that didn't matter to him because he was really and truly in love with her? Betty certainly thought he was.

She was startled too by the tone of the letter. It read like something sent by a suitor in a romantic novel. She speculated that perhaps Victor Bateman's sister, Charlotte, might read such novels and that maybe he had asked her to help write the sort of letter that he supposed a young woman would like to read.

She scanned the neatly flowing handwriting once again and was distracted by the observation that her unexpected and unwanted suitor certainly had a fair hand. But it was not his handwriting she wanted to study, it was the contents of the letter. He said that he loved her and missed her, but he was also making sure that she knew how much to her advantage it would be if she became his wife.

There would be shopping trips to London. She would be able to buy gorgeous fabrics and have them made up in the latest styles, and she would never have to worry about Annette's future. For by talking of business and property and architects, Victor was really telling her that she would be marrying a wealthy man.

And although he had not said so, although there was not one word that even hinted at it, she knew very well that he was telling her how much better off she would be with him rather than a working man such as Daniel Brady.

Marion folded the letter and put it back in its envelope. She laid it aside on the desk and pulled her notebook towards her. She started to prepare the next lesson for her two little pupils but found that she could not concentrate. She was turning the pencil round and round in her hands when she heard the doorbell. Her heart leapt – she laughed at herself for her reaction, but she could not control the hope that the caller might be Daniel.

Like a foolish romantic heroine she rose from the desk and hurried to the mirror that hung over the fireplace. Her hair was tidy, her complexion a little pale, but her eyes were sparkling. She turned as Betty knocked on the door and ushered someone into the room. Marion's hopes died and her smile was replaced by a look of polite enquiry when Betty said, 'This is Miss Dora Gibb, Miss Marion. She insisted on seeing you.'

# Chapter Eleven

The young woman who followed Betty into the room was respectably dressed in a grey woollen three-quarter coat over a grey skirt and neat laced-up boots. She looked the very picture of sedate respectability except for the incongruous emerald-green hat festooned with yellow and orange plumage that was perched on a frizz of recently tonged light brown hair.

Marion saw the way that Betty, from behind the visitor's back, was looking at the tall, improbably coloured feathers with her mouth twitching, and she was hard put not to smile herself. But she realised at once that this young woman had dressed up in her best and should definitely not be mocked for it.

Miss Gibb took her place in the seat that Marion politely indicated and swept the room curiously with her pale blue eyes before looking down demurely at her gloved hands, which she had clasped in her lap. Marion noticed that the gloves, of thick knitted wool, had been darned. After an awkward silence in which the fire crackled and the clock on the mantel shelf ticked away the minutes, Marion said, 'Miss Gibb, what can I do for you?'

The response to her words took her by surprise. '*Do* for me? I haven't come asking for anything. Do you think I'm after a handout or summat?'

'No, of course not.' Marion was taken aback by the rancour in both her tone and the glance that Miss Gibb threw her. She was aware that she was flushing, for it *had* crossed her mind that the young woman might have come to ask for some sort of charity. Henry Brookfield had sometimes entertained such visitors – people who needed to find a respectable job or who had fallen on hard times and needed something to tide them over. He had helped if he could, and maybe that was why he hadn't left as much money to his daughters as he might have done. He could have had no idea that his life would be cut short thus, leaving them in straitened circumstances.

Hoping that her visitor could not read her mind, Marion said, 'May I offer you a cup of tea?'

Miss Gibb, who had been perched on the edge of her chair, sat back and breathed in before saying, 'Aye, you can. We're both going to need it.'

Perplexed by the cryptic answer, Marion rose and pulled the bell cord.

'Is that what you do?' her visitor asked.

'I beg your pardon?'

'You ring the bell for the maid? You divven't actually gan along to the kitchen and make the tea yourself?'

'No, I don't. Does that bother you?'

Dora Gibb looked as though she had not expected such a spirited reply, and her next words were not so confrontational. 'No, I'm not bothered, it's just that I divven't often get the chance to see how the other half live.' There was no mistaking the sneering tone.

Marion found herself wishing that she had not offered tea to this belligerent young woman, for it would only prolong the visit. Thankfully it was not too long before Betty appeared with the tray. Marion got up to place the occasional table between her and her visitor and took the chance to shoot a questioning glance at Betty. Betty pursed her lips and shrugged, as if to say, *Divven't ask me, I'm as puzzled as you are.*

Dora Gibb took off her gloves in order to hook a finger through the handle of the china teacup. Her little finger was held out in what she must have supposed was a ladylike fashion. Marion felt an overwhelming urge to giggle, and averted her eyes quickly. She knew it would have been unkind and ill mannered; Dora Gibb was, after all, a guest.

Dora didn't speak until she had finished drinking, then she placed her cup and saucer back on the tray and looked at Marion coolly. A slight smile hovered about her lips.

Worried by the enigmatic expression, Marion tried to sound both interested and encouraging as she asked, 'So, Miss Gibb, why have you come to see me?'

The answer stunned her.

'It's about Daniel,' the young woman said.

'Daniel Brady?'

'Who else?'

Marion felt a surge of alarm. 'Has something happened to him? I thought as much!'

Her visitor looked at her curiously. 'Why did you think that?'

'He . . . he didn't come to visit when he was supposed to.' She was uncomfortably aware that the girl was watching her through narrowed eyes. 'And he has sent no message.'

Miss Gibb shook her head. 'Poor Daniel. He's been worried about that. Tossing and turning in his bed as he is. That's why he asked me to come and see you.'

She was releasing only the merest nuggets of information, and Marion had the strangest idea that she was deliberately tormenting her. But why would she do that?

'He sent you here?'

'Aye. He wants to tell you that he's sorry.'

Marion wanted to scream, *Get on with it!* But she controlled herself and asked as calmly as possible, 'Why is he sorry?'

'About the papers.'

'My father's papers?'

'Aye. They were stolen the night he was attacked.'

'Attacked? Daniel attacked?' This was getting worse by the minute. Marion rose from her chair, her heart pounding. 'Is he . . .? Was he hurt?'

'Aye, badly. And all for the sake, it seems, of the parcel he was carrying. Of course the thief was not to know it was only papers. He probably thought it was something valuable.'

Marion let that go. She realised that this young woman would not think the papers valuable, and of course they were not compared to Daniel's safety. 'Where is he?' she asked.

'The thief? God knows.'

Marion felt like smacking her. 'No. I mean Daniel. Is he in hospital?'

'Of course not. He's at home where he should be with me and his mam to look after him. Dr Cameron thinks we've done a grand job of it so far, but Daniel isn't out of the woods yet.'

'What do you mean?'

'Well, he's had a blow to his head, hasn't he? Dr Cameron says it's only natural that he should be a bit muddled for a while.'

'But will he . . . I mean, is the damage permanent?'

'The doctor doesn't think so. After all, Daniel is a fine strapping man. Strong as an ox. But . . .' She shook her head.

'What!' Marion almost screamed at her. She felt like closing the distance between them and grasping Miss Dora Gibb by the shoulders to shake the words out of her. Instead she forced herself to sit down and wait for the answer.

'Well, it seems he twisted his leg as he fell. Dr Cameron says he might hev a limp for a while. It could even stop him getting back to work – that is, until he's walking properly again.'

'Is there anything I can do to help?'

Dora stared at her. 'You wouldn't be suggesting that a person like you could help with the nursing, would you?'

Marion felt like weeping with rage. She had no idea why her visitor was being so hostile, but her own feelings were not important. 'No. I meant is there anything I could send – medication, that sort of thing?'

'Daniel doesn't need pills and potions. If he did, his mother would get them for him. What he needs is love and attention, and he's getting plenty of that from his ma and me.'

It occurred to Marion that she had no idea how this young woman was connected to Daniel and his family. Was she a relation of some sort, or maybe just a family friend? She didn't know if it would be polite to ask, but Dora Gibb saved her the trouble.

'I live next door to Daniel, you see. I help me ma at home with the bairns and I put in odd days at the corner shop. But at the moment I'm helping Mrs Brady with Daniel as much as I can.' She shot Marion a look that was almost defiant.

'That's . . . that's very good of you.'

Dora smiled, and Marion had the feeling that this was the moment her visitor had been waiting for.

'Good of me? That's kind of you to say so, but it's my duty, isn't it?' The question was accompanied by a smile that was meant to be sincere but came over to Marion as smugly self-satisfied.

'In what way is it your duty?' Marion asked. She felt anxiety knotting up inside her, and sensed she was not going to like the answer.

'Well, after all, although we're not married yet, it's my place to help in any way I can.'

'Married? Are you and Daniel going to get married?'

Dora Gibb smiled. 'We've been sweethearts ever since we were bairns. Me bottom drawer is just about full up.'

'Bottom drawer?'

'Aye, you know, bed linen, towels, a few pots and pans. Things that women start to put by when they begin walking out with someone.'

Marion gripped the arms of her chair. She felt sick. She'd had no idea that Daniel had a sweetheart. She had never considered such a thing. If she had, she would not have allowed herself to harbour such romantic dreams. Foolishly romantic dreams, she realised now.

She searched her memory for anything Daniel might have said that could have led her to believe he wanted anything more than friendship, and found nothing . . . except surely the way he had looked at her sometimes . . . the expression in his eyes, as if he had wanted to tell her something. Had her interpretation of these moments been completely wrong? Surely not. And yet here was Dora Gibb telling her that she and Daniel were to be married.

The expression in the other girl's eyes told her that she had guessed what her hopes had been and she was exercising her right to put her in her place. Marion was mortified.

Looking and sounding as calm as possible, she said, 'Well then, it seems as though there's nothing I can do.'

'That's right,' Dora said. Then she delved into her handbag and took out a book. Marion recognised it as *The Mayor of Casterbridge*, the last book Daniel had borrowed. 'Here you are, this is yours, I believe.' She held it as though it were something distasteful as she reached out over the distance between them.

Marion took the book. 'Has Daniel finished reading it?'

'Yes.' The answer was short and sharp.

Marion looked down and saw that there was a bookmark between the pages, placed about two thirds of the way through.

Dora must have realised what she was looking at, for she seemed flustered when she said, 'In any case, he won't be reading for a while. He gets headaches.'

'Of course.'

'And I shouldn't think he'll be coming back – erm – for a while.'

Marion realised that what the young woman really meant was 'ever at all'. Not if she had anything to do with it.

In the face of Marion's silence, Dora suddenly seemed

uncomfortable. 'Well,' she said as she rose from her chair, 'that's my duty done. I won't take up any more of your time, Miss Brookfield. I don't suppose you and me will meet again, unless . . .'

'Unless what?'

'Unless you would like to come to the wedding?'

In answer, Marion pulled the bell cord. Thankfully, Betty appeared quickly.

'Miss Gibb is going now,' Marion told her. 'Would you see her out?'

Almost before Betty had closed the door behind them, Marion saw that Dora had dropped her gloves and forgotten about them. She picked them up and contemplated running out into the hall with them, but then she heard the front door close. She gazed at the fire and for a moment was tempted to hurl the gloves – ugly things that they were – into the flames. But she realised that they would in all likelihood make an unpleasant smell as they burned, so instead she dropped them into the waste-paper basket. If Dora Gibb came back for them, Betty could deal with it.

Marion sank down on to her seat and closed her eyes. It wasn't long before Betty returned. Marion had thought she would.

'What's the matter?' the maid asked. 'You look awful.'

'I'm tired, that's all,' Marion replied. 'I don't suppose you would test Annette on her French vocabulary, would you?'

Betty laughed. 'Don't be daft. How could I do that?'

'I'll give you a list of words in English. Just read them out to her and get her to write the French word. I'll check it over later.'

Betty looked doubtful. 'I suppose I could do that,' she said. 'But are you sure it's just tired you are? I mean, it's nothing to do with the young woman who's just called, is it? She hasn't said anything to upset you?'

'Of course not.'

'Are you going to tell me what she wanted?'

'Miss Gibb is a friend of the Brady family. She came to tell me that Daniel has had a fall and that's why he hasn't been here lately. She thought it polite.'

'Yes?'

'What do you mean, "Yes"?'

Betty looked surprised at Marion's curt tone. 'I mean, is that all?' she asked.

Inwardly Marion was seething with conflicting emotions. Daniel had been attacked and was badly hurt. Her first instinct had been to go to him. But Dora Gibb had put paid to that idea. Dora Gibb. Daniel's fiancée. Despite Marion's anguish, anger surged within her. Daniel had deceived her. He had not lied; he had not made false promises. He had simply not said that he was engaged to be married to someone else.

Henry Brookfield's papers had been stolen. That had not been Daniel's fault, but it meant an end to Marion's hopes of finding out what her father had been working on. And if she had had any foolish dreams of a future with Daniel Brady, those dreams had been cruelly shattered. But Marion was too proud to seek sympathy even from Betty.

She looked up at her friend and smiled as she said, 'Yes, that's all.'

Marion must have been successful in hiding her feelings, because Betty, who could usually sense if something was wrong, immediately went about her work and didn't bother her with any awkward questions. In fact Marion sensed that the maid had something on her own mind, for she appeared a little distracted, not to say absent-minded. She kept misplacing the dusters and polishing cloths; one day she searched high and low for the tin of lavender polish before remembering that she had slipped it into the pocket of her pinafore. Another time she stood at the sink daydreaming and went on peeling potatoes until there were nearly twice as many as they needed for the next meal.

'Eeh, look what I've done!' she said. She stared at them perplexedly and then added, 'Never mind, I'll make some soup with the rest. I believe we've got a leek or two in the pantry.'

'Whatever you think best,' Marion told her. But she began to worry about Betty. She hoped that whatever was distracting her wasn't anything too serious.

# Chapter Twelve

One morning, after Annette had left for school, Marion settled in the front parlour to read the newspaper. There was a worrying report of another child gone missing; a pretty little girl of no more than ten years old. It seemed that whoever was taking these children was growing bolder. This time, instead of taking a child from the poorer, meaner streets, he had ventured into the more affluent area around Heaton Park.

The child had been walking in the park with her nursemaid. It was a cold day and the skies were overcast. The lamps had been lit early and they were soon to go home for tea. When the nursemaid stopped to talk to a friend, the little girl ran on, bowling her hoop along the paths between the formal flower beds, until she disappeared into the shadows of the wooded area.

Her nursemaid, realising that she could no longer see her charge, said goodbye to her friend and hurried after her. She found the hoop abandoned on the ground but the child had vanished. She had not been seen since.

Whoever had written the report seemed to be outraged that this could happen to a 'respectable' child. Marion knew that her father would have been equally outraged no matter where the child lived or who her parents were. Love for him welled up inside her and she realised that his murder had been more than a personal tragedy. The world of journalism would miss him too.

Just then Betty popped her head around the door and said, 'Miss Marion, I have something to tell you.'

Marion looked up from the newspaper. 'What is it?'

'Is it all right if I sit down?'

'Of course it is.'

Betty had always been forthright and plain speaking. Now,

something about her hesitant manner alerted Marion. She felt a prickle of unease.

'It's like this . . .' Betty began, and then she stared at Marion nervously.

'Like what? Have you burnt the milk pan? Broken the china tea service? I wouldn't be surprised considering the scatterbrained mood you've been in lately.' Marion was teasing.

Betty smiled self-consciously. 'No, nothing like that. But mebbe it has everything to do with what you call my scatterbrained mood. It's just . . . just . . . oh, heck, I'll just come out with it. Me and Arthur are going to get hitched.'

'So, Arthur has made his intentions clear?' Marion tried to hide her dismay.

Betty grinned. 'Aye. I told you he would, didn't I?' Betty's nervous air had given way to happy confidence.

'You did, but all the same, isn't it a bit quick? I mean, you haven't known him very long, have you?'

'I knew him when I was at school.'

'But not in the years between – oh, you know what I mean.'

'Yes, I do, and I admit it's a bit sudden, but I'm not getting any younger, am I?'

'You're only twenty-two.'

'Twenty-three in January, and all the lasses I grew up with are married with bairns.'

'You're not marrying him because you're afraid you'll be left on the shelf, are you?'

Betty's smile vanished and she looked vexed. 'Miss Marion, how can you think that of me? I'm going to marry him because I love him – and he loves me and we want to be together. I thought you might be happy for me.'

'Oh, I am. I'm very happy for you.' Marion rose and gave Betty a hug. 'Arthur is a good, kind man and if I sounded less than pleased, it's because I love you. I shall miss you. I'm sorry.'

Betty's smile returned. 'Divven't fret. I'll be with you for a while yet. Arthur lives in a lodging house in Shieldfield. We won't be getting married until we find a nice little house to rent; not too far from the police station and not too far from me mam's house.'

'How long do you think it will take you to find somewhere?'

'Mebbe a month or two.'

'A month or two.' Marion tried hard not to sound despondent.

'But. I'll not leave you in the lurch. I'll find someone decent to take my place. I've got a young cousin, Sarah. She's clean and respectable and she's a good cook. I can get her to call, and if you like her, consider it settled. She'll be able to start right after Christmas and I'll stay on to show her the way we do things.'

'I don't think I can afford to pay both of you.'

'You divven't hev to. When Sarah starts, the two of us will work for one wage between us. Sarah will understand that's fair until she's properly trained.'

'But—'

'No.' Betty held up a hand to stop Marion's protest. 'That'll be my way of repaying your father for being the best, most considerate master in the world. He always treated me more like a friend than a servant – and so do you.'

'Will you always be my friend, Betty?'

'Of course I will.'

'And you'll come to see me after you are married?'

'And sit in the front parlour in me best clothes and hev our Sarah bringing me tea and cakes? Try stopping me!'

Betty went back to her duties and Marion tried to concentrate on the newspaper once more, but after a while she realised she was simply staring at the page without reading a single word. She folded the paper and slipped it into the carved wooden magazine rack beside her chair.

Weddings . . . she thought. That's two weddings I have learned about of late. Betty is going to marry Arthur Robinson, and although I will lose her I wish her every happiness. And it seems that Daniel is going to marry Dora Gibb. Marion was shaken by how desolate that made her feel.

Florence Mortimer had a cold. As she bent over her copybook she sniffed continually, and every time she did, Violet Kilmartin looked at her with eyes full of venom.

'Ugh!' Violet suddenly exclaimed. 'There's bogeys dripping on to Florence's copybook. How disgusting!'

Marion saw that this was true and quickly tore the top page from the book and threw it into the fire. 'Haven't you got a handkerchief?' she asked Florence.

'I lost it at school – in the playground.'

'I don't know how you managed that,' Violet said scornfully. 'You sat on the bench all the time instead of running around with the rest of us.'

Marion could imagine only too clearly the scene in the school yard. Florence, hunched into her coat, feeling ill and sitting miserably on the bench watching the others at play. She ought to have been allowed to remain inside until break was over. But perhaps she had been too timid to ask.

'Here you are, dear.' Marion pulled a clean handkerchief from her pocket. 'Take mine.'

The child took it gratefully and immediately blew her nose forcefully, making an unpleasant bubbling sound. Violet, with lips pursed in an expression of disgust, shuddered exaggeratedly and said, 'Honestly, some people!'

Marion noticed that Florence's head drooped more and more as she leaned over her work, and she began to wonder if the child was fit enough to be out at all. She watched her anxiously and suddenly with a flash of inspiration she thought she knew why Florence's work was so poor. The child was short sighted. She decided to suggest this to Mrs Mortimer when she came to collect her.

Violet, meanwhile, was growing ever more restive. She had started swinging her legs to and fro again under the desk, although stopping just short of kicking Florence in the shins. Every now and then she slanted a glance up at Marion as if to see if her behaviour was being noticed.

She's being deliberatively provocative, Marion thought. She wants some sort of reaction from me. Well, she's not going to get one. The best thing to do at the moment is to turn away and ignore her. She'll soon get tired and stop. And thank goodness the lesson is nearly over. Their mothers will be calling for them soon.

Marion contemplated, as she had done before, the years that lay ahead. If all went well with Florence and Violet, the headmistress of the girls' school was going to recommend Marion to other parents. She might end up having teaching sessions every evening. Eventually Violet and Florence and any other pupils she had would move on and others would take their place. Some would be better behaved than Violet, and some worse, and some perhaps would need more care and attention just as Florence did.

And I must do my best for them, Marion told herself firmly. I have a comfortable house to live in and a loving sister. I am so much better off than some of the poor people my father wrote about in his reports. If I have to work hard coaching reluctant children, then so be it. My reward will be to see Annette progress and flourish. She is a gifted artist and must be given every chance.

Marion was shaken rudely from her reverie by a loud shout of 'Stop it!' followed by an ear-splitting scream. She spun round to find that Florence was kneeling on top of the desk and had taken hold of Violet's pigtails. It was Violet who had screamed and it was Florence who had yelled, and was still yelling.

'Stop it! Stop it! Stop it! Stop kicking me!' she bellowed at the top of her voice.

Marion hurried forward and, reaching for Florence, pulled her away, but the child did not let go of Violet's hair. Violet started screaming again as she was dragged across the desk. Marion heard the doorbell ring at the same moment that Violet managed to pull herself free. Florence twisted from Marion's grasp and began to lash out at her tormentor. Then, turning on Marion, she shouted, 'She started kicking me again. She won't stop, and you don't care! Nobody cares!'

At that moment the door to the study burst open and the children's mothers swept into the room, followed by a very alarmed Betty.

'What is going on?' Florence's stepmother said in commanding tones. 'This place is an utter bear garden!'

Violet's mother looked terrified. She had stopped a few paces behind Mrs Mortimer and looked as though she would have turned and fled if it had not been for the solid figure of Betty behind her.

'Miss Brookfield, I asked you what is going on,' Mrs Mortimer said.

'The children . . .' Marion paused. 'The children have had a disagreement.'

'And you allowed it?'

'I – it happened suddenly.'

'No it didn't,' Florence wailed. 'She's been kicking me ever since we started coming here!'

'Who has been kicking you?' Mrs Mortimer asked. 'Miss Brookfield?'

At this Betty uttered an indignant snort, but Marion shot her a warning glance and willed her to keep quiet.

'No,' Florence said. By now she was sobbing. 'Violet is always kicking or pinching or tugging my hair and nobody ever notices, not at school and not here.'

'Florence . . .' Marion began, and completely unexpectedly the little girl threw herself into her tutor's arms.

'I'm sorry,' Florence said. 'I didn't mean that – not the last bit. You are the only person who has ever tried to stop her, but she's sly and spiteful and I hate her!'

Marion had expected that Violet's mother would have leapt to her daughter's defence by now, but instead she hovered uncertainly, biting her lip and looking uneasy. It was almost as if she were afraid of her own child.

Then, astonishingly, Mrs Mortimer snapped at her tearful stepdaughter, 'For goodness' sake be quiet, Florence. That's quite enough. No wonder people lose patience with you. Whatever this commotion is about, I'm sure you were the cause of it.'

'What exactly do you mean by that, Mrs Mortimer?' Marion asked. Florence had stopped sobbing but was clinging to her skirts.

'My stepdaughter always has some tale of this or that person picking on her. She is the unhappiest child I have ever come across. Furthermore, she is slow and clumsy and probably unteachable.'

Marion was shocked to the core. 'Forgive me, Mrs Mortimer, but if a child is unhappy, surely it is the duty of an adult, particularly a parent, to seek a reason, and as for her being slow and clumsy, I think I can explain that. I believe Florence to be short sighted. If you were to have her eyes tested and obtain spectacles for her, you might discover that she's far from unteachable.'

'How dare you speak to me like that?' Mrs Mortimer demanded. 'Obviously Florence cannot continue to have lessons here. Perhaps it was fate that this should happen. I have been persuading her father that the best thing to do would be to send her away to boarding school. When I tell him what has happened here today, I am sure there will be no more argument.' She paused briefly, then addressed Betty perfunctorily. 'Take the girls to get their coats and hats. I wish to speak to Violet's mother.'

Betty looked outraged to be addressed in such a manner, without even a please or a thank you, but Marion inclined her head and the maid shepherded the children into the hallway.

Mrs Mortimer turned towards Mrs Kilmartin, who blanched. Her soft baby features trembled. 'I'm very sorry . . .' she began.

'Please don't concern yourself. I'm sure your daughter acted like a normal high-spirited child. It is entirely Miss Brookfield's fault that things got so disgracefully out of hand. I hope you will agree that she is not a fit person to be in charge of well-brought-up girls.'

'Oh . . . but . . .'

Mrs Mortimer ignored Mrs Kilmartin's attempt to interrupt and continued, 'I intend to advise Miss Clarkson not to send any more pupils to her, and also that I am taking Florence away from school at the end of term. I recommend that you do the same.'

Without waiting for a response, Florence's stepmother swept from the room.

'Aren't you ready yet?' Marion heard her say crossly, then, 'Where do you think you're going? Come back here at once!'

'No, I want to say goodbye to Miss Brookfield.' Florence ran back into the room. 'I'm sorry,' she said. 'You were kind to me and I've made trouble for you.'

'You don't have to apologise,' Marion told her. 'I am the one who is sorry. Now you are going to be sent away to school.'

'That's all right. My father said that if I am to go away I must go to the school where his sister, my Aunt Adeline, is headmistress. Aunt Adeline is kind to me. I will be happy there – and I don't ever want to go home again!' she added with fervour.

Marion decided she had better ignore that sentiment. Instead she said, 'Will you promise me two things, Florence?'

The child nodded.

'Promise me that you will tell your aunt that I think you need to have your eyes examined.'

'I will. And what else?'

'Promise me that you will be happy.'

'I will.'

Florence flung herself into Marion's arms again, from where she was torn by her stepmother, who had come storming into the room.

When they had gone, Marion saw that Mrs Kilmartin was still standing there looking unhappy. 'Well, goodbye then,' she said at last.

'Violet will not be coming back?' Marion asked, although she knew the answer.

'No. I'm sorry. Please don't think I blame you. I know how

difficult she is. I believe you have done your best with her, but it's clear that she's not going to settle. It . . . it would be a waste of my husband's hard-earned money to continue with the lessons. I had a job convincing him in the first place, you see.' Then she sighed and began to apologise all over again. 'I'm truly sorry, Miss Brookfield.'

'Please don't concern yourself,' Marion said. 'I have failed her just as I failed Florence.'

At this Mrs Kilmartin looked even more unhappy.

'We have caused you a great deal of trouble.'

There was nothing Marion could say to this, so she remained silent and Mrs Kilmartin took her leave. Violet had stayed in the hall with Betty. Marion wondered without much hope if the child was ashamed of herself. She heard the front door close after them and sank down into the fireside chair. Betty came back into the room.

'Well?' she said.

Marion shook her head. 'Later, Betty, we'll talk later.'

'Right. I'll bring you a nice cup of tea and we'll hev a good old chinwag when you've calmed down a bit.'

Marion sipped her tea gratefully. She was still upset by what had just taken place, but as the tea soothed her spirits and she began to think more clearly, she remembered with dismay that she had not presented either of the mothers with the bill for the term's lessons. She had the feeling that neither of them would do the honourable thing and send the money to her.

In any case, perhaps she didn't deserve payment. I should have done better for the girls, she thought. Perhaps I am simply not suited to teaching. But in her heart she knew that was not the answer. If she had been better prepared, she was sure she could have devised ways of making even the most repetitive of tasks interesting. Instead she had allowed Violet to disrupt lessons and behave abominably towards gentle, unhappy Florence.

Whatever she did these days, and no matter how hard she tried to stop herself, she would lose concentration and find herself thinking about Daniel Brady and the way he had misled her. I allowed my emotions to get in the way of a professional manner and I am entirely at fault, she told herself.

But all that work for nothing! Marion imagined how she would have told her father about it; how they would have discussed it together, and how Henry would have tried to calm her down and maybe even find some humour in the situation. After a while she did manage to cheer up enough to laugh at herself. But her laughter was mixed with tears.

The day Annette left school she was exuberant. Marion didn't think she had ever seen her happier. 'Just think,' her sister exclaimed, 'I am no longer a schoolgirl. In January I will be a student – an art student. I can't wait!'

Marion tried to smile but her glance was troubled. She knew that it was going to be a struggle to send Annette to art school and she wondered how long she would be able to keep her there.

'And we have Christmas to look forward to!' Annette said. 'Am I too old now to hang up a stocking?' she asked. 'I hope not.'

Her eyes were shining like those of a child, and Marion turned her head away. She could not hide her distress. This would be the first Christmas without their father. It had been Henry Brookfield who had filled the stockings they hung each side of the fireplace. He had waited until they had gone up to bed and then put in each stocking an apple, an orange, a handful of nuts and a small toy.

This had gone on long after they were too old to believe in Father Christmas, and as the years passed the toys had given way to a pretty hair comb, or a brooch, or something for their needlework boxes such as a pin cushion, or some embroidered handkerchiefs.

Who did Annette imagine was going to fill the stockings this year? Marion, her tolerance worn thin by grief, was on the verge of asking her when she heard Annette say in a shaky voice, 'I forgot.'

Marion looked at her sister and saw that there were tears in her eyes. 'Am I wicked?' she asked, and the tears spilled over and ran down her cheeks. 'Am I wicked to have forgotten that Father will not be with us? This will be a dreadful Christmas without him.'

Marion reached for her sister and took her into her arms. 'No, Annette, you are not wicked. You are young and your life is full of excitement and hope. And this will not be a dreadful Christmas. I am sure Father would have forbidden us to be sad and gloomy. We will do our best to enjoy ourselves for his sake. Just you and me together.'

'And don't forget me,' a voice said. Marion turned to see that Betty had come into the room. 'I'll be here, won't I?'

Marion was puzzled. 'No, not on Christmas Day.'

'Try stopping me,' Betty retorted.

'But your mother – your family . . .'

'Me mam's as certain as I am that I should be here.'

Marion saw the resolution in Betty's eyes and smiled. 'Well, I can't quarrel with both you and your mother, can I?'

'I should think not indeed. And I want you to leave everything to me. Every little thing.'

'I will. I promise. But you must promise me that you will take Boxing Day off instead.'

Betty looked as though she was going to protest, but when she saw Marion's determined expression she smiled and said, 'All right.'

Marion couldn't pretend that she wasn't pleased at Betty's decision to come on Christmas Day, and they sat at the table together and drew up a shopping list. When they were satisfied that they had thought of everything, Betty said, 'Erm, there's something else . . .'

'Something we've forgotten?'

'No, nowt like that. It's just, I was wondering if you'd mind very much if Arthur came along for his Christmas dinner. He's not working that day and he has no family left. It will be lonely for him in his diggings.'

'Of course Arthur must come! He'll be very welcome.'

'Right then, that's settled.'

Betty slipped the shopping list into the pocket of her pinafore and resumed her household duties. Marion, knowing that this would be the last Christmas they would all be together, was determined to try and make it a happy occasion, especially for Annette. She drove all thoughts of the future and what it would bring out of her mind. For the moment it was right to live in the present. Her father would want them to be happy and she must honour his memory.

On Christmas Day, Betty and Arthur were in high spirits and their happiness was infectious. They are practising being a married couple, Marion thought as she watched them take charge of the kitchen as if it were their own. But when everything was ready, Arthur went quiet. At first he looked uneasy to be sitting down for the meal in the parlour, but when Betty told him that as the only man present he must carve the meat, he relaxed and began to enjoy himself again.

After they had done justice to Betty's cooking and the table was cleared, there was a moment of awkwardness. Betty and Arthur thought they should retire to the kitchen, whereas Marion wanted them to stay in the parlour until it was time for mince pies and sherry, after which they would be taking their leave.

The problem was resolved when the doorbell rang. A small group of carol-singers had come calling. They were children, and judging from the way they were dressed, they were from the poorer part of town. Marion said that they should come in and sing for them.

When they had sung 'Good King Wenceslas' and 'Away in a Manger', Marion gave them a mince pie and a glass of milk each. Arthur dropped a few coppers into the cap that the eldest boy held out.

And so the day passed. The first Christmas they had spent without their father, and also the first Christmas of a new chapter in their lives. Annette went to bed, warmed by the memories of the day and made happy by the knowledge that in just two weeks' time she would be starting at art school. She slept well.

Marion lay awake. She thought about the last time she had seen her father. She had promised him then that she would look after Annette until he came home. When she'd made that promise, neither of them had known that Henry Brookfield would never come home again.

As she tossed and turned in her bed, she tried very hard to banish thoughts of Daniel. Anger stirred when she remembered the way he had, by a look and a smile, led her to believe that they might have a future together. But the next minute she had to admit that he had never actually said anything – never declared his feelings or his intentions.

Daniel was going to marry Dora Gibb, and Betty, dear Betty, was going to marry her Arthur. Sheer exhaustion made Marion's limbs heavy and pressed down on her eyelids. But before sleep claimed her, she remembered that Victor Bateman was waiting for her answer.

All hope of sleep vanished as Marion lay in the darkness and thought about her life. About her father, who had loved and cared for his daughters, and kept them safe in this neat and respectable little house. About Daniel, who had seemed to care for her, and for whom she would have been prepared to consider an entirely different way of living.

And about Victor. A wealthy, sophisticated and good-looking man who, improbable as it seemed, had declared that he loved her and that

185

he wanted to marry her and take care of both her and her sister. Suddenly Marion yearned to be loved and cared for, to not have to face the daily struggle alone.

She got out of bed, lit the lamp and pulled on her robe. She went quietly downstairs to the study and, taking the writing paper from the drawer, sat at her father's desk. She stared for a moment into the glowing embers of the dying fire and then, taking up her pen, she began to write.

*Dear Victor*, she began.

Hannah Brady was awakened by sounds that at first, still drowsy with hard-earned sleep, she could not identify. She sat up groggily, held her breath and listened. It was footsteps on the stairs. Was it Daniel? Was he all right? He had managed to leave his bed and go down for his Christmas dinner, but by the time Dora had left to go home he had looked strained and tired. She had better go and investigate.

She pulled her shawl around her shoulders, swung her poor old legs over the side of the bed and felt for her slippers. She had barely risen to her feet when she heard the sound of horses' hoofs and a carriage rattling over the cobbles in the street below.

Who could be coming or going in such style at this hour of the morning? She went to the window to look out, but the carriage was already merely a dark shape pulling away up the street.

Already shivering with unease, Hannah lit the candle she kept by her bed and went down to the room that was still filled with the comforting aroma of their Christmas dinner. She saw the object on the table straight away. It was the cocoa tin she kept her savings in; the money they were living on until Daniel got back to work again. The tin lay on its side. Trembling, Hannah placed the candlestick on the table, then picked the tin up and looked inside. It was empty.

Her tired brain tried to make sense of it, and then intuition took her back upstairs. It wasn't Daniel's room she went into; it was Susan's. There was no one there. The bed was empty, and when Hannah turned fearfully, the candle making trembling shadows on the walls and ceiling, she saw that Susan's wardrobe was empty too.

Susan had gone. Left home. There was no other explanation. And she had taken with her all the money that Hannah had left in the world.

# Part Two

# Chapter Thirteen

'I'm sorry, Mr Brady, but I have no idea where your sister is.'

Maisie stood firm behind the counter of the tobacconist's and stared at Susan's brother curiously. He was a bonny fine fellow, she thought, even if he did look a little pale; and when he had walked into the shop he had definitely been limping. She glanced sideways at her reflection in the glass door of a display case and slid a hand up to tuck a stray strand of hair into her upswept coiffure.

'She hasn't been coming to work, then?' he asked.

'Not since Christmas Eve, and I can tell you that Mr Jacobs is more than vexed with her. In fact if she does have the nerve to turn up here again he's given me permission to show her the door.'

'I see,' Daniel Brady said, but it was plain to Maisie that he didn't see at all. 'I guessed she might have left her job,' he said awkwardly, 'but if you know where she is, I ask you for my mother's sake, please tell me.'

His words surprised her. 'Why should I know where Susan is?'

'You are friends, aren't you? I thought she might have confided in you.'

'Friends? What makes you think we are friends?'

Now he looked puzzled. 'Susan told me – I mean, she gave us that impression. After all, she visited your house many times. Why would she do that if you were not friends?'

'She told you she visited my house?'

'Yes. Quite often.'

Maisie stared at him, speechless with surprise. She saw panic forming in his eyes.

'Yes – and you gave her a hat . . .'

'A hat!'

'One you bought for yourself but you didn't think it suited you . . .'

Maisie shook her head.

'And you went to the theatre together and your father promised to see her home.' He stopped and looked at her. His expression was one of desperate resignation. 'It was all lies, wasn't it?'

Maisie had been enjoying the situation, but now, to her surprise, she felt desperately sorry for this decent – and good-looking – man.

'Yes, I'm afraid it was all lies, Mr Brady. My mother and father died years ago from the influenza and I've lived with my married sister ever since. Furthermore, I've never been to the theatre with your sister. It seems like she's been spinning quite a tale.'

Daniel Brady sighed and his broad shoulders drooped. For all her tough exterior, Maisie hated to see a grown man looking vulnerable. She frowned and chewed on her lip as she wondered if there was anything she could do.

He caught her expression and asked, 'What is it?'

'What do you mean?'

'You know something, don't you?'

'Mebbe I do, but I don't know if it will help you.'

'Let me be the judge of that.'

Just then the bell on the door jangled and there was a draught of cold air. Maisie looked beyond Daniel and saw one of her regular customers.

'Good afternoon, Mr Parker,' she said in her most charming tones. 'What can I do for you today?'

She saw the old gentleman's look of surprise. She knew she was putting on airs but she couldn't help trying to impress Daniel Brady.

'The usual, Maisie. You should know by now,' he chided.

Maisie hid her chagrin by bending over the glass-topped counter as she reached for a packet of ten Plain Cut Virginia cigarettes. By the time she straightened up, Mr Parker had already placed his money on the counter.

'Thank you, Miss Collins,' he said, and then his lined, world-weary features cracked into a smile. 'You're a good lass. Always a smile and a nice word, not like that other hoity-toity young madam. She only has eyes for the younger gentlemen, and the ones with a bit money to spare at that.'

Maisie didn't know whether she was pleased or sorry that Daniel Brady had heard this judgement of his sister. She saw how he had stiffened and clenched his fists. How powerful those fists look, she thought. It wouldn't be a good idea to cross him.

Mr Parker had already taken a cigarette from the packet and lit up. He inhaled as if his life depended on it, breathed out slowly and smiled through a wreath of smoke. 'That's better,' he said, and then he began to cough.

Maisie and Daniel watched helplessly until the coughing fit subsided.

'Well, I'd best get back to the office,' Mr Parker said. 'They think I just went to the bathroom.'

Maisie sensed impatience and frustration building up inside Daniel Brady, and she was pleased when Mr Parker finally walked towards the door. But when he opened it, he stopped and looked up at the darkening sky.

'Look at that,' he said. 'It's almost as black as night. Do you think they are snow clouds, Miss Collins?'

'Very likely,' Maisie said. 'You'd best hurry along before it starts. You haven't got your overcoat and I don't want my favourite customer catching a cold, do I?'

Pulling the collar of his jacket up around his ears, Mr Parker hurried out into the cold street and the door banged shut behind him, setting the bell jangling again.

'You were saying . . .?' Daniel Brady said, as though they hadn't been interrupted.

'Well, there was someone . . .'

'Someone?'

'A gentleman.'

Daniel took a step towards the counter, and Maisie had to stop herself from shrinking back.

'Yes, a gentleman. He used to wait for her.'

'Do you know his name?'

'I'm sorry, I don't. Well dressed. He wore a top hat and a cloak on one occasion. Perhaps . . .'

'What is it?'

'Maybe he was going to the theatre.'

Daniel Brady looked at her bleakly. 'With Susan.' It wasn't a question.

'Yes.'

'Do you know how long it had been going on?'

'No. I'm sorry.'

'Thank you for trying to help. I'll go now.'

Daniel turned abruptly and made for the door.

'Mr Brady!' she called after him.

He turned to face her. 'Yes?'

'Don't take too much notice of what Mr Parker said. Your sister was always pleasant to all the customers.'

Maisie hoped she would be forgiven the lie, but for some reason she could not bear this man to be hurt more than he already had been by his sister's disappearance.

'Thank you.'

'And if I hear anything – if I discover anything at all – I'll let you know.'

'That's good of you.'

He turned and reached for the handle of the door.

'But where can I get in touch with you?' Maisie said.

Without speaking, Daniel came back and reached for the notepad that Maisie pushed across the counter. She gave him a pencil and he wrote down his address.

'I'd be grateful,' he said, but before he turned away for the final time, she saw the anguish in his eyes.

Dora shoved her hands deep into her pockets and huddled in a shop doorway as she watched the door of the tobacconist's at the other side of the Haymarket. Since the turn of the year the weather had been bitterly cold, and going out without gloves had caused her to develop chilblains on her fingers.

The small, red, itchy lumps were driving her crazy. Every night she applied a poultice of mashed turnip, grated horseradish mustard and oil, but she could hardly go about with her hands wrapped up in the daytime.

She knew very well where she'd left her gloves, but she'd be damned if she was going to go back for them. No, she'd have to knit herself a new pair; her mother had some spare sock wool, but how could she hold the knitting needles with her fingers in this state? She supposed she could buy a pair, but they wouldn't be as warm or as practical as hand-knitted gloves, and besides, that would be extravagant.

Dora watched as an elderly gent went into the tobacconist's and, after a while, came out again. Surely Daniel wouldn't be much longer. What on earth could he be talking about? Either they knew where Susan was or they didn't. Dora guessed that they didn't. If that sly little madam had had something planned she wouldn't have confided in anyone.

Hannah was in a dreadful state. She seemed to have completely forgotten that Daniel wasn't properly fit and had urged him to go seeking Susan. As soon as Dr Cameron deemed him fit to go out, the first place Daniel had thought to go was the shop where Susan had worked.

Of course Dora had her own ideas. Honestly, Hannah and Daniel were so green. Didn't they know that young women who worked in tobacconists' shops were in a position to meet all kinds of men – men with dishonourable intentions? Many of these lasses were earning a bit extra by being accommodating. Obviously Susan had met someone who was prepared to set her up somewhere. If Daniel ever found her she would hardly be respectable enough to come back home. At least that was Dora's opinion.

And fancy taking all of Hannah's savings! Daniel was going to have to get back to work sooner than was good for him, and until then he'd told his mother not to worry, that he had a bit put by. But why should he have to dip into his little nest egg when that should be put aside for when he got married? Oh, Dora could just strangle that young madam, causing everyone so much bother.

Finally the door of the tobacconist's opened and Daniel came out. Dora's heart lurched when she saw how painfully he was limping. How on earth was he going to manage laying the tramlines? In this weather, without his proper balance, he could so easily slip and fall and do more damage.

Then she realised that he was crossing the market square and coming straight towards her. She turned to open the door of the shop behind her, a pork butcher's, but it was too late. He'd seen her and called her name.

'Have you been following me?' he asked.

'No.' The lie came out quickly and she saw him raise his eyebrows. But to her relief, she also saw that he was smiling.

'Are you sure?'

'All right then, I have,' she said, half defiantly. 'Your first day out of the house and in weather like this. I wanted to make sure that you were all right. Is there anything wrong with that?'

'No, there isn't,' he said, 'but there's no need, you know. I'm not a bairn. I can look after myself.'

'Of course you can! I didn't mean to insult you. It's just that . . . just that I've been so worried about you.'

Daniel looked at her gravely. 'I know you have, and I don't deserve your concern.'

'Oh yes, you do!'

'No I don't, but it's too cold to stand here arguing about it. Come along.'

He turned to go back the way he had come.

'Where are we going? Have you found something out about Susan? Where she is?'

'No, I haven't.'

He looked dejected. Dora had the impression that there was something he wasn't telling her, but she knew it would be no use pressing him. She stepped out of the shelter of the doorway and flinched as the cold wind bit into her face. Daniel took her arm and began guiding her through the wintry flakes drifting down from the leaden sky.

'So, where are we going?'

Daniel turned to look at her and smiled. 'We're going to Alvini's coffee shop for a hot drink. I think we both deserve one.'

Dora could hardly believe she was sitting there. The delicious smells of cooking each time the swing doors that led to the kitchen were opened, the hiss of the coffee machine, the busy waiters with their black waistcoats and their shirtsleeves held up by metal armbands balancing their trays on one hand high above their heads as they moved between the tables.

The other customers, mostly women at this time of day, sat easily, as if they were used to coming here often, their shopping bags beside them on spare chairs or tucked under the table as they gossiped about the new fabrics in the department stores or told each other how well little Johnny was doing at school, or how difficult it was to get a decent char or a maid of all work these days.

Dora sat up straight, pleased that she'd put her best hat on, and tried to look as though this wasn't a new experience for her. Daniel gave her the menu that was propped up between the cruet and the sugar bowl and told her to choose anything she wanted.

'Anything?'

'Anything.'

So Dora asked for hot chocolate and a cream horn. Daniel ordered coffee and something called a Danish pastry for himself. When they were served, Dora realised that she had a problem. Once she started eating her cream horn, Daniel would be able to see her hands and the ugly red splotches caused by the chilblains. She solved the problem by 'accidentally' knocking the menu card over and then putting it back in such a position that it would hide her plate – and her hands.

She noticed that some of the customers were eating their cream cakes with a tiny fork. What a palaver, she thought, but she didn't want to shame Daniel so she did so too. Daniel himself looked so comfortable that she was prompted to ask him, 'Have you been here before?'

'Just once,' he replied.

Dora looked at him questioningly.

'When I took my mother and sister to the theatre I treated them to a pot of tea and toasted teacakes before the show.'

A cloud passed over his face again, and Dora wished she hadn't asked him.

After a while, a waiter came by and asked Daniel if he wanted his coffee topping up, but Daniel shook his head.

'If you're finished, we'd better go,' he told Dora. 'My mother will be anxious to hear what I've discovered. And I'd be grateful if you'd come in with me when we get home. Mother will appreciate your company.'

Dora knew that Hannah would go on and on about her missing daughter and that she would have to put up with it. She must never show her true feelings. But then she told herself that perhaps she should be grateful to Daniel's sister after all. He was so concerned about finding her that he had not mentioned Marion Brookfield again.

'Of course I'll come in and sit with your ma,' Dora said. 'You can rely on me.'

They rose from their chairs and Daniel started to lead the way towards the door. Dora was about to follow him when she saw something that made her stop suddenly. She gasped, and Daniel must have heard her because he turned and looked at her enquiringly.

'Is anything the matter?'

'No . . . it's just that I stood up too quickly,' she lied. 'You know that can make you dizzy.' She smiled up at him in what she hoped was a helpless manner. 'Would you mind if I held your arm?'

'Be my guest.'

Daniel's smile was kind and Dora was almost overwhelmed with emotion. She linked her arm through his and then pretended to stumble so that she had to hold on all the more tightly. Just as she hoped, Daniel was so busy looking after her as he guided her towards the door that he did not notice the two young women in black coats sitting at a nearby table.

When she got to the door, Dora turned round to look at them. One of them, the younger girl, was staring at Dora and Daniel quite openly. The other was making a show of drinking her coffee and pretending that she hadn't seen them. But Dora was sure she had, and it gave her great pleasure to see how rattled Marion Brookfield looked.

'Look, Marion, isn't that Daniel Brady?' Annette said.

'No, I don't think so. And please turn round. It's rude to stare at people.'

'Yes, it is him – go on, look out of the window. There he is at the tram stop.'

There was no need to look. Marion had been aware of Daniel's presence from the moment he had entered the coffee shop, and had studiously avoided looking at him, although she was sure that his companion, Dora, had seen her. Marion knew that Annette wouldn't drop the subject unless she complied, so she looked out of the window and saw the two figures at the tram stop. They were just about to board a tram. Flakes of snow had settled on their coats and on the man's dark hair. Marion watched silently until the tram pulled away.

'I believe you're right,' she told Annette. 'Now drink up your coffee. I'd like to get home before the snow starts to fall in earnest.'

But by the time Annette had finished her coffee and eaten every crumb of her almond pastry, it was already too late. They picked up their parcels and made for the door of the coffee house, and then halted and stared out in dismay. The fall of snow was heavier and they could see the queue of miserably hunched people at the tram stop. Shoppers and anyone else who could had obviously decided to leave town and get home to their firesides.

'Why don't we take a cab?' Annette asked.

'There will be another tram along soon.'

'But there's no guarantee we'll get on it. Look how the queue is growing.'

'That's true. But a cab would be an unnecessary expense.'

'Unnecessary? In this weather? Really, Marion, you behave as though we were poor!'

'We are.'

'Well, maybe so, but not for much longer.' Annette grew impatient. 'You don't want me to catch a cold, do you? Not now when I've just started at art school. And besides, I don't want my portfolio to get wet – and what about your shopping?'

Marion began to laugh. 'I can see I've lost the battle,' she said. 'All right, we'll take a cab. But you're going to get just as wet going across to the cab stand.'

'Not if we run!' Annette said, and they hurried laughing through the swirling snow.

They had arranged to meet at Alvini's at the end of Annette's day at college. And in the hansom on the way home, Annette chattered happily about her work, the lecturers and the other students; those she liked and those she didn't.

'And what about you?' she remembered to ask her sister. 'Did you enjoy your shopping trip? Choosing the fabrics and everything?'

'I suppose so.'

In truth Marion had not enjoyed the day, and if she had not promised to meet Annette she would have hurried around the shops and gone home much earlier.

'It was funny Mr Brady not coming over to say hello, wasn't it?' Annette said suddenly.

Marion was taken unawares. 'He didn't see us.'

'Do you think not? Well, that young woman who was with him did. I saw her looking at you. Do you know her?'

'She came to the house to return a book Mr Brady had borrowed.'

Annette frowned. 'Now that I think about it, she didn't look very pleased to see us.'

'You're imagining things.'

'No, I don't think I am. Who is she, by the way?'

'She's Mr Brady's fiancée.'

'No! Really? How do you know that?'

'She told me.'

'Well, I must say I'm surprised.'

'Why?'

'Well . . . I know Mr Brady is a working man, but he behaves almost like a gentleman, doesn't he? And that person he was with was definitely common.'

'Annette!' Marion was truly shocked. 'You mustn't talk like that. Father did not bring us up to look down on others.'

'I know he didn't, but sometimes it's hard not to.'

Marion did not feel like arguing with her sister, so she lapsed into silence and tried to distract herself by looking out at the passing scene. The street lamps were being lit and light sparkled on the new carpet of snow. How attractive the streets look when they are like this, Marion thought. But not to the poor souls who have nowhere else to go. Now and then she glimpsed the huddled shapes in doorways or alleyways.

Over the winter months, the city filled up with agricultural labourers who had no work or lodgings at this time of year. They came into town looking for employment and somewhere to stay. If they were lucky, whole families of them crowded into one or two rooms in a cheap lodging house. Otherwise they joined the permanent vagrant population on the streets.

Victor was aware of the problem, as were other prosperous businessmen. When he had returned from London, overjoyed to be accepted as her suitor, he had often turned the conversation to her father's work, and he had told Marion that he would do whatever he could to help the city's poor. The sooner the better, Marion thought now, or many of these folk, men, women and children, would not survive the winter.

The next morning, after Annette had left and the breakfast pots had been washed, Betty and her cousin Sarah were upstairs making the beds when the bell rang.

'That's the front door,' Sarah said.

'So it is,' Betty replied.

Her young cousin looked at her across the bed they were making together. 'Shall I answer it?'

'Yes. Gan on.'

'What shall I say?'

'Depends who it is, doesn't it? Oh, get on with you. I'm sure whoever it is won't bite you.'

Sarah was laughing as she hurried downstairs, but when she opened the door her smile faded. A very smart gentleman stood there. He wore riding breeches, highly polished calf-length boots, a black single-breasted three-quarter coat with shiny buttons all the way down the front, and a top hat.

'Yes, sir?' she said.

The gentleman smiled. A sort of superior smile, Sarah thought, as if she had made a mistake of some kind.

'Is Miss Brookfield at home?' he asked.

Sarah sensed her cousin Betty coming quietly down the stairs behind her. She pulled herself together.

'Who shall I say is calling?' she asked.

'Tell her Lady Cressington would like to see her.'

'Oh . . .' It was only then that Sarah looked beyond him and saw the carriage – or was it a coach? Anyway, it had a sort of roof pulled over the top so Sarah couldn't see inside.

'Hurry up, my lass, Lady Cressington is waiting,' the coachman said.

'Sorry – I'll go and ask – I mean tell her. Miss Brookfield, that is.' Sarah turned to go, but then turned back and said, 'Please wait here.'

She was just about to knock on the parlour door when Betty took her arm and said, 'Not bad, pet. But now you go along and put the kettle on. I'll tell Miss Marion who is here.'

Marion was startled. 'What can Lady Cressington want?' she asked Betty.

'How should I know?' Betty smiled. 'Shall I show her in?'

Marion rose from her seat as Lady Cressington swept into the room on a breath of cold fresh air. She was wearing a fur cape with a hood and she had her hands thrust into a matching muff that hung round her neck on a satin ribbon. She drew her hands out of the muff and threw the hood back. She walked towards the fire, where she stood on the hearthrug for a moment warming her hands before she turned and smiled at Marion.

They sat down in the fireside chairs, facing each other. Lady Cressington smiled. 'You look surprised.'

'I am. I wasn't expecting a visit. I'm sorry if I appear rude.'

'Of course you don't appear rude, and furthermore, you have every right to be to be surprised.'

Lady Cressington loosened the ties on her cloak and let it fall from her shoulders. She was wearing an expensive silk taffeta gown of a shade of blue that was a perfect match for her eyes.

'You've been shopping, I see.' Lady Cressington nodded towards the large brown paper parcel that lay unopened on the table.

'Yes.'

'Something exciting?'

'Just some fabric from Bainbridge's department store.'

'Let me guess! For your wedding dress?'

'Yes, and for Annette's gown, too. But how did you know?'

'Don't look so shocked, my dear. I know that you didn't want a fuss – it wouldn't be quite proper while you are still in mourning – but last time I visited Charlotte, she told me.'

'Charlotte? Victor's sister?'

'Yes. Although not exactly friends, we serve on one or two of the same charity committees. Tell me, what do you think of Charlotte?'

Marion didn't think it would be appropriate to discuss her future sister-in-law with a comparative stranger, so she was pleased to be able to say, 'I haven't met her yet.'

'Haven't you? Ah well, that pleasure is still to come.'

There was something about Lady Cressington's wry smile and her suddenly guarded expression that made Marion uneasy.

'But Miss Bateman told you that I am going to marry Victor?' Marion said.

'Yes, and that is why I am here.'

'I don't understand.'

'My dear, don't take offence, but you are all alone in the world.'

'I have my sister.'

'I know, and you have had to become like a mother to her. But you have no one to take on that role for you. I told you last time we met that if you ever needed help you must come to me, and I can't imagine a more appropriate time than when you are planning your wedding.'

'That's kind of you, but Victor seems to be doing all the planning.'

'But he is a mere man! What does he know of wedding dresses and trousseaux? All the clothes and linen, especially items such as nightdresses and underwear, that a new bride needs.'

Marion was embarrassed. 'He – he has been very kind. He insisted on opening an account for me at Bainbridge's and he said I must get whatever I need.'

'And is that all you have purchased?' Lady Cressington rose from her chair and went over to the table. 'This one parcel? May I see?'

Without waiting for an answer, she undid the string and opened up the brown paper. She stared for a moment at the contents and then said, 'Oh, my dear. Is this for your wedding gown?'

'Yes.'

'But grey?'

'I am in mourning for my father.'

'I know, I know, but this dull grey paramatta is not the only choice. How I wish you had asked me to come with you. But it's not too late. Please parcel this up and send it back. We will go together and find something more suitable for a young bride.'

'I don't want to be disrespectful to my father's memory.'

'Your father took his work – his important work – very seriously, but I do not remember him as being austere.'

'No, he certainly wasn't, but—'

Lady Cressington held up her hand to stop Marion speaking further. 'If you truly want to honour your father, just imagine how happy he would be to see you marrying a man like Victor Bateman. How proud he would be to lead you down the aisle; how beautiful he would want you to look. And Annette, too. If she is to be your little bridesmaid, she must look just as beautiful.'

Marion joined Lady Cressington at the table and looked down at the grey fabric. 'But what shall I buy instead of this?'

'Let me think. Purple is allowed for such an occasion during mourning; however, you are too young for purple. But there's also violet, pansy, soft mauve – yes, mauve, that would suit you very well. And it must be silk taffeta, of course, which will rustle in the approved fashion as you walk down the aisle.'

Marion began to relax as she responded to her visitor's enthusiasm. 'How shall I make it rustle?' she asked.

'Petticoats, of course! Petticoats with frills like waterfalls. Oh, how I shall enjoy myself. I'm so glad I've met you! It will be like having a daughter of my own.' She paused suddenly and looked thoughtful. 'I wonder whether it would be appropriate to dress your hair with flowers? Perhaps not. You shall have a darling little hat with a gauzy veil.'

'I hate hats. I wear them under protest because I'm told it's proper.'

'I promise you, you shall not hate the hat I choose for you. In fact you will hardly know it's there when we have perched it amongst the upswept coils of your magnificent hair. So that's settled then.'

Marion felt as though she had been swept along on a tide of enthusiasm. 'Is it?' she asked uncertainly.

'I shall call for you tomorrow morning and we will go and choose some more attractive fabrics – perhaps Annette's gown should be a paler shade than yours. And we will purchase all the other clothing a bride must have.'

'But the expense . . .'

'My dear Marion, Mr Bateman would not have opened an account for you if he had not wanted you to take full advantage of it. We have spoken of your father, but your bridegroom will want to be proud of you too.' She smiled. 'Remember you are marrying a very rich man.'

Lady Cressington returned to the fireside chair and picked up her cloak. 'Will you ring for the girl to help me on with this? Oh, and tell her to parcel that fabric up again.'

Marion rang the bell and wondered who would appear, Betty or Sarah. She hoped it would be Sarah, because she was quite sure that Betty would not think much of being referred to as 'the girl'.

Her silent prayers were heard, and it was Sarah who answered the summons. Her face was flushed and she looked completely over-whelmed as she helped the visitor into her cloak. Once it was on Lady Cressington's shoulders, Sarah hesitated for a moment and then took hold of the ties. But she was all fingers and thumbs, as her cousin Betty would have said, and Lady Cressington knocked her hands away impatiently. However, she softened the moment with a smile.

'Would you help me, Marion dear?' she said. 'The girl can go out and tell James that I am ready to go home.'

'Yes, my lady,' Sarah said, and she actually bobbed a curtsy. 'But who is James?'

'My coachman, of course.'

'Oh, him. I'll tell him, but he's not outside. Betty felt sorry for him waiting out there in the cold so she invited him into the kitchen for a cup of tea.'

'Indeed.'

When the door had closed behind Sarah, Lady Cressington frowned. 'I admire you for being so pleasant – not to say free and easy – with your servants, but that girl! She isn't very well trained, is she?'

Marion smiled. 'She isn't trained at all. Not yet. She is our house-maid's cousin. Betty arranged that Sarah should work alongside her until she gets married, and then the plan was that Sarah would take over here.'

'So what will happen to them now – now that you are to be married and will be leaving this house? They won't be able to come with you.'

'There is no problem. Betty is getting married sooner than she thought she would, and her husband-to-be, Arthur, does not want her to go out to work.'

Lady Cressington's smile was genuine. 'I'm very pleased for her. And the other girl?'

'She's going to work for Betty.'

'A servant work for another servant? I don't understand.'

'Arthur is a police constable and he has just been promoted to the rank of sergeant. Sarah will go to them each day as a daily maid.'

'You must be pleased for them.'

'I am, and I have Victor to thank for solving the problem. I told him that Betty and Arthur could not get married until they found a decent house to rent, and he has made one available. It is not too far from the police station and it has every modern convenience.'

'Victor is a good man.' Lady Cressington laughed. 'Or so his sister Charlotte constantly assures me. If I really were your mother, I couldn't be more happy for you.'

Lady Cressington was not the only caller at the Brookfield house that day. As the carriage drew away, the horses' hoofs and the wheels of the carriage threw up sprays of slushy snow, narrowly missing the man walking up the street.

Daniel stepped back until the carriage had driven by; he did not want his clothes soiled. The weather had been too bad for him to go and seek work today, so he had dressed carefully in his best and set out on a call he had been wanting to make for some time. Even though he was not sure what his reception would be.

He opened the gate and limped painfully up the short garden

path. Each breath he took hurt his still bruised ribcage. The door was opened by a girl he had not seen before.

'May I speak to Miss Brookfield?' Daniel said. The girl frowned as if not knowing quite what to do. 'My name is Daniel Brady,' he added.

'I'll see. Wait here.'

She hadn't invited him to step inside, so he watched as she walked as far as the door to the parlour and knocked. She waited a moment and then entered the room, shutting the door behind her. She came out again almost immediately. She hesitated before walking towards him, and her face was flushed as if she were embarrassed.

'Miss Brookfield says she's not at home.' She raised a hand to her mouth. 'Oh dear.'

Daniel was devastated, but he felt sorry for her. 'I understand.'

He turned to go, and the door closed behind him before he reached the gate. She had not forgiven him for losing her father's papers. Dora had told him that she had called to return Marion's book and worried that she might have given a garbled account of what had happened, he had written to Marion as soon as he'd been able.

She had replied. A single sheet of notepaper told him that she was sorry he had been attacked and that she did not blame him for the loss of her father's papers. She hoped he would soon be well. She had not suggested that he call to see her again, but neither had she told him not to. He had decided to take the chance.

Daniel had not gone far when the front door opened again. 'Mr Brady!'

He turned, smiling. Marion had changed her mind. She would see him after all. It was not the young maid who stood in the doorway now.

'Betty,' he said, walking back towards her. 'I'm pleased to see you.'

She pursed her lips. 'Mr Brady, you mustn't call here again.'

Daniel's smile faded. 'Did Miss Brookfield tell you to say that?'

'Not exactly.'

'What do you mean?'

'Sarah was supposed to say that Miss Brookfield would not be at home if you called.'

Daniel was dismayed. 'How formal that sounds.'

'Sometimes the formal way is the politest way of putting it.'

'Is she angry because I lost her father's papers?'

'No. Not angry. Sad. But she knows it wasn't your fault.'

'So why will she not see me?'

'It wouldn't be proper. Not now.'

'Betty, you're talking in riddles.'

'Miss Brookfield is an engaged lady.'

At first he didn't take it in. 'Engaged? You mean Marion is to be married?'

'Aye, that's right, and to a good man who will take care of her, and Annette too.'

'I can't believe it!'

'Well it's true, and I want you to go now. I don't want you spoiling things for her. Do you understand?'

Daniel couldn't speak. He nodded, but in truth he didn't understand at all. He had allowed himself to dream of a future with Marion, even though he knew how preposterous some might find the idea. But she had encouraged him in his dreams, hadn't she? She had not flirted, not set out to lure him, but the way she looked at him, the natural way they could converse together, surely that meant something? All the time, though, she was being courted by another. It must be so, because otherwise this marriage was too sudden.

Marion had not exactly lied to him, but all the same she had deceived him. Despite his limp, Daniel hurried home. Fuelled by anger, he ignored the pain caused by his injuries. Betty need not worry; he had no wish to call on Marion Brookfield ever again.

Marion heard the front door close, followed almost immediately by the sound of the gate closing. She took Daniel Brady's letter from her pocket. She didn't know why she'd kept it. She read it once more, then crumpled it up and threw it into the fire.

# Chapter Fourteen

The light from the fire reflected in the highly polished furniture and the rich red velvet drapes gave a cosy feel to the room, making it seem a little less grand and intimidating. Susan wandered over to the window, lifted the heavy cream-coloured lace curtains, and looked out. There were lights in the windows of the houses opposite and smoke from the chimneys curled up into the leaden sky.

Jane came into the room to light the lamps and tut-tutted to see Susan standing there. 'Really, Miss Brady,' she said. 'You shouldn't lift the curtains like that. You don't want nosy folk to see in, do you?'

Susan let the heavily patterned lace fall and sighed as she turned round to face the housemaid. 'I suppose not – although I don't see the harm in it. It's a beautiful room.'

'That's just it,' Jane said, and she bustled over to join Susan at the window. 'It's too fine looking for the likes of folk round here. They'll just get jealous. Now if you stand aside I'll draw the curtains.'

Susan stood aside obediently. She had learned to be a little in awe of Jane, who was always respectful, and yet, Susan couldn't help feeling, sometimes acted more like the mistress than the maid.

'I don't mind people being jealous,' Susan said.

Jane turned to face her. 'Pride is a sin, didn't you know that?' If this was a rebuke, she softened it with a smile. 'Now can I get you anything? A little snack to keep you going until the master arrives for the evening meal?'

'Is he coming here tonight?' Susan was astonished. She hadn't seen Gilbert since the day he had brought her here, when he had told her that much as he hated to leave her, he had to go away. 'Has he returned from London?'

Jane's smile grew broader. 'He has indeed, and I'm sure he will be bringing you all the gifts he promised.'

'And so he should,' Susan said. 'I have been so lonely here by myself.'

'By yourself ? What about me? Don't I count for anything?'

'I'm sorry, Jane. You've been good company for me. But you know what I mean. I've never been away from my family before.'

'You knew when you left them you wouldn't be able to go back.'

'Yes. Well, not for a while, anyway. My mother and my brother will be angry with me, but I'm sure they'll forgive me once we are married.'

Jane gave her the oddest of looks. She opened her mouth as if she were about to say something, then changed her mind.

Susan remembered what Jane had just told her. 'How do you know Mr Mason is coming here tonight?' she asked.

'Simple. He wrote me a letter.'

'He wrote to you and not to me? Why would he do that?'

'Perhaps he wanted to surprise you.'

'If that's the case, you've just spoilt the surprise!' Susan said petulantly.

'Now, now, divven't get in a pet. I've told you for your own sake. You'll want to look your best for him, won't you?'

'Hmm. I suppose so.'

'So sit you down like a good lass and read those magazines he ordered for you. All the new fashions for the spring. I'll bring you a cup of tea and a slice of Genoa cake. You like Genoa cake, don't you?'

'Mmm.' Susan felt as though she was being coaxed into a good mood, as if she were a child.

'Then after that I'll help you have a lovely bath and put your glad rags on. All right?'

'All right.'

Susan sat down as she was told and waited for her tea. What else could she do? She wasn't sure what to make of Jane. At first the young woman had been polite and respectful, but as the days went by she had grown decidedly bossy.

Although it had snowed heavily since the beginning of the year, Susan soon realised that it didn't seem to lie long here by the sea. So one morning a few days ago, when the sun was actually shining, she had decided she would go for a walk along the promenade.

Jane was in the kitchen preparing the midday meal and Susan decided not to bother her. She had put her own clothes on since she was a little girl and she didn't need a maid to help her dress now. Although she had to admit that she liked Jane's attentions.

She pulled on her boots, put on her coat and hat and had got as far as opening the front door when she heard a voice behind her. Jane was calling from the door that led into the kitchen.

'Miss Brady! Where do you think you're going?'

'For a walk,' Susan replied. 'You didn't think I was running away, did you?' She had no idea why she had added that remark, but she noticed the effect it had on Jane, who looked decidedly uncomfortable.

'No, of course not. The very idea. Why would you run away from such a lovely house and such a generous gentleman?'

'I was joking, you know.'

Jane smiled, but again Susan thought she looked uneasy.

'I thought I would go for a walk along the prom,' Susan said. 'Do you realise I haven't been out of this house since I first came here. I need to blow the cobwebs away.'

'I'll come with you,' Jane said, and she began to untie her pinafore.

'There's no need.'

'Don't you want a bit of company?'

Susan didn't want company. At least she didn't want Jane to accompany her. In fact she had wanted to get away from the older girl for a while. But she didn't know how to tell her without being rude. Remember, I am the mistress here, she told herself. Or I'm supposed to be. I ought to be able to do what I want. While she hesitated, Jane had shed her pinafore and put on her hat and coat.

'Here you are,' she said as she came towards Susan with a large fringed paisley scarf, which was almost a shawl. 'Let me put this over your head.'

Susan backed away. 'No. It will make me look like an old woman.'

'You don't want that lovely hat to blow off and land in the sea, do you? And besides, who is going to see you? All sensible folk will stay indoors today.'

So Susan had given in, and she and Jane went for a walk along the promenade that curved round the top of the cliffs. Although the sun was shining, Jane had been right about the wind. It was tossing the seagulls high into the sky and chopping up the waves so violently that it made Susan alarmed to look at them.

She grasped the iron rail with one hand while she held on to her scarf with the other. Jane didn't actually say 'I told you so', but Susan could sense that that was what she was thinking. She turned to look at the maid and saw that her nose and her cheeks were bright red. She burst out laughing and the wind caught her laughter and took it out to sea.

Jane scowled. 'What is it?' she asked.

'Nothing. I'm . . . I'm just enjoying being out.'

'Humph,' Jane grunted unbelievingly.

Susan knew it would be cruel to keep Jane out much longer, but before she turned to go home she stared down at the beach. As the waves retreated they left ripples in the sand that glistened in the cold sunlight. She had a sudden memory of a day spent on this very stretch of sand. It was a Sunday when she had been a small child. Her mother and Daniel had brought her here for a picnic. They had come to the coast on the train. A rare treat, as money was tight in those days.

Her mother had spread an old tartan rug and sat down thankfully to enjoy the sun and the sea air. Daniel had made sand pies with Susan and built a castle with turrets and a moat. How she had laughed when the tide started to come in and the moat had filled with water. And then she had cried when the waves knocked the castle over completely. At that point their mother had called them back and given them money for ice creams. Susan had gone home tired and happy. Her eyes filled up as she remembered that day.

'Why are you crying?' Jane asked.

'I'm not. It's the wind.'

'We'd best get along home then.'

'All right.'

And so they had come back to the beautiful little house that didn't seem a bit like home. Once they were safely inside, and Jane was helping her to remove her outdoor clothes, the maid suddenly said, 'Look, Miss Brady, I don't think I've been fair with you.'

Susan looked at her in surprise.

'The real reason I didn't want you to go out was because I was worried that you would be recognised.'

'So that's why you wrapped me up in a shawl! But who would recognise me? I don't know anybody who lives here.'

'The master thinks your brother might be looking for you and he doesn't want any trouble.'

Susan's spirits sank. She knew that Daniel could very well be looking for her. He was almost certain to be, in fact, and if he found her he would drag her home and she would have to face her mother and explain why she had taken her savings. As it happened, she had not needed to. The money was still in her purse. She hadn't been anywhere to spend it, and in any case her gentleman had told her that she could ask him for anything she wanted and if it was within reason he would provide it.

And so he had. Without her asking, beautiful clothes had arrived for her approval. And not just outer garments, but the most luxurious underwear too. Hats, boots, gloves; she had tried them on, chosen what she wanted and sent the rest back.

He had ordered magazines, books, hampers of delicious food. She certainly had nothing to complain about. Except that she was lonely without him, and some days she felt like a prisoner. What was the song? The song about the girl who married for wealth not for love and felt like a bird in a cage – a gilded cage . . .

When she had run away in the middle of the night, she had thought she was going to be married before very long. Why else would her gentleman friend persuade her to elope?

She remembered how excited she had been when he had asked her to leave home, to elope with him. *Elope* . . . that was the word he had used, and that was what sweethearts did, wasn't it? They ran off to Scotland – to Gretna Green, where they didn't need permission from their families in order to get wed. And now that she thought about it, why hadn't he simply asked her mother's permission? Surely her mother would not have refused such a good match for her daughter.

Did he think her mother – and Daniel – would not approve because he was so much older than she was? That must be it. And he must truly love her, mustn't he, or otherwise he would never have set her up in such a beautiful little house. And tonight he was coming to see her. Jane had said that he wanted it to be a surprise. Well, she would play her part. She wouldn't let on that she knew and she would act all surprised and excited when he showed his face.

She would make sure that she looked as beautiful as she could, and he would be so entranced . . . entranced, that was a word they used in the romantic novels she loved . . . so entranced that he would probably propose to her this very night.

210

Her spirits lifted and she was quite ready to forgive Jane for being so bossy.

Susan finished her tea and cake and in a state of high excitement she went up to the bathroom. She looked around the clean cream and blue tiled room with pleasure. A bath with taps and running water, hot and cold; this was better than dragging the zinc tub out from under the scullery bench and filling it with pans of hot water. This was better than having to share the water with her mother, although Hannah always let Susan go first.

She allowed Jane to undress her and pin up her hair and then watched as the maid sprinkled bath salts into the gently steaming water. Parma Violet. The perfume rose and filled the room. The heady aroma aroused her senses. Jane helped her into the bath tub and sponged her down. Then she left her with instructions to relax for a while. Susan lay there and allowed her worries and cares to drain away. Tonight everything would change; tonight would be the beginning of a new life.

Some noise, some movement, disturbed her and Susan tried to open her eyes. Her lids were heavy and her head was swimming. Swimming . . . I am swimming, she thought, but she could not command her limbs, and to her dismay, she felt as though she were being dragged down again. Some current had seized hold of her and was pulling her down under the water. Down . . . down into the murky depths. Except this wasn't the sea, it was a feather mattress.

It was peaceful here, wherever it was. She would have drifted off into a deeper sleep if a pounding noise had not woken her up again. Someone is knocking at the door, she thought, but when she tried to raise her head from the pillow she winced with pain and realised that the pounding was inside her own head.

She was not alone! As her senses returned, she realised that someone was in the room – her bedroom – moving quietly about. She opened her eyes wider and tried to focus. The room was lit only by the gentle glow of the fire and the harsher light of the winter moon that thrust its way through a gap in the curtains. Susan closed her eyes tight as if to squeeze the remnants of sleep away, then opened them again. She looked up and saw the shadows moving on the ceiling.

'I'm sorry, did I wake you?' a voice said, and memories came crashing back, like stormy waves on the shore.

But not fully, and not in any order that made sense to her fuddled brain.

She moved an arm in the bed and felt the warmth of the feather mattress. She turned her head to the side and saw the crumpled pillow next to hers.

It was true, then. It had not been a dream. He had been lying here next to her. She covered her face with her hands and peered out through spread fingers. He was getting dressed. She closed her eyes and tried to block out the sight of him and also all the memories of the night, which were becoming clearer and clearer.

But it was no use. A series of bright pictures flashed across her inner eye.

His arrival. The gaily wrapped presents. The flowers and the chocolates. The dinner table. More flowers. White damask. Sparkling crystal. Polished silver and course after course of the kind of food she had never eaten before.

The wine . . .

At first she had refused the wine. She had never in her life had alcohol, but she had watched the men staggering home from the Raby and she knew very well what it could do to you.

He had laughed. 'My dear,' he had said, 'you needn't be frightened of a little drink. Go on, try this, you will enjoy it.' He held out a beautiful crystal flask. The light from the overhead gasolier sparkled on its many surfaces.

She allowed him to fill her glass. The wine was rich and sweet and had the strangest effect on her as it went down. She began to feel warm inside. After the second glass, delightful sensations quivered through her lower body.

She had asked him why he did not drink the same wine as she, but he had told her that he preferred something less sweet.

And then afterwards . . .

What had happened after the meal?

Jane came in and cleared the table.

No, it wasn't Jane. At least it was, but there was another woman as well. Someone older than Jane. From the way they were talking, Susan realised that she had been helping with the cooking.

Two people to cook a meal for another two people.

Susan remembered that she had laughed when this thought crossed her mind, and Jane and the other woman had looked at her.

212

Then they had looked at each other and raised their eyebrows. Yes, they had raised their eyebrows. Had they been criticising her for laughing? No, she didn't think so. They had been smiling. They had been amused.

How did she get to the front parlour?

Try as she might, she could not remember walking from one room to the other, and yet she remembered sitting there on the sofa and drinking another glass of wine. There had been a tray of something he called petits fours. Little fancy biscuits, some of them with a marzipan taste. He had watched her eat them and then he had taken the tray out of her reach.

'We don't want you to be sick, do we? That would spoil our fun.'

She remembered feeling ashamed. She had been like a greedy child and he would despise her. Without warning tears, began to course down her cheeks.

'There, there,' he said, just as if she were a child. 'There there, my little one. Let Papa comfort you.'

*Papa?*

Yes, he had called himself Papa and he had taken her on his knee. 'You are such a child,' he had said. 'Such a delightful child.' And he began to stroke her bare shoulders. 'What a pretty little gown,' he'd said. 'She's made herself so pretty for Papa that I think she deserves a treat.'

He continued to stroke her shoulders and then, without warning, slipped his hand into her neckline and found her breast. She gasped and tried to pull away but he smiled and drew her closer.

And then . . . and then . . .?

Now, in the dark hours of the morning, Susan began to burn with shame as she remembered how much she had enjoyed his caresses. How she had responded to them with mounting excitement. Then how willingly she had let him lead her upstairs to this very room and how amused she had been when he had pretended to be a lady's maid and offered to undress her.

And how natural she had found it for them to end up in bed together. There was a brief moment of pain, and then . . . and then . . .

She closed her mind to what had followed. She realised that she was sobbing.

'Don't be a silly girl,' he said as he looked down at her. 'Papa will be cross if you are going to be a cry-baby.'

213

Then, without another word, he moved through the shadows, slipped out of the room and left her alone.

When Betty brought Marion an early-morning cup of tea, tears were streaming down her cheeks.

'What is it?' Marion asked.

'I'm so happy for you,' Betty replied.

'It doesn't look as though you are happy.'

'Well, I am, but I'm sad as well.'

Marion, who had slept badly, sat up and sighed. 'I am in no mood for riddles,' she said. 'Would you please sit down and explain yourself?'

Betty put Marion's cup of tea on the bedside table and said, 'Wait a moment, I'll just build the fire up a bit. We divven't want you catching cold today of all days, do we?'

When she had arranged the coals to her satisfaction, she sat down on the bed. 'I've looked after you since you were a bairn,' she said, 'so it's only natural that I should get emotional on your wedding day. I'm pleased you're marrying a good man who will take care of you, and your sister too, but I'm sad that I won't be coming with you to your new home.'

'But you'll be going to your own new home soon.'

'I know. And I owe that to Mr Bateman and I'll be forever grateful.'

After that, with so much to say to each other, they found that they couldn't say anything at all. Marion drank her tea and Betty took the cup back to the kitchen, and soon she called up that breakfast was ready. Marion and Annette had breakfast in their dressing gowns and then everyone busied themselves with the serious business of getting Marion ready for church. And Annette too, of course.

'You look lovely, both of you,' Betty said. 'Those shades of mauve are just right.'

'And all them velvet ribbons and the little glass bugle beads,' Sarah added. 'They don't half look bonny.'

'Are you sure they're not too decorative?' Marion asked.

Marion had intended to take the fabric to the little corner-shop dressmaker in the next street. She had made clothes for the Brookfield girls since they were small children and Marion knew she would have respected her wishes for a classically simple gown for herself and something a little more decorative for Annette. But when Lady Cressington heard this, she had insisted on sending her own dressmaker along.

'My gift to you,' she had said, and Marion had not been able to refuse.

Fortunately the woman had good taste and she agreed with Marion's request for smooth uncluttered lines.

'I shall make your gown as stylish as possible within the constraints of the period of mourning,' she had said. She had persuaded Marion that a passementerie of beads and ribbons in the same mauve shade as the gown would be quite in order, and Marion, who by then was succumbing to the mounting excitement of those around her, had agreed.

'No, they're just right,' Betty said in answer to Marion's question. And then she burst into tears again. 'And as for Miss Annette, she looks just like an angel. If your mother could see her two beautiful daughters now, how happy and proud she would be. And so would your father.'

'Betty . . .' Marion's voice faltered.

'Eeh, I'm sorry, pet. Divven't cry. This is a happy day and neither of them would want to see you like that.'

The two young women instinctively reached for each other's hands, and after a solemn moment Betty said, 'Hawway, let's get on with it!'

The finishing touch was to arrange the minuscule hat, little more than a band of velvet to hold the fine veiling, on Marion's head. Lady Cressington had thought it permissible for Annette to wear a head-band of artificial flowers in shades of violet and lavender, and it was obvious that the younger girl knew how fetching she looked.

'I wish I could draw us both right now,' she said. 'But I'll have to do it from memory.'

No sooner were they ready than it was time to go. Mr Earnshaw, the editor of the newspaper that Henry Brookfield had worked for, called to take Marion and Annette to church. Lady Cressington, who had told him about the wedding, had loaned him one of her carriages.

'I am truly honoured to be standing in for your father,' he told Marion, 'and I hope you will accept these small bouquets. Gardenias for the bride and violets for her attendant.'

Marion was taken aback when they left the house to see many of her neighbours lining the pavement. Miss Cudlip from next door stepped forward and clasped her hands. 'I shall miss you,' she said. 'But you deserve a little happiness.'

At the last moment Marion turned and sought out Betty. 'I wish you were coming to the church,' she said.

Betty looked down at her hands, which were clasped in front of her. 'So do I, pet, but you know Mr Bateman just wants a family affair.'

'Well you're my family and you always will be.'

'Get along with you. You don't want to keep your bridegroom waiting, do you?'

Lady Cressington's carriage was a landau and Marion was pleased that once inside she would be hidden from view, for she could not help feeling that rather than the bonny bride they all took her for, she was really a fraud.

I am on my way to my wedding, she thought as they rattled through the streets, which were still covered with a light dusting of snow. I should be overjoyed. I am marrying a good and generous man who says that he loves me, and who is prepared to look after my sister too.

Marion remembered the day Victor had called to say that he had received her letter accepting his proposal and that he was overjoyed. She sensed that her acceptance had changed him somehow. His physical presence was overwhelming.

'But are you sure you want to marry me?' she had asked him. 'We are so different.'

'It is your difference that attracts me,' he had replied.

She had looked at his handsome face searchingly, wondering if that could be true. Once more she had the feeling that he was saying what he thought would please her, but she had convinced herself that if that were so, it must be because he loved her.

And now I am going to the church to marry him, she thought. And the truth is that I do not love him. But I will do my very best to be a good wife to him. He will never know that I would not have agreed to marry him if Daniel Brady had asked me first.

Just a few short months ago, Henry Brookfield's funeral had been held in this church. The large congregation gathered here on that day had been a tribute to how popular he had been. Today there were only a few people, all connected with Victor, sitting in the front two or three rows of pews.

Victor had promised Marion that the wedding would be a quiet affair, as he knew that there were people who would disapprove of their marrying during a period of mourning.

'If it were not for that, I would have invited the whole city!' he had told her. 'I would want the world to see my beautiful bride and everyone to know what a lucky man I am.'

He had said that with a deprecating smile, but Marion had been embarrassed. It was discomforting to hear him talking like a hero in a romantic novel. But he obviously wanted to please her.

When Marion entered the church on Charles Earnshaw's arm, she was surprised and overwhelmed at how beautiful the old building looked when it was filled with flowers. Victor must have raided every hothouse in Newcastle. And the vases, garlands and swags of blossom were so beautifully arranged.

But as they stood there ready for the signal to walk down the aisle, Marion saw someone in one of the front pews turn towards her and nod and smile as she let her eyes range around the floral arrangements. Lady Cressington. Marion knew immediately it was she who was responsible for the flowers. She remembered her saying that in helping Marion choose the fabric and style of her wedding gown it would be like having a daughter of her own.

Marion sensed Annette's excitement and she turned to smile over her shoulder at her sister just before the organ started playing and Charles Earnshaw led her sedately down the aisle to where Victor was waiting for her.

Marion heard the exclamations the moment she came out of the church on Victor's arm.

'Here she comes!'

'Isn't she lovely!'

A small crowd had gathered, no doubt alerted by the carriages waiting nearby. There were the usual 'oohs' and 'aahs', accompanied by calls of 'Good luck!' Amongst the cheerful crowd Marion spotted two people she knew. Betty and Arthur. Her eyes widened.

'I thought I'd surprise you,' Betty said, and Marion saw that her old friend's eyes were suspiciously moist. 'I arranged to meet Arthur

217

here and I hurried along as soon as you'd left the house. As a matter of fact, we arrived in time to slip quietly into the back of the church and we heard you say your lines.'

'And she sobbed all the way through,' Arthur added, grinning.

'I hope you don't mind, sir,' Betty said to Victor, who was standing patiently by Marion's side.

'I don't mind at all,' Victor said. 'I can see how happy you have made my wife.' Marion still had her hand linked through his arm and he squeezed it gently. 'But now we must go, dear. I believe you are shivering.'

Marion smiled her goodbyes to Betty and Arthur and allowed Victor to draw her towards an open carriage. Annette was to travel with Mr Earnshaw and Lady Cressington. Victor helped Marion in and then turned as a group of children rushed forward. Laughingly, he took a handful of coins from his pocket and threw them on to the pavement for the traditional scramble.

The adults paused and watched, smiling as the children rushed to pick up the coins. The children shouted, 'Hurrah!' and Betty threw a handful of rice. The grains settled in Marion's hair and around the brim of Victor's top hat. Marion looked back and saw Betty smiling and waving. The carriage drew away quickly after that, followed by two others. Victor removed his hat and smiled at her as he shook off the grains of rice.

'It's good of your maid to remember the old tradition,' he said. 'To wish us all life's blessings. But what further blessing do I require now that I have you?'

Marion, made uneasy as ever by this flowery talk, glanced sideways and gave him a keen look, but avoiding her eye, he gazed out at the passing scene and did not speak again.

After a brisk ride through the streets and up the North Road to Gosforth, the carriage, and those behind, slowed down to turn into the semicircular driveway of a large and impressive house. Marion's eyes widened. She had not seen Victor's house before, although Lady Cressington had told her that it was magnificent.

Victor waved the footman away. He leapt down and held up a hand to help Marion from the carriage himself. They walked up the imposing steps together, and as they reached the grand portico the door opened as if by magic.

'Welcome home,' Victor said, and to the delight of the handful of guests who were following them, he swept Marion up in his arms and carried her over the threshold.

Once the others had assembled in the hall and gathered round them, he set her down gently amid the laughter and the congratulations. Marion noticed that although Charlotte, Victor's formidable elder sister, was clapping politely, she was not smiling. Marion was not sure what to make of this.

Charlotte had called on her once and intimated that she was pleased that Victor was getting married 'at last'. An important man should have the comfort of a wife, she said. He should stay at home and take delight in domestic pleasures rather than going out in the evening and staying late at his club.

She had made it obvious that she doted on her brother and that she had thought it her duty to inspect and hopefully approve of the young woman who was about to become his wife. Marion had been left with the uneasy feeling that Miss Bateman did not entirely approve of her, but at least Victor's sister had not been openly antagonistic.

She had actually smiled at Annette, who had been overawed and silent throughout the visit, but even so, Marion could not help remembering Lady Cressington's guarded expression when she had asked her whether she had met Victor's sister yet.

A manservant opened the double doors that led to a large dining room. Victor and Marion went in first and then stood at the doorway to greet the guests formally. Marion was introduced to a town councillor and his wife, Victor's chief architect and his wife, and three formidable-looking ladies, two sisters and a cousin apparently, who were distantly related to Victor and who served with Charlotte on various worthy charitable committees. There were also one or two neighbours from other big houses nearby.

'This won't be much fun for you, sweetheart,' Victor whispered in her ear, 'but once your period of mourning is over, we will have a grand reception and introduce you properly to society.' He laughed softly. 'At least what passes for society here in Newcastle.' His gently mocking but fond smile was meant to reveal that he wasn't really criticising the city he lived in, he was only poking a little fun at it.

Marion would never tell him, but, in truth, she would not have wanted a large wedding reception. She was nervous enough without having to meet too many new people.

Annette appeared by her side, and as Victor hurried away to join the guests, she whispered to Marion, 'What a strange lot these people are. Most of them must be at least a hundred years old.'

'Hush,' Marion whispered, and she took her sister's hand and they walked in together.

Marion had worried that this might prove an intimidating experience for the younger girl, but Victor came over and led Annette to the table, where he gave her a plate and encouraged her to fill it. Then he beckoned Lady Cressington to join them and left them to talk to each other. Marion was grateful to Victor for this, and more than ever persuaded that in marrying him she had done the right thing.

Refreshments in the form of a buffet had been set out on the table; dainty sandwiches, savouries, sweet pastries and several bottles of champagne. At the centre of the display there was an impressive three-tiered wedding cake. Marion found that she could not eat at all, but she was pleased to see that Annette was now enjoying the food and also that she seemed to be getting on well with Lady Cressington. She saw their smiles and could hear them laughing.

Then the time came for them to cut the cake. Two of the maid-servants who had been moving amongst the guests silently removing unwanted plates and filling up wine glasses lifted the tiers down and arranged the bottom tier at the front of the table. One of them handed Victor a knife.

Smilingly, Victor took Marion's hand and led her to the table. He stood behind her so that his arm was round her and they held the knife together. Marion began to tremble and he whispered in her ear, 'Don't be nervous. This is expected of us. I will guide the knife.'

They cut the cake to more applause and laughter. Marion was grateful when her husband moved away again to talk to Charles Earnshaw. She had not been at all nervous about cutting the cake. It was Victor's closeness that had unnerved her. Feeling the warmth of his body behind her, his breath on her neck and the firm grasp of his hand as he guided hers.

Once the cut had been made, the cake was carried off, presumably to the kitchen, and a short while later dainty squares were brought back on a silver salver. Marion heard Charlotte telling her brother that a cake that size had been quite unnecessary.

'Only half the bottom tier was needed for the assembled guests. What will you do with the rest?' she asked.

'I'm sure the servants will enjoy a slice,' Victor said, 'and you are welcome to take what you want to your orphanage.'

Lady Cressington had overheard, and she said, 'What a good idea. May I take some, Victor? I'm sure my poor unfortunates would enjoy a treat.'

Victor nodded and said, 'Of course you may take some, Esmé. I know how you try to help those girls.'

Marion was surprised. Not that Victor had agreed to Lady Cressington's request, but at the casual use of her Christian name and his knowledge of the work she did with homeless girls. Surely Lady Cressington had told her that she did not know Victor very well and that it was Charlotte Bateman she was friendly with.

The guests began to leave. Charles Earnshaw took Marion's hand and said, 'I am happy for you, my dear. You must know how much I respected your father, and the moment I find someone worthy of taking over his work, I shall let you know.'

'Thank you.'

The newspaper editor hesitated and then said. 'Forgive me for troubling you with this matter on your wedding day, but I don't suppose you have found your father's notes, have you? Notes that would help us continue his exposure of the slum landlords and the wicked men who prey on the homeless.'

'No, I'm sorry.'

'That's a shame.'

'What is a shame, Charles?' Victor had come up behind him.

'Marion has just told me that she has not been able to find any of her father's important papers.'

'Ah, that. Perhaps Henry Brookfield didn't make any notes. Perhaps he kept everything in his head.'

'Do you think so?' Mr Earnshaw pondered for a moment with his head on one side. 'Well, he was certainly intelligent enough to remember a great deal of information, and perhaps he thought that was the safest thing to do.'

'Why safe?' Victor asked.

'There would be certain people who would have liked to get their hands on that information. People who would have wanted to stop it ever becoming public. But if you're right, if Henry did indeed memorise everything, then we have lost an opportunity to write a very important exposé. We can only hope that we will find someone ready to start all over again.'

'Indeed, Charles, but I must ask you to drop the subject now. Can't you see you have made my wife unhappy?'

'Oh, my dear Marion, I am so sorry.' Charles Earnshaw was aghast. 'Your wedding day . . . I should not have brought the subject up . . . Please, please forgive me.'

'Of course I do,' Marion said, 'and I assure you that if ever I find anything I think important, I will bring it straight to you.'

Despite her reassurances, poor Charles Earnshaw still looked uncomfortable when he took his leave shortly after. Marion felt sorry for him. She thought Victor had been hard on him but she realised that it was out of concern for her.

The next person to approach her was Esmé Cressington. 'I have a request,' she said. 'May I borrow your sister this evening?'

Marion was astonished. 'Borrow Annette? But why?'

'The child and I have got on so well. We have been talking about – oh, all sorts of things. Fashions, and food, and paintings.'

Marion smiled. She knew very well that Annette was addicted to all three of those.

'And besides,' Lady Cressington continued, 'tonight is your wedding night. You are not going on a wedding journey, but that does not mean that you and your husband should not have some time alone together.'

'Oh, but . . .' Marion's glance strayed in the direction of Charlotte Bateman, who was talking to her three elderly friends.

Lady Cressington smiled. 'Victor has reserved a box at the theatre for them. Some worthy dramatic play by William Shakespeare. And he has suggested that Charlotte goes to stay with them so that they can talk long into the night just as they did when they were at boarding school together.'

'I see.'

'Oh, my dear, don't look so perplexed. It is natural that he should want to be alone with you.'

'I suppose so.' Once more Marion was surprised that Lady Cressington seemed to be on such intimate terms with a man she claimed she hardly knew.

'So may I kidnap Annette?'

'Oh, please say yes, Marion!'

Annette had come to join them. Her eyes were shining. There was no way Marion could deny the younger girl this treat.

'Very well. But your clothes . . .'

'It's all right. Lady Cressington says they have been taken up to my room. She is going to help me change out of this dress and pack what I need for the night.'

Annette flung herself into Marion's arms and hugged her, then, without another word, she hurried from the room with a smiling Esmé Cressington in her wake.

Then came the moment when Marion found herself alone with Victor.

'Do you want to rest for a while?' Victor asked her. 'We will have supper together later.'

'Rest?'

'Yes, my dear. Bertha will take you to our room.'

*Our room . . .*

'Bertha?'

'Your maid. Let me send for her.'

Victor had a word with one of the maids who was clearing the table and she hurried out of the room. A moment or two later a tall, thin woman in respectable grey grosgrain came hurrying into the room.

Victor had a quiet word with her and she came over to Marion and said, 'Please come with me, Mrs Bateman.'

*Mrs Bateman . . .* Marion smiled to herself. She supposed she would have to get used to that.

The room to which she was led was big. Could it really be just a bedroom? A large fireplace with a welcoming fire burning, a massive wardrobe, and a tall chest of drawers, as well as the usual dressing table and washstand. Marion stared around helplessly. She was not sure what she was supposed to do.

'Your trunk has been unpacked and everything put away, madam,' Bertha said. 'I did that last night when it arrived from your former home. I understand your housemaid will be cleaning the house and will send along anything that has been missed.'

'That's right.'

Marion thought how sad Betty must be to be emptying the cupboards of household goods and sweeping and cleaning the house she had been happy to work in for so long. Marion had told her that she must keep anything she wanted, from tablecloths and bed linen to mangles and flat irons, for her own home and give anything else away to people she knew who might want them.

She was not sentimental about pots and pans or even the familiar old dinner and tea services. Her father had never thought such things were important. 'A plate is a plate,' he used to say, 'and although it may be stylish to eat from a dainty porcelain dish, it is what is on it that is important.'

But Henry Brookfield's books and papers were another thing entirely. Victor had been kind enough to say that he would clear out a corner of the room he used as a library and find a desk for her and that Marion could arrange things as she wished. He knew how important these things were to her and he had even come himself to supervise their removal to his home.

'Would you like a bath, madam?' Bertha roused her from her reverie. 'A soak in some nice scented water might refresh you.'

Marion felt like asking the woman she must regard as her own personal maid whether she looked as though she needed refreshing. She couldn't resist a glance in the cheval glass and found that she hardly recognised herself. Tall and always slim, she saw that she had become even more slender over the last few months, but her figure was still womanly especially as it had been enhanced by a little discreet padding.

'Not really a bustle,' Lady Cressington had said when she showed Marion the illustration in the fashion magazine, 'but just enough padding to achieve the fashionable S shape.'

Lady Cressington had also guided Marion towards the mauve silk moiré, the wavy pattern of which would shimmer as she moved.

'Magnificent!' she had said at the final fitting, and Annette, who had been twirling excitedly in front of the mirror in her own bridesmaid's gown of lavender silk, turned and gazed at Marion speechlessly.

'Why, Marion,' she'd said after a long pause. 'You look elegant!'

And now Marion was forced to admit that the gown was very attractive, although she could not go so far as to believe that she herself had changed so very much.

'Mrs Bateman, do you want me to fill the bath?'

'Oh . . . yes please, Bertha.'

And then Marion had to submit to the embarrassment of allowing another woman to help her remove her clothes.

'My robe should be in the wardrobe,' she told the maid.

But the garment Bertha brought her was not her comfortable old flannel dressing gown.

'That's not mine,' Marion said when she saw the rose-pink negligée Bertha was holding.

The lady's maid frowned. 'It is the only gown there, madam.'

'Oh yes, I'm sorry.'

Marion remembered the trousseau that Esmé Cressington had insisted that she buy and that she had asked the shop assistant to send to the Bateman house.

Bertha helped her into her robe and then told her to sit by the fire until her bath was ready. A little later she lay in the rose-scented water and tried to relax, but her mind kept going over the events of the day and then the last few weeks and finally everything that had happened since that dreadful night when her father had gone out, never to return.

After her bath, she allowed Bertha to slip a nightdress over her head and help her into bed.

'You'll be more comfortable that way, madam,' she said. 'I'll come back and help you dress for dinner.'

Marion was tired, but she was far too fraught to rest. She felt like an impostor. *My wife*, Victor had called her repeatedly. And yet she did not feel like a wife. She could not see herself as Mrs Victor Bateman. No matter what vows she had taken in church, in her mind she was still Marion Brookfield.

And yet here she was, lying in this enormous bed, in this luxurious room, supposedly resting before going down for the first meal she would take alone with her husband. And after dinner . . .

Marion thought uneasily about what would happen then. As befitted a young woman of her class, she was completely inexperienced sexually, although she was intelligent enough to know what to expect.

But I am not in love with Victor, Marion thought. She found herself gripping the bedclothes with both hands as a knot of unease tightened within her. Her head began to ache as she fought to control a sense of panic. Then, at last, in a state of nervous exhaustion, she fell asleep.

Marion did not go down to dinner that night. Despite her strange surroundings, she was so exhausted that she slept too long. When she awoke, it was to a darkened room lit only by the flickering of the fire. She lay there puzzled for a moment and then was startled by a gentle laugh.

'Awake at last, my darling?'

Of course. Her husband. She stared at him but saw only a shadowy figure outlined by the firelight.

'Is it very late?'

'Yes, it is. I ate alone.'

'I'm sorry!'

'There's no need to be. I instructed Bertha not to awaken you. I wanted you to be rested for your wedding night.'

Marion was glad of the shadows, because she would not have liked Victor to see the apprehension in her eyes.

'But if you're hungry now, I've had some supper sent up on a tray. Cold cuts, a slice of game pie, a bottle of champagne. Do you want to come over to this little table, or shall I bring the tray to bed?'

'No . . . I'm not hungry.'

'Well at least you must have a glass of champagne.'

Marion heard Victor remove the cork and the slight fizzing sound as he poured the champagne into two glasses. It was only when he brought the glasses over to the bed that she saw that he had removed his clothes and was in his nightshirt.

He gave her one of the glasses, and to please him she drank it all.

'Another glass?' he asked.

Marion shook her head.

'Good.'

Victor got into bed. Whatever Marion might have been expecting, what followed was swift and brutal. She had thought he would kiss her, but without preamble he tugged up her nightdress and covered her with his body. Forcing her legs apart, he entered her, and when Marion cried out in pain, rather than stopping him it seemed to excite him further. She turned her head away and buried it in the pillow, forcing herself to remain silent. When Victor had done with her, he rolled away and sat up. Then he reached for something that he had placed on the bedside table.

'Here you are,' he said. 'Do sit up and take it.'

Marion sat up and he placed a rectangular silver casket in her hands. The sides were embossed with scrollwork and the lid was encrusted with crystals forming flower patterns.

'Go on, open it,' he said.

She raised the hinged lid to find a diamond necklace, brooch and earrings nestling on the pale green velvet lining. She stared at the jewellery speechlessly.

'Don't look so surprised,' Victor said. 'This is my wedding gift to you. I believe something like this is customary. Now, sleep well, my dear.'

But Marion could not sleep. She lay as still as she could so that she would not accidentally touch the man – the stranger – lying beside her. Her head was aching and her body complaining about the way it had just been treated.

Perhaps it is my fault, she thought, because I do not love him. I can only hope that I shall become accustomed to it. I have made my vows and I must abide by them.

She closed her eyes but she could not stop the hot tears from spilling out and running down her cheeks. For even though she tried to deny all thoughts of him, she could not help feeling that the act of love would have been entirely different with Daniel.

Not much later, she sensed Victor rising and leaving the bed. She lay for a while with her breath held, expecting him to come back. But mercifully, he didn't. At last, when dawn was breaking, she drifted off into a troubled and uneasy sleep.

# Chapter Fifteen

The remains of the snow was heaped into piles of soot-stained yellowing slush and the wind was keen enough to cut through to the bone. But after the recent hard weather the men were pleased to be doing a full day's work again. They had greeted Daniel sympathetically, for even though they often looked askance at what they called his bookish ways, they all agreed there was no side to him, and there was no denying that he pulled his weight. Or at least he used to before he had been set upon.

Since he had come back to work, they could not help noticing that he was limping and that sometimes, if his weight was on his right leg, he could not conceal a grimace of pain.

'Are you sure you're up to it?' the foreman had asked him.

Daniel had assured him that he was, even though the effort to keep up with the others was leaving him drained and exhausted by the end of the day. Even so, after he had been home to eat the meal his mother had prepared, instead of resting he had been going out again at night in what seemed like a never-ending and fruitless search for Susan.

Now and then he would go to the Raby with Arthur Robinson. Daniel had never been the sort of man to drown his sorrows in beer, but lately he had realised how comforting it was to sit and talk with a pal. Especially if you were keen to get out of the house.

His mother, although still frantic about Susan's disappearance, nevertheless was suffocating him with attention. In this she was aided by Dora. He was grateful for the way they had looked after him, but he could not help feeling that they were enjoying the power of having a grown man at their mercy.

He didn't want to quarrel with them, especially as his mother was grieving for her missing daughter, but he was determined to escape their ministrations whenever he could. Even though it meant that he had less time with his books and papers.

That night at the Raby, Arthur asked him if he'd had any luck tracing his sister. Daniel shook his head.

'I'm sorry I can't help you,' Arthur said. 'But she isn't a missing person in my book.'

'What do you mean.'

'Well . . .' Arthur looked uncomfortable. 'She ran off of her own accord, didn't she?'

'Yes.'

'It seems likely she knew where she was going.'

Daniel didn't reply, but he thought so too. He hadn't told anyone that Susan had also taken his mother's savings, because that would have made him feel ashamed for her.

Daniel and Arthur talked quietly for a while. Daniel sensed that his friend was trying to cheer him up and he was grateful. After a while he began to relax.

Then Arthur surprised him by going up to the bar and buying drinks all round. Amid shouts of 'Cheers!' and 'Thanks, bonny lad!' he took his seat again.

'What are we celebrating?' Daniel asked. 'Your promotion?'

'Aye, there's that for one thing.' Arthur took a sup of ale and wiped the froth off his moustache. Then he looked around the saloon bar speculatively. 'Mebbe I won't be sitting in here again.'

'Are you leaving the district? I thought you were staying at the Headlam Street station.'

'I am. But now that I'm promoted to sergeant, mebbe you and me should sit in the lounge bar.'

'Whatever for?'

Arthur looked uncomfortable. 'Well, you know, I should mix with a better class of person.'

'Better class of person?' Daniel said. 'Just look around you, my friend. You've known most of these lads since we were bairns at school, and the older fellows too. They are all hard-working men and most of them are decent. You couldn't get a better class of person.'

Arthur had the grace to look abashed. 'You're right, of course. I should follow your example.'

'What do you mean?'

'Well, you're a strange sort of chap, aren't you?'

'Me? Strange?' Daniel made a pretence of looking down at his arms and legs to see if they were the same as any other man's.

Arthur laughed. 'You know what I mean. You're a fine-set-up fellow. Betty tells me that the womenfolk consider you handsome. And you've worked hard ever since you left school – muscles like bell metal. But you've got a brain as well.'

'I believe that's part of the human condition.'

'See what I mean?'

Daniel shook his head.

'Sometimes you talk as if you've swallowed a dictionary. And all that studying.'

'You study as well. You have to for your police exams.'

'That's all facts and figures and procedures. Betty says you read novels – storybooks.'

'So do a lot of people.'

'I know. I like a good yarn now and then. But you talk about it. Betty says you used to go along to the Brookfield house and discuss the stories in the books as if they'd really happened. You have to admit that's strange.'

Daniel laughed. 'Well, it's not quite like that, but near enough. I admit I'm peculiar.'

'And what's more, for all you're brainy, you never get above yourself.'

'Will you stop talking about me? You're making me feel like some specimen in the laboratory.'

'There you go again! But promise me this, even if I rise to inspector, don't you let me get above meself.'

'I promise. Although I suspect Betty will make sure you don't get too bumptious.'

'Aye,' Arthur's smile was wide, 'Betty. And that's the other thing.'

'You've lost me.'

'The other thing we're celebrating. Mr Bateman has given us the keys to the house and we're getting married next week. I hope you'll come to the wedding.'

'I will.'

'And bring your lass. Dora, isn't it?'

Daniel didn't contradict Arthur, but neither did he agree. He took a long sup of his ale.

'Miss Marion will be coming,' Arthur continued, 'or rather Mrs

Bateman as I should call her now. You knew she'd got married, didn't you?'

'Yes.'

'Quiet affair it was. Still in mourning, you know.'

'I know.'

'Is there anything the matter?'

'Why do you ask?'

'You've gone quiet.'

'Yes, well, I'm tired.'

'Of course you are. You've done a hard day's work. Harder work than I've ever had to do. Come along, lad, I'll walk you home.'

'Even you treat me like a bairn!' Daniel smiled.

'Well, it's just that no matter how you try to hide it, it's plain to see that that leg is giving you gyp, and your ma would never forgive me if you took a tumble.'

Daniel pulled a wry face. As if he couldn't look after himself! However, he did his best to smile and they walked down the bank together, saying good night at Daniel's door.

When he went inside, he found that Dora was still there. She was sitting at the other side of the range from his mother and they looked up and smiled in unison.

'Would you like a bite to eat, son?' his mother asked.

And Dora added, 'Do you want to sit here by the fire?'

'No thank you to both questions,' Daniel replied with an attempt at a smile. 'I'd rather go straight up to bed.'

He left the room without another word and went upstairs. Once in bed, he put the oil lamp on the bedside table and propped the pillows up so that he could sit with his books. The short-hand textbook had exercises at the end of each chapter, and he had been working through them and then taking his work to the library, where Miss Bennett had been kind enough to go through it with him.

He tried to concentrate, but tonight his heart wasn't in it. All the worries Arthur's cheerful company had held at bay for a while came flooding back. Susan might have planned her flight, but she was far too young to know what she might be getting into. Daniel was pretty sure that the man Maisie had told him about had persuaded her to run off with him. What kind of man would encourage a young girl to do such a thing? And how far had they gone? Were they even still in Newcastle? Hopeless though the task seemed, Daniel was determined to go on looking for her.

After a few sleepless hours, during which he tried to convince himself that it was only Susan's likely fate that was keeping him awake, he gave up all pretence and admitted to himself that he was also grieving for Marion. Or rather for the loss of his dreams – his impossible dreams. He would have to go to Arthur's wedding. His friend would be hurt if he didn't. And he would have to face Marion there. He didn't know whether he could even bring himself to speak to her.

By the time dawn came, he was more exhausted than he had been when he went to bed. He was truly grateful to his mother for sitting with him as he ate his breakfast. He watched as she made a pretence of eating a slice of bread and dripping. When he was ready to leave, she gave him his bait box and told him to eat everything in it, just as if the years had fallen away and she was seeing him off to school. And looking at her careworn face and the wretchedness in her eyes, for once he didn't mind. He put his arms around her and gave her a hug. He was shocked to discover how thin she had grown.

'I'll be all right, Ma,' he said. 'Don't worry about me.'

The work that day was heavy. They were heaving the tracks into the ready-cut grooves, and although they had grappling tools, it took a lot of brute strength. They had to work as a team and pull together, and Daniel had seen the foreman looking at him doubtfully before they began.

'Divven't fret,' he said, adopting the local way of speaking. 'There's nothing wrong with my arms. I can heave with the best of them.'

And so he did. The work went well, and there was a cheerful mood when they broke to eat their bait. They sat on the ground, on piles of rubble or propped up against the temporary sheds where the tools were kept overnight. After a morning of physical labour, Daniel found that his appetite was returning. He polished off the doorstep-size cheese sandwiches and a pork pie the size of his fist.

Perhaps it was the feeling of returning well-being that made him careless. He felt the usual twinge of pain in his right leg when he got to his feet, but soon forgot about it when the work began again. Then, as they were heaving a curved section of track into place, disaster struck.

He didn't even know how it happened, but his leg gave way and he went down. He fell heavily and upset the balance of the line of workmen. Someone shouted in alarm and then the heavy section of track came crashing down, bringing some of the men with it.

Daniel lay there stunned with horror. He watched the others rise to their feet and was relieved to see that although they were complaining, no one seemed to be badly hurt. But he knew this was sheer good luck. If the track had fallen on someone's leg, the man could have lost it, or even been killed. He got up slowly to see the foreman coming towards him. The two men looked at each other. The foreman's expression was severe.

'You know what I'm going to say, don't you, lad?'

'I do.'

'You could hev killed someone.'

'I know.'

'I'm sorry it's come to this, Daniel, but you're finished here.'

Daniel nodded. He was aware that the others were watching him. No one said anything, but he could tell from their expressions that they wanted him to go.

'Come to the cabin and I'll give you what you're owed. It won't be much but you're entitled to it.'

Daniel collected his jacket and his pay packet and said goodbye.

'What will you do?' the foreman asked.

'I don't know.'

'I could get you a job as a nightwatchman – or mebbe a storekeeper. You've got a good head on you and you're reliable and honest.'

Daniel found himself smiling. 'When I find a job, I'll come to you for a reference.'

'But you divven't think much of my suggestions?'

'No. I'm sorry.'

'Well let's shake hands then,' the older man said. 'I wish you luck in whatever you decide to do.'

'Thank you.'

Daniel suppressed a sense of panic. His heart had not been in this job for many a year, but he had planned to leave only when he could secure a better future for himself. Now it seemed fate had taken a hand, and if his mother was not to suffer, he would have to find other employment as soon as he could.

He began to walk away, but he glanced back at the men he had worked with for so long. It seemed as though none of them could meet his eyes. Soon it would be as if he had never been one of the team.

Marion was having the greatest difficulty adapting to a life where she didn't seem to have anything much to do. She had soon worked out what was expected of her, and it wasn't very much. She had to dress nicely and appear in the dining room for meals with Victor, Charlotte and Annette. She didn't even have any say in what those meals were to be, for that had been Charlotte's province until now, and the older woman didn't show any sign of handing over the reins.

Ever since she had been Annette's age, Marion had had cosy discussions with Betty in the kitchen of her former home about what they thought Henry Brookfield would like for his evening meal and what Annette would like for tea. They had made the shopping lists up together and Betty had made sure that Marion knew the price of everything and where the bargains were to be found.

Sometimes Betty would take Marion with her to the local shops or on the tram into town and a visit to the Grainger Market, where she said you got the best fruit and vegetables – so long as you watched very carefully what was going into the bag. There were those who would cheat you by taking bruised fruit from the back of the display if you took your eyes off them for just a second.

Marion had had some sort of idea that she would be discussing the food shopping with the cook at her new home, but so far she hadn't even met the woman. Charlotte had smiled dismissively and told her not to bother her head about things like that. But what *was* she supposed to bother her head about?

One day she asked Charlotte tentatively if she could help with some of her charity work, but the offer had been refused. Marion had the impression that Victor's sister had her tight group of cronies and they wouldn't welcome a newcomer.

She was also becoming increasingly convinced that Charlotte did not altogether approve of her brother's choice of wife. Marion thought that maybe Charlotte would have preferred to do the choosing herself.

Annette cheered the day for her when she came home from art school. Over a cup of tea and a dainty cake or two she would tell

Marion what she had done that day and explain what her latest assignment was, but then she would try to get an hour or two's work in before Victor came home for dinner.

Her young sister was obviously happy and she was taking her studies very seriously. When Marion remembered the reluctant scholar Annette had been not so very long ago, she couldn't help but be pleased, even though it meant they spent less time together.

Victor had told her that she must order anything she wanted for the house. If she wanted to make any changes in the furnishings or the decor she only had to tell him. But she knew instinctively that that would cause trouble with Charlotte.

And what of the intimate side of married life? She had not been totally unaware of what was expected of her. Once she had become engaged Betty had said that as Marion didn't have a mother to tell her things a bride should know, the two of them must 'hev a little talk'.

After Betty had blushingly hurried through the basic facts of the matter she said, 'But divven't fret, Mr Bateman is a good man. He'll treat you right.'

'Is that what Arthur will do?' Marion had asked. 'Will he treat you right? I mean, is that all it is?'

Betty had looked flummoxed. 'Well no, that's not quite all,' she'd said. 'I mean, a woman's not supposed to say this, but it can be very enjoyable.'

She had refused to say more, and Marion, who on her wedding night had been tormented by longing for Daniel Brady, was still waiting for even a modicum of feeling when her husband made love to her.

*Made love?* was that what he was doing when he came to bed with her? It seemed that the pretty speeches that had once embarrassed her had no place here, and in fact, during intimate moments Victor rarely even spoke to her. Never once mentioned the word 'love'.

He did what he did, sometimes quite brutally, and then he went to sleep, leaving Marion wide awake and wondering if she would be able to endure nights like this for the rest of her life.

Susan looked at herself in her dressing-table mirror and shuddered. I look positively haggard, she thought. Her skin was pale and puffy, there were dark smudges under her grey eyes and even her beautiful

235

raven-black hair looked stringy and lifeless. She flinched when the door opened suddenly and Jane hurried into the room. The maid was scowling.

'Aren't you going to bother to get dressed today?' she asked.

Susan squeezed her eyes shut and opened them again. The headache had not gone. 'I feel bad,' she said.

'In what way?' Susan could have sworn there was a flicker of something – not fear, exactly; concern perhaps – in Jane's beadlike eyes. 'You don't feel sick or owt like that?'

'No – it's my head. It feels too heavy.'

The maid's expression relaxed. 'Well that's your own fault. You shouldn't hev had so much to drink last night.'

'But he kept filling my glass.'

'Yes, I suppose he did. Well, you must learn to drink a little more slowly. If your glass isn't empty then he can't fill it up, can he?'

'But he's always telling me to drink up, to have just a little more, and before I know it I seem to have had a whole bottle of wine to myself.'

'Aye, pet, and more. I'll hev to hev a word with him. If he goes on like this he'll ruin you and that would be a shame.'

'*You* will have a word with him?' Susan was astonished.

'Aye, he pays me to look after you. To keep you bright and bonny.' Jane suddenly couldn't meet her eye. The maid hurried over to the bedside table and picked up the tray that lay there. 'You've left your breakfast,' she said.

'I couldn't face it.'

Jane stared at her for a moment, then said, 'I've got to change these sheets, so why don't you go along and hev a nice bath and then rest downstairs on the sofa until it's time to dress for the evening. I'll help you put something pretty on, one of your new frocks. The master is coming here tonight.'

Susan scowled. How was it that Jane always seemed to know when Gilbert was coming even when she did not?

'Divven't look like that! You'll spoil your bonny face, and you've got to look your best tonight because he's bringing two friends with him.'

'Friends?' Susan suddenly perked up. 'He's bringing two of his friends?'

'That's what I said.'

'But that's wonderful!'

'Why's that?'

'He's going to introduce me to his friends. Surely that means . . .' Susan stopped herself. She didn't want to admit to this strange, sometimes friendly, sometimes bossy woman that she was still hoping desperately that her gentleman was going to marry her.

'What's the matter?' Jane asked.

'Nothing.' And then something else occurred to her. 'Jane . . . you don't think I'll let him down, do you?'

'Let him down?'

'You know. I don't talk like a proper lady.'

'There's no need to worry about that. I'm sure you'll be everything he wants you to be.'


'Please, please say I can go, Marion. It's so important to me!'

They were sitting at the table in the dining room, Victor at the head with Charlotte facing him – she had never given up what she considered to be her rightful place – which left Marion and Annette facing each other across the width of the table. Annette's eyes were shining. She had hardly touched her consommé and it was rapidly cooling in the blue Wedgwood dish. Charlotte glanced at the younger girl and frowned.

Marion was perplexed. 'But you have never been away without me.'

'I'm not exactly going on my own. I will be with Lady Cressington.'

'I know, but . . .'

'What is the child talking about?' Charlotte asked. 'Did I hear that she wants to go to London?'

'Yes,' Victor said. 'Esmé Cressington had offered to take her to London to visit the art galleries, and for some reason my wife is withholding her approval.'

Victor's tone was critical and Marion felt as though she was being isolated.

'But what about college?' she asked. 'Surely you don't want to miss your lectures?'

'Well, no, but a chance to see the Old Masters is surely as good as a week of classes.'

'She has a point,' Victor said.

Marion dropped her head to conceal her irritation.

Charlotte drank her last spoonful of soup and motioned to the young maidservant to clear the table. Charlotte and Victor's plates were empty, Marion's half full and Annette's hardly touched. They remained silent while they were served haricot mutton, boiled potatoes and a macedoine of vegetables. Then Charlotte waved the maid away.

'We'll ring for you when we are ready for dessert,' she said. When the door closed behind the girl, she looked severely round the table and said, 'It is not good for servants to hear their betters disagreeing about something.'

Victor smiled at his sister. 'You are right, Charlotte, as ever. I am truly glad you are here to guide Marion in the matter of etiquette.'

Marion looked sharply at him but found that he was smiling as if he were teasing. Nevertheless, she felt as though he had been disloyal.

Perhaps he sensed her displeasure, because his tone was conciliatory. 'Marion, my dear, I know you take your responsibility for Annette very seriously. But surely you realise that she will be perfectly safe with Lady Cressington?'

Marion could think of no reason to disagree.

'Perhaps you are reluctant to let her go because you will miss her?'

Marion kept silent.

'That's it, isn't it? But don't you see how selfish you are being?'

Marion was shocked into speech. 'Selfish?'

'Yes, my dear. You want to keep your sister by you, and that is natural, but in doing so you are denying her a wonderful opportunity.'

Marion was forced to consider that that might be the case. 'You think I should give her permission to go?' she asked.

'I do. And if you will respect your husband's opinion, you will agree forthwith.'

Victor was still smiling, but Marion did not miss the steely edge to his tone. 'Very well, Victor,' she said. 'Annette may go to London with Lady Cressington.'

At this Annette squealed with delight. Flinging her napkin down on the table, she rose from her chair and hurried to Victor and hugged him.

'Thank you, thank you,' she said. 'I knew you would make her see sense.'

Marion was shocked to the core. Since when had relations between her young sister and her husband become so intimate that Annette could hug him like this? And what about 'I knew you would make her see sense?' Surely those words could only mean that Victor and Annette had discussed this matter previously. Victor had already decided that Annette could go to London. The whole scene that had just occurred had been pointless. A charade.

Dessert was baked apples with whipped cream. Charlotte sat back and allowed the maidservant to heap her dish generously with cream, then said, 'When we are ready for coffee, I want you to take a tray to my room.'

When Charlotte left them, Victor began talking to Annette about her work at art school. Marion felt totally excluded.

Susan gazed in wonder at her reflection in the bedroom mirror. Jane had done such wonders with a few cosmetic aids that you could no longer see the dark shadows under her eyes or the slightly pinched lips – a sign of discontent – that Susan was developing.

Her hair, shampooed with extract of rosemary, was now piled high except for the delicate curling tendrils pulled down to frame her face. Susan had no idea how Jane, a woman who looked as though she would be more at home in a farmhouse kitchen, could be so skilful when dressing a lady's hair. She watched in the mirror as she applied rouge so artfully that no one would be able to tell that Susan was wearing any – at least not by candlelight.

Jane had produced a new gown for her, and Susan stood up and examined her full-length reflection in the cheval glass. She frowned. The daring style, with the neckline cut so low and sleeves designed to look as though they had recently slipped off her shoulders, was strangely at odds with the pure white silk, which would have been suitable for a little girl's party dress.

'You'll do very nicely,' Jane said, and she stood back and looked at Susan as though she was examining a work of art. 'Now come along downstairs and sit in the front parlour while I make sure the table is ready.'

Susan did as she was told. A strange lassitude had overtaken her. She was excited about meeting two of her gentleman's friends, but somehow she could not raise even enough energy to go and peep in the dining room to watch Jane setting the table.

Why am I so tired? she thought. I don't do very much these days. Instead of getting up early and going to work in that poky little tobacconist's shop, I can lie abed as long as I like, and then all I have to do is sit around and read magazines until Gilbert comes to visit me.

Time spent with him never varied. The rich food, the wine that she had grown so fond of, and then . . . Her thoughts skittered away from what happened next. She knew very well that what she was doing was not proper, but she had convinced herself that if she did her best to please him, eventually he would ask her to marry him. If she refused, he might turn her out.

She heard movement in the passage and voices as Jane and another woman discussed the food that was to be served. So the cook had been brought in again. That meant the evening meal was going to be special. This was confirmed when Jane asked her if she'd like to see the table.

Susan had never seen it looking so attractive. The snowy-white damask, the crystal glasses and the silverware were the same as ever, but tonight there were arrangements of white flowers and dark green ivy and a silver epergne bearing an abundance of fruit. Susan realised that the grapes had been arranged deliberately to look as though they were cascading down to the tablecloth.

'They must be special friends,' Susan exclaimed.

'Why do you say that?' Jane asked.

'Well, everything is so beautiful.'

'No doubt he owes them a favour,' Jane said wryly.

'A favour? What do you mean?'

'Never mind. I shouldn't hev said that. I forget sometimes how new to the game you are.'

'Game? What game?'

Jane laughed. 'The game of life,' she explained.

Susan thought that was an unsatisfactory answer and was puzzled by the hint of pity in the maidservant's eyes. Suddenly she shivered.

'Are you cold?' Jane asked.

'No, just goose bumps. I'm nervous, I suppose. I want so much for his friends to like me.'

'No need to worry about that,' Jane said. 'The master wouldn't bring them here if he thought they wouldn't like you.'

\*

240

Marion was glad of the opportunity to sit alone with her books. After dinner, Charlotte had stayed in her room and Marion, Annette and Victor had retired to the drawing room, where Annette settled down on the sofa with a notebook and pencil. She was silent as she became thoroughly absorbed in what she was doing.

Victor sat in one of the large fireside chairs and said, 'I hope you don't mind, my dear, but I have not yet had the chance to read the evening paper.'

Marion sat opposite him and stared into the fire. The only sounds were the rustling of the paper as Victor turned the pages, the crackling of the coals and the ponderous ticking of the large ebony-encased clock on the mantel. She thought of the books waiting for her on her bedside table. One of them was a detective novel that she was thoroughly enjoying. She was just about to go and get it when Victor closed the newspaper, folded it and looked up.

'Nothing of much interest in here tonight,' he said. 'It doesn't seem as if Earnshaw has found anyone to take on your father's work.'

He stood up. 'And now, I hope you will forgive me but I have to meet two of my business associates at the club. We'll probably be late, so don't bother to wait up for me.'

Marion didn't answer, but Annette looked up from her notebook and said, 'Are you going out?'

'I'm afraid I have to, but not before I have a look at what you are drawing.'

'Oh, I'm not drawing,' Annette said. 'I'm just making lists.'

'Lists? Let me see.'

Victor sat next to her on the sofa and held out his hand for her notebook. When she handed it to him he glanced at it and laughed. 'And do you really think you need all these clothes?' he asked. 'Just for one week in London?'

Annette smiled at him. 'Well, I am going with Lady Cressington,' she said. 'You wouldn't want to be ashamed of me, would you?'

Victor laughed. 'Of course not.'

'So may I have them all?'

'I should think so. If you're a good girl.'

'Oh, I will be!'

Annette's eyes were shining and Victor smiled at her indulgently. Marion felt a surge of irritation. He was spoiling her. He had begun to indulge Annette and cater to her whims from the moment they had come to live here. He seemed to be more interested in her than in Marion herself, and sometimes Marion had the craziest idea that he had married her just because she was Annette's sister, but she couldn't understand why.

Once Victor had gone, Annette yawned and stretched and said that as there was nothing to do she might as well go to bed. Marion didn't even look at her. She tried not to feel wounded that her sister didn't consider her worth talking to, but it wasn't very long before she realised that what she was experiencing was not hurt feelings. It was anger.

She couldn't say why, but Susan had imagined that the friends her gentleman was bringing tonight would be a married couple: a man and his wife who were part of local society. She was utterly dumbfounded when two gentlemen walked in. For a start they were old – well, not exactly old, but probably in their forties. They were dressed well.

Susan had learned to judge a man by the cut of his clothes when she had worked in the tobacconist's, and she saw that these men were probably prosperous but not of the first rank. Businessmen, that was what they were.

The pain of her disappointment was almost physical. They were here to talk business, she was sure of it. She was soon proved right. They greeted her cordially, paid her some pretty compliments and then ignored her. As the meal progressed, the whole talk was of stocks and shares and property prices and things that Susan only half understood.

Feeling completely excluded, she turned her attention to each course of the mouth-watering meal that followed. And she allowed Jane to keep filling her glass with wine.

Jane always served their meals wearing a fresh cap and a clean white pinafore over her green rayon, but tonight she was wearing a black silk dress, and her cap and pinafore were trimmed with lace. She brought in course after course and served each one without uttering a word. Susan noticed how much the two guests were eating, and thought them rather greedy. Gilbert on the other hand ate sparingly and seemed to be persuading them to agree to certain business plans of his.

Susan lost interest entirely and grew steadily more bored and miserable. She could not understand why she was needed here.

She was being completely ignored. Was it sheer boredom that was making her feel sleepy, or was it because she was drinking too much wine? She held her crystal wine glass up towards the overhead gasolier and amused herself by twisting it round and round to make the light reflect from the many facets of the delicately etched pattern.

She heard one of the visitors laugh and murmur something to Gilbert, who said, 'Yes, she's very young, just like a child in so many ways.'

The other visitor laughed and said, 'And that's what the attraction was, wasn't it?'

Jane appeared at Susan's shoulder, took the glass from her and placed it on the table. 'I'm serving coffee in the parlour,' she said quietly. 'They won't be very long, so I'll take you up now.'

'Take me up? Am I going to bed?'

Jane didn't reply, but gently guided Susan up the stairs to her room, where she sat her down in front of the dressing table and began to unpin her hair. Susan watched in the mirror because Jane seemed to be taking as much trouble brushing and arranging her hair as if she were going out somewhere and not just to bed.

She felt pleasantly tired and stood up and held her arms out like an obedient child as Jane undressed her and helped her into her nightgown.

'Is this new?' Susan asked when she felt the smooth silk enfold her body.

'Yes. Aren't you a lucky girl?'

Susan began to giggle foolishly. 'Yes, I suppose I am.'

Then the room began to spin and she sat down on the bed abruptly.

'Are you all right?' Jane asked.

'Mmm, just sleepy . . . so sleepy.' Susan yawned and stretched her arms above her head. She felt the cool silk of the sleeves slide down her arms to her shoulders and giggled again.

'Well, don't go to sleep,' Jane said. 'Not yet awhile.'

Susan was about to ask why she shouldn't go to sleep when the bedroom door opened and Gilbert entered. He looked keenly at her and then said, 'You look utterly charming.'

'Are you coming to bed now?' she asked.

'Maybe I will.'

Susan frowned, puzzled by his answer. 'Have your boring old guests gone home?'

'No. Here they are, they've come to say good night to you.'

As he spoke, the two supper guests came into the room. Their faces were flushed and there was a sort of excitement in their eyes.

'Is she ready?' one of them asked.

'She's all yours,' her gentleman friend replied. 'The question is, who shall have her first?'

They all laughed, and Susan's drowsy state vanished abruptly as the three of them began to loosen their clothes.

'No!' she tried to shriek, but the sound came out as a terrified whisper.

She looked around for Jane, but the maid had vanished. She scrambled off the bed in a desperate attempt to make for the door, but the sudden motion caused something that felt like a hammer blow to her head, and the room started to spin violently. She lurched forward, lost her footing and began to fall. Gilbert caught her and pushed her roughly back on the bed.

'Behave yourself,' he said. 'Don't embarrass me in front of my guests. I've brought them here especially to see you.'

Susan lay sobbing amongst the crumpled bedclothes. The fire had died and the room was cold. She had been lying there drifting in and out of a sleep that brought her no rest. When she heard the front door slam she relaxed a little, but her wretchedness didn't abate. Then the door of the bedroom opened and she sprang up in terror, instinctively reaching for the bedclothes and dragging them round her.

'Whisht, lass, it's only me,' Jane said. 'I've brought you some broth.'

The maid put a tray down on the bedside table and lit the oil lamp. Then she hurried over to the fireplace and coaxed the fire back to life.

'Come along now, sup your broth. It will be good for you.'

'I don't want it.' Susan heard her own voice and it sounded ragged.

'Well, I can't force you, but at least you might thank me for bothering.'

'Why should I thank you? You knew what was going to happen, didn't you?'

'Of course I did.'

'And you didn't warn me. You left me all alone with them.'

Jane laughed. 'That was the idea, wasn't it?'

Susan began to weep, deep, shuddering sobs that tore at her throat and racked her body.

'Stop that!' Jane said. 'I want to get to bed tonight and I can't have you behaving like this.'

Susan went on crying, and without warning Jane took hold of her shoulders and then let go with one hand and slapped her hard across the face. The sobs stopped and Susan looked up at Jane in terror.

'It's all right. I'm not going to hurt you. I just wanted you to stop those silly hysterics. Now come along and sup this broth.'

She propped Susan up amongst the pillows and began to spoon-feed her. Susan contemplated spitting it out, but it tasted nice and she found herself enjoying it.

'That's a good lass,' Jane said. 'And in future you'll know not to take on so.'

'In future! Do you mean this will happen again?'

'Of course it will. Why do you think the master brought you here?'

'I thought he loved me. I thought he was going to marry me!'

Jane began to laugh. 'Love you? Did he ever say so?'

'No . . . but why else would he have taken up with me? Bought me such lovely things? Brought me here?'

'You really are an innocent, aren't you? How could you ever think that a rich gentleman like him would marry a common little lass like you?'

'I'm not common!'

'Yes you are. Oh, you're beautiful, there's no denying that, but you come from the wrong part of town, the wrong sort of family. I can tell you for sure that even if he wasn't married already, he would never marry you.'

Susan stared up at her. She began to cry again, silently this time, the tears leaving cool tracks down her burning cheeks. 'Married?' she whispered.

'Aye, and there's something else you should know,' Jane continued. 'I've worked for the master ever since I left my miserable little village and came to work in town. I'm not bonny like you but I'm good at practical things like running a house and keeping everything in order. And I can tell you what a lucky lass you are.'

'Lucky! How can you say that after what has just happened?'

'You're lucky because he's set you up in a house by yourself, not put you in with the other girls. He buys you nice things and is taken enough with you to visit you himself.

'Now take my advice and make the most of it while your looks last. Don't make a fuss, and do as you're told. If you please him, you can ask him to buy you something really valuable now and then – a piece of jewellery, for instance – and put it by to keep you when you're past it.'

Susan stared at Jane with an expression of abhorrence. 'I want to go home!'

'Likely you do. But you can't.'

'Why not?'

'What would you tell your ma? Where would you say you'd been?'

'I . . . I don't know, but I'd think of something.'

'Mebbe you would. I've always suspected you and the truth are often strangers to each other, but your ma wouldn't believe you.'

'Why not?'

'Because the master would make sure that she knew exactly what you'd been doing. How you'd brought shame on your family.'

'How could he do that?'

'Oh, never doubt it, he would find a way of letting your family know about you. He doesn't like to be crossed.'

Jane picked up the tray and walked over to the door.

'Now try and get a few hours' sleep,' she said. 'I'll wake you up with a nice breakfast.'

But long after Jane had left her, Susan lay weeping as she realised the full horror of her situation.


Marion heard the front door close and the murmur of voices as Victor said good night to the manservant. As soon as she judged him to be coming upstairs, she closed the book she had been reading, put it down on her bedside table, and turned down the oil lamb. She felt guilty for the subterfuge, but if Victor suspected she was awake he might come to their bed instead of sleeping in the dressing room, as he did whenever he had been out late.

She lay down but was not able to even try to sleep until she was quite sure that he was not going to join her. She heard him moving around in his dressing room and she wondered, as ever, what exactly he and friends talked about when they went to their club. Business,

Victor had said. Weren't office hours long enough? Marion wondered, and then the thought occurred to her that all kinds of secret deals might be made in less official surroundings. At least that was what happened in a detective novel she had read that involved the murder of a rival banker in the city.

But whatever they talked about, Marion was uneasily aware that she was pleased when Victor stayed out late. She remembered his sister Charlotte saying that she hoped marriage would change Victor's ways and keep him home at night. Well, it hadn't.

Marion tried to relax. The bed was comfortable and the room was warm. Annette was sleeping peacefully just along the corridor. Her younger sister was happy. She loved being an art student and there was no question that she was enjoying living in this grand house and that her future seemed secure.

That was the main reason Marion had decided to marry Victor. He had promised to look after Annette and pay the fees at the art school. But even so, would she have married him if Daniel Brady had been free to marry her? No matter how little they earned, she would have managed somehow to keep her promise to Annette, even if it had meant selling her father's books. She knew some of them were valuable first editions.

Of course, there were those who would be scandalised by such a match between a gentleman's daughter and a labouring man. But she knew instinctively that she and Daniel were right for each other. Or rather she had thought so until Dora Gibb had marched into her father's study that day and told her that Daniel was spoken for.

Angry and anguished she turned her face into her pillow and tried to suppress a treacherous tide of longing. I must not think of myself, she thought. I must do the best for Annette and try to be a good wife to Victor. But she knew the way ahead would be hard.

Victor lay in bed in the dressing room, and in the silence of the early hours he heard his wife moving restlessly in their marital bed. As he had mounted the stairs he had looked along the landing and seen the light that escaped from the bottom of their bedroom door fade and go out. She wanted him to think she was asleep. She had done that before. Poor Marion, he thought, how mortified she would be if she knew that, satiated as he was, he didn't mind at all.

# Chapter Sixteen

'Annette, are you ready?'

The cab was waiting and Marion had expected to find Annette dressed and ready to go with her to Betty's wedding, but instead her younger sister was sitting by the fire in the morning room looking at a fashion magazine. An open box of Turkish delight was on the occasional table next to her chair.

Annette didn't even raise her eyes from the page. 'I'm not coming with you.'

Marion fought the familiar vexation she felt these days when dealing with her sister. 'Please have the good manners to look at me when I'm talking to you,' she said.

Annette looked up reluctantly. 'What is it?'

'We're going to Betty's wedding. You've known about it for some days now and I reminded you at breakfast. Now, I suppose that dress will have to do, but please put your coat on.'

Annette looked mulish. 'I've told you, I'm not coming.'

'But you must.'

'Why must I?'

'Betty has known us ever since we were children. She was like a mother to us.'

'But she never really liked me, did she?'

Marion didn't know what to say. It was true that Annette had often tried Betty's patience, but she was sure their old friend's feelings were not as strong as dislike.

'I'm sorry you feel that way,' she told her sister. 'Betty was always fair and kind and she made sure we had a loving home.'

'That's what our father was paying her for, wasn't it?'

Annette returned her attention to the pages of her magazine and reached languidly for a piece of Turkish delight. Marion felt like tearing the magazine from her sister's grasp and hurling it in the fire. But that would achieve nothing. If she insisted that Annette come with her to the wedding, the younger girl would be rebellious and sulky and her attitude would certainly be hurtful to Betty and Arthur.

Marion stared at her sister and despaired of how much she had changed since they had come to live in Victor's house. Victor indulged her shamefully and Annette had learned to take advantage of it. Had she always been like this? Marion had to admit to herself that ever since she had been a child, Annette had liked to get her own way, and had been quite capable of manipulating their father into giving in to her. But Henry Brookfield had known where to draw the line. Victor seemed not to.

As if to confirm this thought, Annette, realising that Marion was still standing there, looked up again and said, 'Anyway, Victor said I need not go.'

Marion turned on her heel and left the room. She did not trust herself to speak.

Charlotte had commandeered the carriage to take her to a friend's house for luncheon, so the youngest housemaid had been sent to the high street to fetch a cab. Marion tried to calm herself as she walked down the drive to the gateway.

The sun was shining and a brisk wind chased scudding clouds across a pale blue sky. In the borders that lined the pathways early flowers struggled up through clods of damp earth that released a sharp loamy smell. Drifts of last year's leaves had settled under the trees that lined the wall. New leaves were beginning to unfurl in the branches above. It was a marvellous day for a wedding, Marion thought, and if anyone deserved such a gift of nature, Betty did.

The wedding guests were already gathered in the church on Heaton Road. Marion had deliberately planned to arrive late so that she could slip into a pew at the back unobserved. But her altercation with Annette had meant that she had left home even later than she intended, and she arrived just as another cab pulled up and three people got out. They were Betty, her father and her cousin Sarah. Sarah was dressed in her best and carrying a small posy, which she handed to Betty with a reverential look as though she were the attendant to a queen.

Betty took the flowers and checked to see if her skirt was arranged properly, then she saw Marion and smiled radiantly. She was wearing a smart dove-grey two-piece consisting of a flared skirt and a three-quarter-length jacket. A grey hat trimmed with blue feathers was perched on her upswept hair. Marion had never seen her looking so smart – or so happy.

'Go on, get yerself inside,' Betty said to Marion as her father took her arm and drew it through his. Then she looked perplexed and said, 'Where's Annette?'

Marion pointed vaguely towards the entrance to the church as if to indicate that her sister was already inside, and hurried up the steps ahead of Betty. God forgive me, she thought, but Betty would be upset if she thought Annette wasn't here. I'll have to think of some excuse to tell her later.

Betty had written and told her that it wasn't going to be a big wedding, just her immediate family. Arthur had no one to invite except two pals from the police station, one of them Sergeant Wilson. She and Arthur would be paying for everything and they couldn't afford to spend much – not seeing they had the new house to furnish.

Marion slipped inside the church quietly and saw that the guests occupied only the first few rows of pews. She took her place just behind them and tried to appear invisible, for she had seen him straight away. Daniel Brady was standing at the front, waiting for Arthur. He must be acting as best man.

For a moment Marion allowed her gaze to linger on his broad shoulders and his dark hair. Then she closed her eyes tightly in an attempt to banish the emotions the very sight of him aroused in her.

During the service she was reminded of her own wedding. She remembered that the whole occasion had seemed like a dream. But not the usual kind of dream that a bride was supposed to enjoy. No, throughout her own wedding Marion had distanced herself from the proceedings and tried to pretend it was happening to someone else.

In her memories of the day she was an onlooker observing another young woman promising to love, honour and obey the man who stood beside her. She felt a rush of shame. She knew it had not been fair to Victor. Very probably he had soon sensed that she did not love him and that was why the intimate side of their marriage was such a disaster.

After the ceremony, Betty and Arthur led the small procession out of the church. As they approached, Marion edged along the empty

pew towards the side aisle and tried to hide in the shadow of a stone
pillar. Most of the guests hurried after the newly-wed couple so that
they could shower them with rice once they reached the pavement.

When they had gone, Marion left her refuge behind the pillar and
decided to walk up the side aisle. Whether or not she had hoped to
escape detection, her plan was thwarted. Daniel was waiting for her.
They stood and looked at each other in the empty church. A gas jet
flickered nearby, giving an uneven light. They could hear the shouts
and the laughter just outside the doorway. Eventually it was Marion
who broke the silence.

'How are you?' she asked.

She thought there was a trace of a mocking smile as he answered.
'I'm very well, Mrs Bateman.'

Another silence, in which she could feel her heart thudding
against her ribs. Then she said, 'Marion, please.'

'Marion.'

Then they both spoke at once,

'I'm sorry I lost your father's papers . . .'

'I was sorry to hear you suffered an attack – and thank you . . .'
Marion knew she was gabbling.

'Thank you for what?'

'For sending your fiancée to tell me what happened.'

'My fiancée?'

'Yes. Miss Gibb. She told me you were going to be married.'
Marion heard the accusatory tone in her voice and looked down,
unable any longer to meet his eyes.

'Did she?'

There was something about the way he said it that made her look
up again. What she saw in his eyes was anger. Blazing anger. But he
didn't deny it.

'Where's Daniel?' they heard a woman call from outside. It was
Dora Gibb.

His look of anger turned to one of angry resignation. 'I must go,'
he said.

He walked away quickly. For a moment he was illuminated in the
sunshine streaming in through the open doorway, then he was gone.
The church was silent. Marion became aware of the street noises. The
clip-clop of hoofs, the rattle of passing carriages, the call of a
newspaper boy.

She felt faint. There was a table behind the last pew, the surface covered with tottering piles of hymn books from which there arose a faintly musty smell. Marion swayed and leaned back against the table. One of the piles wobbled and came crashing down. Some of the hymn books fell against the other piles and soon they were all cascading gently to the floor. Loose pages slithered out of some of them and Marion stared down in dismay at what she had caused to happen.

Still shaking, she knelt down to start picking up the books.

'Eeh, what's happened here?' someone said as a shadow fell across the stone floor.

Marion looked up to see Betty's mother looking down in concern.

'I . . . I knocked the table,' Marion said. 'Look, the hymn books fell down,' she added unnecessarily.

'Well, let's pick them up again.'

Mrs Sutton knelt down beside her and soon had the books arranged much more neatly than they had been before. She rested a hand on the table and got up slowly, then held out a hand to help Marion up. Betty's mother was out of breath.

'There you are, Mrs Bateman, pet,' the older woman said. 'Now, are you coming?'

'Coming?'

'Aye. To our house. Hev a bite to eat and toast the happy pair.' She smiled broadly.

'I'm not sure . . .'

'Not sure? Why ever would you not come? I mean, Betty will be that disappointed if you don't.'

'Well . . . Annette . . . she's not feeling well.' Marion hated herself for lying. 'I thought I'd better get home and see if she's all right.'

'Not well? It's nothing serious, is it?'

Marion felt even more guilty at Mrs Sutton's genuine concern.

'Oh, no. Just, well . . . you know . . . she's . . .'

Marion strove desperately for some sort of malady that wasn't too serious, and while she did so Mrs Sutton jumped to a conclusion.

'Oh, female problems, eh? Sometimes young lasses take it hard. Well, divven't fret. I'm sure she wouldn't want you to go hurrying home. Now,' the older woman assumed the matter was settled, 'is that your cab waiting outside?'

'Yes.'

Victor had told her to keep the cab; he didn't want his wife to be seen hailing cabs on Heaton Road. Marion thought his attitude was pompous but nevertheless she was grateful.

'Well then,' Mrs Sutton said. 'We were wondering whether you could bring the bairns along?'

'I'm sorry, I don't understand.'

'Betty and Arthur will take a cab down to our house – after all, it's her big day – and the rest of us will walk home. But we thought it would be nice to give our Dinah and Daisy a treat.'

'Oh yes, of course.'

When Marion left the church, she was pleased to see that most of the others had already set off walking. She noticed that Betty's cousin Sarah was chatting happily as she walked with Daniel and Dora Gibb. Dora was holding herself erect, and something about her attitude told Marion that she was not pleased to have Sarah walking with them.

Mrs Sutton shepherded her twin daughters towards Marion's cab, where Mr Sutton was waiting. Mother and father helped them in and then set off to catch up with the others.

'I've told Betty she's not to do anything today and that Sarah will put the kettle on and take the covers off the sandwiches if she gets home before I do,' Marion heard Mrs Sutton tell her husband as they hurried away.

Dinah and Daisy were excited to be traveling in such style, and they laughed and waved to the wedding party as the cab overtook them. How different from my wedding day, Marion thought, and immediately felt annoyed with herself for sliding dangerously near to a state of self-pity.


In the library at Victor Bateman's house, a tall, thin man had emptied all the shelves that housed Marion's books and piled them up on the floor. He was kneeling amongst them and examining them carefully when Victor hurried into the library.

'Well, Samuel?' he asked.

'Nothing. No hidden papers, no notes except those she or her father must have made and used for teaching.'

Victor clenched his fists and paced about the floor. 'Well you'd better put everything back,' he said. 'And I hope you've taken note of each book's position on the shelves. I don't want my wife to realise that anything has been touched while she's been at the wedding.'

'I'm not stupid.' Samuel Burroughs regarded Victor with a certain amount of scorn. 'If I were, you wouldn't employ me.'

He began to replace the books carefully. Victor sat at the desk and watched him. Samuel Burroughs was useful, in all kinds of ways, but he had become a little too cocksure for comfort lately. Victor ruminated uneasily that the man knew too much about him, too much of his business and his affairs.

He was paid well for his discretion, but was it enough to ensure his loyalty and his silence? Maybe he should pay him more. Or when he was sure that there was no more to be found, make sure that he was in no position to cause trouble. That could be arranged.

Victor narrowed his eyes and something of the direction his thoughts were taking must have shown in his face, because when the man had finished and turned round quickly, he looked startled.

'What are you thinking?' he asked Victor.

Victor's expression became bland. 'Why do you ask?'

'The look in your eyes. I didn't like it.'

'No, well that's probably because you haven't found anything for me yet.'

'Yet? Where else is there to look. I went over the Brookfields' house as soon as it was empty. I examined every piece of furniture before you sent it to the salerooms. There were no secret drawers, nothing had slipped down the arms of the chairs, I can assure you.'

'What about the bits and pieces my wife gave to her housemaid?'

'Nothing left the house before I examined it.'

'And the papers you took from Daniel Brady? Are you sure they were all reports of trials?'

'I paid a compliant clerk of the court to transcribe them. You've got the results. You've seen for yourself.'

Victor had indeed pored over the translations that Samuel had brought him. But now he stirred uneasily. 'What did you tell him? This clerk of yours? Why did he think he was being paid to do this?'

Samuel Burroughs sighed. 'I've already told you. Don't you trust me? I told him that I'd found the papers in a house I'd been paid to empty and I wondered if they were important.'

'And he believed you?'

'Of course he did.'

'He didn't suspect anything?'

'Why should he? From what I've seen of the papers, apart from the odd hanging offence, they're all extremely boring. And incidentally, what would we have done if they had been those you are looking for?'

'Then amenable or not, your friendly clerk of the court would have had to be silenced, wouldn't he?'

Victor's voice had taken on a chilling edge and Samuel Burroughs suddenly couldn't meet his eyes. 'Yes, I suppose so.'

Victor adopted a hearty tone. 'Well then, you deserve a drink after all that work – even though the effort was in vain.'

He reached down and opened a drawer in his desk. He took out a bottle of whisky and two tumblers. He smiled faintly.

'Believe it or not, I have to hide this pleasant little vice from my dear sister Charlotte. She's teetotal herself and I shouldn't like her to think that her little brother had gone astray.' Victor poured a generous amount of whisky into each glass. 'Come and sit down,' he said.

Samuel sat at the other side of the desk, noticing its quality and the fact that the top was well polished and free of any papers. Of course Victor kept his business papers at his office in Dene Street. This room and its furnishings were just for show. The sort of room and furnishings a successful man was supposed to have. But as well as success, Victor valued his reputation as a man of moral integrity who was a veritable pillar of the community.

Only I know the truth, Samuel though. The tall man's hooded eyes concealed his uneasy thoughts as he accepted the glass Victor handed him and raised it to his lips. 'By, that's good,' he said.

'Only the best,' Victor said as he raised his own glass.

'Naturally.' After another sip or two of whisky Samuel said, 'There's something I don't understand.'

'What's that?'

'Well, a man like you, rich and powerful, and yet you're frightened of displeasing your own sister.'

Victor laughed. 'I'm not frightened. I'm fond of the old curmudgeon and I choose to indulge her. Besides, Charlotte goes about in society with the most eminent and respectable people. Through her they learn that I am a good brother, a benevolent landlord and an altogether upright citizen.'

'And you don't want anything to get out that might tarnish that reputation, do you?'

Victor's smile vanished and his eyes narrowed. He brooded for a moment and then he said, 'Maybe we have nothing to worry about. Maybe nothing was ever written down.'

'Maybe.' But Samuel didn't look too sure.

'If papers do exist, do you think Brady could have them?'

'If he had, I think he'd have made something of them by now.'

'In what way?'

'Taken them to Charles Earnshaw — or maybe to your wife.'

'You're probably right, but all the same, we'll keep an eye on him.'

Samuel Burroughs laughed. 'You mean I will be keeping an eye on him. Sometimes, Mr Bateman, I wonder what you'd do without me.'

Victor's unease returned. He had allowed Burroughs to become too intimate. The man knew too much. He would definitely have to be dealt with either when Henry Brookfield's papers were discovered or when it was established once and for all that there were none.

But now he smiled and leaned across the desk to fill up the man's glass. 'That's right, Samuel,' he said. 'You've been very useful, but then I've paid you well, and remember, I took you on when nobody else would employ you.'

Samuel Burroughs knocked back the expensive liquor in one gulp and stood up to go. His dark eyes glittered and he drew his lips back in a wolverine smile. 'No, you won't let me forget that, will you? But now I'd best be off. Your wife will surely be home soon, and you wouldn't want to introduce a dangerous felon to her, would you?'

In spite of the jolly crowd of relatives in the Suttons' home, Betty found time to talk to Marion. 'Eeh, I'm glad you came,' she said, and laughed as she had to raise her voice to make herself heard. 'Just listen to them,' she said. 'Why don't you and me go and sit in the yard for a bit and hev a good old chinwag?'

'I can't stay long. I mean, the cab is waiting for me.'

'Divven't worry about that. Me ma's already taken the cabman a cup of tea and a plateful of sandwiches. And no doubt your husband will be paying him well for his troubles. Now, come with me.'

Marion was glad to escape the throng and pleased to find the Suttons' back yard was a little well of sunshine. There was a wooden bench against the coal house and every available space along the walls was filled with plant pots.

'Them's me dad's tomatoes,' Betty said as she nodded towards the tall green growth supported by bamboo canes.

Marion looked surprised. 'Tomatoes? Outside?'

'Aye – you divven't need a greenhouse for this kind. Me dad buys them at the stall in the Grainger Market and they're supposed to flourish outdoors – especially if you've got a nice sunny little spot like we hev. Every year me da hopes for a fine crop, as he puts it, and every year me ma ends up making green tomato chutney!'

Suddenly Marion was overwhelmed with emotion. How wonderful to be part of a family like this, she thought. And what a joyful wedding day Betty would have to remember.

Betty sat down next to Marion but turned her head to look at her and said, 'What's the matter?'

'Why do you ask?'

'You've suddenly gone all serious. Are you worrying about Annette? Me ma said you telt her that she was poorly.'

'Yes.. that's it,' Marion lied.

'Well divven't fret. I'm sure she'll be all right. In fact if I know that little article I wouldn't be surprised if she was putting it on so that she wouldn't hev to come here today.'

'Oh, no!'

Betty took Marion's hand. 'You divven't hev to pretend with me, you know. Annette and me never got along as well as you and I did, and you can rest easy, because I don't mind at all. You are here and that's what matters.' Suddenly Betty looked thoughtful. 'Eeh, who would hev guessed it,' she said.

'Guessed what?'

'That you and me would be married within a few months of each other. And we've done so well for ourselves, haven't we?'

'Have we?'

'Why of course we hev. We've both found ourselves a good man and we've each got a nice new home – and what with my Arthur being made up to sergeant and your husband being one of the richest men in Newcastle, we certainly don't hev any money worries.'

'Is that important?'

'Of course it is! I've seen enough of life round here to know that when poverty comes in at the door, love can fly out of the window.'

'Surely not.'

'Oh yes, pet, I can assure you it's true. I've seen what happens when a family falls on hard times.'

'Do you love Arthur?'

Betty smiled. 'Well, he's not like a hero in a storybook, but aye, I do.'

'And would you leave him if he lost his job? If you fell on hard times?'

Betty looked thoughtful. 'I hope I wouldn't. But we never know what life can bring, do we?'

Marion felt utterly disheartened by this no-nonsense view of life – especially as it had just been expressed by a woman she loved and respected. If I loved someone, she thought, nothing would make me leave him. This made her feel even more dejected. She had already accepted the fact that she did not love her husband, and today she had been forced to come face to face with the man she did love.

'. . . lost his job,' Betty was saying.

'I beg your pardon?'

'I thought you weren't listening,' Betty exclaimed. 'I was just telling you that Daniel Brady has lost his job. He just couldn't manage it now that his leg seems to be permanently damaged.'

'I'm sorry to hear it.'

'Aye, and so's that lass of his.'

'You mean Dora.'

'Yes, Dora. You can tell just by looking at her how keen she is to waltz down the aisle with him. But Arthur says he can't see Daniel tying the knot until he's settled in another job.'

'Arthur?'

'Don't look so surprised. Arthur and Daniel hev become pals since – well, you know, since your poor pa was murdered. They often share a pint and a bit natter together.'

'I see. Your opinion of Mr Brady seems to have changed,' Marion said somewhat sharply.

'What do you mean?'

'You talk about him as if you like him.'

'I do, I always did. But I know what you're getting at. I realised that you were getting fond of him and I just didn't think he was the right fellow for you.'

'Why not?'

'It's obvious, isn't it? He's a working man who left school when he was twelve years old, and you have been brought up an educated lady. Clever as you are, Miss Marion, I couldn't see you managing on a labourer's wage.'

Betty paused and shook her head. 'In any case,' she continued, it seems that he was already spoken for. Arthur says there's been an understanding between Daniel and Dora since they were nothing but little bairns. Dora lives next door to the Bradys, you know.'

A cloud covered the sun and the yard became shadowy. Marion watched a cat walking along the top of the wall. When it reached the next house, a dog's enraged bark made it yowl and leap down into the lane. Betty did not seem to have noticed Marion's silence, or if she had she did not mind, for she took up the conversation again.

'Arthur feels really sorry for Daniel, you know.'

'Why, because he is going to marry Dora Gibb?'

Betty raised her eyebrows at the comment and Marion's acerbic tone. 'Now now,' she said. 'If you were still a little girl I would scold you for talking like that. No, he feels sorry for him because he's injured and won't be able to work again – or not at least until he can find some other kind of occupation that doesn't call for brute strength. And as if the poor man doesn't hev enough to worry about, his young sister Susan has run away from home. Her poor ma is frantic. Daniel goes out looking for the lass whenever he can.'

Marion sat there mutely. There was nothing she could say.

The back door opened and Arthur came out. 'There you are,' he said. 'You'd best come in. Sergeant Wilson has been teasing me that you've run away from me already and he wants to know if he should send out a search party.'

Arthur was laughing. He held out a hand. Betty took it and he pulled her to her feet. For a moment he caught her in his arms. He tried to kiss her but she turned her head away so that the kiss landed on her cheek.

'Give over,' she said, and she laughed. 'What will Miss Marion think of us?'

'It's not Miss Marion now, you know,' Arthur reminded her. 'It's Mrs Bateman.'

He turned to Marion and asked, 'Are you coming in? Sergeant Wilson has sent for a jug of draught sherry from the Raby and they want to toast the happy couple. That's us,' he added unnecessarily before he led his wife back into the house.

Marion followed them in and tried to hide herself in a corner, but when the glasses were handed round and the toast was proposed she found Dora Gibb had come to stand next to her.

'The happy couple!' Sergeant Wilson said.

'Betty and Arthur!' Betty's father added.

'This is lovely, isn't it?' Dora said to Marion. 'I hope you'll be coming to our wedding.'

Marion didn't answer. She gripped her glass more tightly and, resisting the urge to empty its contents over Dora, drank deeply.

Soon after that, two jugs of ale were delivered and the party grew livelier. Marion had gone out to the passage and was sitting on the stairs with the twins, Dinah and Daisy. The little girls had been given lemonade to drink, and every now and then they raised their glasses, said, 'Cheers!' and collapsed into giggles.

When she judged she had been sitting there long enough, Marion told the twins, 'I'm going now. I don't want to interrupt the party, so when you get a moment, will you say goodbye to your sister for me?'

The little girls nodded and held up their faces for a kiss.

'I hope you'll come and see us again,' Dinah or Daisy said. In all the time she'd known them, Marion had not yet learnt to tell the difference.

The other child said, 'You can come and see us when we go to our Betty's house. She has a house of her own now, you know.'

Marion smiled as she promised that she would, then she walked quietly along the passage and out of the front door, closing it behind her. The cab was waiting for her in the street.

When Marion returned to the house she still could not think of as home, she saw the lights on in the library and went in to find Victor sitting at his desk. He was reading the evening paper, but when he heard her he looked up and smiled.

'Did you enjoy yourself at the wedding?' he asked.

'Yes thank you.'

'I'm pleased I was able to find a suitable house for the newly-weds.'

'Yes, they're very grateful.'

'It was the least I could do. After all, Betty looked after you and Annette for many years. I am the one who should be grateful.'

'Why?'

'Marion, my dear.' Victor rose from the desk and came towards her. 'Why are you so surprised? I'm grateful because Betty made a happy home for you – just as I want to do now.'

Marion felt disorientated. Now Victor was talking to her as if he were in love with her again. She was sure that he was not. So why had he married her? Sometimes she wondered if he had been genuinely moved by their plight and was perhaps even fond of her. But other times she suspected it was because Charlotte had told him that it was time he found himself a wife.

Seeing that he was determined to be pleasant tonight, Marion resolved to do her best to lift her spirits and be a good wife.

'Why don't you go upstairs and change, my dear? I've told your maid to get the gown you wore for our wedding day prepared. As we will be dining alone tonight, I think you can lay aside your mourning black.'

'Dining alone?'

'Yes, Charlotte is dining with a friend and Annette has gone to Lady Cressington's. She is going to stay overnight.'

'Why has she gone there?'

Victor smiled. 'Esmé has taken quite a fancy to your pretty little sister. I believe she sees Annette as the daughter she never had. No doubt they will have great fun planning their trip to London. All the clothes they will wear and the places they will visit.' He laughed. 'And no doubt the clothes will be the more important topic of the two.'

'When was this arranged?'

'Why do you ask?'

'Annette didn't tell me she was going to Lady Cressington's. She did not ask my permission.'

'She asked mine. Yesterday.'

'But you knew she was invited to Betty's wedding.'

'Yes, I knew, and I did not think she should be forced to attend. You were going, so honour would be satisfied. *Noblesse oblige* and all that.'

'I went to the wedding because I regard Betty as a friend. I certainly wasn't prompted simply by a sense of duty.'

'Marion, my dear,' Victor said, 'let us not quarrel. If I did wrong in allowing your sister to go to Lady Cressington's instead of your maidservant's wedding, I am sorry. But now we have the house to ourselves. Let us enjoy a meal together.'

Sensing that Victor was becoming irritated and that further argument would serve no purpose, Marion resolved to say no more. 'Very well. I'll go and change my dress as you suggested.'

'Good. I'll peruse the evening paper while I wait for you.'

Suddenly Victor took Marion's hand and raised it to his lips. 'But don't be too long.'

The gesture was meant to be endearing, but Marion was convinced that her husband was playing a part and that the play-acting amused him. She remembered the days when he had courted her with pretty speeches. Even then she had thought that he was saying the things he thought a woman expected to hear; now she was sure of it.

She did not know whether she ought to be grateful to him because he was trying to please her, or angry that he thought her dim witted enough to need such empty flattery.

While she changed her clothes, assisted by her maid, she wondered how Victor could say that they would be alone when the house was stuffed with servants. She wondered if people like her husband even thought of servants as being human at all, or simply automatons whose only purpose was to serve their masters.

At dinner Victor seemed determined to be amiable. He praised Marion's appearance and then flattered her by discussing some of his business projects. He had recently acquired a large plot of land in Heaton and work was to start soon on some more of the soundly built terraced flats that would be affordable to working men.

'I'll put in the latest cooking ranges,' he told her, 'and there will be room to keep a decent-sized bath under the bench in the scullery. Do you approve?'

Marion looked at him to see if his question was serious. 'Of course I do,' she said. 'And I know how pleased my father would have been that you are not going to charge exorbitant rents – unlike some landlords.'

'The landlords that your father intended to expose?'

'Yes.'

Victor insisted that she take a second mutton cutlet and another serving of creamed potatoes. 'You are so slender,' he said smilingly. 'I would hate people to think that I am starving you.'

Marion could not help responding to his good-humoured manner and smiled in return. Is it me? She wondered as she sipped her wine. Am I giving way to moods and looking to find faults with my husband because he isn't the man I wanted to marry?

'Did your father ever talk to you about his work?'

Bewildered by the sudden return to the matter they had been discussing earlier, Marion said, 'I beg your pardon?'

'Your father. Did he talk about his work? I mean, you are an intelligent young woman. Perhaps he asked you to copy up his notes.'

Marion shook her head. 'No, I would have been willing to help – and indeed I had in the past. For example, his reports on how the old buildings near the quayside were disappearing fast to make way for modern business premises and how there were still pockets of slum dwellings in that area. I believe that is what prompted the project he was working on when he died. But he never showed those notes to me. He said they were too distressing.'

'Because of the conditions people are living in?'

'Not just that.'

'What, then?'

'The things that some people . . . women and girls . . . have to do to survive.'

'Ah, I see. Your father was right to spare you and we won't discuss the matter further. Now, shall we tackle this magnificent sherry trifle?'

Victor, perhaps feeling guilty that he had encouraged Annette not to go to Betty's wedding, continued to be charming. He ordered coffee to be served in the withdrawing room. The room was large, cavernous even, but there was an inviting area near the fire furnished with deep leather armchairs and footstools.

They sat without talking for a while. Victor had dismissed the maidservant, saying that he would pour the coffee himself, and he insisted that Marion try a small glass of plum liqueur.

She found it sweet but not unpleasant, and as the glass was so small, she allowed Victor to fill it for a second time. She began to feel drowsy. To her tired brain it seemed as though the shadows hovering in the corner of the room had begun to creep up on them so that the area near the fire became an island of comforting warmth and light. Her eyes closed and only the ticking of the clock on the mantel told her that she was still awake – just.

She heard Victor laugh softly. 'Just like a child,' he said. 'A sleepy child. If only you knew how much more attractive you are when you look like this.'

Then she sensed his shadow fall across her as he rose from his chair and came towards her. He took her hands and pulled her gently to her feet. 'Come along, my dear. It's time we went to bed.'

# Chapter Seventeen

When Marion awoke the next morning she was alone. Only the faint smell of bay rum on the rumpled pillows next to hers betrayed the fact that Victor had also been there. What time had he arisen? Marion could not remember. She had been so tired that she had fallen asleep the moment he had finished with her. She had a slight headache and she wondered if perhaps the plum liqueur had not agreed with her.

Her head cleared a little and her surroundings gradually came into focus. She could hear the coals crackling in the hearth and the wind buffeting the windows. Her instinct was to pull the bedclothes up and go back to sleep, but after a peremptory knock the door opened and someone came into the room. Marion opened her eyes reluctantly and raised her head from the pillows.

Her maid, Bertha, had entered, carrying a tray. The room was dark, the shadows repelled only by a dim light from the dying fire. Bertha placed the tray on the bedside table and went over to the windows to draw the curtains. Rain was streaming down the windows and a gloomy sky hung low over the Town Moor.

'Shall I arrange your pillows, Mrs Bateman?'

The tall, straight-backed woman approached the bed. As Marion sat up, the bedclothes slipped to reveal that she was naked. Embarrassed, she grasped the sheet and pulled it up to cover her breasts as Bertha reached for the silk robe that lay carelessly across a chair. Without a word her maid helped her slip her arms into the robe and Marion hastily pulled it round her body and fastened it.

'Your tray, madam,' Bertha said, and she placed it on top of the counterpane.

'Thank you.'

Marion had not been able to form an easy relationship with Bertha. The woman was polite and efficient but had never attempted to make any sort of conversation. Marion supposed she considered it not her place to do so. But neither did she respond to any pleasantry that Marion attempted. And it was hard to fathom what was going on behind those cold, deep-set eyes.

Once the woman had left the room, Marion poured herself a cup of coffee from the silver pot and spread some butter and apricot preserve on a fresh-baked bread roll. The small ormolu clock on the mantel chimed eight o'clock. Victor must have got up very early.

Marion frowned. She tried to remember when exactly he had left her. A memory surfaced of a cold draught as the bedclothes were moved and then fell into place again. Something nudged at her mind. The clock . . . it had been striking half past the hour. But what hour? Marion had not remained awake long enough to find out.

In any case, what had happened was not unusual. Her husband hardly ever spent the whole night in her bed. More often than not he would leave her and retire to the bed in his dressing room. And there were some nights when he didn't come home at all.

'Where are you going, son?' Hannah Brady put herself between Daniel and the door.

'To the library.'

'On a day like this? You'll get blown away!'

His mother tried to make a joke of it but Daniel could tell that she was vexed.

'It would take a strong wind to knock me off my feet,' he said with a smile, but still she did not make way for him.

'I don't understand why you hev to go to the blessed library all the time. You can bring the books home, can't you? I mean, that's what libraries are for. To lend books to people to read in the comfort of their own home. By their own fireside,' she added, and glanced at the easy chair meaningfully.

'I don't just go to the library to borrow books,' Daniel said patiently. He had told her this many times before. 'I go to sit at a table in the reading room and work there.'

'What do you mean, work? All that writing isn't going to bring home the bacon.'

This was the first time his mother had come anywhere near criticising him for not having found another job. She had every right

265

to be worried, for Daniel was the breadwinner, and when his savings ran out Hannah did not know what would become of them.

'Don't worry, Ma, I won't let us starve. Now, please excuse me but I have to go.'

'*Have* to go?' Hannah said, and at last the anger she must have been bottling up showed itself. 'There's no have about it. If you are going to waste your time with all this scribbling, I don't see why you can't sit here with me and keep me company.'

'No doubt Dora will be dropping by,' Daniel said somewhat acerbically. 'She comes here most days. She will keep you company.'

And this was why he had to leave the house. The reasons were twofold. Firstly, Dora and his mother never stopped talking, interrupting his flow of thoughts, and he could hardly expect his ma to be quiet in her own house. And secondly, since Betty and Arthur's wedding, Dora had become more and more sure of herself and the fact that they would be getting married some day soon.

Daniel was overtaken by the familiar feeling of guilt. He should have told Dora long ago that he didn't want to marry her, but his own feelings had been in such turmoil since Marion had married Victor Bateman that he could not have faced the inevitable scene, the hurt and anger that would be expressed not only by Dora but by his mother too. And he didn't want to make either of them unhappy.

He tried to soften his tone. 'It's not just because of the books that I go to the library. It's because in the reading room no one is allowed to talk, and I need peace and quiet while I'm working. It would be too distracting sitting here and listening to you and Dora chatting.'

Daniel saw from his mother's expression that he had only made things worse.

'Oh, if that's it then you'd better go,' she said. 'It would never do for me and Dora to *distract* you.'

Hannah Brady stepped aside, and when Daniel tried to kiss her cheek she turned away sharply. Daniel walked to the door, but before opening it he hesitated and turned to look at her. 'I'll find a job soon,' he said, 'I promise you, but you must let me follow my inclinations for the moment.'

'That's a laugh,' his mother said. '*Let* you. Since when hev I been able to stop you doing exactly what you wanted?'

This wasn't fair. Since he had been a little lad Daniel had always tried to please his mother and do the best for his family, but he saw from Hannah's set expression that she had made her mind up that she was hard done by. And I suppose she is, Daniel thought. The daughter she loves has run away and her only son isn't following the path she has chosen for him.

'I'm sorry you feel that way, Ma,' he said. 'But I'm going to the library.'

'Would you like a cup of tea, Mr Brady?'

Daniel looked up from the newspaper he had spread out on the table when he heard the whispered question. He had been so intent on his studies that he had not been aware of Miss Bennett coming into the reading room. He was the only person in there but he supposed the librarian was obeying the request for silence out of force of habit. He sat back and eased his shoulders and smiled as he nodded his head.

'Yes please,' he mouthed.

Miss Bennett indicated with a turn of her head that he should follow her. They left the reading room and walked through the main hall of the library, where Mr Chalk was in charge of the desk. The young man looked up and scowled as they passed. He had never liked Daniel and Daniel didn't really know why. Perhaps even though his shiny-sleeved suit and his frayed collars and cuffs betrayed the fact that he himself was impecunious, the young library assistant was one of those people who thought that labouring men should know their place and not aspire to any form of higher learning.

A small fire burned in the hearth and Daniel noticed that Miss Bennett had made the staff sitting room as welcoming and homely as possible. There were embroidered cushions on the two armchairs and a pretty rose-print tablecloth on the small table. He wondered if the library had become more of a home to her than the house she lived in. He could very well imagine that if she was lonely, this world of books would be a wonderful refuge, as it had become for Daniel himself. He sat down in the chair she indicated.

'Here, take this,' she said and she handed him a toasting fork. 'I hoped you would come again today and I brought us some teacakes.' While she was speaking, she had sliced the teacakes nearly in half and put them on a plate on the table beside him. 'Your arms are longer than mine, so you won't have to sit quite so close to the fire. You toast them and I'll butter them,' she said.

Daniel secured half a teacake on the long prongs of the toasting fork and began his task. Miss Bennett spooned tea leaves into the pot. The kettle, which she had placed on the small gas ring on a bench at the back of the room, began to whistle, and she poured the boiling water into the pot.

'There,' she said. 'We'll let it mash a while.'

Daniel thought how cosy the scene would look to any observer; how domestic, as if he and the kindly older woman were family. Mother and son, perhaps. As he turned to slide the last teacake on to the plate, he saw the way Miss Bennett was looking at him.

His eyes widened as he noticed the emotion in her face, and she smiled faintly. 'Yes, I am fond of you, Mr Brady,' she said as if she had read his mind. 'If I had married and had a son, I would have liked him to be just like you.'

'Surely not,' Daniel said.

'Why not? Because we are from different levels of society? Because you are a labouring man? That sort of thing is supremely unimportant to me. You are intelligent, you have a questioning mind, and I believe you are high principled, too. I am sure that if you set your mind to it you could be a force for good.'

Miss Bennett's earnest expression suddenly dissolved into a slightly embarrassed smile. 'There now,' she said, 'sermon over. Shall we eat those teacakes while they are still hot enough to melt the butter?'

'Yes,' said Daniel. 'But only if you will stop calling me Mr Brady.'

Miss Bennett laughed. 'Very well . . . Daniel. However, considering the difference in our ages, I am afraid I cannot ask you to address me as Lavinia.'

As they sat by the fire with their tea and teacakes, Miss Bennett questioned Daniel about the work he was doing. 'I've noticed that you have been going through old newspapers. What is it you're looking for?' she asked.

'I'm reading everything I can find that was written by Henry Brookfield,' he told her.

'Why? Because you knew and liked him, or do you wish to learn something from the articles?'

'I want to learn from them.'

'You mean you want to see if they will tell you how to write, don't you?'

'I suppose I do.'

'Well you must be very careful not to copy his style. You must develop your own style, and you can only do that by writing, not just reading.'

'I know, but I don't know when I will be ready to start.'

'How about right now?'

'Now? But what should I write about? What could I write that other people would want to read?'

'Write about something that interests you.'

Daniel looked perplexed.

'Something you've seen that has intrigued you,' Miss Bennett continued. 'Or something you have done.'

Daniel smiled self-deprecatingly. 'What have I ever done that people would want to read about?'

'Well, for a start, you've been working on the new tramlines.'

'Who would be interested in that?'

'Think about it. Travelling about is becoming easier, the city is being improved, but at what expense?'

'I don't understand. You mean how much money it's costing?'

'I'm not thinking of money. There are other costs to be borne when old gives way to new.'

Daniel looked at his friend, trying to understand, and suddenly he did. 'We're making new roads but in some cases we're destroying the old ones. Buildings that are hundreds of years old have been pulled down to make way for the roads.'

'And do you approve of that?'

Daniel thought for a moment and then said, 'In some cases I do. Some of those buildings were rat infested, overcrowded, insanitary slums not fit for folk to live in. Others, like the little row of shops on Percy Street, were perfectly sound.'

'But they were in the way of progress.'

Daniel sighed. 'That's right. Luckily photographs were taken of them before they were demolished.'

'And I remember that some old artefacts were sent to the museum.'

'Artefacts?'

'Some medieval pottery and even a Roman coin or two.'

'That's right – I was there on the day a hoard of coins was found.'

'But to return to the old slum dwellings,' Miss Bennett said. 'What became of the people who lived there?'

Daniel frowned. 'I believe the landlord offered them other accommodation.'

'Better accommodation?'

'Yes.'

'So why are you frowning?'

'Because many of them couldn't afford the rent in the new houses and God knows what became of them.'

Daniel stared into the fire and Miss Bennett took his cup and poured him another cup of tea. 'There you are, then,' she said.

'What do you mean?'

She looked at him quizzically, and then he smiled and said, 'You're telling me what to write about, aren't you?'

'Yes. Who better to write about the changes occurring in this great city of ours than a man who has been closely involved in bringing those changes about. Not an architect, not a town planner, not one of the city fathers, all of whom see their grand designs on paper, but a man who has worked physically day by day and seen the changing face of the city at close quarters.'

Daniel looked at her intent expression and her shining eyes. 'You think this would be important, don't you?' he said.

'I do. And you must write about the good as well as the bad.'

'You talk as though you believe I am capable of this project.'

'Of course you are. Now go back to the reading room and start writing. And Daniel . . .'

'What is it?'

'This is only my opinion, but I would make the first article sound positive. Accentuate the good things. When you have your readers' interest, then you can start mentioning that there are problems, too. Now finish that cup of tea and off you go.'

Daniel was suddenly filled with a sense of purpose, and an incipient excitement stirred in his soul. 'Very well,' he said. 'But as this is entirely new to me, I would be grateful if you would read my work at the end of each day and tell me what you think of it.'

'Try stopping me.'

Annette came back from London with a trunk full of new clothes and brimming with excitement at the places she had been and the people she had met.

'Lady Cressington took me to a house in Chelsea and introduced

270

me to a real artist!' she said. 'Well, more than one, actually. And they manage to live on the sale of their work – and do you know, Marion, some of them are women! Lady Cressington knows them because of a friend of hers, Sabine Fournier. She's an émigré. That means this isn't her country. She's French but she grew up in Egypt then somehow she ended up in London, and she knows just about everybody!'

'Everybody?' Marion couldn't help smiling at her sister's fervour.

'Well, you know, other artists – important ones. They come to her studio. And Lady Cressington told me I must show them what I could do. So I did some sketches, mostly of people, a flower-seller, a newsboy, some pretty children in the park, and . . .' Annette ran out of breath. She breathed in and the words came tumbling out. 'And Sabine says I'm good and that I must work really hard at art school because I could be a very important artist one day!'

They were in Marion's first-floor sitting room. Marion had come to regard it as her refuge. She had told Victor that she would like to bring some of her books up here as the room was less intimidating than the library. He had wavered at first, and then, shortly after Betty's wedding, had capitulated and provided a bookcase and a small writing desk. While Annette had been in London, Marion had spent many hours in this room with her books, happy in her own company.

Now a ray of late-afternoon sunshine struggled through the heavy lace curtains and illuminated the delicate magnolia, mint green and pink of the Chinese carpet. Annette stood in the centre of the pool of sunshine like an actress in the spotlight waiting for her applause.

And in fact, Marion did feel like applauding. Not her sister, however, but Sabine Fournier, the exotic-sounding artist who had recognised Annette's talent and told her to work hard. Marion was certain that Annette would take this advice, and she didn't mind at all that it had come from a stranger.

'I'm very pleased,' she told her sister. 'And I'm sure she's right. Now shall we have tea together here in my little room?'

'Yes please.'

Annette suddenly sounded distracted.

'What is it?' Marion asked.

'The portrait . . .' She was looking at the portrait of their mother that Marion had placed on the wall to one side of the fireplace. Her expression was wistful, and Marion felt a pang of regret that, unlike herself, Annette had only a hazy memory of their mother.

'Is something the matter with it?'

'No, not at all. It's just that I've never really thought about it before. I mean, we grew up with it, didn't we?'

'Yes. What are you thinking now?'

'Do you know who the artist was?'

'I'm afraid not. It's something I never thought to ask Father.'

There were so many things I should have asked him, Marion thought. So many things we should have talked about. But how could we have known that our happy life together would end so soon and so tragically?

'Well, I don't think he was important,' Annette said, bringing Marion back from her reverie.

'Who?' Marion asked, bewildered.

'The artist. I mean, it's lovely because our mother was so beautiful, but some of the brush strokes are quite crude, aren't they?'

'I wouldn't know.' Marion was amused. 'But whoever painted it, I'm sure it meant a lot to Father.'

'Oh, of course, and I didn't mean to criticise it. It's just that I've had an idea. You are just as beautiful as our mother was and one day I would like to paint your portrait. That is, if I could ever be good enough. Portrait-painting is a special gift.'

Marion was touched both by Annette's desire to paint her portrait and also by the fact that she was humble enough to admit that the skill might be beyond her.

'Well, whether you consider yourself good enough or not, I hope that you *will* paint my portrait. I only wish I had your talent and then I would paint a portrait of you.'

'Victor says I am so pretty that I should have a photographic portrait taken,' Annette said. 'Perhaps we should sit for one together.'

'Perhaps.'

Marion's smile faded. Suddenly the friendly and intimate mood was broken. She wished that Victor would not talk that way to Annette. Not only was he in danger of making her vain and self-important, but there was something else about the way he paid so much attention to her younger sister. Something that Marion had not yet defined, but that was making her more and more ill at ease when she saw them together.

★

'Just look at the pretty new gowns he has sent you!'

Jane had brought the boxes of new clothes into the front parlour, and seeing that Susan had shown no inclination to look at them, she had opened them herself and now the floor was strewn with tissue paper as Jane held up one gown after another.

Susan looked up from the romance she was reading. 'Yes, very pretty,' she said listlessly.

Jane tut-tutted with exasperation. 'You haven't looked at them properly.'

'I don't have to. They are all the same.'

'How can you say that? Look at these fabrics. The finest muslin, mousseline de soie and silk taffeta. And how pretty the colours are. Why, they're just like sugared almonds – the palest of pinks and blues, creamy magnolia and white. So fresh and innocent-looking.'

Susan gave the gowns a long, considered glance through narrowed eyes, then she shrugged her shoulders and scowled.

'I take it you don't like them,' Jane said. She shook her head as if she couldn't understand Susan at all.

'No, I don't. They make me look so young.'

'You *are* young. You don't want to dress like an old woman, do you?'

'Of course not, but I want to look sophisticated. Bright colours are all the rage: deep red, peacock blue, purple, sea green, and even tartan. Oh, you know what I mean. You read the fashion magazines when I've finished with them.'

'Humph, it was a bad idea of the master's to have those magazines delivered to you. They only make you discontented instead of grateful to him for spoiling you the way he does.'

'In any case,' Susan said, returning to her original complaint, 'the gowns may be made from different fabrics but the style is always the same. Those dresses make me look like a schoolgirl.'

Jane didn't reply. She began to fold the dresses and put them back in their boxes. When she had done she said, 'Well, whether you like them or not, the master wants you to wear them, and if you'll take my advice, you should do the best you can to keep him happy. There are plenty of young lasses just as pretty as you who would gladly change places with you.'

'The more fool them!' Susan stood up and her book dropped to the floor. She clasped her hands in front of her and began to sob, and between taking great gulps of air she said, 'If only I'd known!'

Jane looked alarmed. 'Known what?'

'What I was coming to. I thought he loved me, I thought that when he brought me to this house he was going to marry me. I had no idea that I would just be his mistress, and furthermore a mistress that he would share with his friends!'

Jane hurried towards her. 'Whisht, lass,' she said. 'Stop making that dreadful noise. You'll hurt your throat. And if you go on crying like that you'll make your eyes red and your face all blotchy. I've telt you enough times by now that you should go along with what he wants and try and get as much out of him as you can, while you can.'

Susan's sobs subsided and she groped for the handkerchief that she kept tucked up her sleeve. She wiped her eyes and, still sniffing, looked at Jane over the top of the handkerchief. 'What do you mean, while I can?' she asked.

'While you're still young and bonny.' Jane hesitated. 'I shouldn't tell you this, but the master likes them young, and as soon as they begin to show their years, he sends them away.'

Susan was shocked into silence. She stared at Jane through swollen eyes and then she whispered, 'Sends them away? Where?'

Jane was uneasy. She knew she'd said too much. 'I don't know,' she said. 'I pack their bags and off they go. Then I help while the house is cleared and wait to see where he sends me next.'

'You've worked for him before? In other houses?'

'Yes. And let me tell you, this is the nicest little house he's ever provided for his . . . for . . . well, you know. So he must really think a lot of you.'

Susan glared at her. 'You might have told me.'

'Told you what?'

'Told me what you knew about him. Why did you let me go on thinking that he was going to marry me?'

'I did no such thing! I knew you were innocent. He likes virgins. But I never thought that you were so stupid as to believe that he would marry you. I thought you were out for a good time. Out for what you could get and just didn't know the way to go about it. That's why I told you to get him to buy you some jewellery; something that you could sell when he—'

'When he tells you to parcel up my clothes and send me packing.' Susan began to sob again.

'Listen to me,' Jane said. 'You can't change things now. You can't go back. So take my advice and make the most of it. That's what I would do if I was a bonny lass like you.'

'Would you? Would you really?'

'Don't look at me like that, Lady Muck. Don't go all hoity-toity on me. Of course I would. And I'd make damn sure that when the time came that he tired of me, I'd hev a nice little nest egg saved so that I could start some kind of business of my own.'

'Business? What kind of business?'

'I'd set up my own little house with two or three obliging young women who knew where their bread was buttered. It would be a nice classy establishment and we'd take only the best clientele.'

Susan looked at her with an expression of loathing. 'You're disgusting,' she said.

Jane bridled. 'Well, you're no saint.'

Hot colour flooded Susan's face. She was shaking as she replied, 'At least I didn't know what I was getting myself into.'

'No.' Jane looked her thoughtfully. 'I don't suppose you did. And furthermore, I think he's made a mistake with you. You're not suited to this life at all. The sooner he lets you go, the better. And let me tell you, I'll be glad to see the back of you.'

Without another word, Jane began to take the boxes of clothes out into the hall, and Susan heard her carrying them upstairs. She noticed that the maid had not closed the door properly behind her, and she moved quickly across the room and took hold of the handle. She pulled the door open forcefully and screamed, 'That might be sooner than you think!' Then she slammed it so hard that the pictures on the wall shook.

Alone and agitated, she paced about the room as she tried to decide what to do. She hadn't done as Jane suggested. She had no jewellery, nothing valuable that she could sell. All she had was the money she had stolen from her mother. She groaned when she thought how ashamed that made her feel.

Her mother was a good, honest woman, and her brother had worked hard to provide a comfortable home for them. He had annoyed her by being what she considered over-strict, but now she realised that that was because he loved her and wanted to keep her safe.

She could never go back to them. Not only because she had stolen the money but also because of what had happened since. When they discovered how she had been living they would turn her away and never want to see her again. So what should she do?

I can't go back to working for Mr Jacobs, she thought. I let him down by leaving without giving notice. I could work in another tobacconist's, I suppose, but I have no references. And besides, if I worked in any shop in Newcastle I'm sure that Daniel would find me. No, somehow I'll have to get enough money to buy a train ticket to somewhere as far away as I can go. London, perhaps? That's it – I could go to London. And I don't have to wait until I can persuade him to give me some jewellery; I can sell some of the gowns he has given me. I don't need them all and I don't even like them.

Susan's spirits rose as she formulated her plan, but then immediately sank again when she realised that even though she might escape a way of life that was hateful to her, she might never see her family again.

Jane had ignored Susan's outburst, but as she hung the new gowns in the wardrobe her brow furrowed. Without meaning to she had given too much away. If the master found out what she had been saying to Susan, he would be very angry. And Jane had learned from other girls' experiences how dangerous it was to anger him.

If the stupid lass really meant to run away, they would both be in trouble. Susan herself for daring to leave him and Jane for allowing it to happen. She thought uneasily of the other girls she had taken care of. She had told Susan that when the master tired of them she had packed their bags and he had sent them away. But she hadn't been able to answer when the lass had asked where they went, because she didn't know.

On the day they had to leave, they set off in a cab thinking that the master had found jobs for them. Respectable jobs in service or in some select department store. That was what the girls believed. But Jane was not so sure. They might no longer look virginal, but they were still very pretty. They would still be able to attract gentlemen for some years to come. But for her own peace of mind she tried to forget the girls as soon as they had gone and throw herself into moving on to the next nice little house.

She used to wonder why the master always moved on when he found himself a new girl, and eventually she decided that he liked to cover his tracks. He didn't want to lay a trail for anyone who was looking for him. That was why he would be particularly angry if Susan were to run away and tell her family where she had been. Jane realised that she would have to be extra vigilant. Keep an eye on the little madam all day and mix enough laudanum in her bedtime drink to make sure she was incapable of running away during the night.

She hoped to God that the lass wouldn't be witless enough to say something stupid to the master. Perhaps she had better warn her somehow. The master would not be crossed. If he knew Susan was planning to leave, there was no knowing what he might do. Jane had long suspected that his genial charm hid a character as vicious as any to be found in the back streets of Newcastle.

It was to be hoped that Susan wouldn't find out the truth about him the hard way.

# Part Three

# Chapter Eighteen

After the evening meal, in the big soulless house, Charlotte would lead the way into the drawing room, where they would have coffee. Now that the days were lengthening, there was a short period before the lamps were lit when they would simply enjoy sitting there and talking idly about the day's events.

Victor's elder sister had thawed a little. Marion thought she must have passed some unnamed test. She began to suspect that Charlotte might even approve of her. The older woman had come to tolerate Annette, although she pursed her lips and tut-tutted her disapproval when Victor and Annette talked to each other about the younger girl's progress at art school as though no one else was in the room.

Marion knew she ought to be grateful that Victor was showing such an interest in her sister's progress, and she tried not to feel hurt that Annette more often confided her hopes and her plans to Victor than to her own sister.

So while her husband and her sister chatted to each other, Marion would listen to Charlotte talking about the various charities she was concerned with and how pleased she was that Victor was prepared to contribute generously whenever she asked for more funds. Charlotte had every reason to believe that Victor was an honest and successful businessman, a kindly brother and a good husband. Sometimes, though, Marion had the worrying impression that her sister-in-law was trying to convince herself as well as everyone else.

But that was foolish, wasn't it? Quite often these days Marion thought that her husband was playing a part – just as she supposed he had done when he was courting her. But she could think of no reason why he should do this and she was forced to consider the possibility that the fault lay with herself and that her dissatisfaction with her marriage had led her into a fanciful way of thinking.

When the lamps were lit and the curtains drawn, Victor would open the evening paper. He would flick through it idly, sometimes stopping to read an amusing passage out loud to them but more often than not just folding it carelessly and putting it aside.

'They can light the fires with this in the morning,' he would say. 'I only read it out of a sense of duty. As a local landlord and property developer, I suppose I ought to know what's happening in this grand city of ours.'

Not long after that, he would excuse himself and go to the library to enjoy his cigar. Marion suspected that there was something else in the library he enjoyed that he did not want Charlotte to know about, because when he joined her in bed his breath smelled faintly of spirits; whisky, she thought.

One night in late June, Marion noticed that Victor seemed to be paying more attention to the newspaper than usual. He was scowling down at the open pages. He didn't say why he was displeased; he simply folded the paper, put it on the table by his chair and took himself off to the library.

Neither Charlotte nor Annette had seemed to notice that anything was amiss and both were in a good mood when they retired for the night. Marion didn't follow them up. She sat still in her chair while a young maid cleared away the coffee cups, and then she went to the table and picked up the evening paper.

Surely she had not been imagining Victor's bad humour. Curiosity made her scan the pages. She imagined that she would find some story about the city fathers blocking one of his building schemes. Despite his powerful friends, he was not always unopposed.

She turned the pages, looking for a story that would support her theory, then suddenly she became very still. She stared at the printed columns in front of her, scarcely able to believe what she was seeing. There was a report with the title 'The Changing Face of the City', and the name underneath the headline was Daniel Brady.

Was it the same Daniel Brady who had been her father's pupil, or had someone else of the same name written this piece? Marion began to read it and very soon she knew without doubt that it was the Daniel she knew. The writer admitted quite openly that he had been a labouring man and he described the day-to-day life of his fellow workers. He wrote of the excitement he felt when he saw the improvements that were made and his sadness that sometimes this meant the destructions of centuries-old buildings. He admitted that he did not know how to solve this problem.

He mentioned that sometimes the digging-up of old roads led to archaeological finds dating from as long ago as Roman times, and how these object shed light on the way that their ancestors lived many years ago.

In his last paragraph he wrote that this was only the first in a series of articles, and hinted that some of the things he had discovered in the course of his work might offend some readers but that he would try to be honest and fair. Finally he added a line acknowledging the debt he owed to the late Henry Brookfield, a gifted writer and the man he had been fortunate to have as his mentor.

When Marion had finished reading, she closed the paper and folded it. Then, hardly realising that she was still carrying it, she paced about the room restlessly. Daniel . . . Daniel had achieved his ambition to write, and for the very newspaper that her father had written for. She had known that he had the talent to do this, and she thought how proud her father would have been of his pupil.

Her emotions almost overcame her. She felt imprisoned by the boundaries of the room, the walls, the very luxury of her surroundings. Longing to escape, she went to the French windows and pulled one of the brocade curtains aside. She opened the door and stepped out on to the terrace that overlooked the garden.

The night air felt deliciously cool on her skin and the heady perfume of the night-scented stocks planted in the borders assailed her senses. Here in this wealthy suburb the air was fresh and free from the ever-present pall of soot that hung over the city. She knew she was lucky to be living in this comfortable and luxurious house. Even more lucky to have been able, by marrying Victor, to keep her promise to her father that she would look after Annette.

And yet, while she looked out on the beauty of the moon-silvered garden, an ache of discontent rose in her throat. Choking back a cry of frustration, she turned abruptly to walk back into the house and gave a shocked gasp to find Victor was standing in the doorway.

She stepped back, but her took her by the arm and pulled her into the room. He was gentle enough, but the lines of his face were hard and his eyes were narrowed. He let go of her, closed and locked the doors and drew the curtains, then turned to face her.

'I see you've read the paper,' he said. His gaze was directed at the folded newspaper that she still clutched in her hands.

'Yes.'

'And what do you think of it? Of Daniel Brady's attempt to be a journalist?'

Marion sensed Victor's hostility but she would not be intimidated. 'It's very good.'

Victor's eyes narrowed. 'Aren't you being a little indulgent?'

'I'm not sure what you mean.'

'Daniel Brady was a pupil of your father's. I understand you took an interest in his progress. It may be you are being influenced by your . . . liking of the man.'

Marion felt deeply uncomfortable. 'My liking?'

'I believe you encouraged him – in his ambitions, that is – perhaps unwisely.'

'Why unwisely?'

'It's obvious, isn't it? He is not an educated man; that's quite plainly demonstrated by the way he speaks. He will find himself out of place.'

'Daniel Brady speaks perfectly grammatically.'

'I give you that, but his accent is not cultured.'

There was no answer to this except to say that it did not matter. But Marion knew that to men like Victor it mattered very much.

She remained silent, and Victor eased the newspaper from her hands. She had not realised she was clutching it so tightly. Then, in one of his unsettling changes of mood, he said, 'I can see I have upset you and I didn't mean to. You have every right to be proud of the progress your father's pupil has made. If I appear critical, I must confess it is because I am jealous.'

'Jealous? Why?'

Victor smiled. 'You may not believe this – I mean, the notion is absurd – but before we were married I had the idea not only that Mr Brady aspired to better himself but also that he harboured fond feelings towards you.'

'I can assure you he did not! He was already betrothed.'

'I see.'

Victor looked at her searchingly and Marion knew instantly that she had given too much away. Her outburst had betrayed the fact that she had been angry with Daniel, and Victor was too intelligent not to guess why.

'Well then,' he said after a silence that lasted too long for comfort, 'I suppose we must wish him well. And now I mustn't keep you from your rest any longer. I'm sorry, my dear, but I won't be joining you tonight. I'm going to my club. There is someone I must see. A matter of business. It will be late when I come home, so I'll sleep in my dressing room.'

Victor walked into the hall with her and stood and watched as she climbed the stairs. Marion was glad to escape, and her relief that he would not be coming to her bed was almost tangible. She had not been able to reconcile herself to what happened there. Surely all marriages were not like this. If two people loved each other, she sensed that the act of love would bring joy. But she acknowledged bitterly that she would never know such joy, for she did not love her husband, and whatever he might have said before he married her, she was sure that he did not love her.

There was no rest for her. She lay awake for hours wondering if jealousy had truly been the emotion that had prompted Victor's anger. He might not love her but she was his lawful wife. She sensed, though, that there was something else, something about Daniel Brady that had enraged her husband, and she had no idea what that might be.

Victor dismissed the hansom cab near the Central Station and walked across to the opening that led into Pink Lane. Wearing a top hat and an opera cloak, he looked like any other gentleman out on the town and seeking a taste of the low life. Keeping to the shadows, he took care not to antagonise any drunken revellers. He kept his head down, averting his gaze if he sensed anyone looking at him.

A couple of cheap trollops were standing chatting at the corner of a squalid alleyway, and although they seemed to be engrossed in their gossip, Victor knew that they were perfectly aware that he was walking towards them. Without turning to look at him, one of them eased herself into the light falling from the nearby gas lamp and casually hooked one of her legs behind the other. Then she hitched up her skirt just far enough so that Victor could see her price chalked on the sole of her shoe.

He pushed her aside roughly as he walked past and was rewarded with a string of obscenities. He controlled the urge to turn round and bring his silver-headed walking cane down across her shoulders. Her pimp might be watching from some darkened doorway, and although Victor was confident that despite his look of a soft-living gentleman he could see off any attacker, he did not wish to draw attention to himself in case he should be identified.

He turned into a side alley and entered a door next to one of the rowdiest public houses. There was a dark entrance hall, and a little further inside a flickering gas jet illuminated a flight of bare wooden stairs. Although undoubtedly in need of a lick of paint, the surroundings were clean enough, and as he climbed up to the top floor the smell of beer and tobacco emanating from the public house below lessened.

Victor had come up the stairs as quietly as he could, and now he stopped on the top landing and put his ear to the only door. Satisfied with the silence inside, he gave the door a rap with his walking cane. After a few moments it opened just a crack and a voice said, 'Who is it?'

'Are you alone?' Victor asked quietly.

The occupant of the room must have recognised the voice, for the door creaked opened a little wider and Samuel Burroughs said, 'Come in, Mr Bateman.'

Victor entered the room and Burroughs closed the door behind him.

'You keep it hot in here,' Victor said.

He looked around the room. It was furnished more comfortably than he would have expected for a room above a public house, with brown velvet curtains at the attic windows and a matching comfortable plush armchair by the fire that blazed in the hearth.

'I like to be warm,' Samuel Burroughs replied. He watched as Victor's gaze settled on the glass and the half-empty bottle of brandy on the small dining table. 'And I like a bit of comfort.'

'I expect you do, after all those years breaking stones and sleeping in a cold, draughty cell.'

Burroughs scowled. 'No need to remind me of that.'

'Oh, but there is,' Victor said. 'I've had the impression lately that you are not properly grateful to me for keeping your secret.'

The man's scowl deepened. 'I am grateful but I don't think you are.'

'Why should I be grateful?'

'For everything I've done for you. For keeping my mouth shut.'

'You seem to forget, I keep my mouth shut too. I could have turned you in long ago.'

'I suppose you could have. As soon as you discovered that I had escaped from prison. Why didn't you?'

Victor didn't reply. He gazed at Burroughs with an expression of extreme aversion.

Burroughs' mouth twisted into an unpleasant leer. 'I'll tell you why you didn't. You thought I would be useful. And I have been. Very useful, doing the kind of jobs you couldn't trust anyone else to do. I'm surprised a man as clever as you didn't realise how dangerous it was to depend on me like that – to let me learn so much about you.'

Both men were silent, shoulders tense, as they gazed at each other. Then Victor seemed to relax a little. He shrugged and even managed to laugh. 'I suppose that is your way of telling me that you want more money?' he said.

'Yes, it is.'

'Well, I'll think about it.'

'Don't take too long. I've seen a nice little house by the sea, much more salubrious than a place in the middle of town – especially this place.'

Victor's expression hardened. The man was becoming altogether too cocky. But he was right about one thing. It was Victor's own fault that Burroughs thought he could talk to him like this. Well, he'd be damned if he gave in to this sort of blackmail. He couldn't turn Burroughs in to the police – the man knew too much about him. He'd have to arrange a more permanent solution, and in this case it was Burroughs who wasn't being very clever. He seemed to have forgotten that there were some jobs that Victor could do on his own, and, in fact, take pleasure in. One more task, Victor thought, and then I shall give him the reward he deserves.

When he spoke, his voice betrayed nothing but amusement. 'By the sea, eh? Well, perhaps I can arrange things for you. But first I want you to read this.'

Victor pulled the evening paper from a pocket inside his cloak and tossed it to Samuel Burroughs before taking his place in the only armchair. Immediately he drew his cigar case and the necessary paraphernalia from the pocket of his jacket and began the business of lighting a cigar. 'I'll smoke if you don't mind, but go on, man, read it.'

Puzzled, Samuel Burroughs sat down on a wooden chair at his small chenille-covered dining table and opened up the paper. 'What do you want me to read?' he asked.

'Turn the pages. You'll soon see the piece I mean.'

With a rustle of paper Samuel did as he was told, and discovered the article Victor meant. It didn't take him long to read it, and then he folded the newspaper and laid it on the table.

'Daniel Brady,' he said. 'He's writing for the newspaper.'

'I don't need you to tell me what I already know. I need you to do something about it.'

'What?'

'Isn't it obvious? He must have Henry Brookfield's papers.'

Burroughs opened the newspaper again and skimmed the piece he had just read. 'No, it isn't obvious at all. He has simply written from his own experience.'

'But what is he promising to write next?'

'He hints that there are problems. That he will reveal matters that may offend some readers.'

Victor gazed at Burroughs through a haze of cigar smoke. 'Exactly.'

'You think . . .?'

'I do.' Suddenly Victor tossed the rest of his cigar on the fire and stood up. 'He's got the papers, I'm sure of it, and your job is to find them.'

Victor crossed to the door, opened it and pulled his cloak tightly round his body before stepping out into the shadowy landing. Samuel followed him out and stood by the banister rail to watch the dark figure descend into the blackness. The noises from the street, raucous laughter, and a cry of pain from some woman taken too roughly, seeped into the passageway.

Samuel Burroughs returned to his room and closed the door behind him. He was filled with unease. He crossed to the table and poured himself another glass of brandy, but when he sat down by the fire he didn't drink it. Now that he was alone, he cursed himself for the way he had spoken to Victor Bateman.

The brandy must have made him forget for a while what the man was capable of. This is happening too often, Samuel thought. I shouldn't have mentioned the house by the sea . . . it was stupid to drop a hint like that. Luckily he didn't make the connection. I'm getting careless, and that's dangerous when dealing with a man like Bateman.

Well, he would do as Victor asked. He would follow Daniel Brady again and make sure he didn't have those damn papers. If he had, he would get them for Victor and see if the man kept his promise to reward him. If he didn't find anything, he knew he would be in trouble.

Perhaps it was time for him to move on. The problem was that would be very difficult unless he could find some other way of making a tidy sum of money – enough to take him not to a house by the sea but far across the sea, somewhere where neither the law nor Victor Bateman would find him.

Daniel sat nervously on the other side of the desk as Charles Earnshaw read through his second article about the changing face of the city. The editor had a pencil in his hand and he made a mark on the manuscript here and there, but not too many.

Earnshaw remained silent while he concentrated on the document before him. Daniel, aware of a growing knot of anxiety, tried to take his mind off things by glancing round the room, which was on the top floor of the building.

He looked at the bookshelves overflowing with dictionaries, trade directories, editions of *Who's Who*, gazetteers, almanacs and all sorts of other reference books. He looked at the desk itself with its inlay of scuffed green leather, then at the windows, which although they could have done with a good cleaning, gave a fine view over the rooftops and a glimpse of the tall masts of sailing ships docked in the Tyne.

The room was slightly stuffy. It faced south and the summer sun warmed it for much of the day. The bottom half of one of the windows had been raised a little to let in some fresh air, and this also gave entry to the raucous cry of the gulls circling high over the river.

Finally Mr Earnshaw laid down his pencil and looked up. 'This will do nicely,' he said. 'It's a good follow-up to your first piece.'

'Thank you. And you will take more?'

'I think so. There's something else, Mr Brady.'

The editor gazed at him appraisingly. Daniel didn't know why, but he sensed Mr Earnshaw was about to say something that would prove important.

'Yes?' Daniel's throat was dry. His voice was hoarse.

'I'd like to offer you a job.'

'A job? But what . . .?'

Charles Earnshaw laughed. 'Here on the paper – as a reporter, of course.'

Daniel stared across the desk. This was what he had been hoping for, and yet now that the moment had come, he could not believe it.

'But I . . .'

'What's the matter? You do want to come and work for me, don't you?'

'Yes, of course I do. It's just that I have no experience. Maybe I am a little old to be starting an apprenticeship.'

'Right on both counts, and although Henry has obviously taught you well, you could not possibly fill his place.'

'I would never have aspired to.'

'No, you will start like any cub reporter: you will attend council meetings, the opening of a new shop, school concerts and sports days, and also interview any citizen who has achieved success in flower and vegetable competitions and the like. You will find much of it commonplace but you must report on it as if it were a matter of great importance; as it is to the good citizens involved. Do you think you would enjoy this sort of thing?'

'Very much.'

The editor laughed. 'There speaks a man who has never stood in the rain waiting for a dignitary to wield a pair of scissors and open a new footbridge, or at the back of a church hall while some pompous church elder presents certificates to Sunday-school children. But all the while you are doing this you will be learning. And of course you will go on writing these articles for me. That is something I would not trust to any other novice reporter.'

Now Charles Earnshaw smiled, as if he knew he had sounded as if he had been delivering a sermon and now he was going to relax. 'If you can assure me that you are willing to do everything I have just described to you, I would like you to begin work next week. Will that suit you?'

'Very much so.'

'There is one drawback, and perhaps I should have made this clear at the start.'

'What is it?'

'I won't be able to pay you any more than I would pay any other man just starting out on his career – that would not be fair to the men who have been here for years.'

'Of course.'

'At this stage you may reflect that you could make much more money as a labouring man.'

'Not now.'

'Why not?'

Daniel explained about the accident at work and why it had happened. Mr Earnshaw sympathised with him. 'I thought I detected a slight limp,' he said. 'But I understand you are the breadwinner in your household. How have you been managing?'

'I have some savings. They'll last a little longer.'

'Well, each time you turn one of these articles in,' Mr Earnshaw picked Daniel's manuscript up from the desk, 'it would be quite in order to give you a small bonus. It would not be as large as the fee I have already paid you as a freelance, because once you start work here you will belong to the newspaper and so will your work.'

'I understand.'

Daniel's head was reeling. *Belong* to the newspaper. That was what Mr Earnshaw had said. He was aware that he was smiling.

The editor cleared his throat and looked solemn again. 'There is something else I want to say. You know I have been looking for someone to take up Henry Brookfield's work? Well, I think in you I may have found that person. One day, if you work hard, you may become as good a journalist as he was.'

At the end of the summer term the art school held an exhibition of the students' work. There were to be refreshments and Annette had set off earlier than usual that morning in order to help. Marion couldn't help comparing the eager young woman who appeared at the breakfast table without being called with the schoolgirl of a few months ago who almost had to be dragged out of bed.

'You will be there promptly, won't you?' Annette said after she had gulped her tea and placed her cup back in its saucer.

Marion had been buttering her toast but she looked up and smiled. 'I shall be the first to arrive . . .' she began, but broke off when she realised that Annette had not been talking to her.

Her sister rose from the table and went to stand next to Victor. She placed a hand on his shoulder and smiled down at him.

'Don't worry,' Victor told her. 'Nothing would stop me witnessing your triumph.'

Annette laughed. 'Oh, I don't know about triumph. I am just a beginner. Some of the work will be much better than mine.'

'But none will show such promise,' Victor said. 'Now off you go. The cab will be waiting for you.'

To Marion's chagrin, Annette flew from the room without even looking at her. Charlotte had been reading her letters at the table, and she looked up and said, 'You spoil that child. There is no need for her to travel into town in a cab. She could quite easily take a tram.'

Charlotte looked keenly at her brother for a moment. When he didn't respond, she pursed her lips, placed her crumpled napkin on the table, gathered her correspondence together and rose from her chair. Then she surprised Marion by addressing her directly. 'I have a busy day ahead of me, but I should like to go to the exhibition at the art school. Shall we take the carriage together?'

Marion glanced at Victor, who waved his hand casually. 'By all means take the carriage,' he said. 'I'll take a cab into town this morning and I'll be able to walk to the exhibition from my office.'

Victor soon followed Charlotte from the room. He had not spoken to Marion, who was left feeling thoroughly disorientated. There was no doubt that Charlotte disapproved of the way Victor spoiled Annette. Was that why she was prepared to befriend Marion? Charlotte, pompous and opinionated, was an unlikely ally, but Marion found herself pleased that they would be going to the exhibition together.

When they arrived at the exhibition of the students' work, Charlotte swept into the gallery like a ship in full sail. She still favoured the wide skirts of her youth and the swathed loops and drapes made her look like an expensive piece of upholstery.

Friends and parents walked in small groups around the large, airy room, stopping now and then to view the paintings. One or two attracted high regard, some smiles of recognition and approval, but none were disapproved of. How could they be when they might represent the earnest efforts of any of the students present, whose parents might be standing nearby?

Annette, along with some of her fellow students, was standing behind a long table set with snowy damask and serving refreshments to anyone who cared to partake of tea and iced fancies. Marion could not help but notice that it was the most fetching of the girls and the most attractive of the young men who were thus engaged. Whoever had chosen them had wished the scene to be as pretty as a picture. Marion smiled at her own fanciful thoughts, and then, realising that she was alone, looked around for Charlotte.

Victor's sister was with a small group of ladies who were admiring a painting of a group of nannies and children in the park. Marion recognised it as Annette's work.

'Charming,' one of the group said, 'and I'm pleased to say that the children are not at all sentimentalised.'

'This student is head and shoulders above the rest,' another said. 'Let me see . . .' She peered at the name card displayed below the painting. 'Annette Brookfield.'

Charlotte looked pleased. 'Did you know, the girl's older sister is married to my brother. He spotted her talent at once and is keen to encourage her. In fact . . .' She leaned forward as if she was about to convey something confidential, and this prompted her companions to draw closer together. 'Victor is paying for her to study here.'

Marion had been about to join them, but that last remark made her turn away. She was pleased that they had praised Annette's work but embarrassed that Charlotte had found it necessary to tell them that Victor was paying Annette's fees.

I am a hypocrite, she thought. That was one of the reasons I married Victor – so that I would be able to keep my promise to Annette that she would come to art school. And yet when it is mentioned I feel embarrassed. Is it because I worry that anyone should learn the truth about me? That I married Victor under false pretences?

The parents and families of the other students were obviously enjoying the exhibition, and those young people who were not helping with the refreshments were mingling sociably.

How Father would have loved to be here today, Marion thought, how proud of Annette he would have been and how thankful that I have been able to make this possible.

She looked at some of the other students' paintings but found she could not concentrate. The crowd around her formed groups, parted and regrouped as they moved from painting to painting. Their voices echoed in the high-ceilinged room, and Marion gradually began to distance herself from her surroundings.

And then she caught sight of Victor. She had known he was coming, of course, but she had not been aware of the moment he had arrived. He was standing in the far corner of the gallery talking to Esmé Cressington. Marion thought that she ought to join them, and began to make her way towards them, but something about their stance – the way they were standing so stiffly – made her stop and draw back. She had not needed to hear their words to know that they were angry with each other. So angry that Lady Cressington abandoned discretion and raised her voice.

'I've told you, Victor, you must leave the girl alone!'

Victor's shoulders had been tense, but now they eased a little and he laughed. 'Are you jealous, Esmé?'

'No . . . yes, but not for the reason you are implying. I am genuinely fond of the child. She is like . . .'

'The daughter you never had?'

'Don't mock!'

'I'm not mocking. I believe I am stating the truth.'

Lady Cressington drew herself up and faced him squarely. 'So you are. And because I regard her as a daughter, I will not have you corrupting her.'

'Corrupting her? Because I'm paying her fees? I recognise her talent, that's all.'

'That isn't all and you know it. Remember, I know your predilections—' Esmé Cressington broke off. She had suddenly seen Marion standing not far away from them. 'Ah, here is your wife,' she said, and smiled radiantly as if she had not just been furiously angry.

'Marion, my dear, there you are,' Victor said. 'I couldn't find you when I first arrived. Have you seen Annette's paintings? You must be proud of her.'

'Yes, I am,' Marion managed to say.

But inwardly fear and apprehension surged through her veins. What had Lady Cressington meant when she had told Victor to leave the girl alone? And why had she accused him of wanting to corrupt Annette? The voices receded again and the room began to spin as the implications of what she had heard came home to her.

# Chapter Nineteen

A parlourmaid showed Marion and Annette into Lady Cressington's drawing room. Marion noticed that her sister seemed to be quite at home. Annette flopped down into one of the satin-brocade-covered armchairs and reached for a magazine that was on a small table nearby. She had not questioned Marion's sudden decision to visit Esmé Cressington; rather she had been delighted to pay a visit to a woman she seemed to admire above all others.

'What a pleasant surprise!'

Lady Cressington swept into her drawing room. Although they had probably broken some rule of etiquette by calling without being invited, it seemed to Marion that she was genuinely pleased to see them – or at least to see Annette. Annette had risen from her chair, carelessly letting the magazine fall to the floor, and Lady Cressington hurried towards her and kissed her on each cheek in the French manner.

Then she stepped back and said to the younger girl, 'I'm so glad you came today, for I want to talk to your sister about a plan I have for you.'

'What is it?' Annette's eyes were shining like those of an eager child who sensed there was a treat in store.

Their hostess laughed. 'No, I shan't tell you until I have talked to Marion. Now . . .' She went over to the French windows and opened the door. 'Why don't you go and sit in the summerhouse? Take that magazine with you. No . . .' She raised a hand when she saw that Annette was about to protest. 'I insist that you be patient. Now off you go.'

Without further protest, Annette did as she was told. Esmé Cressington watched her fondly, much as an indulgent parent regarded an adored child. But when Annette was a sufficient distance from the house not to be able to hear anything that was said, the older woman turned to Marion and her smile was replaced by a troubled frown.

'Why have you come?' she asked.

'To see you.'

'Don't pretend this is a normal social call. I sensed how fraught you were the moment I entered the room.'

Marion had lain awake all night planning what she was going to say, but now that she was here, she forgot all her carefully rehearsed words and blurted out, 'I heard what you said to Victor yesterday.'

Lady Cressington was silent for a moment. Then she said, 'I thought maybe you had.'

'I would like an explanation.'

Lady Cressington turned her head to look out into the garden, where Annette in her simple white muslin dress could be glimpsed at the other side of the lily pond. After a silence in which she seemed to be making up her mind about something, she faced Marion again and said, 'You had better sit down.'

They sat opposite each other in chairs arranged at either side of the hearth. There was no fire today. Instead, a large arrangement of garden flowers in a blue and white earthenware vase obscured the grate. The heady perfume of the blooms scented the room, and for a moment, with the sunlight streaming in, the atmosphere seemed languidly peaceful. But then the thud of a small bird flinging itself against one of the windows shattered the mood.

'Poor thing,' Esmé said. 'I don't know why they do that. I hope it isn't too badly hurt.'

But she made no move to go and discover the bird's fate. Instead she looked straight at Marion and said, 'Your husband likes very young women. Even younger than you are. Girls who have barely put their schooldays behind them. And sometimes they have not.'

'Likes?' Marion gripped the arms of her chair, half knowing and yet dreading the answer.

'I'm sure you know what I mean, otherwise you would not be here.'

Marion met Esmé's chilled gaze for a moment and then turned her head to stare at the flowers in the grate. She watched as a petal detached itself from an overblown crimson rose and fell on to the marble hearth. After a while she looked beseechingly at Lady Cressington. 'What have I done?' she whispered.

The older woman sighed, and her tone was gentle as she said, 'Try not to worry too much.'

'How can you say that? I thought I was acting in Annette's interest when I accepted Victor's proposal, and instead I've brought her into a . . . a dangerous situation.' Marion's voice shook with anger. Her rage was directed not only at her husband but also at herself. 'I'll never forgive myself!' she said.

'Marion, my dear, you are not to blame,' Lady Cressington said. 'You were totally ignorant of Victor's true character. And now you must be thankful that you have had your eyes opened in time to do something about it.'

'What *can* I do?'

'For a start, you must be vigilant. I am sure that is why you brought Annette with you today. You did not want to leave her alone in the house, did you, in case Victor came home for some reason?'

'No.' Marion could not meet Lady Cressington's gaze.

'Secondly, time is on your side.'

Marion looked up, her eyes widening. 'I don't understand.'

'Annette will grow up. In fact, since leaving school and becoming a student, she is growing up fast.' Lady Cressington paused, and a faint smile hovered over her lips. 'Some young women never do grow up properly, do they? They retain their childlike ways until they appear ridiculous. Such women are either scheming or are simply not as intelligent as Annette. But soon your sister, beautiful though she may be, will look like a young woman rather than a girl, and Victor will lose interest. Until then, I will do anything I can to help you.'

Marion stared at her. 'I did not realise it at first,' she said, 'but I now know that you are a friend of Victor's. Why should you help me?'

A spasm of irritation marred Esmé's beautiful face. 'You heard what I said to Victor yesterday, so you must have heard what he said to me.'

'That you regard Annette as the daughter you never had.'

'Your husband was mocking me, but nevertheless, it is true. Forgive me if I tell you that in my opinion your sister is self-centred and wilful—' She held up a hand to stop Marion's angry interruption.

'No – that is how she appears to nearly everyone but you.

297

Nevertheless, Annette has found probably the only warm place in my cold heart.' Esmé Cressington laughed self-deprecatingly. 'Maybe it is because she reminds me of myself when I was a girl. And maybe that is why I am determined no harm shall come to her.'

'Harm!' Marion almost choked on the word.

'You know what I mean.'

Esmé suddenly looked thoughtful.

'What is it?' Marion asked. 'What are you thinking?'

'You know, we may be worrying in vain. Victor has a reputation to protect; he wouldn't want to foul his own nest. For some reason he particularly likes his sister, the formidable Charlotte, to think well of him.'

'Charlotte has already told him that he shouldn't treat Annette as a child,' Marion said.

'Has she?' Lady Cressington sounded surprised. 'Do you think she knows about his attraction to young girls?'

Marion could barely conceal her revulsion, but she answered as calmly as she could. 'No, I don't think so. She disapproves of the way Victor indulges Annette.'

'That may act in our favour. Charlotte's presence may keep him in check, except that . . .' Lady Cressington paused, and the troubled look returned.

'What is it?' Marion asked.

'I've sensed of late that Victor is losing control of the darker side of his nature.' She paused. 'He may even have taken a step towards a place from which he cannot return.'

The temperature in the room seemed to drop.

'What do you mean?'

Esmé Cressington shook her head slowly. She stared into the mid-distance as if she were seeing something – some scene – that troubled her greatly. Then she said, 'I cannot tell you, but I pray that I am wrong.'

Something about the words sent shivers down Marion's spine.

Lady Cressington shook her head as if trying to dismiss some fearful picture from her inner eye, and then she looked at Marion and said in a steady voice, 'But to return to the problem of your sister: Victor almost certainly knows it would be foolish in the extreme to seduce her, but he may not be able to help himself. And that is why I am going to help you.'

The word had been said, and Marion felt sick. 'What will you do?' she asked. Her throat was dry and her voice rasped.

'I shall take her to London and keep her there until the autumn term begins. I shall tell Victor that Annette must visit the galleries and the latest exhibitions. And also that she must continue to meet and socialise with other artists. He won't argue with me.'

'How can you be sure?'

'I know too much about him.' Her mouth twisted into a wry smile. 'And no, I am not going to explain myself any further.'

Lady Cressington stood up. 'Now let us go and join Annette and tell her that I will be calling for her in the morning and taking her to London. I'm sure that will make her very happy. And Marion, my dear . . .'

'Yes?'

'If I were you, I should act as if you know nothing – suspect nothing.'

'Why?'

'Trust me, it's for the best.'

Esmé looked at Marion's bewildered face and found room in her cynical heart to be truly sorry for her. No doubt the girl had married Victor Bateman because she and her sister had found themselves orphaned, and when Victor had befriended her she had been truly grateful. She had obviously believed him to be respectable and kindly. That was the persona he presented to the world in general.

And I am to blame for encouraging the match, Esmé thought. I cannot plead ignorance of Victor's character. But I am so used to doing his bidding that I gave no thought to the welfare of the Brookfield sisters. Now I must endeavour to make amends.

But now that Marion had glimpsed the darker character behind the amenable façade, it would be altogether better if she remained ignorant of how truly ruthless Victor could be.

'When was this latest trip to London arranged?'

Victor stood in the wide oak-panelled hall of his home and watched as Annette's trunks were brought down. Annette herself was rushing up and down the stairs excitedly, giving the servants orders, which only added to the confusion.

'Yesterday. I have already told you that,' Marion answered with a smile, trying to conceal her nervousness.

299

'But when *exactly*?'

'We called to see Lady Cressington after lunch. That's when she suggested that she should take Annette to London for the summer.'

'I did not know that you were in the habit of calling on Esmé. What prompted you to do so?'

'She sent a note inviting us – I told you.'

This was what Lady Cressington had told Marion to say, and Marion, new to the game of deception, hoped that she had made it sound convincing. Esmé had also told her to behave as though she knew nothing of Victor's perversions, and her manner had convinced Marion to heed the warning, at least until she found a way of escaping the trap she had so blindly walked into.

Victor was staring at her coldly.

'I see,' he said.

At that moment the doorbell rang and Lady Cressington herself was shown into the hall. Marion observed the look of suppressed anger on her husband's face and the way in which Esmé Cressington returned his glare with an expression of cool defiance.

Without preamble Victor said, 'Annette is not of age and she is in my care. I could forbid this trip, you know.'

'You are not Annette's father,' Lady Cressington replied.

'However, I am her guardian.'

'Who appointed you as such? Surely Marion is responsible for her sister.'

'Marion is not yet twenty-one. She cannot act as Annette's legal guardian. As Marion's husband, that duty falls to me.'

They looked at each other, each determined not to admit defeat, but at that moment Annette came racing down the stairs. 'Isn't it marvellous?' she said to Victor. 'Thank you, thank you, thank you!'

Victor looked bemused. 'Why are you thanking me?'

'For allowing me to go to London again. Esmé said she was sure you would.'

'Esmé?'

Annette looked embarrassed. 'Lady Cressington. But she said I should call her Esmé.'

'Did she indeed?'

Victor smiled, and Marion knew how much that smile had cost him. He had been outmanoeuvred and he did not wish to appear a tyrant in Annette's eyes.

'Well, well,' he said, 'so you are leaving us for a while. Going to London, where you will meet Lady Cressington's bohemian friends.'

'Lady Cressington's friends are mainly from France, not Bohemia,' Annette said.

In spite of his black mood, Victor smiled at her. 'I did not mean people who came from the country that bears that name. The word can also be applied to people – often writers, actors, artists – who do not live according to the conventions of society. I can only hope that you will be the same sweet child when you return to me.'

At that Annette flung herself into Victor's arms and Marion watched uncomfortably as he kissed her sister on the top of her head. But Annette was in too much of a hurry to allow the moment to linger, especially as just at that moment Lady Cressington said sharply, 'Annette! My carriage is waiting. If we are going to catch the morning train, we must depart immediately.'

Before leaving, she turned to Victor and said, 'Believe me, Victor, I have every intention of protecting Annette; both from my bohemian friends and from anyone else who may be a malign influence.' Then she took hold of Annette's hand and led her out into the sunshine.

The servants carried Annette's luggage out to Lady Cressington's carriage and then disappeared to their domain behind the green baize doors. Marion and Victor were left alone in the silent hall.

A shaft of light fell through the still open door, the sunlight revealing a few floating dust mites that had been set free from the rugs on the floor by the furious bustle that had just taken place. Marion became aware of the ticking of the long-case clock that stood against one of the panelled walls. The rhythmic swinging to and fro of the pendulum was uninterrupted by any human activity.

She looked at her husband to find that he was staring at her as if trying to read her mind. Then, with a scowl and a shrug, he walked out to where his own carriage was waiting to take him to his office.

Marion had been unaware of Victor's manservant standing in the shadows behind the open door, so she gave a start when the door began to close seemingly of its own accord. The man gave Marion a slight bow and then left the hall the way the other servants had gone: through the door that led down to the domestic offices.

Fleetingly, Marion wondered what he and the other servants talked about when they were together. She was mortified to acknowledge that although they were living, breathing people just like the other inhabitants of the house, they seemed to exist in a different plane – another world that had been created for the sole purpose of serving the likes of Victor and his sister. And me too, she realised.

Her thoughts flew to other, happier times. A time when she and Annette and their father had lived in a much smaller and yet comfortable house with Betty, who although she was their servant was also a friend. Suddenly she knew where she would go today. She would go to see Betty.

But she would not burden her old friend with her grief and anxiety; she would simply take comfort from sitting and talking. For a few hours at least she knew she must get away from this house where the atmosphere was becoming more and more oppressive – and threatening.

Neither would she tell Betty that Annette, in her eagerness to go to London with Lady Cressington, had blown a kiss to Victor but had quite forgotten to say goodbye to her own sister.

'What do you think of this, then?'

Betty stood in the living room of her new home and invited Marion to look around her.

'I think it's wonderful,' Marion said, and she meant it.

The house with its recently plastered and newly painted air about it was neat as a pin. The range, where Betty also did the cooking, was highly polished, the rugs and curtains were cheerful, and on the table the deep red chenille cloth with its silky fringe added a touch of newly-wed luxury.

'You needn't hev brought these.' Betty looked down at the bunch of flowers that she held in her hands. 'Just hevin' you here is treat enough for me. But hawway into the scullery, let's get these bonny blooms into a vase.'

Betty led the way through a door into the scullery, where there was a wooden bench with a sink set below the window and rows of shelves on the opposite wall.

'That's wor bath,' Betty said as she drew aside a green and white gingham cloth hanging on a wire stretched along the edge of the bench. 'Arthur pulls it out and sets it afore the range there.' She nodded towards the room they had just left. 'Nice and cosy it is for the two of us to take a bath by the fire of a Friday night.'

Her eyes took on a dreamy expression for a moment, and then, as if sensing that she had given something away, she looked abashed, her cheeks reddened and she let the curtain fall again. She laid the flowers on the bench and turned round to face the shelves. 'Now, let's see, which vase will be best?'

Marion stared up at the neatly kept shelves. The familiar pots and pans, the stoneware dishes, the baking tins and various jugs. She felt grief rise in her throat. She was not aware that she had made any sound, but she must have done because Betty turned to face her and said, 'What is it?'

'I . . . Nothing.'

Marion averted her gaze from the shelves but not before Betty had realised what she had been looking at. 'Eeh, Marion, hinny,' she said. 'I know what's fretting you. But you said you wouldn't need any of them and I was to take what I wanted.'

'I know – and I'm glad you did. It would be dreadful if all those things – part of our happy home – were just thrown out. I'm glad they're being used and I'm glad that they've found a home with you.'

Betty looked at her searchingly, and when she had assured herself that Marion was not going to cry, she turned back and reached up to take a cut-glass vase from the top shelf.

'Pretty, isn't it?' she said as she held it up to catch the sunlight streaming through the window on to the bench. 'Arthur gave it to me as a wedding present. And do you know, every now and then he actually remembers to buy me flowers to put in it!'

Marion remembered her own wedding present from Victor. The silver casket containing the diamond jewellery that she had never worn.

She watched as Betty filled the vase with water and trimmed some of the leaves off the flowers before arranging them. The discarded foliage gave off a sharp, almost bitter smell, and Betty wrapped it up in a sheet of newspaper before putting the bundle in an enamel pail that was used as a rubbish bin.

'Now where shall I put them?' Betty said as she led the way back into the living room. 'I know – on this little table. It was the table your father said was kept for the jardinière – whatever that was. I never found out.'

'It was a large decorative plant pot,' Marion told her. 'My mother used to keep a house plant in it – I think an aspidistra – but when Annette started to crawl she knocked it off the stand and it was broken. That was before you came to work for us. She got such a fright, poor child. I can see her now, sitting there surrounded by broken foliage and lumps of soil. My father never got round to buying another one.'

'I daresay he would hev done if your ma had been there to remind him!'

The mention of her mother evoked in Marion the usual ache of regret. Regret that her father had been deprived of a wife he adored, and that she and Annette had not been able to grow up with a mother's love to guide them.

But they had been blessed to have Betty to care for them and to run the little household, and it was natural that she should have come to Betty now just as she might have gone to her mother. But for all the love and care Betty had lavished on Marion and Annette, she was *not* their mother, and Marion did not feel able to tell her of her grave doubts and worries.

When the flowers were placed to her satisfaction, Betty spread a clean white cloth on the table and they had tea and a slice of marmalade cake.

'Arthur's favourite,' Betty confided. 'The poor man hasn't had good home cooking for years, and you should see the way his face lights up when he comes home to be greeted by the smell of a good pot of stew on the range and a fresh-baked cake cooling on the table.'

'I'm glad you're happy, Betty,' Marion said.

'Happy as the day is long. I can't tell you how grateful we are to Mr Bateman for letting us hev this house, of course. Do you know, there's a waiting list for nice new places like this.'

'No, I didn't know that.'

'Well, there is. And me and Arthur know very well that we got to the top of the list because of you.'

'Because of me?'

'Eeh, lass, you're slow today. Because Mr Bateman loves you and he wanted to please you.'

'Oh . . . yes.'

Betty finished her piece of cake and glanced up at the clock on the mantel shelf. 'Now you just sit there and hev another cup of tea if you like, but I've got to pop along to the shops to get a few bits and pieces for the meal tonight. I've promised Arthur some dumplings in the mince, so I need fresh suet from the butcher's.'

She took a notepad from a drawer in the sideboard and wrote a shopping list.

'You're going to be busy. I'd better go,' Marion said.

Betty looked affronted. 'I'll never be too busy to talk to you. Sit and drink your tea like a good lass and we'll hev a bite of dinner – lunch, as you call it – and a good old chinwag when I gets back.'

Betty took her shopping basket from the scullery and hurried out. As the front door opened, Marion heard her cheerful greeting to a neighbour, and then the door closed and the house was silent.

Marion drank a second cup of tea and carried the cups and plates through to the scullery, where she washed them carefully at the sink. She left them draining on the board and then returned to the table and reached for the writing pad Betty had left there. She had decided not to wait for her old friend to come back from the shops.

She knew that the promised chinwag would include questions about her life and her happiness, and she would not be able to answer them. Betty had encouraged Marion to accept Victor Bateman's proposal of marriage, and if Marion were to even hint at Victor's true character her old friend would be horrified. Marion did not want Betty to feel guilty.

Betty and Arthur were so happy in their new home and they were grateful to Victor. Victor gave them this home to please me, Marion thought, and that made her doubly uneasy. She tried not to think what Victor would do if she left him. Would he turn Betty and Arthur out? Or put up the rent so that they would not be able to afford to stay here? But he wouldn't do that, would he? After all, everyone said what a good landlord he was.

Marion tried to dismiss these uneasy thoughts from her mind, and picked up the pencil. She wrote that she had remembered that she had to go into Bainbridge's in the city centre and choose some curtain fabric. How good I am becoming at lying, she thought. She placed the note in the middle of the table and left the house, pulling the door shut behind her.

It did not matter if Betty had not taken her door key with her. Marion had seen the key hanging on a string by the letterbox. This was something many people did. She wondered if the policeman in Arthur approved of the practice.

Marion walked along the pleasant street towards Heaton Road. She did not want to return to the house in Gosforth yet and she

305

thought she might sit in the park for a while. She wondered whether she would meet Betty coming back from the shops, and had her apology ready, but she was totally unprepared for the person who rounded the corner of the street and walked towards her.

If she was shocked to see Daniel Brady, then he seemed more so. He stopped within a few yards of her and stared as if he couldn't believe his eyes.

'I was on my way to Arthur's house,' he said as if he thought she deserved an explanation.

'I've just come from there, I've been visiting Betty,' Marion said in the same vein. 'Arthur isn't in.'

'I know. I was supposed to be having a drink with him tonight but I can't go; I'll be working. I was going to leave a message with Betty.'

'She's gone to the shops. I shouldn't think she'll be long.'

Suddenly, despite her lingering anger with Daniel, Marion saw the funny side of it. The two of them standing yards apart from each other exchanging information in a stilted fashion like amateur actors in a stage production.

When she smiled, he did too.

'I'll leave a note,' Daniel said. 'I must tell Arthur that I shall have to forgo the pleasure of sitting with him in the Raby in favour of the much more exciting prospect of a ladies' charity supper in the assembly rooms in Gosforth. I believe it has been organised by a Miss Charlotte Bateman.'

'My sister-in-law.'

Victor nodded. 'Apparently they are raising money for those they call the "poor benighted heathen".'

They smiled at each other awkwardly.

'Oh well . . . I should be going,' Marion said

She started to walk forward again, apprehensive of the moment when she would have to pass him and hoping that he would step aside. But he didn't move, and when she reached him she halted. Daniel took her arm.

'Wait,' he said. 'I'll drop a note through the door, then I'll walk with you to the tram stop – or are you getting a cab?'

She stood there uncertainly, and he must have taken her hesitation for an answer of sorts, because smiling over his shoulder as he went, he hurried to his friend's house. Marion watched as he took a notebook from his pocket, hurriedly wrote something on the top page, then tore it off. He posted the note through the letterbox and came hurrying back to her.

There was an awkwardness between them and they walked without speaking until they reached Heaton Road.

'The tram stop or the cab rank?' Daniel asked.

'I – I'm not going home immediately. I thought I would walk in the park for a while.'

'Good,' Daniel said, and Marion flushed when she realised he had taken this for an invitation.

But she didn't say anything, and she allowed him to take her arm and guide her across the busy road. They stood on the central island while a smart carriage rattled by, and then they stepped on to the road again and were nearly bowled over by a delivery boy on a bicycle who seemed to appear out of nowhere.

'Have a care, lad!' Daniel shouted after him.

'Sorry, mister,' the boy yelled over his shoulder.

Marion clutched at Daniel's arm when she saw the bicycle begin to wobble.

'He's caught the wheels in the tramlines!' she said.

'It's all right,' Daniel replied. 'Look, you can open your eyes – he's safe.'

Marion, who had not realised that she had closed her eyes, opened them and saw that the boy was indeed quite safe and was pedalling away as furiously as ever.

'We can't stand here,' Daniel said. He took her hand. 'Now hurry, we'll just make it before that tram!'

They were out of breath and laughing when they reached the other side, and somehow they forgot to let go of each other's hands as they began to walk towards the gates of the park.

Neither of them was aware of the two people who were watching them. Betty, who had noticed them as she walked back towards her street, stopped with her shopping basket over her arm and gazed after them with an expression of shock and dismay. Oh, Marion, hinny, she thought. What are you thinking of? She shook her head and sighed before she turned the corner and made her way home disconsolately.

As Betty walked away Samuel Burroughs lowered the newspaper he had appeared to be scrutinising and folded it. He had been standing on the corner of the back lane that ran down behind the shops, and now he moved forward quickly. He had been close enough to hear them when they had talked about going to the park, and now that they were safely across the road he set out after them.

Well, well, he thought. This is something I didn't expect to see. And neither did Victor Bateman, I'll be bound. He set me on to follow Brady because he still thinks he's got some papers that he wants; he can have no idea that Brady is meeting his wife. This could be more interesting than I thought.

Maisie was trying to smile and act normally as she chatted to the customer she was serving. She did not want the two gentlemen to know that she was straining to listen to their conversation. She had served them with the very best cigars just a moment ago, but as they were about to leave, a sudden shower of rain made them wait inside the shop.

The reason she was listening to them was because she had caught the words: 'Yes, it's the girl who used to work here. The one who looked like a schoolgirl dressed up in her mother's clothes.'

'I remember her well. And it's a nice little place by the sea?'

At that moment Maisie's customer handed her the payment for his packet of ten Plain Cut Virginia cigarettes.

'Thank you, Mr Parker,' she said. 'Oh dear, you're going to get wet on the way back to the office, aren't you?'

'Afraid so,' he said as he tucked his cigarettes into an inside pocket. 'Don't want them ruined, do I?' He smiled at her.

He turned to go, but Maisie called him back.

'Wait a moment,' she said, and she vanished into the back shop.

He was standing there looking puzzled when she returned carrying an umbrella.

'Take this,' she told him.

'That's very kind of you, Maisie. I'll bring it back after work tonight.'

'Have you got an umbrella of your own?'

'I did have, but I seem to have left it somewhere.'

Maisie smiled. 'Well, you'd better keep that one.'

'Oh, I can't do that. It's a very fine umbrella. Does it belong to your employer?'

'I have no idea who it belongs to. A customer left it here. That's always happening. We keep them for a month or two, and if no one claims them we give them to the next needy customer. We have some fine walking sticks, too. Now off you go.'

Mr Parker thanked her again and hurried out into the rain-swept street. Maisie took a soft cloth from a drawer behind her and started to polish the glass top of the counter. The task was genuine enough; customers were always leaning on the counter and leaving their finger marks there, but all the time she was working she was endeavouring to hear what the two gentlemen were saying.

They were so engrossed in their conversation that they hardly noticed that the shop was empty and their words might be heard by the shop assistant.

'That all sounds very nice to me. And you've actually been there?' the more portly of the two said.

The other man, slightly younger with a broad, self-satisfied-looking face, replied, 'Yes. I told you.'

'Why you?

'He owed me a favour.'

'Favour?'

The younger man laid a finger against the side of his nose and leaned towards his companion slightly. 'Planning permission.'

'Oh, I see. I must say I'm surprised. I always thought he was a sanctimonious sort of chap. All this stuff about it being his duty to build decent affordable housing for the working man, et cetera. And besides, it's not too long since he married, is it? A decent young woman, so I hear.'

'Come, come, don't you think a man deserves a little treat now and then? I mean, I've told you, it's all very tasteful. It's not like going to a cheap whorehouse. And as far as I know, he's always been discreet about that sort of thing.'

'Well, well, I suppose it does no harm. Oh look, the rain has stopped. We can go now.'

'Where are you off to?'

The younger of the two had opened the door and stood back to let his companion go first.

'Board meeting. And you?'

Maisie didn't hear the answer because the door had closed behind them. She put down the cloth, abandoning her cleaning activities, and stared out through the window at the busy scene in the Haymarket. People hurried by, some stopping to shake and close their umbrellas

309

and women clutching their skirts and raising them above their ankles as they stepped over the puddles that had formed during the brief shower.

The skies were clear now. The rain had washed away the usual pall of smoke that hung over the city. The respite would be temporary. Maisie's brow was furrowed. She had never liked Susan Brady, with her little-girl ways and her empty-headed chatter, but she was woman enough to feel sorry for the girl if it was really her the two gentlemen had been talking about.

What on earth had the silly lass got herself in to? Maisie didn't doubt that Susan had been misled by the man in question. She had probably even thought that he intended to marry her. Instead he had made her his mistress and ruined her further by sharing her with a friend. Maybe more than one.

Maisie shivered; not with cold but with repulsion. Now what was she going to do? She stared down at the glass counter, where she could see the reflection of her own troubled face. She had promised to tell that decent man Daniel Brady if she discovered anything about Susan's whereabouts. But would he want to know that his sister was little better than a whore? Many a family would never want to see such a girl again. Maybe it would be better if she didn't tell him.

'Daydreaming, Maisie?'

Maisie looked up to see one of her regulars smiling down at her: a shop assistant who worked in a gentlemen's outfitters.

'You didn't even hear me come in, did you?' he asked. 'Well, I hope you were dreaming about me.'

'Get away with you, you cheeky young devil.'

Maisie's spirits revived as she dealt with his request for a packet of Abdullahs. She listened patiently to his usual joke about wanting to whisk her off to his harem, and by the time he left the shop she had almost convinced herself that Daniel Brady would be better off not knowing what his sister had sunk to.

The sudden shower of rain sent them hurrying into the Pavilion Café, where Daniel managed to secure a table before the place filled with damp, laughing customers.

'I'd better get to the counter promptly,' he said. 'There's already a queue. Tea or coffee?'

'Hot chocolate!' Marion said.

'Right-ho.'

Marion watched Daniel walk to the counter and observed his slight limp. Someone was desperate to get hold of my father's papers, she thought. Papers that don't seem to exist. But they were prepared to leave Daniel for dead.

'Why so solemn?' Daniel asked when he returned to the table with a tray.

'Oh . . . nothing. I was just thinking how quickly the weather can change.'

'Were you?'

It wasn't a question, for Marion could see that he didn't expect an answer, but neither did he believe her. Thankfully he did not pursue the matter any further.

'Hot chocolate and iced buns,' he said as he placed the contents of the tray on the table.

'Wonderful!' Marion said. 'How did you know that I love iced buns?'

Daniel smiled at her. 'I guessed. Susan always said that the iced buns here were the best in town. Better even than Alvini's.'

'Susan?'

'My sister.'

'Oh, of course.'

Daniel sat down and turned sideways to place the empty tray on a vacant chair. When he straightened up and faced her, Marion was shocked by the change in his expression. A moment ago he had been cheerful – exuberant, even – but now he looked haunted.

'Daniel, what is it?' Marion asked.

'My sister. She's missing.'

'Of course. Betty told me. I'm so sorry.'

'We haven't seen her since Christmas Day.'

His distress was painful to see, and Marion cradled the tall cup of hot chocolate with both hands and looked down at the swirl of cream floating on the top.

'My mother is heartbroken,' she heard Daniel say. 'She grieves for Susan every day.'

'No doubt your fiancée will help comfort her.' She had said that without thinking and she couldn't believe how waspish she had sounded.

'My fiancée?'

311

'Dora. Surely you haven't forgotten her name.'

'Marion, I am not engaged to Dora. I never have been.'

She looked into his face, searching for the truth.

'Then why did she tell me that you were going to get married?'

'Because . . . because she thought we were.'

'I don't understand.'

'Dora and I were childhood friends. But even then I didn't seek her out. She lives next door and she always seemed to be waiting for me – to tag along even when I was playing with the lads. They used to tease me about her and everyone – my mother included – assumed that we would get married one day.'

'Did you ever ask her?'

'Never.'

'You just let her believe that you might some day.'

'I didn't intend that – I just didn't want to hurt her.'

'But don't you see, you already have hurt her by allowing her to hope?'

'I realise that now. You know, I always hoped that she would fall in love with someone else. I mean, she's bonny enough and she will make a good wife.'

'How can you be so stupid? No other man would approach her if he thought she was already engaged to you. And she probably told everyone that she was!'

'Don't, Marion.' He sounded anguished. 'If I've behaved badly . . .'

'You have!'

'. . . then I have already been punished.'

'Punished? How?'

'By losing any chance of making a life with you.'

They stared at each other across the table, aghast at the realisation of what they had lost. Then Marion picked up her cup and raised it shakily to her lips. The drink had gone cold and the chocolate tasted bitter. She put it down again and started picking miserably at the iced bun.

Then, locking everything they had just talked about somewhere deep inside her, she said, 'I'm sorry about your sister. I hope you are able to find her.'

'Thank you.'

They drank their cold chocolate and took the buns outside to break up and scatter for the birds.

'I'll walk with you to the cab stand,' Daniel said.

'All right,' Marion replied listlessly, and they set off towards the gate that led on to Heaton Road.

Neither of them spoke, and neither did they notice the tall, thin man who had left the café just a moment or two behind them.

Samuel Burroughs watched Daniel Brady help Marion into a hansom cab, and then he followed him to the tram stop. They were both going into town, Daniel no doubt to the newspaper where he worked, and Burroughs to Victor Bateman's offices, where he had much to tell him.

# Chapter Twenty

Samuel Burroughs got off the tram at the corner of Newbridge Street. It would be no good going to Victor's office now. Victor would be busy and wouldn't thank him for showing his face when there might be some important people there.

All sorts and conditions of people came to see Victor. He was a rich and powerful man. Even a titled gentleman or two danced to his tune when they wanted a favour. Equally, Victor knew how to get favours in return. Many a good citizen thought Victor Bateman a splendid chap and never realised that he had got from them exactly what he wanted. Sometimes Samuel thought that Victor should have been an actor.

No, he would have to wait until the business day was nearly over and most of the office staff had gone home. It was a time Victor reserved for appointments with those people he did not wish others to know he was dealing with. And those same people might not want it known that they were associated with Victor.

Victor kept a comfortable suite of rooms on the top floor, where he would retire at the end of most business days, with only his most trusted clerk to show his visitors in. It was here that he preferred to meet with Samuel Burroughs.

Hannah Brady sat at the table with the newspaper spread out before her. She used a finger to follow the words and her lips moved slightly as she read them. The words she kept returning to were *Daniel Brady*. They didn't always appear. Daniel had explained to her that it was only his articles, as he called them, that had a byline. She hadn't needed him to tell her that that meant 'by Daniel Brady'. But of late he had pointed to little stories that he had also written, and his name didn't appear there at all.

'Not important enough,' he had told her.

Hannah thought that a shame. She had never thought to see her son's name in print in a newspaper and her feelings were a mixture of pride and regret. Pride because here was proof that her son was a clever lad, and regret because she had never encouraged him in his ambitions.

Of course he wasn't earning as much as he could as a labouring man, but since he'd been set upon and his leg injured, that way of working had become closed to him. And Daniel had explained that he was still learning how to be a reporter and therefore he was lucky to be paid at all.

'Like an apprentice,' he'd said, and Hannah had understood that.

But he'd assured her that soon he would earn more – enough to keep them more comfortably than before. And he wouldn't have to give up work when he got older and his limbs got stiffer. They could even look forward one day to moving to a better part of town.

Hannah hadn't liked it when he had said that. This was where she had been born and lived all her life. When she'd repeated the information to Dora, however, the lass's eyes had lit up.

'Mebbe we could get one of those nice new houses like Daniel's friend Arthur has,' she'd said.

Hannah had often thought about that and the way Dora had said 'we'. The lass obviously thought that she and Daniel would get married one day, and although just a short while ago Hannah had wanted nothing more for her son, now she wasn't so sure.

The kettle started to boil and Hannah sighed and folded the paper and placed it on top of some others. She rose to make a pot of tea, and at that moment Dora came in.

'Here, let me do that,' she said.

Hannah sat down again and watched as the girl got the teapot and the tea caddy and a couple of cups and saucers. She looked perfectly at home as she moved about the room and then into the scullery to fetch the milk from the pantry. But I don't know if I like the way she just waltzes in here without knocking, Hannah thought. And immediately felt guilty because she had been glad of Dora's easy familiarity over the years.

She had dreamed of how nice it would be to have the lass as a daughter-in-law and how Dora would look after her in her old age. But Dora had changed lately. Hannah couldn't put it into words.

Instead of giving Hannah the respect that was due to an older woman, she had begun to treat her as if . . . as if what? Suddenly Hannah realised what had been bothering her. Dora was treating her as if she were an *old* woman. Someone to be humoured, certainly, but also someone who could be chivvied about and told what to do.

They sat at the table and drank their tea, and then Dora asked Hannah if she would like her to peel the potatoes.

'Potatoes?'

'For Daniel's supper,' Dora said, and she said it slowly and clearly as if having to explain to someone who was not as sharp as they used to be.

Hannah sighed. 'That would be good of you,' she said. 'I thought I'd make some broth with the scrag end in the larder. There's some leeks and carrots in there and you'll find a bowl of barley soaking on the bench. I should hev got it on a while since, but Daniel won't be back for a bit yet.'

'What time will he be home?' Dora asked.

'I don't know. He's working late.'

'Let's hope that's all he's doing,' Dora muttered.

'What do you mean?'

Dora pursed her thin lips, looked as though she might say something, changed her mind and shrugged. 'Nowt. It's just that he keeps such peculiar hours these days.'

'It's part of the job.'

'If you say so. Now,' she hurried on, 'why don't you sit in the easy chair, put your feet up on the cracket, and mebbe close your eyes for a while. I'll see to the broth.'

It sounded more like an order than a suggestion, but Hannah did as she was told. She always felt tired these days. So much so that Daniel, much against her wishes, had fetched the doctor to her.

Dr Cameron had looked into her mouth, sounded her chest, taken her pulse and pronounced that he didn't think much was wrong with her. He put his stethoscope into his little black bag and Daniel saw him to the front door.

'Your mother is not ill,' he told Daniel quietly. 'I believe she's unhappy. It's as though she's grieving.'

'She is,' Daniel told him.

Dr Cameron raised his eyebrows.

'For my sister.'

316

'Susan?' The doctor looked shocked.

'No . . . she's not dead. She left home.'

'Ah . . . well . . . that will be it then. You'll just have to look after your mother, Daniel. See that she eats properly. Do little things to please her.'

He was about to step up into his waiting carriage when he turned and said, 'When people have seen the doctor they like to be given some sort of pills or potions. I could sell you one of my own tonics – iron and quinine – but she doesn't really need it. Why don't you buy her a bottle of tonic wine? Give her a wineglassful three times a day. It's pleasant-tasting and it might even do her some good.'

Daniel had bought the wine and had found the one wine glass they owned. He didn't know where it had come from, but ever since he had been a child he had seen his mother use it to cut circles in the dough when she was making scones. Hannah had sipped the wine obediently, but Daniel could see that she didn't care for it and he gave up trying to make her drink it when there was more than half a bottle left.

Now, as Dora began to wash and peel the vegetables in the scullery, Hannah was happy enough to close her eyes and pretend to be asleep. That way she wouldn't have to talk to the lass. But pretend sleep turned to a short spell of real sleep, and she actually felt refreshed when she opened her eyes again to find Dora sitting opposite her.

'All done?' Hannah asked.

'Aye. The pan's on the range, there.'

And so it was. The lid was rattling gently and the steam rising from the pan carried a delicious and comforting smell. Hannah's sigh was one of regret. In so many ways Dora would have made a good wife for Daniel, but Hannah was sure now that wasn't to be. And she wasn't altogether sorry.

Dora glanced up at the clock quietly ticking on the mantel shelf. 'He's late,' she said.

'Aye.'

'Well I suppose I'd better go or me dad will come seeking me.' Dora rose reluctantly and said good night. 'Are you going to wait up for him?' she asked Hannah.'

'Aye, I think I will.'

'What will you do?'

'I'll hev another bit read of those newspapers. Will you pass them over, hinny?'

Hannah thought Dora gave her a strange look, but the lass took the newspapers of the table and handed them to her as requested.

'Well, I'll be off,' she said.

'Wait a moment. Is there another paper there? The one I was reading when you came in – it should hev been on top of the pile.'

'It was.'

'Was?'

'I used it to wrap the vegetable peelings in before I put them in the bin.'

'You what?'

Dora looked uncomfortable. 'Don't look at me like that. It was only an old newspaper.'

Hannah remained silent, and after an uncomfortable pause Dora took herself off. Once in the back lane, she stopped and clenched her hands to her breast. Hannah was no longer her ally. By her own thoughtless action she had lost the support of the one person who might have helped her persuade Daniel that she was the right wife for him.

Raised voices warned her that she was not alone. She looked up to see a couple, a man and a woman, coming down the back lane towards her. They were arguing. Or rather the woman was shouting at the man, who was laughing foolishly. He was drunk. And maybe the woman was too.

Dora leaned back against the wall and watched their unsteady progress. They made a comical sight, but the tears that streamed down Dora's cheeks were not tears of laughter. They were tears of despair.

'It is quite in order for my wife to visit her former maid.'

Samuel was dumbfounded. He had expected anger, fury even, but Victor sat calmly behind his desk, a wreath of cigar smoke obscuring his face, his voice betraying no emotion other than a slight amusement.

'But I've told you, she met Daniel Brady there.'

'In the street, you say?'

'Yes.'

'If the meeting had been prearranged as you suggested, surely they would have met inside the house?'

318

'Well, even if it wasn't arranged, they still went for a walk in the park together.'

'It was a pleasant day and my wife is a kindly soul. She probably wanted to know how her father's former pupil was prospering. Especially as he is now working for the *Journal*.'

Samuel stared at Victor, then shook his head slowly. Victor laughed.

'Did you think you had brought me some important piece of information?' he asked.

'Yes.' Samuel's tone was surly.

'Well, thank you anyway. It shows you have my interests at heart.'

'And am I to continue to keep an eye on him?'

'Yes. In fact it was careless of you not to stick closely to him today.'

'He was only going back to the office. He told her so.'

'And tonight?'

'He's reporting on some charity function. Your sister's going to be there.'

Victor smiled. 'Ah, Charlotte. She has a good heart. Perhaps that makes up for my failings.'

Samuel could have sworn that Victor was pleased about something. He had no idea what it could be. He got up to leave, but then paused at the door. 'Have you thought about that other matter?' he asked.

'Other matter?'

Samuel felt like cursing him. Victor Bateman knew very well what he was referring to but was just playing with him.

Before he could frame a suitable reply, Victor said, 'Oh, you mean the money, don't you? You think I should pay you more for your services?'

'I do.'

'I'm still thinking about it. Now off you go and get back to your duties.'

Samuel Burroughs kept a rein on his anger until he had left the building and stepped out on to the pavement. But then he couldn't help turning to look up at the lighted window of Victor's office. The look on his face was one of frustrated rage. He had existed too long in an underworld of crime and violence not to know he was worth much more than Victor had been paying him. He would bide his time, but not for much longer. It was time to move on. But not before someone had paid him well for what he knew.

Victor stood to one side of the window and looked down at the street below. Sure enough, Burroughs looked angry. And if he was angry, he might become dangerous. Perhaps he ought to give in and give him more money, but Victor didn't like to be browbeaten. If he paid up now, Burroughs would see it as a victory. But whatever he decided to do, it must be soon.

He went back to his desk and poured himself a whisky. He thought about the information that Burroughs had brought him. He didn't think there had been any prearranged meeting between Marion and Brady. She was too honourable to do anything like that. But ought she have refused to walk with the man? Yes, perhaps she should have. Were they too friendly? Yes again. But what Burroughs had not realised was that this could work to Victor's advantage.

He had known from the start that Brady was in love with Marion, and although she was married, a man like that would not stop caring for her welfare. If he really had found Henry Brookfield's papers – that is, if they existed – and if they contained any information that was damaging to Victor, Daniel would not be able to stop himself from telling Marion. And from Burroughs's account of their meeting today, she had not appeared to be angered or alarmed at any point.

He finished his cigar and drained his glass. He refrained from pouring a second drink. He had been planning to go to the coast tonight, but that could wait. No, he would go straight home and have dinner with his wife. Apparently his sister was going to be out at a charitable function and Annette was in London. Marion and he would dine alone. Perhaps he had been neglecting the poor girl.

Charlotte had asked for the carriage, and Victor, thinking that he might go to the coast by train, had agreed that she should have it. He left his senior cleark to lock up, walked downstairs to the ground floor and asked the nightwatchman to run along and get him a cab.

'You can ride back in it,' he said genially.

When the cab arrived, he tipped the watchman generously and said a pleasant good night. On the way home, he started to think about how he would deal with Marion. He knew he must be subtle. But he enjoyed play-acting, and as the cab carried him northwards out of the city, he was rehearsing what he was going to say.

Marion had been waiting nervously for Victor to return from the office. She was never sure exactly what time he would come home;

often he didn't bother but went straight on to some meeting or other at his club. Charlotte would wait only so long and would then summon the parlourmaid and tell her that dinner was to be served straight away.

'If he comes home while we are eating or after we have finished, then he will just have to be content with what Cook can warm up for him. Children who are late for the table,' she would add incongruously, 'are lucky to be given anything at all.'

Marion realised that Charlotte in many ways had not truly acknowledged that her younger brother was a grown man and that he was responsible for his own behaviour. And she had also realised that Victor indulged Charlotte in her fantasies.

But tonight, Charlotte was not dining at home. She was at some charity function at the Assembly Rooms in Gosforth. Previously, when Marion had found herself in this position, she had waited longer than Charlotte would have done before ordering the meal to be served. And when she did, she was made aware of the servants' disapproval, although naturally, none of them would grumble out loud.

Tonight she had just decided that Victor must not be coming home and that she faced the prospect of dining alone. She was about to pull the cord that would set a bell ringing in the kitchen below when Victor arrived, full of smiles and apologies.

'I'm so sorry, my dear,' he said. 'I forgot Charlotte was going out tonight, otherwise I should have made the effort to return sooner.' He came towards her, took her hand and kissed her. It took all her self-control not to push him away. 'How lovely you look tonight,' he said. 'What a waste it would have been if there had been no one to admire you across the dinner table.'

Marion looked at him levelly. He was acting again, and she was mortified that he thought her foolish enough to be impressed by his insincere compliments. Thankfully he did not seem to expect a reply.

'My dear, I've noticed you never wear your diamonds. Did I make a mistake?'

'Mistake?'

'Are they too sophisticated for a young woman of your age?'

'Oh, no . . . I mean, I don't know. I've never owned any jewellery. At least not as valuable as that.'

Victor pulled the bell rope and then took her hand and led her to the table. 'I should have realised. I can see that I will have to buy you some more – and we will go shopping together.'

'No, please . . .Victor . . .The diamonds you gave me are beautiful. It's just that I've never been used to wearing such lovely things. But if you want me to wear them, I will.'

Victor smiled at her but was prevented from saying anything more by the appearance of the parlourmaid.

'You can serve dinner now,' he told her peremptorily, and then held out a chair for Marion to sit at the table.

He seemed to be in a good mood and he kept up a flow of inconsequential but amusing conversation. He even made gentle fun of Charlotte and her good causes. Then, having mentioned his sister, he said, 'Do you know, I rather like this. Dining alone, just you and me. Maybe I have been neglecting you lately. I promise I shall mend my ways.'

Marion wondered if he could have any idea how much she despised him and how uneasy it made her feel that his mood seemed to change almost from one hour to the next.

Victor did not withdraw after the meal for his cigar and whisky. Instead he went with her to the drawing room and sat with her while they drank their coffee.

After a while he stopped talking and, sighing contentedly, sat back in his chair and half closed his eyes as if he were relaxing. The coals crackled and shifted in the hearth, the ormolu clock on the mantelpiece ticked ponderously as if time were slowing down and Marion suddenly became aware of all her days stretching out ahead of her. Days spent in this house that didn't feel like home waiting for a husband who had become an enigma.

She was not aware that she had been staring into the mid-distance with unfocused eyes and was startled to hear Victor's voice. She looked up to find him standing over her.

'What are you thinking? You look so sad.'

'No, I'm not sad.'

'Are you sure?'

There was something about the way he asked it that alerted Marion. Had he read her thoughts?

'Well . . . yes, I am a little sad,' she told him.

'Have I done something to upset you?'

'No, not you. It's Annette.'

'What has she done?'

'Nothing except be herself.' Marion feigned a smile. 'I miss her, you see, and I wish she weren't so happy to go away with Lady Cressington instead of staying here with me.'

'Ah, I see. You care very deeply for your sister, don't you?'

'I do.'

'Poor Marion. I shall have to do my best to distract you.'

Marion, who could hardly have told her husband that it was the prospect of life with him that had dismayed her, saw to her relief that he seemed happy with her answer. It's not completely untrue, she thought. I do miss Annette, but how good I am getting at dissembling.

She felt guilty that such duplicity had become part of her life; nevertheless, she smiled at Victor and did her best to convince him that she was enjoying his company and, indeed, was grateful for it.

Victor held out his hand to her and raised her to her feet.

'Come,' he said. 'Let's go to bed.'

In bed, Marion's flesh cringed at his touch and she wept with relief when he left her to go and sleep in the dressing room.

Victor was as insensitive to his wife's feelings as ever. He was satisfied that he had done the right thing in not questioning her about her friendship with Daniel Brady. In fact he was quite happy to let the friendship continue. For even though she might harbour romantic yearnings for Brady, Victor was convinced that she was too moral a human being to be capable of physical infidelity.

He was quite aware, however, that Brady was in love with Marion and would be concerned about her welfare. Therefore if he discovered anything that might make him suspicious of Victor's business dealings – or worse – he would be bound to tell Marion; to warn her, perhaps. Tonight, Victor slept easily, secure in the belief that Brady had not laid his hands on any dangerous information.

Daniel knew that he deserved the rebuke that Marion had given him. Paradoxically, he had treated Dora badly because he had not wanted to be unkind. He remembered what his mother would say to him if he was sick when he was a child and she administered some foul-tasting physic. If he twisted his face or bellowed in outrage she would tell him, 'You've got to be cruel to be kind, pet.'

Then he had not really understood, but now he did. He would have to talk to Dora. And once he had made up his mind, he knew he should not delay things any longer but must do so at the first opportunity.

Usually when he came home from the office he would find Dora sitting with his mother, but for the last few days she had not been there. Eventually he asked Hannah outright why Dora had not called lately.

'I'm not sure,' Hannah said, and Daniel saw that his mother was troubled. 'Why do you ask?'

'I . . . I need to talk to her.'

The anxiety on his mother's face deepened. 'You're not . . . I mean . . . you're not going to ask her to marry you, at last?'

The way his mother emphasised the last two words made Daniel feel all the more ashamed.

'No. I'm sorry.'

'Why do you say you're sorry?'

'Because I believe that's what you want for me. To have Dora as a wife.'

Hannah was sitting in the battered old armchair and she had spoken without ever taking her eyes off the comforting glow of the fire. But there was no comfort in the haggard lines on her face. Daniel knew that almost every minute of the day, and probably the long nights too, his mother grieved for Susan

After a long pause Hannah said, 'Mebbe I did. For many years that's exactly what I hoped for. But now I'm not so sure.'

Daniel was surprised. 'Why's that?' he asked.

'I hev me reasons, but divven't bother us now, lad.'

Daniel stood looking at her for a moment, and then said, 'I'd better go and talk to Dora.'

'Aye, you'd better.'

He waited for Hannah to say more, but it was obvious that she was lost in her own wretchedness. He left quietly by the back door and walked the short distance to Dora's house.

When he had called for her, all Dora's hopes came flooding back. She had been in the scullery washing dishes when he knocked at the back door. Expecting it to be the coalman's wife coming for payment, she had wiped her hands on her pinafore, taken the money her mother had left on the windowsill and opened the door. Her eyes widened when she saw who was standing there.

'Daniel . . .' she breathed. Then, after a moment or two of staring at each other awkwardly, she added, 'Are you going to come in?'

She held the door and stood back to let him pass, but he made no move.

'No,' he said. 'Dora . . . could you step out for a moment. Maybe we could stand here in the yard. It's a pleasant evening.'

Wordlessly she replaced the money on the windowsill and took her shawl from the hook on the door. She wrapped it round her shoulders, then closed the door behind her. She was aware that her heart was beating violently. Had he come to propose? Had he noticed that she had stopped coming to see Hannah, and had her absence made him realise that he missed her? Here, in the twilight, were her dreams going to come true at last?

She looked up into his face and knew immediately that far from coming true, her dreams were about to be dashed for ever. When he began talking, his voice was low and tender. He spoke of the years they had known each other and the pleasant times they had had.

*Pleasant!* Was that all they had meant to him?

Very soon he got on to apologising. Saying it was all his fault and that he didn't deserve her. That he was grateful for all the help she had given his mother and he hoped they could still be friends.

All too soon he was gone. There, with the clouds scudding across the darkening sky, and a cool breeze drying the tears on her cheeks, Dora's heart hardened and despair turned to rage. She had loved Daniel for as long as she could remember. He had filled all her hopes and dreams. She wiped her face with the corner of her shawl and turned to open the back door of her home. Even before she had closed the door behind her, love had turned to hate.


'How are you getting on with the shorthand?'

Daniel looked up to find Miss Bennett standing beside the table where he was working. Mr Chalk, who was shelving returned books, looked round and frowned. He clutched the remaining books in the crook of his arm and with the other hand pointed exaggeratedly towards the notice that said: SILENCE.

Miss Bennett and Daniel looked at each other and smiled. Daniel could have sworn his friend was suppressing a burst of mischievous laughter. Her tired old face softened until Daniel could see clearly the merry schoolgirl she might once have been.

There was no one else in the library, but Mr Chalk was clearly a strict disciplinarian as far as the rules were concerned. Daniel had come here as he did many evenings after work, thankful that the library kept hours to suit the working man and thus encourage people to read and to study.

'Come for a cup of tea,' Miss Bennett whispered. 'You've been working nonstop for the past hour. You could do with a break.'

Daniel gathered his papers together and put them into his dispatch case. After his cup of tea he would go home. Now that Dora no longer called to see his mother, Daniel felt guilty about leaving Hannah too much alone. He followed Miss Bennett to the staff rest room. This had become a haven for him as much he guessed it was for her. He looked forward to their friendly chats, and since he had started at the newspaper, Miss Bennett had questioned him eagerly about his work, showing interest even in his reports on the flower and vegetable shows.

This evening she had the small table set and waiting. Instead of the teacakes they usually had, there was a temptingly golden cake.

'Sponge cake,' Miss Bennett said. 'The Queen's favourite. They say she has it served every single day at teatime. I made it myself, and I hope you don't mind, I prefer a lemon filling to jam and cream.'

'I don't mind at all,' Daniel assured her.

He could see she was too modest to ask how he found the cake, and when he bit into the sweet, buttery, airy confection he was relieved to find it delicious, and said so.

Miss Bennett looked down at her plate to hide her smile of pleasure. 'Another slice?' she asked. 'Oh, do say yes.' She cut one and eased it on to his plate. Then she took another for herself. 'I suppose I'd better leave some for Mr Chalk,' she said. 'Not that he deserves it after being so rude. But I suppose he is practising for the day he will be in charge.'

'Mr Chalk in charge of the library?'

'I'm retiring soon.'

Daniel's dismay must have shown in his face.

'When I have gone, I hope you will not allow that young pup to discourage you from coming here.'

'I won't. But what will you do?'

'I'm going to India.'

Daniel was aware that his jaw had dropped. He recovered himself, placed his cup carefully on its saucer and said, 'India?'

'Yes. To Amritsar, to be precise, in the Punjab.' Miss Bennett was smiling at the effect she had caused. 'Shall I tell you why?'

'Please do.'

'A friend has asked me to go and work in a mission school.' Her expression changed and she grew serious. 'I will miss you,' she said.

'And I will miss you.'

'But we will write to each other, won't we?'

'Of course. When do you go?'

'In two weeks' time.'

'So soon?' Daniel was dismayed.

'I've sold my house. There was no point in waiting.' She laughed again. 'I've waited long enough, don't you think? But now I think we need a fresh pot of tea.'

Miss Bennett also insisted on Daniel having another slice of cake, and they began to talk of nothing in particular. Then she said, 'Daniel, may I look at that dispatch case of yours?'

'Of course.' He lifted it up from where it was resting against his chair and she took it and put it on her knee.

'It's very fine,' she said.

'I know. It was Henry Brookfield's.'

'So you told me.'

She smoothed the padded leather cover with her hand. 'My father had one just like this.' Then she added, surprisingly, 'May I look inside?'

'Of course.'

Miss Bennett loosed the catch and opened the lid. 'Yes, it is just like my father's dispatch case. His had the same pocket on the inside of the lid for pencils and rubbers and the like. Would you mind if I took your papers out?'

'Go ahead.'

Daniel watched curiously as his friend lifted out his papers and put them on the table. Then, to his surprise, she began to run her fingers along the edges of the red silk lining.

'Here it is!' she said. 'Just like my father's.'

'What have you found?'

'Come and see.'

Daniel went to stand behind her chair and leaned over to look into the case.

'Do you mean to say you've never noticed this piece of red ribbon at the front, just behind the catch?'

'No, I haven't.'

'Here – take hold of it and pull it up.'

Daniel did as he was told, and to his amazement the bottom of the case lifted up to reveal another shallow compartment. Lying there were several sheets of paper.

'What is it, Daniel? You look shocked.'

'I am.'

His hands trembled as he took out the papers and examined them.

'Something important?' Miss Bennett asked.

Daniel nodded speechlessly. Even one quick glance had revealed that these were notes and reports that Henry Brookfield had made of the last case he had worked on.

'Yes,' he told Miss Bennett. 'I think they will prove very important.'

A little while later, Daniel left the library and set out for home. Knowing that Miss Bennett would soon be leaving for India and they might never see each other again, he had stayed longer than he had intended and he hoped that his mother would not reproach him. He was too preoccupied to notice the two people who were following him.

Samuel Burroughs followed Daniel because he had been told to. He didn't think he was going to discover anything worthwhile, not now. And perhaps it was because his heart wasn't in it that he didn't notice the anonymous-looking woman with a shawl pulled over her head.

If anyone had asked Dora Gibb why she was following Daniel she would not have been able to tell them; at least not in a coherent fashion. Once she had followed him because she loved him and was suspicious of his involvement with Marion Brookfield. When Marion married Mr Bateman, Dora had thought that Daniel would come back to her. But he hadn't. Instead he had made it plain that he did not want to marry her. Perhaps he never had.

So why was she following him now? Because I hate him, she thought. I hate the way he has changed ever since he met the

Brookfields, father and daughter. Loving hopelessly herself, Dora believed that Daniel still hankered after Marion, and that was why he hadn't come to his senses.

All this working late and going to the library instead of coming straight home. There must be a reason, and that reason must be Marion Brookfield.

Dora fought down the bile that threatened to choke her. In her lucid moments she knew she wasn't thinking straight. A virtual prisoner to her obsession with Daniel, she had not yet come to accept that they had no future together.

# Chapter Twenty-One

Daniel had walked as far as Shields Road when he decided not to go straight home. He was keen to look at Henry Brookfield's papers, but no matter how much he was involved with his work, he was constantly haunted by the knowledge that his younger sister was missing and he had failed in his quest to find her.

He realised that for his mother, not knowing what had happened to her daughter might actually be worse than knowing she was dead. If the latter was the case, Hannah – and Daniel – could grieve properly. But as it was, he knew they would be in perpetual torment.

His mother would fret if he was late home, but if he could bring her any news of Susan – anything at all – she would forgive him. If he hurried into town he might just catch Maisie before she went home.

He took the tram that crossed Byker Bridge. Once in town, he alighted and hurried up Northumberland Street to the Haymarket. The streetlights were already lit, and he was so lost in thought that he did not take much notice of the woman who had followed him all the way from the library. But even if he had looked at her directly, he might not have recognised her, because she had covered her head with her shawl and pulled it forward so that her face was in shadow. She looked like any other woman of her class. Anonymous to all but those who knew and loved them.

Maisie, who was about to leave the shop and go home, saw him as soon as she opened the door. She hesitated. She could always hurry back in and hide in the back shop. Mr Jacobs, who always took over for the late hours, when a different sort of customer was about in the Haymarket, would tell Mr Brady that she had already gone home. Her employer had done that before if a gentleman customer had become troublesome.

'Another one of your followers, Maisie,' he would say. 'But why should I complain if your pulchritude attracts gentlemen and brings them into my shop like bees to honey.'

Maisie wasn't quite sure what pulchritude meant, but it was obviously a compliment, and she would laugh and say, 'Get away with you!'

But now, by wavering, she had left it too late for any retreat. Daniel Brady had seen her and he was dodging across the tramlines to get to her as quickly as he could.

'I'm glad I've caught you,' he said.

'I was just on my way home.'

'May I walk with you a little way?'

'There's no point. I – I've nothing to tell you.'

The hesitation, slight as it was, had given her away.

'Miss Collins. Please.'

'We–ell . . .'

'What is it?'

Maisie was troubled. Although she had decided that it was better if Susan's family did not know what she had sunk to, she found that she could not deceive this patently decent man.

'There's not much I can tell you,' she began.

'But you have discovered something?'

'Yes. You're not going to like it.'

He looked into her troubled eyes and his expression, already grave, now became anguished. 'She's not . . . not . . .'

Maisie could not bear to see him suffering, and she reached out and placed a hand on his arm. 'Quiet yourself, Mr Brady. Your sister is not dead, if that's what you are afeared of.'

'Tell me, then. Tell me what you know.'

'It's not much,' she repeated.

A portly man in an overcoat and carrying a briefcase brushed by them and made his displeasure plain. 'You're blocking the way,' he muttered.

Daniel Brady was oblivious to the man's annoyance, but Maisie took hold of his arm and drew him gently towards the doorway of an office that was already closed. She had never thought of herself as sentimental, but even before she began to speak, she could guess at the grief she was about to cause when she told him that Susan, although still living, was as good as dead to any decent family.

Dora, pressing close to a wall, kept her back to Daniel and the woman from the tobacconist's shop. Standing like this meant that she could not hear every word, but she learned enough to shock her profoundly.

She had never liked Susan, mainly because the younger girl had ignored her for most of the time. If she had nothing better to do she would sit and gossip with Hannah and Dora for a while, but Dora could see that the girl's mind was always elsewhere. Thinking of clothes and how to get the money to buy them, no doubt. Well, it would seem that Susan would have clothes enough now, but what a way to earn them.

Dora half turned and watched as Daniel seemed to stagger. The lass from the tobacconist's put out an arm to support him.

'I'll call and see you again,' Dora heard Daniel say. 'Promise me you'll try and find out the name of the man who is – who is keeping Susan.'

'I'll try,' Maisie said, 'but no promises. I can't come right out and ask, you know. I'll just have to keep my eyes and ears open if anyone discusses the matter in the shop.'

'God bless you, Miss Collins,' Daniel said.

'Mr Brady, please don't hope for too much.'

Daniel didn't respond. He took his leave so suddenly that Dora was caught unawares. But she had no need to worry. She didn't think he noticed her as he hurried by. As she watched him go, some instinct made her look back to where he had been standing, and she saw that the woman he had called Miss Collins was watching him too. And then, as the Haymarket became busy with folk intent on spending a night in town, Miss Collins shook her head, turned and was soon lost in the crowd.

Dora walked away slowly. Shaken and sickened by what she had just heard, she did not want to risk meeting Daniel now. But lost in thought, she didn't see that he was waiting for her at the tram stop.

'Dora,' he said, causing her to jump back, startled. 'Why have you been following me?'

She felt herself flushing. 'What makes you think I've been following you?

'Why else are you here?'

'I – I've been shopping.' And then, seeing him looking at her quizzically and realising that she wasn't even carrying a basket, she added, 'Window-shopping.'

She stared at him belligerently and he didn't argue with her. Instead he smiled and said, 'Well then, shall we go home together?'

'No. I don't want to go home with you.'

'Why?'

'I heard. I heard all that about Susan.'

'I thought you did.'

'She's little better than a whore! When your mother finds out, she'll die of shame.'

'My mother isn't going to find out,' Daniel said. 'Unless you tell her.'

He looked into her eyes, and Dora raised her chin and stared back defiantly. He remained silent, and eventually she lowered her gaze and said, 'No, I won't tell her.'

'Thank you.'

'Nor anyone else,' she added.

Daniel looked surprised.

'No one else will hear anything from me,' Dora said. 'I've been in and out of your house all my life and I wouldn't want anyone to think that I was tarred with the same brush.'

'Dora . . . don't. Don't talk like that,' Daniel said. 'We have been friends since we were children.'

'Friends?' Dora said and her tone was bitter. 'That's all we've ever been, isn't it?'

'What do you mean?'

'I thought we were sweethearts until you made it plain that I wasn't good enough for you.'

'I never said that. And in any case, it isn't true.' Daniel looked anguished. 'Dora, I'm sorry. So sorry. I know I've hurt you. I wish there was something I could do to make amends.'

'There isn't. But divven't fret. I won't be bothering you again.'

As she spoke, a tram rattled up to the stop. They both climbed on and Dora, without another word, sat as far away from Daniel as she could.

Daniel wondered if he should go and sit beside her, but Dora had made it plain that she did not want him to. And, in any case, what could he say? They would only sit in awkward silence all the way home.

As the train rattled and swayed through the city streets Daniel realised how fatigued he was. He found himself closing his eyes. As the sounds of the real world faded, he thought he could hear the shouts and laughter as he and his pals, as children, had kicked a tin can down the back lane. Dora would always run after them, keen to join in the fun. It seemed that everywhere he went in those days Dora was not far behind. The other lads often teased him about it.

The tram halted at a stop and the resulting jolt made him sit up straight and open his eyes. The remembered laughter faded, but as the scene vanished from his mind it left a lingering sense of shame. He must have known how much he meant to Dora and yet he had done nothing to discourage her. Marion had been right the day she had told him he had behaved badly, and yet his sin had been one of omission.

And now Dora had vowed never to set foot in the Bradys' house again. Daniel was ashamed of the sense of relief this gave him. But he could only hope that his mother, who imagined that the girl was a true friend, would never find out what Dora had said about Susan.

When Daniel arrived home, his mother was sitting in her usual place by the fire in the range. She looked up and smiled and it took all his resolve to smile in return. If only I could tell her that I've had news of Susan, he thought. But what news! She must never know what I've discovered. It would break her heart. And even when I do find my poor sister, can I ever bring her home again?

Without a word, Hannah rose from her chair and busied herself setting his supper on the table.

'There's a nice pie from the pork butcher's for you,' she said. 'Full of jelly. And mind you eat it all.'

'Thanks, Ma. You're spoiling me.'

'And so I should. While I've been sitting here, I've come to realise that I've been neglecting you lately. You've always been a good son, none better, and I know in my heart that you've done your best for me and for . . .' Her voice broke, but she quickly recovered. 'And for your sister. In my grief I think I forgot to show how much I love you, Danny boy.'

The sad smile on her face and the use of the pet name she had for him when he was a bairn almost unmanned him. He smiled and gave her a hug and insisted on making the pot of tea himself. He put two cups on the table and asked her to sit with him and talk for a while. Her pleasure at his invitation in turn made him feel guilty for all the times he had wished her to be silent.

She asked him to tell her more about the kind of work he was doing now, and he did not think her interest was feigned. She told him how proud it made her to see his name in the newspaper and that she could not bring herself to throw any one of those papers away.

The fire crackled and the gas lamp hanging above the table hissed faintly; the curtains were drawn against the night, and Daniel knew that any stranger walking in would have found the scene peaceful, a haven of content. But that stranger would not know of the grief and torment that lay under the surface.

While Hannah washed the dishes she could not conceal her yawning, and it was easy for Daniel to persuade her to go to bed. She grumbled a little. She said that if he was going to stay up late and work he might like her to keep him company. She promised to be quiet.

She rallied when he teased her that she needed her beauty sleep and told her to go upstairs. He filled the stone hot-water bottle for her and followed her. She was already sitting up in bed and had pulled her shawl round her shoulders. Even so, he could see how thin she had become and his heart ached. He kissed her brow and before he left her he blew out the candle.

As he went downstairs, it crossed his mind that their roles were changing, becoming reversed, but he was only too pleased to look after his mother just as she had cared for him when he was a child.

Daniel took off his jacket, slipped it over the back of his chair and sat down. Then, with the house quiet, he opened his dispatch case and took out the papers Miss Bennett had discovered. These were undoubtedly the notes Henry had been making when he had been working on what had proved to be his last investigation, and what Daniel was to read was shocking.

Some of the notes were written in longhand, and to Daniel's newly experienced eye they looked like the first drafts of articles that Henry Brookfield intended to write. Other work was in shorthand, and Daniel took his own notepad and a pencil and began to make notes as he read. As he worked, his expression became increasingly bleak.

335

One part of the investigation was concerned with the slum dwellings that were a disgrace to Newcastle, one of the most prosperous cities in Europe. Henry Brookfield's mind had been sharp and his writing incisive. Daniel learned things about his home town that he had never known before.

Henry's style as he exposed the worst of the crowded, rat-infested, insanitary living conditions was unforgiving, and despite the lack of sensational language there was no disguising his sense of outrage. Henry had set himself the task of discovering and exposing the slum landlords who more often than not hid behind some anonymous company. Not even the clerks in the offices knew who the owner of the company was.

And neither did the rent collectors Henry had spoken to. The men who went weekly round the streets taking more than they could afford from people who thought themselves lucky to have a roof over their heads, no matter how ramshackle and decaying it was.

As he read on, Daniel felt his own anger growing. But there was worse to come. During Henry's forays into the areas where the very poor lived, he had become aware of the growing incidence of children, mostly girls, simply vanishing from the streets. And it was not only very poor children who disappeared. It seemed that any pretty little girl who wandered out alone or was left unattended was also in danger of being – being what? Abducted? Yes, abducted, Henry had decided.

This was not a murderer at work, else where were the bodies? Too many had vanished for at least one or two not to have turned up in the river or one of the deserted buildings down by the Ouseburn. Henry had decided that the girls were being taken for the purposes of child prostitution. There were men who would pay well for young virgins, especially as they believed this was a cure for venereal disease.

The clock on the mantel shelf chimed midnight. Daniel, sitting at the table in his shirtsleeves, glanced at it briefly and then returned his gaze to the papers spread out on the table before him.

At some stage Henry's instincts had alerted him to the fact that he was being followed. Daniel read:

Tonight he was no more than a few paces behind me. I could hear the footfalls but, whenever I stopped to look behind me there was no one. I think he wants me to know that he is there. Is he trying to frighten me?

Daniel thought this might be the case, but then Henry had written:

He allowed me to find him tonight. It was dark and he kept to the shadows. When I took a step nearer to him, he thrust out an arm and hissed, 'Come no nearer.' I stopped and backed away a little. 'What are you after?' he asked me.

I peered at him closely but all I could see was a tall, thin figure with his hat low on his forehead and his coat collars pulled up to conceal the rest of his face. I had no intention of confiding in him and I asked him why he wanted to know. His answer surprised me.

'Because I might be able to help you,' he said.

'How can you help me?' I asked him.

'I know who you are,' he said, 'and I think I know what you're up to. You're going to write about the slums, aren't you?'

I kept silent, and after a moment he said, 'Well, answer me or not as you please, but that's why you're here.' He paused, then added, 'There's something else, isn't there?'

'What else could there be?'

'Don't play clever. I know you've been asking folk about the children.'

I could see there was no use denying it and I merely nodded.

'You want to know who's responsible, don't you?'

I nodded again.

'Would it surprise you if I told you it's one and the same person who owns most of these godforsaken rat-runs?'

I had already suspected that was the case, so I simply shook my head.

'I thought not. I thought you were sharp enough to work it out.'

'Are you going to tell me his name?' I asked him.

'Mebbe.'

'Do you want money?'

The man's mocking laughter conveyed contempt for my naivety.

'How much?' I asked.

But he wouldn't tell me. He told me where to meet him and when, and to bring as much as I thought the information was worth. He would tell me if it was enough and then give me a name. Before I could say more, he seemed to melt into the shadows.

Daniel laid down his pencil and sat back in his chair. He rubbed his eyes wearily, but tired though he was, he had no intention of going to bed until the work was done. His head was aching and his eyes were smarting. He rose from the table to make himself a cup of tea.

But the tea grew cold as he ignored it and carried on with his work, noting street names, the names of people who had been willing to talk to Henry and the names of people who had lost a child.

When a pale light made its way through a gap in the curtains and the street rang to the sound of booted feet as men made their way down to the shipyards, Daniel eventually put down his pencil, gathered up the papers and put them back into the bottom compartment of his dispatch case.

Henry Brookfield had not discovered the name of the slum landlord who was also responsible for taking children off the streets and placing them in brothels. But he had been very close. He must have been. For Daniel was convinced that that was why he had been lured to his death.

He remembered his conversation with Arthur Robinson in the Raby that night. Arthur had not believed they had hanged the right man for the murder of Henry Brookfield. Neither had Daniel. And now, more than ever, he was convinced of it. Whoever had murdered Henry Brookfield had placed his belongings in the pockets of the poor drunken wretch who had been taken to the gallows. Indeed, he had probably supplied the man with the bottle that had made him drunk and insensible.

He must be found, Daniel thought. I don't know how I'm going to do it, but I must find a way of completing Henry Brookfield's investigation.

Victor Bateman and Samuel Burroughs looked at each other across the wide expanse of Victor's desk in the house in Gosforth.

'I told you never to come to the house unless I sent for you,'

Victor said. 'Both my wife and my sister are at home this evening, and Charlotte, at least, will want to know why I have been bothered with a business matter at this time of night.'

'Bothered?'

'That is how she will see it. She will ask who you are and I will have to invent some lie.'

'That should come easy to you.'

'You forget yourself.'

Victor's eyes narrowed and his icy stare caused Samuel Burroughs to shudder. Someone walking over my grave, he thought. He tried to outstare Victor, but he could not free himself from the notion that he had just put himself in great danger.

Victor reached into a drawer of his desk and took out a bottle of whisky and two glasses. He poured himself a measure and then deliberately put the other glass back, empty, into the drawer.

'You won't be staying long enough,' he said.

Burroughs watched Victor savour the whisky. He could have done with a tot himself. Anything to warm the wintry feeling that was beginning to course through his tall frame.

'Well?' Victor said. 'What's so important?'

'Brady. He's still looking for his sister.'

'What's that to me?'

'He's been talking to the woman in the tobacconist's. She overheard something, it seems.'

'Overheard what?'

'Two of her customers. One of them was talking about the Brady girl.'

Victor took time to light a cigar, and when it was burning to his satisfaction he said, 'Go on.'

'The fellow in question had done someone a favour – something to do with planning permission – and had been rewarded with a visit to this nice little house by the sea.'

'And why do you think that has anything to do with me?'

Burroughs was overcome with resentment. Resentment that Bateman should think he was so stupid. 'That's where you keep her, isn't it? That's where you keep Daniel Brady's sister. In that nice little house by the sea.'

'I don't know what you're talking about.'

'Yes you do. Brady might not have been able to find his sister, but

I've known for some time that you have her and where you keep her, *Mr Mason*.'

There was a slight pause before Victor said, 'I don't know what you're talking about. You're talking nonsense.'

'No I'm not. I followed you there and it only took a few discreet enquiries to discover that it was a Mr Mason who bought the house.' Burroughs stopped, appalled both with himself and at the way Victor Bateman was looking at him.

'Why would you do that?'

'Because . . . because . . .'

'You want to get more money out of me. Blackmail me? Is that it?'

'No, not blackmail. I wouldn't put it like that.'

'Well I would.'

The two men stared at each other. The silence lengthened. Then Victor poured himself another whisky and stared into the glass thoughtfully.

'All right,' he said, without looking up. 'On reflection I suppose I do owe you a — shall we say a bonus, for the work you've done for me. All those pretty little children you managed to take from the streets unseen and undiscovered.' Victor laughed. 'They got that wrong, didn't they?'

'What do you mean?'

'"The Toff", the press called you, and they dressed you in a cloak and a top hat.'

'The cloak was right.'

'Yes . . . the dark cloak so you could melt into the shadows. But you never wore a top hat. Poetic licence. It made a better story, I suppose.'

'I don't know what you're talking about.'

'Well, no matter. Tell me, I'm interested, did it never bother your conscience?'

'Probably as much as it bothered yours!'

'Well, well. We are getting bold, aren't we? Very well. You've forced me to recognise what I owe you. Don't come here again — ever — and don't come to my office. I'll visit you in your cosy little room above the public house and I'll bring you a reward that I believe you will find satisfactory. There'll be enough for you to take yourself off, if that's what you want. Will that do?'

'I suppose it will have to.'

Victor's mood changed and he laughed. 'Come, come, Samuel, don't look so gloomy. We've struck a deal and to seal it let's have a drink.'

He opened the drawer and took out the second glass. He poured a generous measure and pushed it across the desk. Burroughs took it and found that his hand was shaking. When he drank, he slopped some out of the glass and it ran down his chin. He wiped it with the back of his other hand and looked up to see Victor watching him appraisingly.

'When will you come?' Burroughs asked, aware that he sounded surly.

'Shall we say soon? Don't go out. Lie low, stay in your room and wait for me. All right?'

'I suppose so.'

'Right.' Victor rose from his chair. 'Drink up and away with you. I must get back to my family.'

He smiled genially, but Burroughs noticed that the smile did not reach his eyes.

Samuel Burroughs knew that things had gone badly wrong. Bateman had no intention of bringing him money. A bonus, he had called it. And if he was not going to pay him, then there was only one other way to keep him quiet.

I'll have to go, Burroughs thought. Get out of town and as far away as possible. But what am I going to use for money? I should have saved something. Bateman has paid me well, but I've spent it all. What can I do?

'Thank you for coming.'

Daniel met Marion at the gates of Heaton Park and, taking her arm, began to lead her towards the Pavilion Café.

'Betty said you needed to see me urgently.'

'Yes.'

Betty had been a most reluctant go-between. Daniel had had to convince her that the only reason he wanted to see Marion was to discuss her late father's work and that he had no intention of doing anything dishonourable.

'I saw you the other day,' Betty had said. 'Going into the park. Were you discussing Mr Brookfield's work then?'

Daniel could have lied to make it easier, but he sensed that Betty was far too astute to accept anything but the truth.

'No, that was a chance meeting.'

Betty had looked at him long and hard. 'I divvent't want anything or anyone to harm the lass,' she'd said.

'I would never do that.'

'No, I don't think you would. But why can't you just go and see her at home?'

'Mr Bateman doesn't like me. I wouldn't get past the front door.'

Betty had given in and agreed to take a note to Marion. And now, here she was. Daniel found them a table.

'Would you like a cup of tea?' he asked.

'Anything.'

A short while later, when both had sipped their tea without really tasting it, he told her that he had found her father's papers, and something of what was in them.

'What would you like me to do with them?' he asked.

'I promised I would give them to Mr Earnshaw,' Marion said.

'I could do that. After all, I work for him.'

'Very well. But I would like to see them first.'

'I'm not sure if your father would have liked you to see all of them.'

'Why not?'

'The subject of some of his work is . . . is harrowing.'

'And you don't think I'm capable of dealing with it?'

'Not only harrowing but . . . repugnant.'

'I see.'

Daniel wondered if she did.

'Will you trust me?' he asked.

'Trust you to do what?'

'To keep the papers for a while and carry on with your father's work?'

Marion stared at him. 'You?' she asked.

Daniel flushed. 'Why not me? Do you not think I'm capable?'

Instinctively Marion reached across the table and took his hand. 'Please don't misunderstand me. I wasn't questioning your ability, far from it. I think it's a wonderful idea. And I know my father would choose no one else.'

'Do you think so?'

'I know so.'

'Then I promise I will do my very best to honour his memory.'

Marion smiled at him and then said, 'But what about Mr Earnshaw? Will he agree to let you do this work?'

'I shan't tell him until it's done.'

'A fait accompli?'

'If that means what I think it means, yes.' He smiled broadly. 'And furthermore, I shall tell him that I had your approval.'


'So your former maid called to see you this morning?'

Victor smiled pleasantly at Marion across the dinner table. They were alone, Charlotte having gone to one of her charity functions.

'Betty, yes. How did you know?'

'Bertha mentioned it to me.'

'Why would she do that?'

'I beg your pardon?'

'Why would my maid report my daily activities to you? Have you set her to keep watch on me?'

Victor laughed. 'My dear Marion, of course not. I merely asked the woman if my wife had a pleasant day. She said she presumed you had because your old friend had called and not much later you left the house. You missed lunch, in fact.'

'Yes, I did. And yes, thank you, I have had a pleasant day.'

'And are Sergeant Robinson and his wife quite happy with their new home?'

Marion looked at him and her eyes widened. Was there a hint of a threat in that reasonable question?

'Very happy,' she said.

'I'm pleased. Let us hope that they will have long and happy lives there.'

Now definitely uneasy, Marion took a bread roll from the basket and began to drink her soup. Of late, she'd had the feeling that Victor was watching her closely, as if he were waiting to discover something. Even now, although he had smiled and shrugged good-naturedly, she could not shake off the feeling that he was scrutinising her through narrowed eyes.

What would he do if he learned that Betty had acted as a go-between her and Daniel? Would he give the Robinsons notice to quit the home they loved? Marion's feelings were complex. Not only did she hate this man who took pleasure in corrupting young girls, and who had even set his sights on Annette, but she had the feeling that there was more to learn about him. And she must be cautious. She had just realised that she thought it better to hide the discovery of the papers from Victor. She could not explain why.

Victor made an effort to be charming but he knew something had changed. Not simply because Marion had been so curt with him but also because he had the distinct feeling that she was hiding something from him.

If only I hadn't told Burroughs to keep to his miserable lodgings, he thought. He would have been following Brady today – for I'm pretty sure it was Brady that Marion went to meet – and maybe he would have had news for me.

So what is she hiding? I'm forced to assume that Brady has found her father's papers. And if so, how incriminating can they be?

The second course was served, and he watched as Marion pushed the fillet of lemon sole around her plate. He deduced that although she was uneasy, as her lack of appetite showed, she was not frightened. And if the papers had contained anything incriminating, she would be.

No, Henry Brookfield could not have discovered the name of the man he had been pursuing so determinedly. And Samuel Burroughs, who knew far too much for his own good, must be dealt with before he revealed the truth.

# Chapter Twenty-Two

Samuel Burroughs knew that he would have to act quickly. Before he left, he packed most of his belongings into a carpet bag light enough to carry if he was in a hurry and stowed it under his bed. Then, before the town had properly come awake, he set off to find his first mark.

He walked eastwards over Byker Bridge. He had wrapped a muffler around his face and wore a cap like any working man. He mingled with the crowd going down to the shipyards until he reached the turning that led to the back lane of the street where the Brady family lived.

From long observation he had learned that Daniel Brady left by the back door when he went to work in the mornings. He had done that as a labouring man in his working clothes, and now that he was a reporter, dressed more like a gentleman, his habits had not changed.

Burroughs lifted the latch, opened the door and slipped into the back yard.

Daniel was startled when he saw the tall, thin figure of a man push himself up from where he had been leaning against the wall of the coal house.

'Who the hell are you?' he asked and took a step towards him

The man shrank back. 'Go easy, I mean no harm.'

'Then what do you want?'

Daniel frowned as he gazed at the sharp nose and the glittering eyes that were all he could see of the man's face.

'I want to help you.'

'How can you help me?'

'I have information that you would be glad of.'

'What information is that?'

'You've taken over from Henry Brookfield, haven't you? Mebbe I could tell you something that he never managed to find out.'

'And that is?'

'A name.'

Daniel's heart began to race. 'What name?'

'It'll cost you.'

'I have no money.'

'Can't you get any?'

Daniel remembered what Henry had written. A man, nameless, had offered to sell him information. That man in all probability had lured him to his death.

'It was you, wasn't it?' Daniel said.

The man backed away nervously. 'What do you mean?'

'You lured Henry Brookfield down to the Ouseburn that night and killed him.'

'No, you've got it wrong!'

'You asked him to meet you there. Don't deny it. You offered to give him a name – the same offer you've just made me.'

'How do you know that?'

'I know. Then, whether he gave you any money or not, you murdered him.'

'No, it wasn't me!'

'You're lying.' Daniel took a step towards him.

The man backed up against the wall. 'Well, mebbe I got him down there, but I didn't murder him.'

'Who then? Who were you working for?'

Daniel took a further step forward.

'Stop! Stop right there or you'll never know.'

'Go on, then.'

'I've told you. It'll cost you.'

Before the man realised what was happening, Daniel had grabbed him, spun him round and bent one arm up behind his back.

'Let go!' the man screeched. 'You're breaking my arm!'

'It's your neck I should be breaking. Tell me now, or I'll march you up to the police station in Headlam Street.'

Daniel's prisoner tried desperately to break free, and proved himself stronger than he looked. At last, with one pull that must have caused him agony, he got away, opened the door and fled out into the

346

back lane. Daniel lunged after him, but all he managed to grab was the trailing end of the man's muffler.

This only stopped his flight for a moment, because with one hand the man unwound the muffler, the action setting his cap flying. He left both cap and muffler as he ran. Daniel started to chase after him, but his damaged leg stopped him. When the man reached the top of the lane, he turned and regarded Daniel mockingly.

'There's something else I could have told you,' he shouted, 'but you'll never know now!'

Then he vanished around the corner.

Daniel, cursing the leg that had let him down, steadied himself by reaching out with one hand and leaning on a wall. As he stood there, he thought back to the brief glimpse he had had of the man's face when the cap and muffler came off. Surely he had seen this man before?

Samuel Burroughs cursed himself for a fool. Why on earth had he imagined that Daniel Brady would have any money, or even if he had that he would part with it willingly? Perhaps he had chosen Brady because he was the easy option. And after this miserable failure to extort money, he couldn't help thinking that if he had started by telling the man he knew where his sister was, he might yet have succeeded.

Well, there's only one thing left for me, he thought. It's risky, but it's the last throw of the dice.

Samuel Burroughs went back to the room above the public house in Pink Lane for the last time. He smartened himself up, took his carpet bag from under the bed and closed and locked the door behind him, even though that wouldn't stop Victor Bateman from discovering he'd fled for as long as the time it would take him to kick it open again. The landlord would have to whistle for the last month's rent.

'There's a gentleman asking to see you, Mrs Bateman.'

Marion looked up from her escritoire, where she was writing a letter to Annette. 'A gentleman?' she asked. 'Is it Mr Brady?'

She knew immediately how foolish it had been to ask that. Daniel would not call here.

'He didn't give his name, madam,' the maid replied. 'He said he was a business associate of Mr Bateman's. I told him that the master would be at his office until this evening, when he would return for dinner, but the gentleman insisted that it was you he wanted to see.' The maid paused, waiting for an answer. When none was immediately forthcoming she added, 'Will you see him?'

Marion was puzzled, but she thought she had better agree in case Victor had sent the man. Although she couldn't imagine why he would.

'Yes, I'll see him. Would you show the gentleman into the library?'

When she entered the library, the caller was standing by the window with his back to the light, so that she could not quite make out his features. But she thought she had seen that distinctive figure before, although she could not remember where. She hesitated for a moment, not knowing what to do, and then decided to sit at Victor's desk and put its broad expanse between her and the mysterious stranger.

'Will you sit down?' she asked, and indicated the chair on the opposite side of the desk.

The man did so but offered no explanation for his presence.

'May I know your name?' Marion asked.

'You don't need to.'

His answer was so unexpected and his tone so intimidating that Marion immediately glanced towards the bell cord at the side of the fireplace.

'There's no need for that,' the stranger said. 'No need to summon help. I'm not here to harm you. I've come to help you, in fact.'

'Help me? Has . . . has Victor sent you?'

The man's thin-lipped mouth curled into a sneer and it sounded as if he choked back a laugh of derision.

'No, your husband hasn't sent me here,' he said. 'In fact Mr Bateman would be most upset if he knew I had called on you.'

Marion rose quickly to her feet and with her eyes measured the distance to the door and then the bell pull. Which would be nearer?

'Sit down,' the man said. 'I've already told you, you're not in danger. I've come to help you. To give you some information. Something I imagine you'd really like to know.'

Marion sat down again. She was intrigued by what he had told her, but as she stared across the desk into his coldly glittering eyes she could not help but compare herself to a frightened rabbit.

'And what is that?' she asked.

'Well, there's a couple of things I could tell you, but it depends on how much you're prepared to pay.'

'Pay? You want to sell me information?'

'That's right.'

'But why should I buy it?'

'Because it concerns someone you . . . How shall I put this? It concerns a man you are very fond of, and I don't mean your husband.'

Marion felt herself flushing. 'I have no idea who you could mean.'

'Really? Look, let's stop this play-acting. The man I'm talking about is Daniel Brady, and the information concerns the whereabouts of his little sister.'

Shocked, Marion caught her breath, and her words when they came were hardly more than a whisper. 'You know where Susan is?'

'I do. Interested now?'

'Yes. Please tell me.'

'It'll cost you.'

'You've already said that. But I have very little money.'

For an answer the man looked deliberately round the room, letting his eyes linger on the oil paintings and the luxurious furnishings.

'Very little money of my own,' Marion amended.

Burroughs controlled a spurt of rage. He realised that Bateman's wife was probably telling the truth. It would be just like the mean streak in Victor to give her only the smallest of allowances, keep her on a tight rein.

'You must have something,' he snarled. 'Jewellery, perhaps? Surely he gave you a wedding gift?'

Marion sat back in her chair and considered his words for a moment. Then she looked up at him and said, 'Yes, he did.'

'There you are, then. Don't trouble yourself over the principles of the matter. The jewellery was a gift. Yours to do what you please with. And surely Susan Brady's life is worth saving.'

'Her life?'

'Yes. The man who's got her will tire of her sooner or later, and then, I promise you, she will simply disappear. He's done it before.'

'Who is he, this man? Do you know?'

Marion thought that the man gave her the strangest of looks, as if he were considering something, then he said, 'Of course I do, but you don't have to know. You'll find out soon enough. Now, if you want me to tell you, go and get the jewellery.'

This was not the moment to ring for a maid. Marion decided to go to her room and get the jewellery herself, but when she opened the door she came face to face with Bertha.

The woman didn't even blink. 'I just came to see if you needed me, madam.'

Marion didn't believe her for one moment, but she smiled calmly and said, 'No, that's all right. You may go.'

It seemed to Marion that her personal maid was reluctant, but eventually, as Marion herself did not waver, Bertha turned and crossed the hall, disappearing through the door that led to the servants' quarters.

Marion stayed where she was until she could be reasonably sure that her maid was not coming back, then she raced upstairs.

When she returned to the library, her visitor eyed the object she was carrying expectantly. She could not help but notice the gleam of avarice in his eyes.

'Is this all you have?' the man asked when she opened the lid of the silver casket and revealed the diamond necklace, earrings and brooch nestling on the green velvet lining.

'Yes.'

'Well, I suppose they would fetch a tidy sum.'

'You want me to sell them?'

'No, not you, there isn't time. I'll take these now as payment and be gone.'

For a moment it looked as though he was going to snatch the casket from Marion's hands, but she retreated to the other side of the desk and sat down again. 'First of all you must complete your side of the bargain,' she said.

He laughed unpleasantly. 'Of course. Give me a notepad – you'll find one in the top left-hand drawer.'

When Marion opened the drawer and found the notepad she said, 'You've obviously been here before.'

He nodded.

'Are you a business associate of my husband's?'

'You could say that.' His eyes glittered malevolently.

She pushed the pad across the desk and watched as he took a stump of pencil from his pocket and began to write. Underneath the address he drew a rough map.

'That's where you'll find her,' he said as he tore off the top sheet of paper and reached across the desk to give it to her.

Marion was about to take it when he snatched it back. 'Give me the jewellery.'

'How do I know this isn't a trick?'

'You don't. I can't even give you my word because my word means nothing to honest folk like you. But I'll swear on it anyway. You've never harmed me and I wouldn't swindle you.'

They stared at each other for a while, and then Marion made the decision and handed over the silver casket, at the same time taking the sheet of paper from his other hand. She stared at the address and the map.

'It's about a quarter of an hour's walk from the station,' the man said. 'If I were you I wouldn't get a cab. If you're going to do this without telling your husband about it, it's better not to leave a trail.'

Then he put the casket in an inside pocket of his jacket and rose from his chair. 'You won't see me again,' he said. 'Don't ring for the maid, I'll see myself out.'

Marion sat where she was and stared at the address the man had written down. The house was on the coast, in Whitley-by-the-Sea. It meant nothing to her. She supposed the man could have tricked her. She might have handed over her jewellery for nothing, but she had an inner conviction that he had been telling the truth.

She also decided that for some reason the man hated Victor and this action of his had been prompted not only by cupidity but by a desire for revenge. She went over everything he had said and was filled with the conviction that without actually saying so, he had been telling her that the man who had taken Susan away from her family was her own husband, Victor Bateman.

Marion was shaken, but she knew she did not have time to ponder further. She fetched her hat and coat herself and asked one of the maidservants to run along and get her a cab.

Only a short while after that, Bertha put on her own hat and coat and set out to walk into the city.

Marion asked the cab to wait while she called in at the newspaper offices. The man who had sold her the information had told her to waste no time, but Daniel deserved to know where his sister was straight away. He would want to come with her to the address she had been given in Whitley-by-the-Sea.

But the clerk on the reception desk had bad news. 'Mr Brady isn't in the building,' he told Marion. 'He'll be coming back with his story but I couldn't say when that will be.'

Marion was dismayed but not deflected. She told the cab driver to take her to the station. She would go alone.

Meanwhile, in Victor Bateman's office in Dene Street, Bertha Soulsby sat and waited impatiently in an anteroom. Bertha had been grateful when Mr Bateman had remembered her and given her the job of personal maid to his new wife. She had always been well spoken and more of a lady than some of the other women who had worked for him, and it amused her that now she was to keep an eye on his wife rather than one of his little mistresses.

The Bateman family home was infinitely more luxurious than any of the houses she had worked in before, and the money and the pickings were good. And all she had to do was look after Mrs Bateman, who was no trouble at all, and at the same time report if anything out of the ordinary occurred.

Well, Mr Bateman would certainly want to know what had happened today. It was a pity that Mrs Bateman had opened the door and found her there. But Bertha had already heard enough to know that the master should be told immediately.

Mr Bateman was in a meeting, but fortunately Bertha didn't have to wait too long. When she told him what she had heard, he literally went white with rage, and stormed out of the room without even thanking her.

Well, no matter, if this was to be the end of a pleasant interlude, she had been careful to put a little by to tide her over. And, of course, as a precaution, she had made sure that Mr Bateman had already written a glowing reference for her, which she kept in a locked writing chest in her room. She would be all right.

Something told her it would be better to leave now. Go to another city. She sensed that Victor Bateman's house of cards might be about to fall down. And from the look of him as he had stormed out of the room, God help anyone who crossed him today.

When Marion left the station at Whitley-by-the-Sea, she stepped out into a fine but persistent drizzle. The sky was grey, and when she looked ahead of her, down the hill towards the promenade, it was hard to distinguish sky from sea. As she hurried through the damp air she thought about what she had to do and hoped that it wouldn't take long to persuade Susan to come away with her.

The route took her down to the promenade and then along the sea front. A low mist hung over the sea, and the eerie sound of a foghorn moaned across the water. Marion could hear the waves breaking on the shore and dragging back across the shingle. Not many people were about, and the smoke rising from the many chimneys suggested that the more sensible were sitting at home by their fires. Maybe this weather signalled the end of the summer.

The terrace was neat and the gardens tidy. In one or two of them wind-battered rosebushes hung on to their brown-edged blooms. The garden of the house Marion stopped at was neatly paved, with an ornamental sundial in the centre but not a flower or a leafy plant in sight. Marion opened the gate and walked up the short path, nerving herself for what lay ahead.

'What do you want?'

The maid who answered the door was unlike any maid Marion had ever met in her life. Not that she had met many until she married, but she knew that no servant in a respectable household would speak to a caller like this, no matter how unwelcome.

'I have come to see Miss Susan Brady,' Marion replied.

'You've got the wrong house,' the young woman said, and was about to shut the door when Marion stepped forward and placed one hand firmly against it.

'I don't think so,' she said. 'Now, are you going to let me in or shall I call a constable?'

Marion noted the flicker of fear in the woman's eyes. 'A constable? Why would you do that?'

'Because I believe you are keeping Miss Brady here against her wishes.'

Marion had no idea if this were true. For all she knew, poor Susan was quite happy to be here, which was exactly why she hadn't informed the police. She wanted to get inside, see Daniel's sister and somehow persuade her of the danger and make her see that she should leave at once.

Two women with shopping baskets over their arms hurried up the street and glanced towards them. The maid glared at Marion steadfastly. Marion guessed that the woman who was barring her way did not want to attract attention by making a fuss. Taking advantage of this, she acted swiftly and pushed her way into the house.

'Here, come back!' the maid shrieked after her as Marion walked past.

But now that she was inside, Marion was perplexed as to what she should do. She would have to look in every room until she found Susan. The maid was coming up behind her quickly, so Marion took hold of the doorknob of the first room she came across and entered as quickly as possible.

At first she thought there was nobody in there. The sky outside was growing dark, and heavy lace curtains obscured what light there was. The room had a sweetly stale smell. A small fire burned in the hearth, and suddenly Marion saw a movement from a figure sitting at one side of it. As her eyes became accustomed to the dimness, she saw that the figure was a young woman. It must be Susan.

The girl lifted her head and looked at Marion. 'Are you going to light the lamps now?' she asked. 'I don't like sitting here in the dark.'

'Susan? Is that you?' Marion asked.

The girl looked puzzled. 'You're not Jane. Where is she?'

'Right here.' The voice came from behind Marion. 'And this lady is just going.'

'But who is she?'

'She's no one you need bother about.'

'Then why is she here?'

Marion noticed that the girl's voice was slurred. She was either ill, very tired or had been drugged. Most probably the latter.

'I'm a friend of your brother,' Marion said.

The girl uttered a harsh cry and dropped her head in her hands. Without looking up she asked, 'Does Daniel know I'm here?'

'No, he doesn't.'

'Please don't tell him. He will be so ashamed.'

'Daniel loves you, you must believe that. He will not condemn you.'

'Yes he will. And my mother will never want to speak to me again.' Susan's shoulders began to shake.

'Here, this has gone on long enough,' the maid said suddenly. 'Whoever you are, can't you see you're upsetting the girl? Now go home before the master gets here or you'll be in trouble.'

'When I go, Susan is going with me,' Marion said.

'And who the hell are you anyway, coming in here and giving orders like this?'

'I'm Mrs Victor Bateman.'

The maid's horrified reaction told Marion all she needed to know. It was equally obvious that the name meant nothing to Susan. Feeling thoroughly sickened, Marion turned to Daniel's sister and held out her hand.

'Come now,' she said. 'Let me help you up. I know you don't want to stay here. Come away now, before . . . before the master arrives. I have a cab waiting.'

Susan allowed Marion to help her to her feet, and stood swaying for a moment before she said, 'Where will you take me?'

'Somewhere safe.'

'And my brother?'

'He will want to see you.'

The girl became agitated. 'No . . .' she began.

'But I shall tell him to wait until you are ready to see him.'

Susan looked around her uncertainly. 'What about my clothes?'

'Leave them.'

'Oh, but . . .'

Marion would never discover whether she could have persuaded the poor confused girl to leave her clothes behind, because at that moment Victor burst into the room.

'What you doing here?' he shouted.

Marion drew herself up and faced him. Susan cowered behind her and the maid started edging towards the door.

'I've come to take Susan away,' Marion said.

'How dare you!' he bellowed. 'How dare you interfere?'

'And how dare you keep her here!'

'She's hardly unwilling,' Victor sneered.

'I am!' Susan cried. 'I know I came here of my own free will – and how foolish that was – but I thought you were going to marry me.'

355

'Marry you?' Victor looked incredulous. 'A man like me, marry a little trollop like you?'

'I'm not a trollop!' Susan began to sob.

'Oh, but you are. Does this fine lady – this friend of your brother's – know what you have done? How you have shared your bed not only with me but with other men as well?'

'You forced me to do that.'

Tears were streaming down Susan's face. Marion felt sickened.

'If you were so unhappy with the arrangement, why did you stay here?' Victor asked.

Susan turned fiercely on the maidservant who hovered uncertainly by the door. 'She kept me here,' she said. 'She watches me all the time. And besides . . .'

'Besides what?' Victor asked scornfully.

'I – I have nowhere to go.'

Susan looked utterly defeated. Marion had sensed from the moment she entered the room that the poor girl had probably been kept docile with drugs, and her anger rose.

'You have now, Susan. You're coming with me.'

Victor laughed. 'And where are you going to take her?' he asked. 'Surely not to your husband's house?'

'Her brother will find somewhere for her,' Marion replied.

At this Susan roused herself. 'No,' she moaned. 'No, not Daniel.'

'It's all right, Susan,' Marion said. 'Trust me.' She took hold of the girl's arm. 'You must come now.'

Victor stepped forward. 'Let go of her. She's not leaving this house!'

'Yes she is,' Marion said firmly.

At this, Victor advanced towards Marion with one arm raised, and before she could avoid him he struck her so hard that she fell to the floor.

'No – don't hurt her!' she heard Susan say.

This infuriated Victor all the more, and he turned on Susan. Speechless with rage, he advanced towards her, and Marion, her head spinning, tried to push herself up and at the same time catch at his legs. He turned and kicked her in the ribs. She felt as though every ounce of breath had left her body. The room went black for a moment and she had to concentrate very hard on trying to breathe.

Her vision faded, but she saw Susan stoop and pick up something from the hearth. The fire tongs. The girl grasped them by the pincers, and while Victor was still recovering his balance after kicking Marion, she brought the heavy steel ball that formed the ornamental handle down on his head. He fell heavily and made a grunting sound.

Marion was aware of movement in the doorway, and she turned her aching head just in time to see the maid vanish from the room. She dragged herself up and went over to Susan.

Daniel's sister was standing looking down at Victor. He was not moving. Marion knelt swiftly and placed her hand on the side of his neck. She thought she detected a faint pulse, but she could not be sure. Overcoming her revulsion, she laid her head on his chest and listened for a heartbeat.

As she knelt there, she heard Susan scream, and a moment later two powerful hands closed around Marion's neck.

'You bitch,' Victor breathed hoarsely, and he began to throttle her.

Marion struggled desperately to prise his fingers away from her neck. As she began to lose consciousness, she saw a blurred shape standing over them. Susan. The younger girl raised the fire tongs high in the air and then brought them down on Victor's head so forcefully that Marion heard the bones of his skull crunch.

Incredibly, his hands closed around her neck even more tightly, but that lasted only for a second and then his grip slackened and his hands fell away from her. She heard a rattling in his throat and raised her head to see a stream of blood issuing from his mouth. He shuddered and was still.

When she rose from her knees, Susan was still standing there gazing down at him. Her lips were trembling. 'He was going to kill you,' she said. She was trembling. The fire tongs slipped from her grasp and fell with a dull thud to the floor.

'I know,' Marion said.

'I was frightened. I thought he was going to kill me too. I had to stop him.'

As they stood looking at each other in the darkening room, Marion became aware of frantic activity on the floor above. A moment later she heard someone hurrying down the stairs and along the narrow passage. Marion was shocked into activity. She strode to the door just as the maid, dressed in her hat and coat and carrying a suitcase, was about to leave the house.

'Where are you going?' Marion asked.

'As far away as I can get,' the woman replied. 'I don't know what happened here, and I don't want to know. You won't hear any more from me.'

With that she vanished, leaving the front door open. Marion closed it, and then went back into the front parlour to find that Susan hadn't moved. She raised her head and looked at Marion.

'What are we going to do?' she whispered.

'We must go to the police station.'

'No! We can't do that!' The younger girl sounded panic-stricken. 'They'll hang me.'

'No they won't. He was going to kill me. You saved my life. I shall tell them so.'

'And do you think they'll believe you? When it gets out what kind of person I am – how I've been living – they'll say I'm a bad lot and they'll hang me. And maybe they'll hang you as well. They'll say we did it together. We've got to get away from here.'

Marion looked uncertain. 'But it would be wrong to run away.'

Susan was getting more desperate by the minute. 'Look, I saved your life, didn't I? I didn't do that so that they could lead us to the gallows. Please, please believe me. We can't tell anyone about this. Ever. Promise me you'll never tell anyone – anyone at all.'

Marion fought with her conscience only a moment longer before she said, 'I promise.'

She had accepted what she must do.

'Is there anything in this room that belongs to you?' she asked.

Susan shook her head.

'Come along then. We'll go and pack some of your clothes.'

Marion strode towards Susan and took her by the hand. She held it as the girl stepped carefully round the body and then led her upstairs.

'Which is your room?'

Susan didn't object when Marion allowed her to pack only a minimal amount of clothes. Marion chose them herself, taking only two of the plainer, more sensible dresses. Along with some underwear, she threw them roughly into a laundry bag that she found in the bottom of the wardrobe. Then she made Susan check to see if there was anything personal in the room. There wasn't. It seemed the clothes Susan had been wearing when she arrived had long ago been disposed of.

Marion agonised over whether she should close the front door behind them. The thought of Victor's body lying undiscovered for any length of time filled her with horror. She decided to leave the door open. Holding the laundry bag in one hand and taking Susan's arm with the other, she hurried down the street towards the promenade.

There was a cab waiting round the corner. Guessing that it was waiting for Victor, Marion hesitated for only a moment and then forced herself to walk at a normal pace, chatting to Susan as if they hadn't a care in the world. Susan responded only with monosyllables, but that would have to do.

When they reached the station, the lamps that hung over the platforms had been lit. Marion was worried by the look in the girl's eyes. She had no idea what lay in store for Daniel's sister, but she was determined that no further harm should come to her.

Meanwhile Daniel Brady, leaving the courthouse where he had been reporting on a murder trial, remembered where he had seen his mysterious early-morning visitor before. And who he had been with.

# Chapter Twenty-Three

Esmé Cressington was taking morning coffee in her suite at one of the best hotels in Mayfair. After breakfast she had sent Annette off in a cab to Sabine's studio in Chelsea, and she intended to do a little shopping in Bond Street before collecting her and returning in time to get ready for the theatre. She hadn't decided as yet whether to go to the Savoy and see the latest offering by Gilbert and Sullivan, or try to find something more serious minded and dramatic.

Esmé loved the theatre and would have been happy with either choice, but she was trying to think what would please Annette. So she had rung for the morning paper and was about to peruse the theatre listings.

But she never got that far. She had only turned a couple of pages when her eyes opened wide in horror. She reached for her coffee cup, but her hand was shaking so much that it slipped from her hand and fell to the floor, the spilled coffee spreading out and staining the pretty Persian rug.

Her attention had been caught by the headline:

MYSTERIOUS MURDER IN NORTHUMBERLAND
LOCAL BUSINESSMAN BRUTALLY KILLED!

The story, originally reported in a local paper, apparently, had been picked up by the national press and treated sensationally. As the story unfolded, Esmé's horror grew.

She read on and learned that Victor Bateman had been murdered in a small house in a respectable terrace in Whitley-by-the-Sea. A cab-driver whom he had instructed to wait for him had eventually got worried and gone looking for him. Seeing a front door open, he had entered cautiously and found the body on the floor in the front parlour.

The cab-driver had told the police that while he had been waiting he had seen only three people leave the street. A young woman had come hurrying away not very long after the gentleman must have entered the house. He said that she looked as though the devil was after her. A little later another two women emerged from the same street and strolled by chatting amiably. He didn't think they could have had anything to do with it.

Apparently the police had no suspect but were still investigating and had already discovered that Victor Bateman had not been as respectable as he had appeared to be.

Esmé let the paper fall to the floor. She sat back in her chair and thought long and hard. So they were investigating Victor. How much would they discover?

She rang for a second pot of coffee. 'As strong as you can make it,' she said. As she drank it, she tried to pull herself together. She would have to go and get Annette straight away. They must return to Newcastle. Although she admitted to herself that if it hadn't been for the girl, she might have abandoned everything and headed for Marseille and then on to Egypt, where she had once lived with her father.

Samuel Burroughs had taken a risk coming to London. After all, he was an escaped convict with a price on his head. But he did not know of anywhere he could get a better price for Marion Bateman's diamonds.

He watched the crooked jeweller, an associate from long ago, examine the gems for a moment before he looked up and said, 'I'll have to get my father's opinion, Samuel.'

Before Burroughs could protest, the man went through a door that led to the back shop. He heard voices and a door opening and closing. The minutes ticked by and Burroughs grew uneasy. He was on the point of leaping over the counter and going to see what was happening when the door behind him opened.

He turned to see the shop filling with uniformed men. He had been betrayed.

'How much have you told Annette?' Marion asked.

Marion and Esmé Cressington faced each other across the wide space of the drawing room. Marion sat in one of the wing chairs by the hearth while Lady Cressington roamed about nervously. She could not settle.

'Only as much as she needs to know.'

'And that is . . .? Lady Cressington, will you please sit down!'

Esmé looked startled by Marion's abrupt tone, but she did as she was told and sat at the other side of the hearth. A small fire burned in the grate but did little to take the chill from the atmosphere that had settled over Victor Bateman's house like a pall.

'I told her that Victor was dead,' Esmé Cressington said.

'Just that?'

'No. I felt it best to tell her that he had been murdered, and that was why we must hurry home.'

'How did she take it?'

'She was heartbroken. What did you expect?'

'And you left it at that?'

'No. Once the storm of sobbing was over, I thought it best to at least hint that Victor was not the good man she thought him to be, and that was probably the reason why somebody had killed him, although we may never find out who it was.'

Marion dug her fingers into the velvet padding on the arms of the chair. 'Do you think not?'

'Well . . . everyone seems convinced that the young woman who hurried away from the scene is the culprit. But even if that's true, I'm sure we'll never find her.'

'What makes you so sure?'

'Anyone connected with Victor's more nefarious dealings will be well away by now.'

'You knew about those?'

'I beg your pardon?'

'About Victor's "nefarious dealings", as you put it?'

'I did.'

'And were you part of them?'

'No! Never part of them. My sin was venal. I needed money and I allowed Victor to bribe me.'

'I don't understand.'

Esmé Cressington sighed. 'You know how I like to live in style. My late husband's money ran out long ago. When I met Victor, I was on the point of bankruptcy. I had decided that my only course of action was to flee my debtors.'

'What has Victor to do with this?'

'He was . . . How shall I put this? He was attracted to me.'

'You became his mistress?'

Lady Cressington flinched. 'For a while. But that didn't last very long.' She smiled wryly. 'I was too old for him. My youth had already started to fade and he very soon lost interest.'

She paused and stared into the mid-distance as if focusing on past troubles.

'But by then he had paid off my debts,' she continued, 'and he was happy to go on providing me with a generous allowance so long as I never revealed what I had discovered about him.'

'How could you keep quiet about something like that!'

Her visitor laughed, a dry little laugh. 'Victor pointed out to me that much of the money he had given me was the profit from the – those places. I was as guilty as he was, he said. And if I ruined him, I would be ruined too. I would be hounded out of society and maybe even imprisoned as an accomplice.'

Marion looked at her with revulsion. 'So you kept quiet.'

'I am very ashamed to say that I did. But I won one concession from Victor. When the girls were too old and he would have thrown them out to fend for themselves, or . . .' she paused, and her eyes filled with horror, 'or worse, I persuaded him to give them to me. I . . . I cleaned them up, fed them wholesome meals and found positions for them as servants in large houses – as far away from this city as possible.'

'But you went on taking his money?'

'I did.'

'On the day of my father's funeral, Mr Earnshaw told me that you had helped him with his work. Is that true?'

'I did.'

'Did my father know of your connection with Victor?'

'Of course not! When I learned of his work with the homeless, I approached him and offered my help. It . . . it eased my conscience, I suppose.'

Marion and Esmé Cressington stared at each other. The fire flickered, the clock on the mantel ticked, and outside the wind blew the first of the fallen leaves across the lawn and against the window.

Eventually Lady Cressington sighed deeply and said, 'I am giving my house to the church. I intend that it should be used as a home for the motherless children who roam our streets. When that transaction is complete, I shall leave this city. Leave the country, in fact.'

Marion could think of nothing further to say, so she rose and rang the bell for the parlourmaid.

Lady Cressington laughed softly. 'I don't suppose you would allow me to see Annette just one more time before I leave.'

'No.'

'I didn't think so. I came to really love her, you know.'

Marion bowed her head and remained silent as the maid showed Lady Cressington out.

The next caller that day was Daniel.

'I'm sorry, Daniel, Susan still refuses to see you,' Marion said. 'She feels so ashamed.'

'Tell her there's no need for that. She was young, she was foolish, but whatever she has done, she is still my beloved sister and I will never reproach her. She has been punished enough.'

'I've told her all that.'

'Have you also told her that she's breaking her mother's heart?'

'Yes.'

'And that Ma need never know exactly where she has been or what she has been doing?'

'What have you told your mother?'

'Only that Susan ran away because she was bored with her life and wanted to find something better. I said that she was working in a house at the coast.' Daniel flushed and looked uncomfortable. 'Ma thinks Susan was a lady's maid.'

Marion looked at him. She knew it would be too painful to express the thoughts that were going through their minds.

'I think you should tell your mother that Susan is ashamed that she caused so much grief, that she is staying with a good friend who will take care of her and that she will come home as soon as we can persuade her.'

Lines of worry were etched in Daniel's handsome face and Marion wondered if he had any idea what had really happened that night in the little house by the sea. She imagined that he thought Marion had taken Susan away before Victor had been murdered and that the murderer was probably the mysterious young woman the cab-driver had described as hurrying away as though the devil was after her.

Marion knew that she could never tell Daniel who had struck the blow that had killed Victor. She had made a promise, and Susan's secret was safe with her, even if it meant that she could never be entirely truthful with the man she had come to respect and care for above all others.

'Does Susan know that you were married to the man who took her away from us?' Daniel asked.

'Yes. I had to tell her, but fortunately she believed at once that I had no part in it. In fact I think she sees me as a victim too.'

She saw Daniel battling with his anxieties, but he managed to smile when he asked, 'What does Susan do all day?'

Marion smiled. 'I can hardly believe this, but Charlotte has taken her under her wing. Both Susan and Annette. The three of them spend their days in my sister-in-law's sitting room, reading and talking about nothing in particular as far as I can see. They are all bruised souls and I think they are taking comfort from each other's company.'

'Does . . .' Daniel's expression was one of acute embarrassment, 'does Miss Bateman know that Susan was . . . why she was in that house at Whitley-by-the-Sea?'

'Yes. Charlotte deserves that we be honest with her.'

'And she doesn't . . . I mean, she is willing to befriend Susan?'

'Totally.'

'And Annette? Have you told Annette?'

'My sister doesn't need to know, and thankfully, she has not asked.' Marion's smile was rueful. 'It seems there is some advantage in her being self centred – or rather, so single minded about her art.'

They smiled at each other for a moment, but then Daniel looked uneasy again. 'The stories in the newspapers will not give them any comfort,' he said.

'No.'

'As details of Victor's life emerge, some of the tales will be sensational. For example I believe either Victor or, more likely, his paid accomplice was the man the newspapers called "The Toff".'

'I had already come to that conclusion,' Marion said gravely.

'I also believe it was the same wretch who attacked me in order to get hold of your father's papers,' Daniel said. 'Victor was worried about what they might reveal.'

'This man who worked for Victor was the same man who told me where Susan was, wasn't he?'

'I believe so. He and Victor must have fallen out.'

'We must be grateful for that,' Marion said and they smiled at each other briefly.

Then Daniel became serious again as he said, 'Marion, there is something I feel I must warn you about.' He paused while the seconds ticked away in the silent room. Then, unwillingly it seemed to Marion, he continued, 'I think it almost certain that it was Victor Bateman himself who murdered your father.'

Marion stared at him. There was so much hurt in her eyes that he wanted to stride across the space between them and take her into his arms. But there was also something about her, some sense of her innate pride, that prevented him from doing so.

'I think I had already guessed that,' she said. There was another long pause while Marion looked as though she was trying to suppress some nightmarish vision. Then she sighed and asked, 'Would it be possible for me to see my father's papers?'

'As soon as you like. Most of them are in longhand, but I know enough shorthand now to be able to transcribe the rest.'

She surprised him with a smile. 'And that's another thing. Daniel, do you think it would be possible for me to learn shorthand?'

'Of course I do. But why?'

'Oh, it's just an idea I've had. An idea of what I should do with my life.'

'Are you going to tell me what it is?'

'No, not yet. But I promise you will be the first outside this household to know.'

Another funeral, Marion thought. This time it is my husband's, but unlike at my father's funeral there are only three mourners.

The stories emerging in the newspapers had been enough to persuade Victor's former friends and business associates to stay away. And Marion would not have come either if Charlotte had not begged her to accompany her.

So it was only Marion, Charlotte and Victor's solicitor Mr Gilchrist who followed the coffin to the grave. Herbert Gilchrist, solemn in unrelieved black, thought it his duty to be there. Before the service began, he had smiled encouragingly at Marion and assured her that he would assist her in any way that he could.

At this Charlotte had sniffed audibly and, leaning towards Marion, whispered, 'Victor's affairs have been lucrative for Mr Gilchrist. He obviously hopes that you will retain his services.'

But Charlotte had not objected when the solicitor offered her his arm as they negotiated the winding paths that led to the newly dug grave.

'I can't . . .' Marion whispered when one of the gravediggers handed her the silver shovel bearing the clods of earth.

Charlotte stepped forward to perform the duty, and although she was heavily veiled — as was Marion herself — Marion thought she could see the glint of tears in her eyes. The revelations about Victor's true character had shocked Charlotte deeply, but she had loved her younger brother and the torment she was suffering must be grievous.

They had both thought it best that Annette should not come to the funeral. She was at home with Susan. Betty had volunteered to come to the house and sit with them.

Ever since learning the dreadful truth about Victor, Betty had been overwhelmed with guilt. 'I encouraged the lass to marry that evil man,' she told Arthur. 'How could I have been so blind?'

Arthur had assured her that Victor Bateman had taken many people in, 'pulled the wool right over their eyes', he said, and that she was not to blame herself.

'But I do,' she had replied. 'And I swear that for the rest of my life I shall do anything I can to help that poor lass.'

On the day of the funeral she had arrived early enough to harass the household staff and make sure that a good meal was provided for Annette and Susan, and also that the formal table in the dining room was laid out with the appropriate funeral meats just in case there were any mourners.

Many of the servants had already asked Charlotte for references and were planning to find new employment as soon as they had learned whether they had been mentioned in the master's will. When the funeral party returned from the church, Mr Gilchrist went down to the servants' hall and was able to assure them that they would receive the usual bequests. Marion and Charlotte waited in Victor's study.

While they were alone Charlotte spoke. 'There's something I must say.'

Marion did not know what to expect. She looked at Charlotte anxiously.

'I find this difficult, but I will come straight to the point. When Victor married you I did not welcome you as I should have done. I wanted my brother to get married but I was hoping that he would choose a bride from what they call a good family. I am ashamed to say I did not think you good enough for him. How wrong I was. The truth is, it was Victor who was not good enough for you. Not nearly good enough. Marion, my dear, I hope you can forgive me.'

For the first time that day, Marion found that she had tears in her eyes. She reached for Charlotte's hand and squeezed it. 'Of course.'

'Thank you.'

They sat in silence until Mr Gilchrist came to join them.

Victor's will was simple. He had no children, so Marion, as was to be expected, was the main beneficiary. He had provided generously for Charlotte, even though she had ample money of her own left to her by their father.

Marion sat white faced and silent throughout, and it was only after Mr Gilchrist had gone that she said quietly, 'You realise I can't take any of it.'

'Why not?' Charlotte asked.

'How can you even ask? When I think how that money was made!'

'Some of it was made quite legitimately. Think of the new homes that replaced the squalid slums.'

'And think of those very same insanitary hovels where your brother collected extortionate rents from the poorest members of society. And think of the children he stole from the streets and placed in brothels – another source of his great wealth!'

Charlotte flinched and raised her hand as if to ward off Marion's words. 'I *have* been thinking about that. I cannot stop thinking about it. I don't know if I'll ever be able to forgive myself.'

Marion was surprised. 'What have you to forgive yourself for?'

'For being blind, and not only to what my brother was doing. For years I have been raising money for charities overseas – and I do not reproach myself with that – but I have been blind to the poor and needy in my own city. I am determined to find some way to make reparation both for my own failings and for my brother's sins.'

The two women were alone in the dining room. Betty had insisted that they go there and she had poured them each a cup of tea. The tea grew cold and the food Betty had provided lay untouched on the table.

'How will you do that?' Marion asked.

'The brothels must be shut down immediately and the poor girls and women taken care of. After that, something will have to be done about the conditions some of our unfortunate citizens live in. There's so much to do, and as yet I have no definite plans. But whatever I do, I will have to do alone.'

'Why alone?'

Charlotte's smile was bitter. 'Because those I thought of as my friends have deserted me.' Suddenly she looked anguished. 'You won't desert me, will you, Marion?'

'Of course not. But you must realise that I cannot stay in this house.'

'I thought you would say that, but where will you go?'

'I have a plan,' Marion said, and she allowed herself to smile. 'But today is not the day to discuss it.'

Charlotte looked hopeful. 'At least tell me if your plan includes me.'

'If you would like that. But now I must go and see Annette. She is very sad and confused.'

'The girls are in my sitting room,' Charlotte said. 'I will stay here and persuade your friend Betty to make me a fresh pot of tea. Oh, and send Susan down to keep me company.'

Marion expected to find her sister weeping, but when she walked into Charlotte's sitting room she was taken aback to find Annette busy with her sketchpad. She was drawing a pencil portrait of Susan Brady.

'Susan,' Marion began, 'I'd like to talk to Annette. Do you think you could leave us for a while.'

Annette didn't look up from her pad as she protested, 'Oh, please not now, Marion. Susan is such a good model. Come and see.'

Marion went to look over Annette's shoulder, and saw at once how Annette had captured Susan's beauty but also the haunting sadness that never left her eyes these days.

She also saw how Annette had taken refuge in her work – her talent being the one thing she could be sure of. Her younger sister was not yet ready to discuss what had happened and Marion wisely decided to leave things be. She turned to go, and was surprised when Annette laid down her pencil and reached up and caught her hand.

'Wait a moment,' she said.

'What is it?'

Annette looked up at her, her eyes brimming with tears. 'I love you,' she said. 'And I am very grateful for everything you have done for me. I'm not sure whether I deserve it, but I couldn't have a better sister.'

Marion, almost overcome herself, leaned down to kiss her sister's brow, and then walked from the room to go and have tea with Charlotte.

In the days and weeks following the funeral, Marion and Charlotte agreed that together they should set up a trust with the money that Victor had left. Charlotte herself would be happy to direct funds into housing projects and hospitals, and Marion, who still had a tiny income inherited from her mother, would follow the dream that had been growing within her for some time now. They would live together on the untainted money that Charlotte's parents had left her, and Charlotte also insisted on paying Annette's fees at art school.

'I am so grateful that you have not cast me off,' she told Marion. 'Not one of my former friends will have anything to do with me. They treat me like a leper. It seems that they cannot believe that I knew nothing of Victor's criminal activities. I have no one now except you and the girls. I hope we will be like a family.'

Charlotte knew that Susan had been rescued from her brother's clutches. But, like Daniel, she did not know the true story of that fateful night, and Marion intended that she never should.

Susan still refused to go home, and each time Daniel visited he was made painfully aware that there was a coolness growing between him and Marion. He had no idea what could have caused it.

By the time Christmas came, all the servants had left, most of the rooms had been emptied of furniture and Betty and her cousin Sarah came in daily to help Marion with the housework and the cooking.

Betty and Arthur came to spend Christmas Day with them, but the mood around the table was subdued as everyone there thought back to happier times.

Eventually, as spring began to give way to summer, the house was sold, and Marion, Charlotte, Annette and Susan were able to move into the large house in Eldon Square, in the centre of Newcastle, that

Marion had deemed suitable for the project that was close to her heart.

Daniel called to see them in his lunch hour and caught them by surprise. Susan, who was helping with the unpacking, came face to face with her brother. She turned and fled up the stairs. He called after her, but she did not reply.

Marion found him standing in the hallway. 'You've come in time to unpack the books and arrange the desks and typewriters,' she said, and she laughed.

He looked puzzled. 'Books I can understand, but desks? Typewriters?'

'For my school. I didn't want to tell you until it was all arranged, but I am going to start a sort of business school. A place where young women can come to learn office skills. Those who can afford it will pay fees, but if they can't it doesn't matter. We will buy their books for them and even provide free accommodation if they need it. Those who cannot come in the daytime because they need to earn a living will come for evening classes. Young women whose prospects would otherwise be bleak will be able to train for respectable employment.'

'So that is why you asked me if I thought you could learn shorthand!'

'Yes. We shall be employing properly qualified instructors, of course, but I feel it is only right that I should be able to master what our pupils are expected to learn.'

Marion's eyes were shining. She was filled with enthusiasm, and Daniel thought that whatever barrier it was that had lain between them had vanished at last.

'And I have some even more wonderful news,' she said. 'Susan is going to be one of my first pupils. She's really keen.'

Daniel remembered the evening, so long ago it seemed now, when Susan had shown interest in his shorthand book. 'That is wonderful,' he said. 'I have much to thank you for.'

They stood in the hallway for a time just looking at each other. They were alone. The sounds of the house receded and Daniel took a step towards her. Marion's eyes widened and it seemed to Daniel that she would welcome his embrace. But then, suddenly, the barrier came down again and she moved away from him.

'What is it, Marion?' he asked. 'What has come between us? Is it the articles I'm writing for the newspaper? Is it because I am revealing more and more about your husband's affairs? I realise that must be painful for you.'

'I can ease the pain by making sure that Victor's wealth is given back to the people he has wronged. And I am very glad you have taken up my father's work.'

'Then what is it?'

'I don't know what you mean.'

She stared at him obdurately and Daniel knew he was defeated. He returned to the newspaper office vowing that rather than risk further rejection it would be best not to see her again.


Marion had been aware of Susan's flight, and now she went upstairs thinking she would find the girl on the top floor where their bedrooms were. But instead she found her hovering on the first landing. Daniel's sister looked troubled.

'What is it?' Marion asked her.

'I was listening to you talking to Daniel. I'm sorry if I was eavesdropping, but . . . but . . .' Susan shot her a look of anguish.

Marion was shocked. 'Don't you trust me?' she asked. 'Do you really think I would betray you and tell your brother what happened that night? I made a promise. That is your secret and mine.'

Susan, her eyes brimming with tears, flung herself into Marion's arms, hugged her briefly than hurried up to the room she was to share with Annette.

The room, which had once been a dormitory for housemaids, stretched along the front of the tall house, and Susan found Annette looking out of one of the dormer windows that jutted out from the roof.

'Come here,' Annette said without turning round. 'Come and look.'

Susan joined her at the window. 'What are you looking at?'

'The city. Isn't it amazing?'

'Is it?'

'Of course it is. Tell me what can you see.'

'Buildings, roofs, chimneys, smoke.'

'And what else? Look up.'

Susan, puzzled, did so. 'Sky, clouds, birds.'

'That's right. And we are up here amongst the birds and we can look at the city as I've never seen it before.'

'I suppose you're going to say it will make a marvellous picture,' Susan said. She left Annette at the window and walked over to sit on her bed, which was still heaped with the clothes she had not yet put away.

'Many marvellous pictures,' Annette corrected her. 'I'll be able to watch the city at all times of day, in all kinds of weather, in every season.'

Susan didn't respond, and Annette turned from the window to look at her. 'What's the matter?' she asked.

'Nothing.'

'Yes there is. Tell me.'

'Your sister . . .' Susan began.

'You're not going to say Marion has been mean to you, because I won't believe it!'

'Of course not. She's an angel. But, well, I've just heard her talking to my brother.'

'You were eavesdropping?'

'I suppose I was.'

'Well, you know what they say: "Eavesdroppers never hear good of themselves".'

'It's not that at all!'

Annette, seeing that Susan was truly and deeply distressed, came and sat beside her. 'I'm sorry if I sounded flippant. Tell me what is troubling you.'

'I'd like to ask you something, not tell you something.'

'Ask away.'

'What do you think of your sister and my brother? I mean, do you think they like each other?'

Annette frowned. 'Do you know, I'm not sure. I mean, I can't speak for your brother, but my sister seems to want to keep her distance, doesn't she?'

Susan, biting her lip, nodded. 'Yes, she does. And I think I know why.'

'Why? Tell me.'

'I can't, not yet. Perhaps not ever. But I'm going to try and do something about it.'

Despite Annette's pleas, Susan would say no more, but later that day, when everyone was exhausted and could do no more than sit and chatter idly, she put on her coat and hat and slipped out for a walk.

Hannah Brady had just taken the dirty dishes through to the scullery, and now she came back, poured Daniel and herself cups of tea and sat with him at the table.

'Are you sure she's all right?' she asked. This was a question she asked almost daily.

'Believe me, Ma, she's fine. I saw her today and she's as bonny and blooming as ever.'

'Did she say why she won't come home and see me?'

'No, she didn't, but I'm sure she will in time. Furthermore, I have some good news. Miss Brookfield – that is, Mrs Bateman – is starting a school for young women who want to work in offices, and Susan is going to be one of the first students.'

'Our Susan? Work in an office?'

'Yes. Are you pleased?'

'I suppose so.' She sighed. 'I never realised until lately that I had such clever bairns. It won't be long now until you're both off and you'll leave your old ma far behind.'

Daniel put down his cup and looked at his mother's sad face. 'I'm not sure what you mean by that, Ma,' he said. 'I can assure you that I'd never leave you behind in any sense of the word. Wherever I go and wherever I live, there will always be a home for you with me.'

They were so intent on their conversation that neither of them had heard the back door open or the soft footsteps coming through from the scullery. It was only when they heard a muffled sob that both turned to look at the figure who was standing behind Hannah.

After a few seconds of stunned silence, Hannah Brady rose falteringly to her feet and drew her errant daughter into her arms.

'Ma, I'm so sorry,' Susan sobbed. 'Can you forgive me?'

'Of course I forgive you, pet,' Hannah said. 'I'm just so pleased to see you!'

Susan pulled away from her mother's embrace and turned to face her brother. 'And you, Daniel? Can you forgive me?'

Daniel hugged his sister tightly. 'Susan, Susan,' he said. 'How can you doubt it?'

By now all three Bradys were weeping, and Daniel, man though he was, was not ashamed of his tears. Hannah wiped her face on her pinafore.

'Daniel, put the kettle on,' she said. 'We'll hev a cup of tea and a bite to eat. Our Susan's come home.'

'No, Ma,' Susan said quietly, 'I haven't come home to stay. I'm not brave enough to face the sort of gossip that must be keeping the tongues wagging round here. I'm going to stay at the school and learn everything I can, and as soon as I can get a proper job I'll find somewhere decent where you and I can live together.'

Hannah was still wiping her eyes, but at this she laughed. 'Well now, there was I thinking I was a useless old woman that nobody wanted, and in the space of a few minutes both me bairns have said I can come and live with them!'

Susan laughed shakily. 'Until then,' she said, 'you can come and visit me in Eldon Square. I know Marion will agree to that.'

'Marion, is it?'

'Yes: Marion, Annette, even Charlotte. There are no formalities. We are like a little family.'

'Can you stay awhile tonight?' Hannah asked anxiously. 'There's some apple pie to eat up.'

'Yes, I'll stay for a while. But before I eat your apple pie – which I've sometimes dreamed about – I want to say that I'm truly ashamed for all the grief I've caused you. Even taking your money. What a wicked thing to do.'

'That's all right, pet. Daniel's told me that you've well and truly learned your lesson, and I promise you we'll put it all behind us. We'll never speak of it again.'

If Susan was thinking of all the other things that must never be spoken of, she tried not to show it.

When it was time for her to go, she asked Daniel to see her back to the house in Eldon Square.

'You've made Ma very happy,' he said as they set out.

'Yes, and I'm happy too, although I don't deserve to be. Marion has been so wonderful. In fact, you don't know just how wonderful she has been, and I've decided it's time you did.'

As yet there were no live-in staff at the house in Eldon Square. Charlotte and Marion had decided that they would engage a cook-housekeeper and a general maid who would both have their own room, but the rest of the staff needed for a house this size would come in daily.

So it was Marion herself who answered the door when Daniel brought Susan home. She saw two people standing at the top of the stone steps, silhouetted in the lamplight of the square. After a pause, when her eyes had adjusted to the twilight, Marion said, 'Susan, I didn't know you had gone out.'

'I'm sorry. I should have told you. I went to see my mother.'

'Oh Susan, I'm so pleased.'

'And now I'm very tired. If you don't mind, I'll go straight up to bed.'

Marion was surprised when Susan pushed past her, throwing her brother a meaningful look over her shoulder before hurrying along the passage and almost running upstairs.

'Well . . .' Marion said. 'I suppose we should say good night.'

'Wait,' Daniel said. 'I need to talk to you.'

There was a long pause before Marion asked, 'Do you want to come in?'

'It's a lovely night. Shall we walk in the garden?'

'Well . . .'

'Please, Marion.'

She paused only to take her coat from the hallstand, and hatless, she walked with Daniel to the enclosed garden of the square. Daniel opened the wrought-iron gate, and they set out along one of the pathways, although neither seemed to know where they were going.

Birds, disturbed by their progress, squawked indignantly and rustled the leaves of the branches above them. Without warning Daniel stopped walking and turned round to face Marion. 'You know that I love you,' he said. 'I've loved you from the moment I first saw you, and at one time I hoped that you loved me.'

His words were so unexpected that without thinking, Marion replied, 'I did.'

'I would have looked after you. Annette as well. We would have managed somehow. So what went wrong?'

'Dora, remember? She told me that you were engaged to be married.'

Daniel groaned. 'So you married Bateman.'

Their faces were shadowed by the patterns of the leaves, but when Marion looked up at him he saw the sadness in her eyes.

'And now?' he asked. 'What is it that has come between us now?'

'I can't tell you.'

'You don't have to.'

'What do you mean?'

'Susan has told me everything. She told me what happened that night and she told me that you had promised to keep her secret. To tell no one, not even her brother. I believe that, straightforward and truthful as you are, you could not allow yourself to get close to me if you could not be honest with me. You could not have borne to have such a secret coming between us. I'm right, aren't I?'

Marion nodded mutely.

'But now there is no secret to keep us apart. And now I can take you in my arms, like this.' He did so, pulling her gently towards him. 'And I can kiss you . . .'

The noises of the city, the rattle of carriage wheels over the cobbles, the voices of revellers come into town for an evening's entertainment, were all around them, and yet seemed as far off as if they were part of another world.

For the moment, this was Marion's world. Safe in Daniel's arms, she could at last look forward to their future together.